Deep Cover

Other Books by Brian Garfield

Fiction

THE ARIZONANS

THE LAWBRINGERS

VULTURES IN THE SUN

THE VANQUISHED

THE LAST BRIDGE

VALLEY OF THE SHADOW

SLIPHAMMER

THE HIT

SWEENY'S HONOR

THE VILLIERS TOUCH

WHAT OF TERRY CONNISTON?

Non-fiction

THE THOUSAND-MILE WAR:
World War II in Alaska and the Aleutians

Editor of WAR WHOOP AND BATTLE CRY
(An Anthology of Short Stories)

Deep

by Brian Garfield

Cover

DELACORTE PRESS / NEW YORK

For Shan and Z M

Man is a pliable animal, a being who gets
accustomed to everything.

FYODOR DOSTOYEVSKY
The House of the Dead

War is such a terrible, such an atrocious, thing,
that no man has the right to assume
the responsibility of beginning it.

LEO TOLSTOY
War and Peace

And nothing can we call our own but death;
And that small model of the barren earth,
Which serves as paste and cover to our bones.
For God's sake, let us sit upon the ground,
And tell sad stories of the death of kings.

WILLIAM SHAKESPEARE
King Richard II

Deep Cover

☆☆☆☆☆☆☆☆☆☆ ☆☆☆☆ ☆☆☆☆☆☆☆☆☆☆ ☆☆☆☆☆☆ ☆☆ ☆☆☆☆☆☆

Prologue

September 1954

The file on Viktor Rykov was open on the desk and Yashin did not look up from it when Grigorenko came in. The general entered the office with outstretched arms and the grumbling voice of a Russian bear: "Comrade Secretary—always a pleasure to see you," and Yashin let him stand there with his hands out over the desk. Finally he looked up and the smile on Grigorenko's face had gone rigid, so that it no longer concealed the deceit of his courteous greeting.

Yashin removed his rimless glasses. "Be seated, General." His pointing arm was serpentine. Behind the pane at his right a summer drizzle misted the turreted onions of St. Basil's and the heavy towers of the Kremlin. Yashin reached for the cord and drew the blind. "Well then, Oleg."

Grigorenko waited politely.

"It appears Rykov has a plan to offset the American superiority in strategic weapons."

"Rykov always has a plan," the general said.

"You don't trust him, do you?"

"Not always."

Yashin said, "He insists he knows precisely how many years ahead of us the Americans are in long-range bombers and guided missiles and nuclear capacity. I forget his exact figures."

"Is Rykov a scientist now?"

The lamps pushed at the gloom without dispelling it. The siren of an emergency vehicle brayed faintly from some indeterminate direction and Yashin watched the general's broad face. A year ago Lavrenti Beria had been executed, and Grigorenko had expected to get Beria's job, but Marshal Zhukov had blocked him and Grigorenko was still Second Secretary, GRU (Air).

Yashin said, "Your wife is well?"

"Oh yes. Thank you."

"Your sons in the Air Forces?"

"Both very fit. Igor is in China, training pilots."

"Yes, I know." Yashin liked to change the subject swiftly and see how neatly balance was regained: "Rykov's newest scheme has come to the attention of Nikita Khrushchev. Without the express endorsement of Rykov's immediate superiors." He watched the general shift mental gears.

"Rykov would have ways of doing that," the general said.

"Evidently Secretary Khrushchev approves. I understand they've cleared Rykov to proceed with his scheme."

"What about Comrade Malenkov?"

"I think as time goes on it won't matter what Malenkov thinks," Yashin said.

" . . . I see."

"Rykov has hundreds of people in training."

"I know how his programs work. It's the pattern of his old China scheme. What is it this time, Japan?"

"America." Yashin watched the general absorb it. "Rykov's whimsy is to call his training camp Amergrad." His praying-mantis body curled over the desk. "That's what Rykov wants to do—another deep-cover scheme."

"His schemes have worked before, you know."

"Never on this scale."

Grigorenko looked uncomfortable. "It hasn't been tried on this scale. Hundreds of people, you said."

"You're defending the man?"

"I don't trust him. I said that. But you must admire his successes. He made it work in China."

"He used Chinese agents. Born in China. He has no American-born agents for this one—where would he get them?"

Grigorenko spoke reluctantly. "Rykov is thorough. I've never faulted his attention to security."

"He's persuaded Khrushchev he can account for every detail. But what of it? Hundreds of men and women party to the secret—any one of them can destroy it."

"I'd need to know more about it," Grigorenko said. "One must assume he's screened all of them exhaustively."

Yashin was patient. "Rykov would have us all believe he knows as much about strategy as Clausewitz. What do you think will happen if he's left alone to his Machiavellian intriguing?"

"I suppose the risk is high."

"Indeed." Yashin reached for his meerschaum; he did not light it. "Dangerous to the Party and dangerous to Mother Russia, *n'est-ce pas?*"

"Quite possibly so, Comrade."

Yashin pushed the Rykov file across the desk. "He's arrogant. He's convinced he has the only way of doing things. You worked with him against the Germans early in the war—more than once you disagreed with him on tactics; you were superior to him both in rank and in the chain of command but every time there was a dispute Rykov managed to get the ear of someone with the authority to force you to go along with Rykov. More than once his schemes failed, but he was never reprimanded—he has a talent for covering his tracks, he always has a sacrificial goat nearby to take the blame." The pipe lifted like a pistol. "But this time if he fails we all suffer and if he succeeds it could undermine your position and mine as well."

"Could it?"

The general had to be played with care. "If the Politburo keeps digging holes in our funds so they can finance Rykov's expensive schemes, our performance will suffer and of course Rykov will be able to suggest that our responsibilities be combined under his command."

The general answered slowly. "I suppose that could be the case."

Then Yashin brought out his heavy artillery: "You know of course that it was Rykov who blocked your hopes to take Beria's place." And watched the general's face change.

When the Zis limousine stopped at the platform Viktor Rykov leaned forward in the back seat to bring the depot clock into view.

From the end-of-track station the rails glittered along the south Russian steppes toward Dzhezkazghan. The weather-beaten building might have been an isolated Siberian Railway stop. Southeast, two thousand kilometers across the Kirghiz, lay China: six hundred years ago Genghiz Khan's Mongols had drummed across these steppes, invading without warning, and one day the new Mongols of Mao's China might attempt it again.

The woman in gray uniform got out from behind the wheel and came round to open his door. Viktor Rykov's boots crunched the cinders as he dismounted and went up the wooden steps. His eyes swept the platform quickly. Two soldiers marched sentry paths, rifles across their shoulders; no one else was in sight except the dispatcher in his window by the turnstile.

The advancing train was less than a kilometer away and Rykov could feel its rumble through the soles of his boots. A long plume of coal smoke trailed back from the engine.

Andrei Bizenkev spoke behind him and Rykov turned with a quick snap of his thick shoulders. Andrei had emerged from the dispatcher's office. His face was young, Slavic-broad. "I was afraid you'd be late."

"A flock of goats on the road. There are always delays in this rancid country."

The troop lorry came rutting down the road and stopped by the platform a hundred meters away. The driver got out on the running board and straightened his cap and waited without moving. Andrei turned to Rykov: "I'd like to bundle the bastards right back on the train and send them back with boot prints on their asses."

"They haven't destroyed me yet. They've tried before." Rykov spoke Russian with a strong Georgian accent. He was a superb linguist; he had a colloquial command of eight languages and his thick harsh Russian was deliberate, a reminder of roots necessary to a man made rootless by history. Stalin's accent.

"Andrei."

"Yes?"

"We don't want our guests denouncing us for lax discipline. Observe the proper formalities of address with me while they're here."

"Da, Tovarich." The crooked smile of complicity did not fit quite right on the wide young face.

The train slid in with a hissing scrape of brake shoes. The engine driver had been briefed: normally the train would stop its goods wagons nearest the platform, leaving the passengers to walk a hundred meters on cinders, but today the first-class carriage halted directly opposite the station turnstile. Andrei straightened his tunic, and Rykov watched the carriage doors swing open and decant a handful of soldiers who ranged themselves along the platform. A young Red Army ensign walked around very stiffly barking commands at them, and Andrei said peevishly, "The whole absurd performance is guaranteed to attract attention."

"Whose attention? There's no one."

"Just the same. The Army's got no subtlety. No sense of security."

"Perhaps it wasn't the Army's idea. Men like our friend Yashin see an assassin beneath every stone. Never mind—let them have their games."

The soldiers moved clear of the carriage doorway and a

cadaverous figure appeared: Yashin stepped onto the platform incuriously, not smiling when his glance fell on Rykov. His face was gaunt and scored and his spidery fingers held a gnarled pipe, unlit.

Yashin was followed immediately by Colonel General Oleg Grigorenko who was in mufti. The two visitors walked forward in a lockstep, the general exactly one pace to the rear, as befitted his subordinate status to that of the Comintern First Secretary.

At the turnstile Yashin, with ritualistic formality, flashed his internal passport past the dispatcher's window and allowed Rykov to submit to his orthodox bear hug of greeting. Rykov could smell the pipe tobacco on Yashin's coat before he turned to grip the general's shoulders and repeat the meaningless pantomime. Afterward Rykov led his visitors down to the car. "Your bodyguard detail will ride behind us in the lorry. With your consent they'll be quartered in truckers' barracks just outside the *kolkhoz.* You understand we can't permit them inside."

He saw with satisfaction that he had provoked Yashin but the First Secretary's face did not change expression, except for the eyes, and Yashin turned without comment and stooped to enter the car. Grigorenko followed and Andrei came down the steps to get in after Rykov; Rykov caught the dry glint in Andrei's young eyes when he settled on one of the jump seats and smiled at the visitors.

The engine popped and began to growl. The Zis left the graded cinders and began to rattle when it struck the stony ruts of the dirt road. General Grigorenko reached for the strap loop. Andrei made casual talk about the sparse landmarks out here in the bear's corners and Grigorenko made a few monosyllabic responses in a voice heavy as coal lumps rattling down a metal chute; neither Yashin nor Rykov spoke at all. Rykov used the time to measure his guests—for confirmation, not discovery: he was quite certain he already knew their intentions.

Fyodor Yashin's hawked features were arresting and elegant: he was a striking figure, heads turned when he came into a room, and his success in the Party was due in part to the physical accident of his appearance. He had the genius of a Rasputin and his vigilant silences could be more disquieting than the harsh brutality of a Malenkov or the sly sarcasms of a Vishinsky. He spoke euphonious Leningrad Russian and wore expertly fitted suits that had not come from stock. A silk shirt and a preference for first-class rail passage in the class-less state: vanity was a weakness that could betray a man, and Rykov considered ways of making use of Yashin's.

By contrast General Grigorenko wore an old suit, double-breasted, with dark pinstripes and baggy cuffs; it bulged where his shoulders had begun to thicken. On his lapel he wore the Order of the Red Star. Clearly he was uncomfortable in civilian clothes: he had an imposing beefy presence, the stiff erect carriage that went with the habit of command. He had a remarkably cubic skull and his pale facial hair was all but invisible against the skin, so that when he cocked his eyebrows the expression showed mainly in the changed shape of his eyes.

Almost certainly Grigorenko had been told it was Rykov who had kept him from taking Beria's post. Rykov knew the persuasions Yashin must have used: *The choice was between you and Tolubchev. Khrushchev consulted Rykov, and Rykov put Tolub-chev's name forward, obviously because Rykov knows he can manipu-late Tolubchev. When Tolubchev is gone Rykov will take his place.* As a matter of fact it was all true except that no one had ever seriously considered Grigorenko for the post. Even Marshal Zhukov, who had always favored the military, had not en-dorsed Grigorenko. If you sought a captain for your chess team you did not seek him among those who did not under-stand the moves of the game. Grigorenko was a satisfactory bureaucrat but when it came to strategy and decision his mind was rudimentary.

It was natural that Yashin and Grigorenko would try to put Rykov away: that was why they were here today, he was cer-tain. The fact-finding visit was only a smoke screen. Yashin and Grigorenko needed to be able to demonstrate that they had taken the trouble to examine Amergrad on the ground, which was something no other high officials had done. Once they returned to the Kremlin they would be in a position to spread any lies they chose and there would be no one to dispute them. Between Grigorenko's GRU network and Yashin's control of sixty Communist Parties the two men carried enough weight to persuade the shaky ministerial cabinet to abandon the Amergrad project and put Viktor Rykov on the shelf—give him a listless series of outpost appointments until retirement.

. . . Following leisurely, the troop lorry was a faint heavy shape through the limousine's dust. Rykov lit a brown cigarette and reflected on his choice of weapons. The Zis climbed a steady slope and from the summit they overlooked a surprising green valley locked away from the world, a bowl ringed by thick tall trees.

"The forest hides us from the casual eyes of nomadic herders. We have nine hundred square kilometers inside the security wall. There is only the one gate and we patrol the wall with guards and dog squads, but there's also an electronic detection net. You can't get within two hundred meters without tripping off an alarm."

"You're always thorough," General Grigorenko conceded.

Fyodor Yashin said, "No one denies the months of routine and the endless careful planning. But the complexity of it— a secret isn't a secret when more than one person knows it. If two people know, it's going to be known by others, sooner or later, and if it's known by hundreds in the first place, you can't keep it secret for any time at all."

The road took them down through the trees past a wooden sentry watchtower. Yashin said, "It ought to make a superb detention camp." They were baiting him but Rykov did not rise to it.

At the roadblock they had to step out of the car and hand their papers to a sergeant while a soldier searched the car. Grigorenko muttered an oath and Rykov said, "An inconvenience, but I can hardly make exceptions to my own standing orders, can I." Finally the sergeant clicked his heels and let them pass.

Grigorenko spoke irritably:

"Don't you think your precautions are excessive?"

"We don't want anyone coming inside who's likely to forget himself and speak Russian to the Illegals."

"They've heard Russian before. They *are* Russians."

"That's what we're teaching them to forget."

Yashin's eyes flicked him. "And what if they forget too well?"

The wall was twelve feet high and crested by electrified barbed wire. The Zis stopped by a barracks and the woman driver opened the door for them. "We change cars here," Rykov said. "Your luggage will be brought along." He took them past the checkpoint, through the gate. Between the outer and inner walls they showed papers to a guard in an olive-drab American uniform with an Eisenhower jacket. A yellow Chevrolet waited, tended by a man in denim jacket and a greasy yellow cap; the car had an Arizona license plate and a "Tucson Yellow Taxi" decal on the door. Rykov put the visitors in the back seat and climbed into the front beside Andrei, twisted around with his left arm across the back of the seat and said, "I'll have to remind you, please, not to speak to anyone we see along the way."

Yashin said, "My objective is to interview some of your people. You know that."

"We've got to keep you separated from them. You'll conduct your interviews through soundproofed glass. There'll be simultaneous interpreters—you'll see the men and women you're talking to, but they won't hear your voice. Do you speak English?"

"Only in self-defense." Yashin did not smile at his little joke.

Rykov said, "The Illegals you'll meet here are the survivors. We've screened out nine out of ten before they get this far. You understand we can't afford the slightest slip at this stage. Once they come here from the primary training centers they need speak only a single word of Russian, even in their sleep, and they're given the sack. I must ask you to humor my regulations."

The taxi took them through the woods on a four-lane stretch of highway divided centrally by a grass strip. Large yellow signs in English announced PAVEMENT NARROWS—EXPRESSWAY ENDS 1000 FEET, and they bumped past a row of flaming oilpots onto a temporary macadam surface full of chuckholes. They turned abruptly into a district of warehouses and automobile junkyards and repair shops, a utility plant, another patch of woods and a street of pleasant small houses with trees arching the sidewalks. A man stood in a driveway washing down a Buick with a garden hose, and a cocker spaniel cavorted on the sloping lawn. The house was all on one level and had large picture windows. They passed a small U.S. POST OFFICE van and a slow-cruising police car with a red dome light and came to an intersection with filling stations—Mobil, Texaco, Union 76—on three of its four corners. The traffic signal suspended on cables above the middle of the intersection turned from yellow to red and Rykov got out of the car to pick up a newspaper from the unattended corner stand. He left a five-cent piece beside the iron weight that kept the newspapers from blowing away and returned to the car before the traffic light had turned. "The Tucson *Daily Star.* We get it through Tass. It's about ten days late, but that hardly matters. Yesterday we developed the major news stories from it and designed our radio and television broadcasts around it."

Traffic in a wide street sucked them into its flow. The curbs were lined with parking meters. Rykov pointed out Regan's Drugs, the movie theater, Woolworth's, John's Men's Shop, a beauty salon, real-estate and insurance offices. A red light halted them beside an open-fronted lunch counter and Johnnie Ray was singing "Walkin' My Baby Back Home" on the jukebox. They went on past a Safeway Market with an enormous asphalt car park and General Grigorenko said, "You don't see as many motorcars on the streets of Leningrad. What was the cost of this?"

Rykov pointed off to the left. "The nursery school. We allow Illegals with children into the program if the children are younger than eighteen months. They're raised in English."

Yashin's wintry expression never changed. "One might suspect the Americans grow enough of their own."

The taxi slid to the curb by a big Spanish stucco edifice,
FEDERAL OFFICE BUILDING engraved in concrete above the entrance. Rykov preceded them through the revolving door and
saw the general give the device a narrow look full of nervous
distrust. Yashin gave the surroundings no more attention
than he would have paid a Moscow worker's flat. Andrei trotted to the elevator bank and inserted a key and the car took
them to the fifth floor.

"Your quarters are at the rear. We'll try to anticipate your
needs but you'll have to regard yourselves as confined in
quarantine."

"I'm sure it's all quite necessary," Yashin said.

Rykov took them into his office and closed the door. Andrei
arranged chairs, and from the way General Grigorenko's eyes
followed Andrei around the room it was evident Grigorenko
didn't like his being there, but if Yashin could bring a witness
Rykov was entitled to the same privilege according to the
rules of protocol. Rykov pressed a button under the lip of his
desk and sat back. "We can begin right away if you like."

"By all means," said Yashin.

An old man brought in a large tray and set it down and
left the room. Chilled glasses of vodka, dishes of smoked
whitefish on bread, and sour pickles. Andrei passed them
around.

Rykov settled his elbows on the desk and steepled his
fingers. "You'll want a general briefing, but first let's clear the
air. When you return to the Kremlin there will be nothing to
prevent you from remembering a great many ugly things that
did not happen here. You might try to persuade the Politburo
that my operation here is slipshod and worthless, nothing but
a danger to the Soviet Union and a grave drain on her resources. When men in your position make such statements,
rebuttals from men in my position mean little."

Yashin murmured, "You forget your superior. What about Tolubchev?"

"Naturally his assurances would be discounted because ultimately the responsibility for Amergrad is his. He authorized it and he has no choice but to defend it. Who would believe him?"

The narrow face did not change. "You have a lively imagination."

"Have I."

"What do you want, Comrade—my assurances of support?"

"Only your assurances of an open skepticism. I never ask the impossible."

"Show us what you have to offer. Then we'll see."

"In a moment. It remains to be said that the state security files are at my disposal at all times."

Yashin didn't stir. It was Grigorenko who stiffened. "You're threatening us with blackmail?"

"You? Hardly."

"Never mind," Yashin said. He appeared remote, detached. He understood well enough. The government was unsteady, the post-Stalin purges had stripped the top levels of functionaries, and those who remained were a meager cadre intent on training a new generation to fill the bureaucracy's vacancies. Yashin and his comrades could not afford the loss of further Party executives. Yet Rykov's threat was explicit: destroy Rykov and you risk destroying men whose services are vital to the Soviet Union. The ammunition waited in his NKVD files.

He was offering Yashin a simple trade and making it clear he was not asking for support, only indifference.

Yashin lit his pipe. He had not conceded yet. "We'll see," he said again. "You may proceed."

Rykov sat back. "Andrei?"

Andrei clasped his hands behind him and assumed a gentle *ex cathedra* manner. "The first group of trainees is to matriculate in three weeks' time. They'll be seeded in at discreet intervals over a period of eighteen or twenty months. These agents may not be called on to act for many years, and in the meantime their whole concern will be to behave like Americans. That's why their training here has to be exhaustive, and incidentally expensive. Once in place they will have no contact with active Soviet field agents. Their instructions will come from Moscow—directly, without the use of established *rezidentsii* or safe-houses.

"When and if a Moscow Control is sent out to activate them, he'll have to make contact without the use of any ritualistic devices like codes and countersigns—they can't be expected to remember obscure passwords over a span of ten or twenty years.

"When contact is made the procedure will be simple. Control will address the agent by his real name, his Russian name, and he'll supply the names of both the agent's parents. In turn the agent will give him the full names of all four of his grandparents. Any enemy agent who gets deep enough into things to learn those names and their proper use will know so much about us that nothing would add to the damage already done.

"No agent is to take into his confidence anyone outside his own immediate cell, even if it's someone he thinks he met here at Amergrad. If he's not a member of the same cell he's to be treated as if he's a real American. The only communication between cells will be between cell leaders and of course agents and leaders will know only what they need to know for the execution of their own missions."

Andrei shifted his stance and his voice changed slightly. "They're going to be seeded into a place called Tucson, in the Southwestern desert. Population around fifty thousand. Industries, at the moment, cattle, copper mining, tourism. The town provides services and transport for the surrounding agricultural and mineral districts."

"Cowboy country," Grigorenko said. "Why?"

"Our analyses indicate Tucson will become an important defense center within a few years. It's in the same part of the country as the aircraft and missile plants in California and Utah, it's not far from the Alamogordo test range, the nuclear laboratories at Los Alamos, and the Nevada nuclear testing sites. It's four hundred miles inland from the nearest coastline, which makes it invulnerable to naval air attack, and the weather and topography encourage year-round aircraft and missile operations. The Army has a sophisticated artillery and electronics testing facility nearby at Fort Huachuca and in Tucson itself there are two Air Force bases—Davis Monthan, part of the Strategic Air Command, and Marana, a pilot-training field. We feel Tucson will become a vitally important base for intercontinental bombers and long-range rockets armed with nuclear warheads, as well as a center for research and weapons factories."

Yashin said, "Of course that's an opinion. You can't be absolutely certain it will develop that way."

He was talking to Rykov, and Rykov answered him: "We deal with probabilities, indications, suggestions."

"Circumstantial evidence."

"Yes. When you've got enough of it and it all points in the same direction, you can be fairly sure you're on the right track. But absolute certainty? No. That's beyond our power."

"Then you're committing the Soviet government to a course of action based on guesswork." Yashin's face shifted toward Andrei. "You may proceed."

Color flooded Andrei's face. "As I said, our Illegals will be seeded into Tucson on a steady basis. The infiltration will continue into 1956, by which time we expect to have seeded nearly three hundred highly trained Amergrad agents into the city."

Grigorenko sat up. "Three hundred agents to spy on one town?"

"Spy on it? No. We're not concerned with cloak-and-dagger charades. Our people are under orders to do nothing which could jeopardize their cover. Even if they see a chance to obtain secret information—even if they think it's vitally important—they're not to touch it. In fact if they discover a Soviet agent spying on secret activities they have orders to do their patriotic duty as Americans by turning the spy in to the American authorities."

"Absurd," Grigorenko said. "Madness." He turned his face toward Yashin.

Yashin said only, "Go on."

Flexor muscles contracted Andrei's hands but he went on gamely, his smile fixed and meaningless, and Rykov let him handle it by himself because Andrei would never learn how if someone was always there supporting him.

"We've projected a heavy multiplication of military installations in Tucson over the next twelve years. The purpose of the Rykov plan is to have our agents in place before the installations are even built—the Americans won't suspect people who are already entrenched important members of the community."

"Important members?" Grigorenko lifted his hand and turned it over. "Overnight?"

"People come from everywhere to the Southwest. For their health, retirement, a lazy bourgeois life. Our Illegals will be part of the stream."

"You said 'entrenched.' You can't just walk in and overthrow the power structure."

Andrei twitched but he did not look at Rykov. "It's a transient city. There's no traditional hierarchy—very few old families, no settled political structures taken for granted. We expect the population of Tucson to double in six years and that will give us an immigration of new voters who weren't there before and therefore can't be counted on to support old-time politicians. In American municipal politics the party labels have no meaning, all the candidates spout the same capitalist rubbish, but individual faces come and go constantly and our people will have no difficulty insinuating themselves into both major parties in five or six years."

Yashin stirred. "You talk as if you intend to take over the entire city."

"Yes, quite. Not only the city, but the Air Force bases, the aircraft plants, and the guided-missile installations—as they are built. They'll all be looking for personnel, particularly administrators and engineers with military experience. That's why we've recruited quite a few of our people from the Red

Air Forces. We'll be in control of the entire war machine in that sector of the United States—our people will be established in every echelon from military officers and plant executives all the way down to flight-line mechanics and factory janitors. When the final stage of the Rykov plan takes effect we'll own the Tucson military complex as if it were a Russian air base on the outskirts of Moscow."

☆☆☆☆☆☆☆☆☆☆☆☆☆☆☆☆☆☆☆☆☆☆☆☆☆☆☆☆☆☆☆☆☆☆☆
Chapter One

March 197-

The red scrambler operational telephone was always in the
corner of his vision. Smith turned the page of the specifications manual and shifted his buttocks on the hard seat of his
chair and checked his watch again to remind himself that
boredom was finite: his shift in the subterranean doomsday
room would end and presently he would return to sunshine
above ground. Smith had an earnest young face and an
AFBSD patch on his Air Force uniform. Smith, Arthur, NMI,
First Lieutenant USAF, 036754991.

The windowless room was sealed like an orbital capsule and
the sterile console panel glittered with screens, toggles, dials,
buttons—all the self-conscious set-decoration of computer
technology. Antiseptic air whispered from ducts in the thick
walls and there was a subliminal rumble of life-support ma-

chinery; the recirculation systems were designed to keep
Smith alive long enough to do his job after the atmosphere
above ground had been rendered poisonous by CBW or nuclear attack.

There was a big pane of reinforced bulletproof glass to his
right and beyond it was a mirror duplicate of his cell occupied
by Lieutenant Haas, Martin G., who had a bald spot and a
mild case of facial acne, Omnidirectional microphones fed
into cross-circuited PA systems so the two men could talk with
each other but couldn't reach each other physically. Around
their necks on dogtag chains hung magnet-coded keys; to
unleash the power of Silo Six, both lieutenants had to set their
controls identically, insert their keys and simultaneously turn
them. It was thought, or at least hoped, that this duplication
would prevent Unauthorized Implementation, which was a
euphemism for what happened when a man went off his nut
and decided to set the world on fire by himself. No one man
could launch the birds. The firing locks were separated by
twenty feet and impregnable glass and the initial contact had
to be made simultaneously (half-second leeway), so that even
if one man somehow neutralized the other and obtained both
sets of keys, he couldn't lock down one key and walk over and
turn the other one. There was no way around it: it took at least
two people to destroy the world.

If the order came down it would come by way of the scrambler telephone, melodramatically red, dialless. The phone
would buzz and its light would flash and when it was picked
up it would speak in a series of code letters which had to
match the codes sealed inside the heavy envelopes that lay in
the rectangular trays beside the phones. The codes were
changed regularly and at the end of each shift the envelope
was destroyed, unopened, in a security shredder which made
confetti of it, incinerated the scraps and then fed the ashes
into an acid bath. Except in training simulation Smith had
never been authorized to open a code envelope and he believed he never wanted to, just as those who had designed the
ultimate weapon believed they did not want to find out what
would happen if it was used.

The system which ended with Silo Six began with the bil-lion-dollar Ballistic Missile Early Warning System (BMEWS) and its ultrasensitive radar scopes designed to single out hos-tile missiles coming over the top of the world. Once an attack was detected, the warning would be fed into the sixteen-million-mile system of electronic circuits that led into the fourteen vast computers of the North American Aerospace Defense Command (NORAD), buried in a five-acre command post 1,500 feet beneath the granite summit of Cheyenne Mountain, thirteen miles south of Colorado Springs near Pike's Peak.

Preliminary Yellow Alert signals would go out instantly to all operational stations—Polaris and Poseidon submarines, airborne SAC bombers, aircraft carriers, military bases on four continents, and the Missile Wing Commanders of each ICBM and Safeguard ABM base. Simultaneously, signals would go out by microwave scrambler to activate the cased radiotelephone that was carried by a Secret Service agent who was never more than ten paces from the President of the United States.

If an incoming attack was confirmed the Red Alert condi-tion would be flashed to all stations. The identity of the at-tacker would be known by the trajectory of the incoming missiles: NORAD's computers could analyze paths of ap-proach and decide within milliseconds where the missiles had been launched.

Intercontinental war moved at eighteen thousand miles per hour and under most foreseeable circumstances the President would have little more than eight minutes to order retaliation.

The President's order would be transmitted directly to NORAD and to Strategic Air Command's *Looking Glass* air-borne headquarters—an aircraft orbiting in a random flight path and carrying sufficient high-ranking Air Force generals to guarantee temporary survival of the command structure, even if NORAD should be destroyed.

From NORAD or *Looking Glass* the order would be for-warded electronically through circuit relays to each opera-tional commander on station. In Tucson the order would be received by the Missile Wing Commander, who was on twenty-four-hour call.

Tucson's missiles were kept in eighteen separate complexes, which were grouped in six Residency Operations Groups. Each ROG had a Launch Commander, whose command post was an underground blockhouse, its horseshoe wall crowded with radar and closed-circuit television screens in tiers above a curved desk where console operators with earphone headsets and chin microphones sat in tilt-back swivel chairs.

Almost everything was turned over to computers; the men in the blockhouse were there mainly to monitor procedures and make sure nothing went wrong. Target information would be coded automatically onto magnetic tapes and programmed into the Minuteman Integrated Command and Control System (MICCS). The Launch Commander and his officers would complete their final drill—verification procedures and double-lock systems—and issue the coded final command over the red buzzer phones of the two Launch Operators in each silo. At any point up to actual ignition the procedure could be halted immediately by a countermand from the President.

The ROG which serviced Silos Four, Five and Six occupied a massive network of space and machinery radiating out from the command blockhouse in low underground caverns connected by ringing concrete corridors and miles of pipes and cables. Ventilator blowers made a soft muted roar and massive machines stood ready to slide back the topside reinforced trapdoors to expose the ICBMs for launching. In Communications, reels of tape poured out of decoding machines. Hundreds of men monitored incoming data. And in Silo Six the two lieutenants hovered over their red telephones.

On Friday, March 29, Jaime Spode left the Rayburn Building and turned his topcoat collar up. A knot of filthy cars went by in the slush, snow tires humming, white exhausts spuming. Spode picked his way across the mess and tramped along the rim of Capitol Hill toward the new Senate Office Building. He could have taken the subway but he wanted to avoid the girl he had seen going down the Rayburn entrance.

The sky was a dense slab of lead and the cold air was viscous as syrup. Breckenyear's remark still hung vivid in his skull because there was no place to hide it away. "You ought to be able to figure that out for yourself, a smart redskin like you." Breckenyear had smiled and the crafty aged eyes had disappeared into the wrinkles to indicate he was just joshing but the old bastard had known Spode would take it as an insult.

Spode couldn't remember two dozen words of Navajo. He'd been only nine years old when his father had packed up the family and moved to Willow Run to help build B-24 Liberators. If he went back now they'd laugh him off the Reservation. But he was still and always an Indian, even if sometimes he almost felt like a white man. Almost.

The girl he had sighted going down to the subway was one of those complaisant blondes who had turned out afterward to be a Groupie and when she had shown him her score card —diplomats and flunkies of every known skin hue—he had politely shown her the door; it had been weeks ago but the bad taste was still in his mouth. It did not please Spode to be a number on a list of Costa Rican chauffeurs and Tanzanian Second Secretaries. In the right company he was prepared to joke about his Dignity as a Noble Savage but neither the blonde nor Breckenyear was right company by Spode's definition.

He went down the third-floor corridor to Senator Forrester's door and found Lester Suffield in the outer office eating a cheese sandwich. The secretary's desk was unoccupied and the door to the Senator's empty private office stood wide open. Spode said, "There's three sizes of nuclear bombs. Large, extra large, and where did everybody go. Did somebody set one off in here?"

Lester Suffield gave him a bleak glance of recognition. "That's a sensitive subject around here. We don't make jokes about it." He exposed his wrist watch and shot his cuff. "He's down on the floor. There's a flap on."

"The Court nominee?"

"They're taking the vote. He'll be back, I guess, if the Dixierats don't start a filibuster."

"I'll wait." Spode parked his briefcase and shrugged out of his coat. His brown suit needed pressing. He unbuckled the galoshes. "Les, you wouldn't have another half-sandwich you could spare?"

"Help 'self." Suffield proffered a waxed-paper wedge. "I'm supposed to be on a diet anyhow." He was a big florid man, shaggy with a soot-gray pelt, but his eyes were clever like a terrier's.

When Spode walked over to him the open buckles of his galoshes chinked like Mexican spurs. He unwrapped the sandwich and held the waxed paper under his wide blunt chin to catch crumbs while he ate. "Where's Gloria? Lunch hour?"

"Gone for good. Buying her trousseau."

"I forgot."

"He still hasn't hired a replacement."

"Figures," Spode said. *He always took sergeants for granted, too.*

"I think I've got a girl lined up," Suffield said. "Remember Veronica Tebbel?"

"Ronnie Tebbel? Sure. Isn't she still running the home office? What makes you think she's willing to move back East and take a demotion to common secretary?"

"I asked her, son. That's the first rule of detective investigation. You spooks could save a lot of sweat if you remembered once in a while that the easiest way to get an answer to a question is to ask it."

"Us investigators don't look at it that way," Spode said. "Us investigators figure the less questions you ask, the less you get lied to."

"Which may explain why you never find out anything worth knowing."

"It could explain that, come to think of it."

Suffield settled a wistful glance on the empty chair behind the secretary's desk. "Sic transit Gloria," he said.

"Oh Christ." Spode crumpled the waxed paper in his fist, launched the wad toward the wastebasket, and missed by two feet.

Suffield said with mild interest, "For a spook with your second-story history, you're about the most spastic excuse for a human being I ever saw."

Spode leered at him. "White man, you want to go five rounds with me, I'll call the gym and tell the medics to stand by to haul your carcass away." His look traveled up and down Suffield. "God knows you could use the exercise. Look at the gut on you."

"Sure, Jaime. A nice fair fight. My high-school boxing and your karate."

Spode snorted and went over to put the wadded waxed paper in the basket. "Karate. Christ."

"Didn't they teach you that stuff in the spooks?"

"You've been looking at television."

"No, I'm serious."

"Maybe we learned a little hand-to-hand. It was a long time ago."

"Did the Senator get the same kind of training?"

"The Senator wasn't in the spooks with me."

"The hell he wasn't. He told me about it once."

"That was military counterintelligence. A thousand years ago—Korea. We were kids, it was one of those games they told you to play when they put the uniform on you."

"But you stayed in and he didn't."

"Because he's got brains and money and I'm dumb and poor and anyhow what else could I do? You're right, you do like to ask questions."

"Let's swap jobs, then. You be the Senator's aide and I'll be his investigator."

"Forget it, I know when I'm well off."

"Then you're not as dumb as you look." The corners of Suffield's wide mouth turned down. "Sometimes I feel as if I'm wet-nursing a mental retard. Will Rogers must have had our private Senator in mind when he said every now and then an innocent man gets sent to Congress. I hate to think of what's going to be left of us when Webb Breckenyear and Woody Guest get done dribbling the Senator's head on the table like a basketball."

The Senator came in grinning. "No way to talk about me behind my back, Les."

Suffield turned a dismal glance on him. "I'm glad you think it's funny."

"Nothing cheers me up like enthusiastic optimism." The Senator's tough gold-flecked eyes pivoted to Spode. "How're they hanging, Top?"

"Loose and shriveled," Spode replied. The Senator had called him Top for twenty years. It was a habit Spode had stopped trying to break him of.

Senator Alan Forrester walked into his private office and peeled off his topcoat. Went around behind the big desk and pawed through the litter of papers to see if anything had been added to it in his absence. Spode strolled into the office behind Suffield and sank into a chair. The Senator pulled his chair out and said, "God, what a grim day."

The Senator had a deep tan, made ruddy by the chill wind outside, and all his bones were big. His patrician good looks masked a hide as tough as a dollar steak. He had the Forrester grin that, on the face of his eminent father, had appeared eleven times on the covers of *Newsweek* and *Time* when the old man had owned this Senate seat. There was a lot of the old man in the young Senator—and of the grandfather who had come to Arizona in the 1880's with a Yorkshireman's canny acquisitiveness and in twenty years had built an empire of mines and ranches and railroads. But Alan Forrester was his own man and nobody had known that better than the late Senator Hayden Forrester.

The Senator sat with one arm hooked over the back of his chair. He had enormous hands—but Spode had seen how gently they held newborn calves and voters' babies. The creases that bracketed his mouth had grown deeper since Angie had died.

The Senator said, "Report, Top."

"I ain't got much." Spode admitted it apologetically, spreading his palms.

"Such as it is, let's have it."

"I spent two hours over at the Rayburn, standing in line in Webb Breckenyear's waiting room. The old bastard ought to sell tickets—he'd make a fortune. For a senile politician with a two-horse constituency he's got a fan club can't be beat."

"Lobbyists or down-home folks?"

"Lobbyists. Panting around for scraps from the pork barrel."

"Did you talk to him?"

"Let's say he talked to me."

"Get anything?"

"After he asked after you with plenty of affectionate chuckles, he made it clear the Honorable Webb Breckenyear is still Chairman of House Military Appropriations, and until the pit-viper liberals and the pinko-pacifist disarmamenters pass a Constitutional Amendment putting military affairs in the hands of Junior Senator Alan Forrester—and I emphasize 'Junior'—until that time, the Constitution provides that military appropriations are the bailiwick of the House in general, the Committee in particular, and Webb Breckenyear in person. I think I'm quoting him more or less verbatim."

"In other words, no dollar figures."

"For a wild-eyed revolutionary radical redskin like me it would've been easier to get General Custer to pin a patriotism medal on Sitting Bull."

The Senator's face hardened. "Is that the way he treated you, Top?" He sat up straight.

Spode waved his hands. "Forget it. I don't want to start a civil-rights sit-in on the old curmudgeon's doorstep. Forget I said it."

"No."

"I wish you would. Maybe I'm just using it as an excuse because I didn't get anything out of him."

The Senator settled back slowly in his chair. "I'm sorry you had to waste your time."

"You pay me by the week."

"At least he can't come back at us later and push his old ferret eyes wide with innocence and say, 'Why didn't y'all jist come rat out an' *aisk* me?' " A smile touched the Senator's mouth. "Sometimes I take pleasure in knowing Breckenyear would like to see me right where I'd like to see him. No satisfaction in hating a man if he won't hate you back."

Les Suffield stirred in his chair. "Breckenyear's in a position to hate pretty hard."

"Good. I'm tired of knocking down straw horses."

Suffield said slowly, "You want this fight, don't you?"

"Why not? I feel like busting a few heads."

"You'll only bust your own. You know that."

Spode looked from one to the other. They were staring at each other like pugilists before the bell. Through the door Spode heard the dim sounds of junior staffers returning from lunch to their desks in the bullpen office across the way, to handle the Senator's routine paperwork, talk to the Senator's constituents, answer the Senator's phones, stuff the Senator's newsletters into franked envelopes, and in general keep trivia off the Senator's back.

Spode sat back in the chair. He crossed his legs at right angles and laced his hands together behind his head and told himself, *I am going to keep all the way out of this.*

The Senator said, "You've had it in your craw for a while, Les. You may as well cough it up now."

Suffield's shoulders dropped, as if with relief. "All right," he said. "I will." He was beginning to perspire. "You've been right in there waving all the right flags. Right in there reforming welfare, civil rights, getting a fair shake for the chicanos, whipping the tails of the nasty bad guys behind environmental pollution. It's all fine by the voters—our voters, we haven't got any thick-smoke industries down home and they don't build cars in Arizona. You went out on a limb pushing tax penalties for big families but you probably picked up enough support from the anti-population-explosion crowd to offset the damage you did with the diehard Catholics. You get high marks right down the line as the perfect image of the crusading young progressive Republican. The right amount of stir in the press about standing you for President in a few years' time. In short, an impeccable record, a toothpaste smile, broad-based popularity, and no skeletons in your closet. No mortal enemies either. You've never made the mistake of pushing anybody into a corner he couldn't get out of gracefully. The extremists won't vote for you, but they won't spend their every last dime fighting your reelection. Nobody's got a chance in hell of unseating you this November. With the right stand-off at the next convention, you could walk right into the presidential nomination, and who have the Democrats got who could beat you for the White House?

"Those are the stakes," Suffield continued, "and you want to forfeit. You want to tie the rope around your own neck and hand the end of it to Woody Guest and Webb Breckenyear."

The Senator smiled. "In other words, don't rock the boat."

"Rock it my ass. You're hell-bent to sink it. Don't I make any sense to you at all? Don't you see what happens when you go after Breckenyear's hide? For openers you'll get Senator Guest on your ass, and when you get Woody Guest on your ass you get Woody Guest's friends on your ass. You have any idea how many friends he's got?"

The Senator murmured, "It happens to be a simple question of right and wrong."

"This is no simple question of right and wrong. This is a question of the precedence of one right over another. Go after the old guard now and I guarantee you, come November they'll hand you your head. Then you're out of office and how many wrongs can you right from there?"

"You're talking like a campaign manager, Les, and this isn't—"

"I *am* your campaign manager!"

"—the time for it. I'm not running for anything right now. The primary campaign doesn't open till June. A lot can happen in three months."

"Hell, the minute you got elected five years ago you were running for reelection." Suffield leaned forward, elbows on knees, earnest and intense. "You want to monkey with the sacred cow of National Defense—why don't you just lie down on the floor right now so you won't have so far to fall when they stick the knife in you? Down home in Tucson and Phoenix the Pentagon stands for Daddy Warbucks and Santa Claus

and Jesus H. Christ all at once—and you want to charge right
in on your horse and break your lance against it!"

Spode studied his galoshes. A little pool of melted snow
was drying into the carpet beneath his foot.

Suffield hunched farther forward on the edge of his seat.
"Without the defense establishment your whole constituency
would dry up and blow away. It was fine for Ike to bleat about
the military-industrial complex—he was retiring, he wasn't
looking for votes from the good people of Arizona. Am I
getting through to you yet?"

"You're waving an empty gun in my face, Les. I'm sorry.
I've never attacked legitimate defense needs. There's a difference between real needs and phony boondoggles."

"Try that persuasion on a voter with a four-second attention span."

"I will."

"You say one unkind word about the Pentagon and all
they'll remember is who got them their jobs."

Forrester looked at him and smiled a little but he wasn't
amused. "All right. You've had your say, now I'll have mine."

Spode studied the hard jut of the Senator's face. Alan Forrester went on, "If Breckenyear's buddies have a little accident and it happens to set the planet on fire then it'll make
just a whole lot of difference how well the civil-rights fight
goes in Arizona, won't it."

"We've been over all that before. They're not going to have
any little accidents. They never have before, why should they
now?"

"The odds have caught up. The mathematics is no good."

"That's what Moskowitz told you, but he's just one scientist. Look, suppose you're right, suppose Moskowitz is right
and they're going to blow up the world if they get Congressional authorization. Then suppose I tell you you're still
crazy. You open you mouth in public and you'll get an ICBM
crammed right down your throat, multiple warhead and all."

"You can't always go by that."

"Look, I'll tell you what, you're so dead set on this, at least
keep a low profile till November—get reelected first."

"That would be too late, I'm afraid."

"Too late for what?"

"Too late to stop the Pentagon from building the Phaeton Three system."

Jaime Spode sat bolt upright and blinked. The Senator added, "They'll be rolling on it by then. The appropriation is scheduled to come out of Breckenyear's House committee in May, eight weeks from now."

Spode interrupted. "Where'd you get this?"

"Sometimes it helps to be in high places, Top." The Senator went back to Suffield. "Unless we make a great deal of noise between now and May, Breckenyear will follow his usual pattern: draw up the bill by himself, walk into the committee with copies already printed up, pass them around the table and give the committee half an hour to discuss it and eighteen hours to get up a minority report before he shoves it out onto the floor as a rider to some harmless bill. He'll get it to a vote before anybody knows enough about it to start a floor fight. He's always operated that way. And Woodrow Guest will ram a carbon copy of it through the Senate in exactly the same way."

Suffield's upper lip was pinched between his teeth. The Senator said, "It'll add thirty billion dollars' worth of redundant hardware to the capacity we've already got for overkill. It'll multiply the chance of an accidental nuclear explosion by a thousand times. I don't think we need that kind of protection, Les."

Suffield scowled at the floor. "And you're willing to stake your political future on it."

"Yes."

"Then you're still a fool. All right, look, do it off the record. Leak it to the press, let them send up a trial balloon, see what the public thinks. Find some lame-duck Congressman on Breckenyear's committee and get *him* to make the indignant speeches and feel out the reaction. There's a hundred ways to do it without showing your own face. You've got to stay out of it—you just can't afford to be the one who pulls the plug. Not on the record."

"I can't do it that way," the Senator said, and smiled because he was anticipating Suffield's inevitable reaction.

"Sure," Suffield said obliviously. "Now tell me how you're too honest and red-blooded and forthright to work behind the scenes. You that was born in a smoke-filled room with a silver campaign promise in your mouth."

"No comment, but it's beside the point. Suppose we leak the information. Suppose the public takes off with it. Now, I'm a member of the Senate Military Affairs Committee. I'm supposed to know about things. When the disclosure hits the press, it's going to be assumed I know all about the Phaeton program. At that point I've got no choice but to speak out, because if I keep my mouth shut my silence has to imply acquiescence with the Pentagon party line. No. I'd have to speak out anyway—and I may as well do it right in front. At least that way if it catches on I can run with the ball and not get left back with the pack."

"You're a gold-plated idiot. If you feel the urge to make a stand, wait till November and make your stand on the next new Pentagon toy. Let this one go through."

"I can't."

"You've got to."

"Les," the Senator said slowly, "I am the only one who tells me what I've got to do."

The Senator's eyes swiveled toward Jaime Spode. "What about it, Top? Where do you stand?"

"Let's see." Spode ticked off fingers. "I hate funerals, I hate Pentagon mental retards, I just work here, none of the above."

"It's no time to be flip," said Les Suffield.

"The hell," Spode replied. "The air was getting blue." He uncrossed his legs and smiled vaguely in Suffield's direction.

The Senator said, "All right, Top. Now answer the question."

"I'd rather keep my politics to myself."

"Crap," the Senator said amiably.

"Look, you don't want my grass roots opinion. If you're asking for moral support you want me to agree with you, and if you want to see if I can pick holes in your arguments then you want me to fight. Either way, it stinks."

"When I want a directed verdict I'll ask for one," the Senator snapped. "All I want from you is a straight answer. Quit jumping to confusions about my motives."

Spode sighed in his chest. "All right, put it this way. Private opinion. I always thought it was a psychotic kind of game to play where you pass out nuclear toys to all the players and then tell them not to use them. I never met a kid yet who'd obey that kind of rules for long. And we are talking about kids and games, aren't we. End of speech, end of private opinion."

"If I'm reading that correctly between the lines, you're agreeing with me. Does that mean you're with me regardless of consequences?"

"I'm with you right up to the lynching, but who cares about me? I don't swing any weight up on the Hill."

"Maybe he wants the Indian vote," Suffield said dryly. "Any warheads up on the Window Rock Reservation, Jaime?"

The Senator said, "I don't want anybody doing a job for me if he doesn't believe in it." The gold-flecked eyes switched back to Les Suffield. "You get the point of this, Les?"

"I do." Suffield scowled at a point somewhere near the base of the desk and Spode could see the quick mind at work behind the broad face. Spode had never known him to confuse political expediency with the reality of his own beliefs. Suffield ate, breathed and sweated politics; it was his life, to the exclusion of all other interests. His dedication was to the intricate moves of the back-room game, the interplay of forces behind the scenes, the exercise of hidden leverage. He was at his vital best in the crises of a hair-close campaign when it was coming down to the final wire. He was like the compulsive big-time gambler to whom the stakes meant nothing intrinsically—they were only chips in the game; but the game itself counted—and how well you played it.

Finally Suffield spoke. "I'm not deserting the ship. You'll have to throw me overboard if you don't want me on deck."

"Even though you're convinced I'm wrong?"

"Where my friends are concerned, I value personal loyalty higher than political planks."

Spode wondered if Suffield actually believed that. More likely it was the obvious challenge that stimulated him.

"Make sure," the Senator said. "Take your time. I can't afford to have you do half-assed work when things get tight."

Suffield spread his hands wide. "What do you want me to say? Did I ever tread water on you?"

The Senator pinned him with a long silent scrutiny and Suffield met it with eyes slightly stirred to anger.

The Senator said, "I'm calling a press conference at five this afternoon. I'm going to lower the boom. All the way. Does that make you change your mind?"

"No."

"Does it make you even want to hesitate?"

"It makes me want to puke. But I'm not going to sell you out. And I won't walk out of here and leave you with nothing but yes-men."

Spode grunted. Suffield flung him a glance and said, "No offense intended. But somebody's going to have to be the loyal opposition around here, play devil's advocate every step of the way to keep you both from making asinine mistakes. I won't come quietly, but I'll come."

"Good enough," the Senator said. "Then I'm putting you right to work. Tomorrow's Saturday—book me on the morning flight to Tucson. Let the press know I'm going; I'll want reporters at the airport."

"What's the trip for?"

"Fact-finding. I've got work to do, so get the word out I won't be available. No testimonial luncheons or dinners for the social-climber crowd in the foothills. I intend to caucus with the military brass and the industrialists to find out how they're going to react. Learn if there are lines of attack I might use to get if not cooperation at least a minimum of vocalized resistance."

"I can tell you how they'll react right now."

"You might be surprised."

"By what?"

The Senator smiled. "That's what I'm flying out there to find out, isn't it."

Jaime Spode said, "You might get one break. Bill Ryan took over the Air Force Base a few months ago. He's a bird colonel now."

"I know."

Suffield asked, "Who's that?"

"Ryan used to fly Top and me around Japan and Korea."

"Back in the spook days," Spode said with a round glance at Suffield.

Suffield shook his head. "Don't go counting on a twenty-year-old friendship to put any Air Force colonels in your camp. All he'll do is tell you how foolproof their fail-safe systems are and how we need all the hardware we can get to fight off the monster of the International Communist Conspiracy."

"They're not all of them Patton-leather neanderthals, Les."

"Just don't count on anything, that's all."

The Senator reached for his interoffice intercom. "Gloria?" A crease furrowed his forehead and he released the button. "Damn. Slipped my mind completely. Les, do you mind calling the airport yourself and taking care of the other chores?"

"I don't mind. But you'd better get yourself a new girl pretty quick or take a secretary pill. I don't mind staying aboard the sinking ship but I'll be damned if I'll take a demotion from first officer to cabin boy."

"I know—I know. There's been too much to do around here to spend the days interviewing applicants."

"Ronnie Tebbel," Suffield said. "She's worked for you long enough to know the ropes and she's the brightest bird this side of Margaret Mead."

"And a mite better-looking," Jaime Spode remarked.

"I've thought about it," the Senator said. "My only question is, who'll run the Tucson office if Ronnie comes back here with us?"

"The way things are going you won't have a Tucson office

long enough to worry about it." Suffield stood up, went through to the outer office and reached for the phone.

The Senator said, "Shut the door a minute, Top. Let's talk."

Spode pushed the door shut and came back to his chair. "What do we get to talk about?"

"Webb Breckenyear's office. You spent a couple of hours over there today. You've got good eyesight. How good are the security arrangements?"

"You're kidding."

"Am I?"

"Look, you hired me to snoop. All right. But there's snooping and snooping."

"As Les has been pointing out, I'm going into a tough son-of-a-bitch fight. It happens that I'm doing it, to use the hoariest phrase I can think of, for the good of my country and it also happens that if I win it may propel me right onto the presidential launching pad. But if I lose, I lose the whole bag of marbles. So I'm laying everything on the line. And I need to use every means I can to reduce the odds against me."

"I can see that. But the risk, if you get caught—"

"If *you* get caught."

"Put it any way you like. If I get caught it's you they'll roast, not me. Breckenyear knows who I work for."

"Then don't get caught. I won't have any chance at all unless I know more than the opposition knows. I've got to stay ahead of them—and the more ignorant they are of how much I know, the better chance I've got to trip them up in public. I need exact appropriations figures on the Phaeton program from Breckenyear. That's your job."

"Couldn't we get that from the request for appropriations the Pentagon sent up? At least that's on the record."

"Budget requests don't mean a thing. They always request five million dollars' worth of paperclips because the committee has to cut something out of the request to show how hard they're guarding the American taxpayers' interests. I need the hard figures—the appropriations Breckenyear and Guest actually intend to ram through Congress."

"Just the Phaeton stuff?"

"That's number-one priority. But get anything else you can. The more waste we can find, the more weight our case has. And if I challenge them on more than one item it'll give us room to negotiate later—something we can give up on, to make it look as if we're compromising."

"Isn't that exactly what you just accused them of doing?"

The Senator smiled. "Think of that."

Spode grunted. Then he sighed. Finally he shook his head. "All right. First off, I'll need to find out whether he keeps it locked up in the office or takes it home nights to work on."

"You know the drill a lot better than I do."

"You used to handle it all right."

"A long time ago, Top."

Spode stood up. "You'll be in Arizona all week. What do I do with the stuff if I get it before you come back?"

"You damn well better have it before that. Hop a plane and bring it out to me."

"Right." He turned toward the door, stopped, and swung one foot up on the arm of the empty chair to buckle his galoshes. "You weren't expecting the originals, I hope."

"You've got a camera. Use it. We hardly want him tipping to the fact we've burgled his files."

"Not even you could be that dumb," Spode said. He grinned and went out and nodded to Suffield who was still on the phone.

☆☆☆☆☆☆☆☆☆☆☆☆☆☆☆☆☆☆☆☆☆☆☆☆☆☆☆☆☆☆☆☆☆☆

Chapter Two

Alan Forrester drove home past the reservoir and along the Potomac in a gloom of lightly falling snowflakes. The desultory thump of the windshield wipers exacerbated his mood.

He drove up the curving slope of Arizona Terrace and ran the car into the garage, wondering whether he would have to dig the driveway out in the morning.

Mrs. Thomas had left the place immaculate. The bed had been turned down, his slippers set out and two wooden hangers left pointedly on the bed for his overcoat and suit. He hung up his things and went down the half-flight of stairs to the kitchen. Mrs. Thomas had left a note taped to the refrigerator door: *Phone me or send a wire before you come back from the Wild West so I can stock the frigidair with milk & eggs. S. T.*

He filled a small glass with ice cubes and Chivas Regal and

carried it into the living room. He could hear the muted crack of icicles from rafters and trees. Only one lamp burned and the forty-foot room was lonely with gloom. He went around turning on lights and saw himself reflected in the wide glass patio doors, his slippered feet hidden in the deep jungle of the shaggy orange rug that Angie had bought over his protests. All the chairs and paintings were loud, vital, bold with primary colors; the room was full of her and Forrester felt savage with loss. It all came back in a piece—the apologetic telephone voice of the intern on emergency service, the bewildered rush across Washington to the hospital full of black faces and the burly cop, awkward and ill-at-ease: *This fellow come through the red light, Senator. No, he don't seem to've been drunk. Drivin' a real old Chrysler, one of them big tanks with tailfins, of course we'll know more when we get the wreckage sorted out but right now it looks like as if he was hittin' maybe forty, forty-five and those brakes just plain give out on him. Hit your wife's car not exactly head-on, sir —sort of catty-corner on the front bumper, she was comin' through there on the green light. Dumped Mrs. Forrester's car right over on the roof and skidded it right up against that building on the corner. The man driving the Chrysler, he's back here too, they got him under oxygen but there ain't a chance he'll pull through either. I wish there was something I could do for you, Senator—I have to report these things every other day to somebody and there's never been a one where I didn't wish there was some kind of wand I could wave to bring the people back. Ain't nothing I could say to you right now that would help make any sense out of this, sir.—I guess I won't even try.*

It had been almost a year ago but he still remembered the cop's voice; he had clung to it as the only reality of that ghastly day, the voice of the man in uniform who in those fractured moments seemed the only authority, the only possible wisdom. Later the reason had come to him slowly: the event had made him once again the fourteen-year-old boy whose father in Army colonel's uniform had taken him aside in the hospital corridor and told him his mother was dead. The two women in his life, gone under circumstances eerily similar. And at Angie's funeral on a sun-bright Tucson day that had mocked the solemnity of the ritual he had watched the casket descend into the grave and wept because he had no son to whom he could try to explain it. Her voice had echoed in him, accusation beyond reply: *We can't just keep putting off till it's convenient, darling. You're forty years old, I'm thirty-four, we've been married almost six years. To hell with all these rationalized procrastinations—to hell with the damned population explosion. I want to get pregnant.* When the old Chrysler had smashed brakeless through the red light she had been four months pregnant.

Her face had been full of joy those few months and he had humored her desire to redecorate the house flamboyantly; infected with her mood he had laughed at the growing discomfort of the colleagues and wives who came every other Wednesday to the traditional cocktails *chez* Forrester. Angie had been the compleat Washington hostess; she had delighted in the social hysteria of the capital, the Embassy Row receptions and Georgetown dinner parties at which lobbyists wheeled, wives gossiped, and much of the country's political business was done.

There had been no gatherings in the house since the accident. The room remained empty of everything but Angie's bright colors. Washington society had honored the Senator's grief by granting him a mourning moratorium on invitations. But gradually, because he had to and not because he enjoyed it, he had begun to resurface, to accept the cards and calls. The newspaper chat columns had waited a decent interval and then had begun to describe him as "Washington's most devastatingly eligible bachelor." Hostesses had begun to pair him off with this Desirable Single Girl or that. He remained quite immune because he could by closing his eyes create a vision of Angie that was almost tactile. The way she pinched her lower lip with her teeth and arched her eyebrows into triangles when she was earnest; the casual elegance of her walk; the way she tossed her head, the way her chestnut hair shone in sunlight. She had often been contentious, stubborn; she was more exciting than cuddly, more challenging than comfortable; but it was the brightest light that lingered longest in the retina.

The old bell-shaped Seth Thomas that Angie had bought

at a Maryland country auction rang the hour and Forrester switched on the television and stood in front of the screen, sipping his drink, debating whether to look at ABC or CBS or the NBC version, and then recalled fielding four or five questions from the CBS reporter which made it a good bet that that network's coverage would be heaviest.

The color screen warmed up; the announcer was revealing the crash in Spain of a Concorde with eighty-nine people on board and there was half a minute of film shot from a copter and relayed by satellite.

Television terrified him, he was appalled by the thought that tens of millions of people could be prodded by simultaneous stimuli into laughter and tension and applause and, irrevocably, opinion. But he had invited television coverage of the press conference because if the cameras didn't cover an event it hadn't happened; without television's stamp of recognition it did not exist, and what did not exist could be disregarded.

A correspondent stood against a background of palm trees and campus buildings and did forty seconds on the skull-smashing arrests of fourteen black students who had attempted to close down the administration building. Four commercials extolled forgettable products and Forrester's eyes strayed toward the glass doors and the surly wintry evening beyond. An avuncular newsman recited a report of guerrilla strikes and government counterstrikes in the hills behind Djakarta. The anchorman uttered unemployment and inflation figures and summarized in brief sentences the daily serial catastrophes of a world in unchanging flux, talking through a capped-tooth smile of destruction and disaster. A slow day for news. That was good, he thought dispassionately, a big story would have crowded him off the air.

He saw his face on the screen, squinting against the portable kliegs like a Hollywood horseman; his own appearance always startled him because he never felt subjectively as tall and rangy-rugged as the lean image on the screen. The voice sounded lower than his own, a silver rolling resonance that only just escaped being guttural.

They had edited him down to essentials but the result did not displease him because they had kept the context intact, which indicated that the news-bureau chief was probably on his side, and for openers that was a good sign.

"It's been brought to my attention that the Pentagon and its tame mouthpieces in both houses of Congress intend to sneak their new Phaeton Three program through passage in the form of riders casually attached to unimportant defense bills. I think the people of this country need to be warned of this attempt to stifle legitimate discussions and inquiries. . . . We're talking about offensive weapons, not defensive systems. We're talking about a terrifying new form of MIRV —multiple independently targeted reentry vehicle. We're talking about deploying a system where each single missile can deliver more than sixty miniaturized nuclear warheads on more than sixty separate enemy targets—and each one of these mini-warheads will have twice the destructive power of the bombs that wiped out Hiroshima and Nagasaki. We're talking about a defense establishment that's so arrogant it expects to ram down our throats a quantum jump in the arms race—an apocalyptic program—that they want us to swallow without a murmur of dissent."

They cut the rest of it and jumped to the Q & A period. There was some narrative commentary by the reporter and they had edited it neatly up to the beginning of the interviewer's question: "Senator, you've never associated yourself with the disarmament people before. Would you say this stand of yours is a new departure?"

"I'm a firm supporter of national defense. The Pentagon wants us to believe that anybody who questions their hardware salesmen must be a coward who wants to appease the other side the way Chamberlain appeased Hitler. The fact is we have the military capacity to destroy the Soviet Union utterly—we can overkill them forty times over—and we simply don't need another new weapons system that could prove more dangerous to us than to them."

"Senator, you've referred to that 'danger to ourselves' several times now. What danger do you mean?"

"Two things. First, what kind of weapons will the other side be forced to develop to counteract ours? And second, what about the risk of accidental detonation? The Phaeton system would deploy thousands of armed hydrogen warheads where we now have hundreds. Multiply the stockpile by a hundred and you multiply the risk of unintentional explosion by a thousand. A calculated risk is only justifiable when you've got something to gain from it, and we've got nothing to gain by this. The odds aren't acceptable. I'm saying it's time, right now, to stop giving the bomb merchants free rein."

"That's pretty strong talk, sir."

"I feel strongly about it. We hear a lot about boondoggles and pork barrels and Federal giveaways. I say let's not give away another thirty billion dollars for doomsday toys nobody needs."

The screen cut away and the moderator said deadpan, "There has been no reaction yet from the White House or the Pentagon to Senator Forrester's remarks." A kitchen cleanser replaced the moderator's face and Forrester switched the set off and smiled broadly when he heard the telephone ring: whoever it was, he wasn't wasting any time, but Forrester let it ring four times before he picked it up.

It was Woody Guest.

The elder Senator's voice was affable and hearty. "Nice little minstrel show you put on there, boy. Marvelous coverage, too. Did you catch yourself on CBS?"

"They gave it more time than I'd expected. How are you, Senator?" Forrester settled hipshot against the corner of the writing desk and sipped his drink.

"A mite ruffled. Candidly, young friend, you caught me off guard."

Think of that.

"If I hadn't had an off-the-record tip," Woodrow Guest continued, "from a journalistic acquaintance, I'd have missed your performance altogether."

"That would have been a shame."

"It would."

"Since you evidently want me to ask, what's on your mind, Senator?"

"You didn't play fair with us, son. Why didn't you come to me first?"

"Would it have got me anywhere?"

"Might have. After all, in our exclusive little club we have traditional ways of handling the decision-making process and getting things ironed out. You break with tradition, young friend, you make things uneasy for everybody."

"In my judgment this is no time for clubhouse rules."

"No issue's too important for decent courtesy, son. You've made a bad error." Guest's voice changed. "God damn it, Alan, have you got your brains up your ass or what? What in God's name got into you? Just what did you have in mind?"

"How about saving the Treasury thirty billion dollars, for openers."

"Balls. You're forgetting where you come from. I won't be able to hold up my head in Phoenix after tonight."

"I'm sure you've got time enough left to compose your suicide note."

Guest ignored it. "I had my suspicions but now I'm sure of it. You've joined the liberal losers at last—the ones who find success vulgar. I should have seen it coming."

"I haven't joined the crazies just yet, Senator."

"You may as well. Nobody else is going to give you a place to hang your hat after this little display."

"Not even you?"

"Not even me. Thank God I'm not the one who's up for reelection this year. At least I won't have to boot you off my ticket."

"I take it that means I'm not to count on your venerable support in the primary."

"You can put that in the bank, son. And you won't get much support from the Republican machinery anywhere."

"All right, Senator. We'll just have to wait and see how it all develops, won't we."

"Nothing to wait for, young friend. We've dealt with mavericks on the Hill before. It's not your private ball park up here

—you came into our ballgame, son, you play by our rules or else you get out of the park."

"Receipt acknowledged, Senator."

"You think about it, that's all. I'll get back to you after you've had time to mull it over. Take care now."

Forrester depressed the cradle button and waited with the receiver in hand until it rang again as he knew it would. He was smiling a little. "Forrester here."

It was Les Suffield. "I'm still at your office and the phones are jumping off the desks. What do I tell the ink-stained hacks?"

"You have nothing to add to what I said at the press conference. You're not empowered to speculate on questions I didn't cover."

"Maybe. Christ, you didn't half sling it all into the fan, did you?"

"If you pull punches you don't get much coverage."

"Too much coverage, Senator. Too much. You take the lid off the honey jar, you're bound to get all the predators swarming around. Just what effect did you expect to get, breathing fire like that?"

"Not as much as I'd like. It will roll off the ones who want to stay indifferent, it'll appear true to those who want to believe it, and it'll be dismissed as a pack of lies by those who've committed themselves to their own pack of lies."

"All right. So why did you do it?"

"Let's just say it was a fiendish impulse."

"Christ on a crutch. All right, you're on the nine-o'clock flight in the morning out of National, tickets at the VIP lounge for you to pick up. If I were you I'd leave the phone off the hook, otherwise you won't get any sleep."

"Senator Guest has already been heard from. I'm unlisted so there won't be too many more."

"What did he say? As if I can't guess."

"I've been drummed out of the party and he's about to bust my saber across his knee."

Suffield laughed unpleasantly and hung up. Forrester put the phone down properly because there was one more call he had to take tonight and he would know it when it came. The instrument began to ring immediately but he ignored it after the third ring and went into the kitchen feeling aggressive and alive, up on his toes, full of anticipatory adrenalin. He made another drink and sorted through the refrigerator to find the makings of a supper; the phone kept ringing angrily but he shut it out and thought of Angie, half-wishing she could be here for this fight and half-angry with himself for wishing it because he was very close now to putting her all the way behind him, and he knew he had to cover the last sprint toward escape even though it made him feel as guilty as if he were abandoning her. He supposed another woman would make the escape easier but no casual one-night stand would do it and he was not ready for anything deeper than that yet.

He let his free associations ramble and so he was presently thinking about Top Spode because Top was one of those easygoing philandering grasshoppers who never stored up winter food and went through life regarding women the way most men regarded good cigars, as something to be treasured briefly and discarded when they had served their purpose. Actually he was thinking about Top because he was expecting Top's call. He kept listening for it but it didn't come until after he had finished scraping the dishes and putting them in the dishwasher. Then he heard it, two rings and a pause, then two rings and another pause, and he headed toward it when it began to ring again.

"What have you got, Top?"

"A bad case of ring-around-the-rosy. Subject does not have the nitty-gritty. The job's been subcontracted out."

"Subject" was Congressman Webb Breckenyear, and "nitty-gritty" meant the specifications and budgetary breakdown on the Phaeton Three program. Breckenyear had farmed the assignment out.

"Why the hell would he do a thing like that?"

"I've only been on the job a few hours. What do you want out of me?"

"You'd better come out here. We'll have to talk."

"I'll pick you up in twenty minutes."

Forrester made a face. "All right, if you think it's necessary."

"Color me paranoid but let's don't take chances."

Forrester jiggled the button until he got a dial tone, left the
receiver off the hook, and went up to the bedroom to get his
overshoes and coat. He went right past the framed photo of
Angie on the chest of drawers and then abruptly turned back,
took the photograph down and put it away face-down in the
top drawer. It made him feel as if he had just made an important decision. He shouldered into the coat and went out the
front door, working his gloves on while he took long slow
breaths of the cold night air. It had stopped snowing and the
fresh lie looked puffy and clean on the sloping lawns and
roofs. He left overshoe spoor behind in the thin white crust
on the brick walkway when he went out to the curb and stood
waiting in the wind, enjoying the crisp bite of it.

The reflected glow of headlights appeared at the road crest
and the sleigh-bell chitter of tire chains reached his ears.
Coming over the hill the lights seemed to bounce wildly
before they settled down, stabbing him. Spode drew in at the
curb and leaned across the front seat to open the door.

Forrester got in. Spode switched off the lights and engine;
the windows immediately began to steam up. Forrester said,
"I don't see why your car's any safer than my basement."

"I go over it every other morning for bugs. Can you say the
same thing for your basement?"

"I suppose not, but it's pretty far-fetched to think—"

"I don't think," Top said mildly, "I just assume."

"All right, then. What's this about Breckenyear farming it
out? Farming it out to whom?"

"That information wasn't included in the price of my ticket.
But I could make a pretty good guess, and so could you."

It took a while for Forrester to work it out but in the end
he said, "Ross Trumble."

"Got to be."

It fit. Trumble was a sophomore Congressman—Representative from the Second Congressional District of Arizona,
which included Tucson and the southern counties, not ex-

cluding the defense plants, Davis Monthan Air Force Base, Fort Huachuca missile-test range and CBW laboratories, and the Tucson wing of ICBM and ABM silos. In his freshman term on the hill Trumble had made friends with Webb Breckenyear because Breckenyear chaired House Military Appropriations and Trumble was the property of the Arizona military-hardware manufacturers who had financed his campaigns. Now in his second term Trumble was a junior member of Breckenyear's committee and since it looked as if the Phaeton contracts, once let, would go to Arizona corporations, Trumble was the obvious man to draw up the bill.

Webb Breckenyear was a Democrat and it would help show his bipartisan altruism to let Trumble handle the chore. Trumble was a Republican, somewhere to the right of Senior Senator Woodrow Guest; he had received Guest's support in the election and no doubt would continue to receive it: Guest knew that if you demanded loyalty up, you had to show loyalty down, even when you didn't like some of the players you had to root for. Besides, in less than four years on the Hill, backed by Breckenyear's Southern Democrats and Guest's centrist Republican wing, Trumble had insinuated himself powerfully. If there was another right-wing surge within the party like the ones that had taken off in 1964 and 1970, it was not beyond belief that Ross Trumble could wrest the Arizona Republican machine out of the Senior Senator's grasp, and Guest was not going to make it easier for Trumble to try by backing Forrester's leftish move. As far as Woody Guest was concerned, everybody except himself was expendable, but Senator Forrester was more expendable than Congressman Trumble. Forrester was in the fight all by himself and whatever support he was likely to get would come not from his own party but from the opposition, and in this election year even that would be muted. In traditional political terms Forrester's move was suicidal, but politics was no longer as traditional as it had been. Of course his odds were still rotten but that was what made it an interesting fight.

"Ross Trumble," he said. "All right, I don't see any problem. Get them from him."

Top was sitting up straight as he always sat with his long arms folded across his wide flat chest. The reflected light of the street lamp made highlights in his long glossy black hair. He said, "It's so damn easy to tell a fellow to run it on up the flagpole when you don't have to figure out how to stitch the flag."

"If it was an easy job I wouldn't need to have you do it."

"Now you're trying to flatter me."

"And succeeding," Forrester said. "What's the flap?"

"Trumble used to be an FBI agent. He won't be easy to crack."

"He can't keep those papers in his pocket twenty-four hours a day."

"But he probably keeps them in a lock-up. You happen to know any unemployed safecrackers looking for work?"

"You may be making problems for yourself where there aren't any to begin with. Maybe Trumble had security training once but he's gone off the wagon and he's got a lech for anything that wiggles. Why not get one of your lovely young friends to fry him while you take his place apart?"

"Two problems. One, the only girls I could trust with that kind of caper are Agency employees. But I don't work for the Agency any more and the Agency frowns on its people free-lancing. And two, Trumble's leaving Washington day after tomorrow—back to Tucson for an indefinite stay. Like you."

"Will he take the papers with him?"

"I guess that's what he's going out there for. To check out the details with the people at Matthewson-Ward and Shattuck. He wouldn't be likely to leave the papers back here on top of his desk."

"Then tail him out to Tucson and stick to him until you can pry open his files."

"Yeah. Listen, you happen to know Diego Orozco up in Phoenix?"

"No."

"Private detective, runs a confidential agency up there. I could maybe hire the use of one of his female operatives but it would cost you seventy-five a day plus travel and expenses.

Eight cents a mile round trip Phoenix-Tucson, that's twenty bucks, and expen—"

Forrester's laugh cut him off and Spode darkened and said, "Sometimes I forget you're a rich son of a bitch. But it'll have to come out of your pocket, you can't very well charge it up to the Government. And I'm still not clear just how vital this package of papers is to whatever you're planning to put across."

"Vital enough. I thought you heard me the first time. I intend to use every stick I can get my hands on to beat this insanity to death, because if somebody doesn't Trumble and Breckenyear and the hardware merchants won't be satisfied until they've blown the world up from under us."

"You've already got my vote, you know. I didn't ask for a speech—all I want to know is how badly you want Trumble's file. You want it even if it has to come with my head in a basket?"

"Make your own judgment, Top."

"Like I said, I just work here."

The Senator's face moved. "I want to live and if I ever have a kid I want him to live. That's what it breaks down to."

Spode brooded at him. "It's not just politics anymore, is it? You mean that."

"I mean it."

"Then I'll get the papers for you. But maybe you ought to have the meat wagon and a crash crew ready to collect me." Spode grinned with his teeth and reached for the ignition key and Forrester got out and watched the car drive away.

☆☆☆☆☆☆☆☆☆☆☆☆☆☆☆☆☆☆☆☆☆☆☆☆☆☆☆☆☆☆☆☆

Chapter Three

Forrester changed planes at Chicago. The jet broke through the smog overcast and the top of the snowcloud layer was a soft cotton mattress beneath the motionless belly of the airplane. The stewardess brought him a cup of hot black coffee and smiled. "My folks live in Phoenix, Senator—they voted for you."

"How about you?"

Her laugh stirred her short blond hair. "The first time you ran for Congress I was fourteen. Anyhow I live in Los Angeles —I can't vote in Arizona. But I would if I could."

She went forward, emphasizing the sway of her long hips because she knew he was watching. Her kind had voted him into office because by accident of birth he had the looks and charm that worked in a society which equated celebrity with importance and which favored a candidate who was at his amusing best on late-night television.

As always, Les Suffield had booked two first-class seats for him so that he wouldn't be disturbed. The Washington *Post* lay on the empty aisle seat beside him. It had given him a three-column spread across the middle of the front page. HOUSE-PENTAGON COLLUSION CHARGED. *Forrester Alleges Secret Phaeton Power Play.* There were sidebar heads: *Breckenyear Denies Charges; Pentagon Says "No Comment."* The editorial inside was cautious: "If what Senator Forrester charges is true, then certainly the public deserves, and should demand, full disclosure in open hearings." At least, he thought, it had served to redden Webb Breckenyear's face.

Under the wings the weather cleared and the land began to heave and buckle, and the plane began its slow descent while still over New Mexico. Sprawls of weathered aridity, puckered by brown mountains of rock and pale earth. Another high stretch of desert, another mountain range, snow on the peaks; the plane banked and began to spiral in earnest. Mount Lemmon, bald with snow, could be recognized easily from the air: Tucson's ten-thousand-foot landmark. Davis Monthan Air Force Base was a great grey expanse: it had been built well beyond the southeast edge of the town but Tucson had grown with swift carcinoma and now the curving rows of mass-produced tract houses and shopping centers all but encircled the base. Population 375,000, median income $8,200, nine percent of its housing units substandard, 33,000 people earning less than the poverty level—numbers meant nothing in human terms but served to placate Washington's insatiable mania for columns of figures. Tucson was not a simple place and could not be dismissed by computer statistics.

The newcomer saw what he expected: the plastic holy land of the Good Life, warm dry winters, palms and cacti, constant sunshine. Until World War II there had been nothing but railroad yards, dude ranches, tuberculosis sanatoriums and thirty thousand or so people. Then had come the Cold War and the population explosion. SAC had moved in and the defense plants—Matthewson-Ward, Shattuck Industries, and the smaller ones. The onetime cowtown was now the second largest city in Arizona and contained nearly a third of the state's population within its metropolitan area.

The boosters still hung banners across Broadway, "A Community on the March." You still heard how Tucson was a grand place to raise a family. It was still a Middle American town, a joining town—Rotary, the Elks, the Lions, the Jaycees, the Eastern Star, the Ladies' Auxiliary of the American Legion, the Knights of Columbus; it was a seller's market for the *Reader's Digest* and the Book-of-the-Month Club. But it was also a high crime center, a metropolis jammed with automobiles, a suburbanite sprawl with its old downtown center crumbling into slums. Alan Forrester could see the smog plainly, a well defined brown murk into which the plane descended.

The 707 landed with a lurch on the black tire smears that planes had left before it. It taxied toward the long west wing of the terminal and from his window Forrester could see the reporters waiting just inside the glass doors of the building. The jet engines unwound and passengers crowded into the aisles but Forrester kept his seat. He watched them go down the portable stair and cross the sun-blasted concrete to the door. The cluster of reporters broke in half like the Red Sea to let the passengers by, and Forrester's attention focused on a tall long-haired woman fighting her way against the tide with frequent distracted smiles of apology as she squeezed through the door and came outside. It was Ronnie—Veronica Tebbel.

She had high strong bones and large eyes and she moved with graceful economy. The dark hair fell loose to her shoulders and she stopped to comb it back from her eyes with her fingers while she looked for him in the windows. He moved his hand back and forth against the plexiglass until she smiled and nodded and came along to the foot of the boarding stairs to wait for the crowd to thin out. Then she came up the stairs, long-legged and slender and full of vibrant energies. She had to be thirty-six or more but in the sunlight she moved like a twenty-year-old.

Forrester stood up in the aisle and lifted his briefcase onto the seat—that ancient expandable briefcase, its leather tough and creased with age lines, which his father had carried to the United States Senate before him.

The stew let Ronnie come aboard and Forrester saw her squint against the gloom inside the fuselage. She came to him with a smile and an outstretched hand. Forrester stared at her until she blushed and he said quickly, "I'd forgotten how lovely you are."

She smiled, but it was incomplete. Something had come up behind her eyes. She withdrew her fingers and spoke in a soft low contralto. "I thought I'd better come on board and warn you."

"The reporters? I saw them."

"They're waiting for you like the Mexicans outside the Alamo."

"I've been besieged before. What kind of mood are they in?"

"Edgy—your plane's two hours late. But some of them smiled at me."

"Anybody'd smile at you, Ronnie. That's the cross you bear."

"When a cougar bares his fangs it doesn't pay to assume he's giving you a friendly smile. They only wanted to pump me. You'd better fix your tie, they've got TV cameras—here, let me do it."

Her touch at his throat was light and cool and her face hovered before him. "There," she said, and smiled. Forrester felt defensive. He reached across the seat for his briefcase and glanced out through the window. The strong warm sun slanted down, the tarmac had emptied of passengers; and he could see the reporters stirring impatiently. A tiny woman in a trim grey suit, with wire-grey hair and a simian face, had come outside and stood pointing toward the door of the plane, and a camera crew beside her circled forward to focus their portable television apparatus on the top of the boarding stairs. The woman was Nicole Lawrence, KARZ-TV's political reporter and professional gadfly; she had traveled with him on the campaign and he knew her tart caustic tongue. "I see they've sent out the big guns."

"What did you expect? You uncovered your own artillery last night," Ronnie said.

"You don't approve, do you?"

Her smile was evanescent and nervous. "I only work here."

"That's what Top Spode said. I didn't let him off the hook and I won't let you off either."

"I hate to admit this," she said, "but anything you do is all right with me." She seemed to have surprised herself because she added with an impatient toss of her head, "Senator, I don't—"

"Alan."

It had been a silly thing to say; this wasn't the time for it. It only made her withdraw. "Maybe," she said, not looking at him. "I'll have to think about that. In the meantime before you go out there and let them stand you up against the wall, you need to know this—they're going to hit you with questions about the primary campaign. Have you got an answer for them?"

"Id est, am I ready to announce my candidacy. No. I'm not."

"Because you're not sure if the Phaeton thing will turn into a banana peel?"

"Maybe."

"The mood of the press," she said deadpan, "is such that they're assuming if you don't declare for office now it's because you're scared the party will scuttle you over the Phaeton issue. One of them asked me if you intended to run as an Independent. Have you thought about it?"

"No."

"The funny thing is, I believe you. But they won't."

"They wouldn't anyway. Candidates always deny they're going to be candidates. That's rule one of the great American game."

"Then what will you tell them?"

"That I haven't made up my mind."

"They'll call it a cop-out."

"Let them," he said. "We'd better go."

He took her arm but she disengaged herself. "It wouldn't look right, would it? You'd better go out alone and let them take your picture on the stairs. I'll creep out afterward and collect your luggage and meet you out front with the car. Will you be staying at the ranch?"

"Not for a few days. I had Les call the Pioneer for a reservation."

"I could have somebody drop your bags at the hotel if you want to stop by the office first."

"Good. I'll want to get on the phone before dinner." He walked toward the door, and stopped. "Dinner. Are you busy tonight?"

"Is it important?"

"Sometimes I'm not sure what's important," he said, and elaborated it with a lie: "There's a lot we'll have to discuss and there may not be time at the office. I'm going to work you hard for the next week or two."

"In that case I'll break my date." Her eyes were dark with a sort of reserve he couldn't place. She had been married once, but her husband had been dead ten or twelve years. Still, it was possible she felt his presence, as Forrester felt Angie's, a memory which crowded out the desire for further affinities.

She was watching him with a soft wide expression, her lips slightly parted and her head tipped to one side. He gave her a quick smile and stepped out into the warm blaze of sunlight.

He sat back with a huge yawn and a slow two-handed combing back of his hair. Through the doorway he saw Ronnie with a telephone receiver on her shoulder, head tilted against it to free her hands, listening to the phone and jotting on a brass-framed calendar pad. She had lovely eyes.

She cradled the phone and ripped the top page off the pad and came into his office talking briskly:

"I tracked down Frank Shattuck at the Mountain Oyster Club. He'll be on the golf course in the morning but he said he'd be home by three if you'd care to drop in then." Her voice was dry with irony. "Easy enough to see how the wind blows, isn't it? He won't come to you—you have to go to him."

"After all," he said, "tomorrow's Sunday." Frank Shattuck was board chairman of Shattuck Industries, which manufactured ICBM components in its plant two miles from the gate of Davis Monthan Air Force Base.

She poked the note into his breast pocket. "Don't miss the appointment." But the gesture contained an intimacy she evidently hadn't intended and she stepped back quickly.

He spoke to fill the silence. "We'll have to take a raincheck on that dinner-for-two. I just talked to Colonel Ryan. He'll skin me if I don't come to his house for dinner. I included you in the invitation—I hope you don't mind?"

She turned her face: a quick smile. "No."

"Have you met Bill Ryan?"

She shook her head and the hair flowed softly back and forth.

"I expect you'll like him."

Through the window he could see the courthouse square, pooled by street lamps. A couple stood in the square with two young children, pointing and talking, the father in dungarees and a zippered windbreaker talking with wide sweeps of his arm and probably explaining to the kids the functions of the courthouse.

He felt Ronnie's weight beside him and moved aside to give her the view. "That's what it all comes down to—giving them something to believe in."

She gave him a brief warm smile.

On the way out they passed a few night workers—pale civil servants and fluttering clerks. Forrester smiled at them with his candid eyes and answered their greetings, addressing them by name as a political animal must, and when they reached the sidewalk Ronnie laughed at him. "Did you see the way they looked at you? You've got those votes sewed up."

"Hitler had charisma. I don't altogether approve of the personality cult in politics—even if I do owe it a great deal."

"You can't make the rules, can you?" There was something grave in her voice.

They walked up the quiet street without speaking. Occasionally her arm brushed his. She meant nothing overt by it; he was beginning to know that she was a woman in whom very little was obvious. She had come to work for him during his last campaign and he had become well acquainted with her, but only as one would become well acquainted with one's military subordinate—clearly, but at a distance. He knew the quickness of her mind, the good efficiency of her talents. The rest was unanswered.

They crossed an intersection under a street light and he stole a direct look at her. He thought of the cliché of the oblivious boss who has never really looked at his adoring and beautiful secretary before. Like all clichés it was worthless because it oversimplified reality. He had never been blind to Ronnie's sexual attractions. He wouldn't have hired her if she hadn't caught his eye. That was the way he had always been: he liked to surround himself with decorative women. Angie had known that and Angie had never held it against him: in her own way she took a certain pride from the fact that of all the attractive women in his life she alone had held him. Now and then she had made a tart joke about it and he had composed a ritual reply: "Just because a man's on a diet doesn't mean he can't read the menu." They had laughed the way healthy people laugh who are sure of themselves and of each other. Angie had been complete in her femininity, men had always given her a second look, and he had enjoyed it as much as she had: it had confirmed his proprietary pride, which took pleasure from other men's envy.

He caught Ronnie's short half-smile when they turned the corner. He was intensely aware of her electricity; aware, as well, that she liked him and was pleased by his attentions. She hadn't tried to rebuff his interest by displays of indifference: she gave off none of the signals of misogamous frigidity he had discovered in otherwise coquettish women; still, curiously, she had surrounded herself with tensile barriers and by setting limits she had challenged his masculine determination. He felt like a small boy confronted by a new mechanical device: he would not be willing to quit prying it apart until he found out what made it work.

"Here we are." She handed him the keys. He unlocked the

door for her and went around to the driver's side and slid in under the wheel. "Why a station wagon?"

"I paint," she said, and it was only after a moment that she seemed to realize it required further explanation. "I'm a Sunday painter. Oils—landscapes, mostly. I like to drive out in the country. I need the space in back for my easel and canvases and paintbox and palette—all the impedimenta of the amateur dauber."

He drove west toward the freeway, moving against the incoming tide of Saturday-night traffic. "I often wondered what you did with your off time. Not that you seem to have much of it. I've caught you in the office on the phone at ungodly hours some nights."

"You have a bad habit," she said lightly. "You always forget the difference in time zones between here and Washington."

It was a casual remark and he almost let it go by but then the significance of it struck him. He shot a glance at her. He couldn't make out her expression; the light was poor. He said, "Do you mean to tell me you wait around the office every night of the week on the off-chance I might telephone from Washington?"

"Well, it's not only for that. We're understaffed; usually it takes me till eight or nine to clear the decks for the next day's action."

"Why in hell haven't you said so? We can hire another secretary."

"It didn't seem important," she said vaguely. "I haven't had anything better to do, anyway. You can't paint at night."

"But what about your social life?"

"I lead a very quiet social life," she said, and added nothing to it.

He made the turnoff and followed the flyover ramp up onto the freeway. He pushed the accelerator down and moved out into the left lane to pass the slower traffic. The station wagon was a big one, heavy and no better designed than most of its kind: everything rattled slightly, the steering and braking controls were not precise, and at high speed it tended to wag its tail and bounce with a lunging seasick sway. Forrester liked to drive; he had behind him a youth filled with the roar of sports cars, the memory of rallies and gymkhanas.

He said, "Les Suffield asked you if you'd be willing to come to Washington and run my office there. Have you thought about it?"

"I'm still thinking about it. I imagine I'll do it, at least until November. If you decide to run again and they put you back for another six years, I may decide to come home. I've been in Washington before. I don't like it very much."

"It's a one-company town," he said. "If you don't like the company it's not much of a place."

"That kind of social whirl doesn't appeal to me, I'm afraid."

He found the turnoff, corkscrewed down under the highway and drove north toward the base. The white stripe of the road ran as straight as an architect's line. "You said you lead a quiet life. Forgive me if I'm prying, but is that because you're a widow?"

"That's part of it."

"What's the rest?"

"It's hard to put into words."

"When Angie died I didn't want to face people either— nothing seemed worth the effort."

"Because you had no one to share it. I know." She turned in her seat—she was far over against the door. "I knew what you were going through last year when she died but there wasn't anything I could say that would have helped. You understand? But it's been eleven years since my husband died. I'm not still carrying a torch."

"Then it's something else."

"Really, I'd rather not talk about it."

"Another time then."

She put her feet flat on the floor and looked straight ahead and the next time she spoke it was to say, "We must be almost there."

The air-base gate was an open entrance—there were AP's on duty but passage was not restricted and they drove through it slowly. Somewhere ahead was an interior perimeter beyond which unauthorized visitors could not go. Forrester had been here before on various occasions and knew the general area he sought, but he had to stop and ask a woman pushing a stroller where the base commander lived. Most married officers lived off-post in civilian houses but the base commander was on twenty-four-hour call and had to live on the base. The best the Air Force had done by way of privacy was to put his house behind a dusty hillock away from the other buildings. The last piece of road was indifferently paved and the wheels churned up a gritty dust that quickly got into Forrester's nostrils and teeth but he didn't mind; he had grown up on the taste of it. Beyond the hill he turned into the graded circular drive.

It was an ultramodern house of glass, open to the space about it, not especially large; one of those Southwestern houses without basement or attic, temporary-looking because it was temporary.

The front door of the house opened, throwing a splash of lamplight across the steps, and Colonel Bill Ryan came out beaming.

Ryan had always been big and now he was a big man with a belly on him. He had thick shoulders and a deep chest; a square head anchored on a wide neck. He was wearing a loud Hawaiian shirt, white tapered slacks, white loafers, no socks. He was crowding fifty but he had the kind of durably boyish face often discovered on mercenary soldiers and airplane pilots. The hair on top, sandy and going thin, was combed carefully over the pink scalp.

"About God damn time you remembered to call on your old friends." He marched forward to pump Forrester's hand and clap him violently on the bicep.

Ronnie was getting out of the car and Forrester saw the way Ryan's unsubtle grin widened with the quick shift of focus that bracketed them both in the single frame of his vision. "Yes indeed," Ryan said, full of approval, bowing over Ronnie's hand with an amusingly courtly gesture. Ronnie smiled pleasantly and said she had heard a lot about him. Ryan's laugh expanded his throat. "That's a shame—I was hoping we could be friends."

There was a shriek of lusty delight from the house and

Forrester wheeled in time to see Alice Ryan rush breathless down the steps. "Why didn't you *tell* me they were here? Alan, *dar*ling, it's been so *long!*" She planted a warm wet kiss full on his mouth. Her assault almost knocked him back against the car and he laughed, untangling himself, but when he caught Ronnie's glance he felt color flood his face. Alice Ryan stepped back and looked him up and down, and then Ryan cleared his throat and introduced her to Ronnie. Forrester saw the way Alice's expression changed immediately, became speculative, the assessment of the predatory female for one who might prove to be a competitor. Alice was a small fluffy blonde, husky and pneumatic, with a sun-whacked face that tended to pout. Her aura was frankly sexual; she gave an impression of greedy appetites and single-track intentions. She wore a pleated black skirt and a bolero half-jacket, bare at the midriff, with slinky black sleeves that covered her plump arms. She was slightly overweight but it hadn't gone to her waist; it only emphasized the roundness of her hips and buttocks, the ripe thrust of her breasts. She had the hoarse breathy voice of the casual alcoholic.

They went inside amid a great deal of chatter, both Ryans trying to talk at once. Forrester felt curiously detached, unable to enter into the spirit of hearty reunion; he had always liked Bill and Alice, had always been at ease with them, but up to now they had been friends with no outside issues to color the relationship.

The room was self-consciously new, deliberately underfurnished, with large expanses of parquet floors and vastnesses of plate glass. The obligatory display case of a commanding officer; but in it, Bill Ryan looked alarmingly out of place.

There was a mild confusion of choosing seats and talking loudly across the room while Ryan mixed strong drinks and served them with Alice trailing him around distributing napkins and appetizers from a wooden tray. Forrester marked the contrast between all this and the cluttered pillowy comforts of the quarters Ryan had inhabited in his throttle-jockey youth. In those days they had sat around a kitchen table drinking beer from cans.

They were feeling each other out like strangers. Alice's bouncy enthusiasm was forced, she was drinking too fast, and Ryan was putting on a hearty front but he was searching for things to talk about and there was too much postmorteming of old times. Ronnie was the only real stranger here but it wasn't her presence that made for the awkwardness; Ronnie seemed to fit in more easily than any of them—perhaps because she did not try too hard.

Alice fluttered nervously in and out of the kitchen, preparing to serve dinner. Once Forrester heard the crash of porcelain from the kitchen and Alice's explosive curse. Ronnie hurried to the kitchen door—"Won't you let me help?"—but Alice snapped at her: the kitchen was too small for two, she had everything under control; the words did not convey the meaning in her shrill tone. Ronnie returned to her seat, subdued, and Ryan made a clumsy effort to cover the moment with a hurried joke. But when Alice appeared Forrester did not miss the tight-lipped turn of Ryan's face or the sulky glance Alice threw him.

Dinner was equally awkward and Forrester felt saddened by the sense of disintegration. Prism lights, recessed in the fake-beamed ceiling, threw too much bland illumination across the table, showing up the tremor of Ryan's hands as he ate, the telltale thread of moisture on Alice's pouty upper lip. The meal was delicious and perfectly served but Alice hardly touched it; she sat pushing her ice cubes around with a wooden chopstick. Ryan tried to keep a conversation going but Forrester caught him gritting his neat white teeth.

In the end Forrester felt ashamedly stupid: it had taken him too long to realize they were nervous and upset because they were in the presence of a United States Senator. He made the discovery in a remark Ryan let drop; a moment later he could no longer remember the remark itself but he knew what he should have known all along. They were commoners in the presence of royalty; Ryan was an unhappy Falstaff whose Hal had become king.

He took no comfort from the discovery; he could see no way to put them at their ease. It made him quietly miserable. Over coffee he caught Ronnie watching him with kind compassion: she understood, but it was not her place to break the ice. Nor, he realized, was it his. He was in fact a Senator and there was no way on earth to deny it or change it.

Ronnie wanted to help with the dishes but they wouldn't let her. Ryan helped his wife carry things out to the kitchen. Forrester heard water running in the sink, the clatter of washing up, the hiss of Ryan's sibilant berating, Alice's strident, contentious, carelessly drunken reply: "All *right!* Just once, let's do things *my* way, all right? Get back in there and act like a host."

Forrester turned away when he heard Ryan's step; he began to speak to Ronnie, pretending he hadn't heard. Ronnie put her hand on the table, forming a loose fist; he had the feeling she would have touched his hand if they had not been separated by the width of the dining table.

Ryan came in red-faced, trying to beam. "How about a little snort of brandy to go with that coffee? Whaddya say, buddy? Mrs. Tebbel?"

"Please call me Ronnie. No, no brandy for me, thank you."

"How about you, buddy? Not going to let me down, are you?" Ryan's grin was painful. He had started to clap Forrester on the shoulder but thought better of it. He wheeled furiously toward the bar without waiting an answer. "Got some real fine Havanas here. Old buddy of mine flew them in from Guantánamo."

They left the table and settled around the phony brick fireplace. Forrester heard the click of the refrigerator door and in a moment Alice arrived from the kitchen, unsteady on her feet, carrying a tall glass full of ice cubes and whiskey. Ryan launched into another Good Old Days monologue with heavy jocularity but rapidly ran down, dragged on his cigar and jetted smoke, and finally squirmed in his chair and said, "Time to go from the preamble to article one. This damn house hasn't got much more than this one room. You want to exile the ladies to the bedroom or take the cigars out on the patio?"

Alice muttered something unintelligible and Ryan pro-

fessed not to hear her; he got up and said, "You gals mind
entertaining each other for a while?" and marched toward the
sliding glass doors at the back of the room.

Ronnie smiled up at Forrester. "Go on, now. We'll get
along fine." It was a lie and everyone knew it except Alice,
who was filing her nails with an emery board, sulking, nearly
drunk enough to pass out or go into a crying jag. Forrester
did not want to leave Ronnie with that on her hands but this
was important. He said, *sotto voce,* "I'm sorry, Ronnie," and
went out onto the patio after Ryan.

Ryan had turned the outdoor lights on. "No bugs this time
of year. I love it out here on the flagstones. But if you get
chilly I'll hunt up a sweater."

"This is fine, Bill."

Ryan slid the doors shut, closing them out. "Sit down, sit
down. Want another drink before we start the brouhaha?"

"No, thanks."

"Neither do I. Well then, old buddy, let's have at it."

"You don't like this, do you?"

"Oh, hell, don't mind any of this. I don't like anything right
now. It's a bad patch. Alice and me, I don't know—it seems
to've become nothing more than some kind of incessant bargaining. And this stinking job of mine . . ."

"What's wrong with it? It's a pretty important job."

"Nuts. I'm just marking time here. It's a dead end. This
command's supposed to belong to a brigadier general, you
know. I'm just filling in until they find themselves the right
general to take it over."

"Maybe they'll give you a star."

Ryan snorted. "I don't expect to get another promotion
before World War Four."

"Why not? You've got a good record."

"As a pilot, buddy. As a pilot. But I started in P-51's and
that's the kiss of death; now I'm overage and I'm just an
embarrassment to have around. They take people like me and
shuffle us around from one boondock job to another until it's
time to retire us gracefully and forget us. I'm just sitting
around waiting to be put out to pasture; but by God I hate

rown out like an old shoe. I hate it. Do you know what wn here? A pencil pusher. They've got a SAC wing nder to run operations and an ICBM wing commander the silos and all I do is take care of the real estate for them.

"You're not an old man. You can do anything you want. A new career with your retirement pay for a cushion. Look at all the retired officers who've made successes of themselves."

"Doing what? Figureheading some corporation with hot defense contracts? Playing politics with the old buddies in the Pentagon to keep those contracts up? Not me. I'm an airplane jockey and that's all I've ever been. You know that last Pentagon tour of duty cooked my goose. If you're a colonel in this business and you want to be a general you've got to charm the generals' wives and when it comes to that I'm about as adroit as a bull in a china shop. I hate every bit of it—I always have. Always having to choose your friends by rank. You can never win a game of golf or a game of bridge against a superior officer but you've always got to know how to play well enough to make it look good. You can't get mad if a drunken superior starts to paw your wife. You spend your whole life going to drinking parties where nobody's got anything to say and you watch them turn your wife into a rank-conscious drunken bitch."

Ryan took the cigar out of his mouth. He had bitten it in two. He spat the stub into his hand and hurled it over the patio wall into the night.

"Look, buddy, do me a big favor. Forget everything I just said. Once a year a guy has a right to get maudlin but I didn't mean to dump it all over you. I swear I won't do it again. Now let's talk about what you came up here to talk about. I saw you on the TV last night—that little speech of yours must've shook the striped pants off some diplomats."

"Did it shake yours off?"

"I'm on your side. I think the fat cats are too fat. About time somebody talked about trimming some of it off."

"What do you know about the Phaeton system?"

"Enough."

"How much is enough?"

"Buddy, I am bound by Title Eighteen of the National Security Act."

"I'm cleared for Top Secret information. Do I have to show you my clearance?"

Ryan flushed. "Of course not, Senator."

"Don't do that. I didn't come up here to muscle you."

"Exactly what did you come for?"

"Two things. First, where do you stand on Phaeton?"

"Personally? I just told you. I think the damn thing's a waste of time, a waste of money, and a potential catastrophe."

"Will you testify to that effect in front of a Senatorial hearing?"

"No."

It made him sit up. "No?"

"Maybe if I had three stars I could get away with something like that. Just maybe. But I don't have three stars. Just a pair of scrawny turkey buzzards on the shirt collars of my uniforms."

"You're a front-line operational officer, Bill. You're in command of a strategic base. You're more closely in touch with the immediate problems of this kind of thing than anybody else. Why shouldn't your word carry weight?"

"Because in my business we're not allowed to have public opinions unless they happen to coincide with the official line of the department. Even the liberal politicians insist on keeping military types out of politics. If I open my mouth in public hearings there'll be nothing left of me but a small wet spot on the pavement."

"You're not trying to tell me they'd court-martial you."

"What do you think they cashiered Billy Mitchell for?"

"For God's sake, Bill. That was more than forty years ago."

"And you think they've changed any in that period of time, the big boys with the omelettes on their hats?"

"Come on, Bill. You've got to do better than that."

"It's a taut community. People don't like to hear any questions about anything at all. They particularly don't like to hear questions from snot-nosed junior officers. Mitchell was a brigadier, Alan. I'm not even that high on the totem pole.

Maybe they wouldn't court-martial me but they'd make it so life wasn't worth living, in or out of the service. They'd see to it I couldn't get a job doing so much as grease-monkeying a cropdusting plane anywhere in the country. You better believe it, buddy. Rank Has Its Privileges, and among those privileges is the good old blackball. One twitch of a government digit and my head rolls—that's all it takes. No. You don't get me to testify. And I won't use this as an excuse but I'll mention it for what it's worth—even if I did testify for you I'd do more harm than good. They'd scrape up enough embarrassing items from my record to discredit me as a reliable witness and they'd probably throw in eight scientists and fourteen four-star generals to counteract my testimony anyway. You think about that, because this little job you've picked is about as easy as trying to mate a chimpanzee with a porcupine. No way, buddy, *no* way."

Ryan sank his teeth into the remains of his cigar and blew a rancid cloud of smoke. "Now what was the second thing you came for?"

There was no arguing with him, he had the stubbornness of an elephant in heat.

"I want to inspect the missile complex."

"Why not? That's your privilege—you're on the Military Affairs Committee."

"This isn't just a junket for the benefit of the press. I want to go through the whole system with a fine-tooth comb."

"What for?"

"Holes in the system."

"You won't find any. There's no leaky radioactivity and you won't find any loose buttons lying around where some kook could set them off."

"I know all about the fail-safe systems. I have a feeling they can be cracked."

"What do you mean by cracked?"

"Any security system can be breached."

"Who by? What for?"

"The country's crawling with extremists at both ends of the spectrum. You don't have to look too far to find a crowd of

jokers with wild-eyed notions—how many officers have you
got on this base right now who belong to right-wing fa-
natic groups, the ones who see Communists under every
rock? Look at the equipment they've got here at their fingertips."

"Nuts. If the command doesn't come down from the top the
system doesn't fire."

"Right now it doesn't but I can't believe a security system
that tight can be applied to anything as complex as the Phaeton. Rednecked right-wingers or left-wing activists or sheer
accident—it doesn't matter what triggers it off. The system's
just too unwieldy."

Ryan shrugged elaborately. "I hope you're wrong. I'll get
in touch with Fred Winslow, he's the Deputy ICBM Wing
Commander—we'll get passes for you to inspect the setup.
When do you want it?"

"As soon as you can. I'll want to bring a couple of people
along—one of my staff people and a scientist."

"They cleared for Top Secret?"

"Yes."

"Who's the scientist?"

"Moskowitz."

"He was on the Titan development program, wasn't he?
What makes you think he'll play along?"

"I've talked to him."

"Who's the other one?"

"Jaime Spode."

Ryan beamed. "Top Spode? He still around?"

"Still around, still the best."

Ryan nodded. Evidently he had run out of things to say.
Forrester got to his feet. "If you like I'll come to your office
next time—I didn't mean to upset anything for you and Alice.
I know this is awkward."

"You didn't upset anything that wasn't upset before. Forget
it. It's not that you're a Senator, it's that we're none of us the
same as we used to be. Which leads me to ask what it is that
you expect to get out of this Phaeton fight besides a lot of
bruises and an early retirement."

"Maybe I'm tired of going through the motions—maybe I just feel like making waves for a change."

"Nuts. I think you want the top spot and you're gambling that this will buy it for you."

It pulled Forrester's head around: he caught the sudden brightness of Ryan's fierce grin.

"Well? Isn't that it?"

"You're off base by a mile."

He despised his evasiveness but that was the way the game was played. What could he say to Bill Ryan now—that he thought Alan Forrester would make a good President, that with the radical polarization of strident extremists the only hope was for a calm, decisive, rational, patient middle-of-the-roader to come out of the woodwork before the country splintered altogether into factions and brought a führer to power?

His good-humored denial hung suspended and Bill Ryan's face settled slowly like coffee dregs. Without further comment Ryan said, "Come on inside, getting chilly out here," and slid the glass door open. Sand scraped in the aluminum track.

When Forrester crossed the weatherstrip he heard a phone begin to ring with shrill demand. "That's for me," Ryan said and hurried by, leaving him to close the door.

Alice was sitting up straight with careful attention to her balance; when she reached for her glass she took a long time to get her fingers around it, and when she lifted it, it did not follow a straight course toward her lips.

Forrester stopped beside Ronnie's chair. She gave him an upturned questioning smile and he nodded in reply: it was time to go and he did not sit down. Ryan had turned his back to the room and had been speaking inaudibly into the telephone. Now he hung up and came about, and made a face. "I don't know what was so important he had to call at this time of night. Pete Chandler." He was scowling at Alice.

Alice's smile changed slightly but she did not speak and after a little while Ryan shifted to Forrester. "My chief of security. It seems you've got friends in the young generation. Some university kids had a meeting and there was some talk about showing support for your anti-Phaeton plank by having a little sit-in on the runway."

"*On* the runway?"

"Yeah. Sometimes these kids don't think ahead too good. I don't suppose you've ever seen what a human body looks like after it's been exposed to a few seconds' worth of jet exhaust. Nothing much left but cinders."

"I gather they didn't get that far."

"No. Six or eight of them showed up at the gate and Pete told the guards not to let them in. They sat down on the road outside the gate and he wanted to know whether to call the cops and have them removed. I told him to let them sit there. It's a wide pavement, the cars can steer around them. They'll get tired and hungry after a while and go home. Why make an incident out of it?"

"Smart," Forrester said. "Not everybody shows that kind of restraint."

"Pete wanted to call out the cops and beat some heads," Ryan said. "He's a bit of a flag-waver. I suppose it's a good thing he did call me first."

Alice said, "The little bastards deserve a few lumps. Who do they think it is that protects them so they can have the freedom to sit down in the middle of the road?"

There was no point in trying to explain to her the contradiction in her statement; she was drunk and belligerent, her eyes had lost focus. Forrester cleared his throat and said it was time to be going. Ryan went with them to the door; Alice didn't get up from her chair. She waved and said something vague and Ryan came outside and said to Ronnie, "I'm sorry about that."

"We all get under the weather sometimes," she said politely.

Ryan frowned into space briefly before he remembered his joviality; he put a grin on his face and pumped Forrester's hand. "Bring this little lady back with you next time you come, buddy. She does light up the place."

"They're nice people, really, but they seem to have made an awful mess of it, don't they?"

He said, "I get the feeling that marriage is all burned out. It's a shame."

They drove toward the gate and when they turned into the approach road Forrester could see the kids cross-legged on the pavement beyond the guard post. Two helmeted AP's were keeping an eye on them. A white city patrol car with the gold Tucson Police stripe down its sides was parked on the far side but the officers were only sitting inside watching. When Forrester braked at the guard post, he saw the big KARZ-TV mobile news van approaching from Twenty-second Street; he extinguished the speedometer panel lights to reduce the illumination within the car.

Ronnie said, "Aren't you going to talk to them?"

"Who? The television truck or the kids?"

"The kids, of course. They're out here on your account."

"I can't do that now." He drove past the kids with his face averted; the KARZ-TV truck was drawing up and the two city cops were getting out of their car, wise enough to know that if the kids intended to make a scene they would most likely do it when they had television coverage.

A block away Forrester began to accelerate. "You think I copped out."

"Shouldn't you have talked to them?"

"With the TV people hanging on every word?"

"I thought you wanted publicity."

"Not that kind. What kind of grass-roots support do you think I'd get if I gave the impression I was encouraging the lunatic fringe?"

"Lunatic fringe? They're only good-hearted kids and they're honestly concerned about the issues."

"In politics realities don't count—you have to work with appearances. You have to disavow the support of the extremist groups whether you happen to agree with them or not. Guilt by association, don't you see? I can't afford to be identified with a bunch of picketing kids unless I know more about them. They're supporting my side of the Phaeton question but for all I know those six or eight kids back there are card-carrying Weathermen or Maoist pamphleteers. Not knowing who they are, I can't afford to associate myself with them. Now

if they're still there tomorrow we can run a check on them and
if they turn out to be harmless and well-intentioned I can set
something up and go out there and have myself photographed shaking hands with them. But you can't go into that
kind of thing blind."

"I suppose you're right."

He drove west and north, dog-legging along the boulevards. "If I take you home you'll be stuck without your car.
It's not gallant but I think I'll drop myself off at the hotel and
let you drive yourself home."

"Of course. You've had a long day."

She was sitting back, tired and relaxed; she appeared less
tense than she had earlier. He felt a quiet sense of easy intimacy and risked a question: "What about that dinner for two
we promised ourselves?"

"When?"

"Tomorrow?"

"I was planning to drive up to the Catalinas tomorrow.
Painting. I usually don't get back from my expeditions in time
for dinner—I pack sandwiches and a thermos."

"During the week, then?"

She hesitated. "All right."

"You're nervous, aren't you? Why?"

They passed a jammed parking lot beside a big low stucco
night spot. The neon sign had a few dead letters: ATOM C BAR
& GRIL E—DINE & D NCE—LIVE MUSIC FRI & SAT NITES. The
lettering was outlined by the neon shape of a Titan missile.

Ronnie said, "It sounds childish, I suppose, but I just don't
want to let it get to be intense. I don't want to get to a point
where I can even suspect I'm leading you on. Right now I
don't need any complications in my life."

"Maybe you're making too much of it. I like your company,
Ronnie, but I haven't suggested building a fence around
you."

She laughed. "That's bold enough."

"Monday night, then. How about it?"

She gave in. "All right, Alan."

It pleased him absurdly—that she called him by name.

He drove into the city along East Broadway's sputtering fizz

of neon. Low-down-payment car lots, franchise eateries. An
Air Force Phantom jet went over at low altitude with a racket
like the sound of ripping canvas, and pickup trucks driven by
men in cowboy hats waited at the red traffic lights gunning
their souped-up mills. University kids crowded into the beer
joints eight to a car, hoping their forged age cards would be
acceptable to tolerant bartenders.

His father had maintained a permanent suite in the Pioneer
and Forrester still kept it. The hotel was busy with a Hollywood crowd, a film crew making a Western on location in the
nearby hills. They were on the sidewalk, a pack of them,
half-drunk and loud. Forrester stood smiling until Ronnie slid
across the seat under the wheel and drove away with a casual
wave.

Forrester went up to the seventh floor in the elevator and
down the long wide corridor with its muffling carpet. In the
suite he found the bed turned down and a cut-crystal bottle
of whiskey waiting for him with an ice bucket. He had a drink
and showered and when he came out of the steamed-up bathroom the phone was ringing.

It was Ronnie. "I'm sorry to disturb you."

"I'm still up. What's the matter?"

She sounded angry. "I just had a call from Frank Shattuck's
secretary. She's been trying to reach us all night."

"To cancel the appointment tomorrow?"

"Three guesses why. It seems he's been taken suddenly
busy. Called away to a conference in Los Angeles or some
such lie. What'll you bet he's out on the Country Club links
big as life tomorrow morning?"

"Never mind, Ronnie. Don't let it get your goat. I'll get to
him sometime during the week—it's not urgent."

"The longer you let it wait, the longer he'll have to sew up
his mind tight against you," she said. "Shattuck Industries
swings a strong lobby in Washington, Alan."

"So do I. Thanks for your concern, Ronnie, but it's not the
end of the world."

"I'd like to strangle the smug fool."

"It's all right. It'll give me a chance to get out to the ranch
for the day. You wouldn't want to come along, would you?

We've got some magnificent scenery up there, fine for painting."

"I know. I was there once or twice during the campaign."

"How about it, then?"

"Well—all right. Of course. Thanks for inviting me. Shall
I pick you up? It'll save you renting a car."

"Fine. Is seven too early?"

"I usually get away even earlier—I don't like to waste the
daylight."

"Six-thirty, then."

"Good," she said. "Good night."

"Good night, Ronnie. Sleep well." When he cradled the
phone he kept his hand on it, as if to retain the thread of
contact with her.

He switched off the light and lay back and grew drowsy with
a constraining ennui, the listlessness that followed a day of
long travel across time zones. Somewhere in the ensuing run
of time, between wakefulness and sleep, a vivid picture came
into his mind—Angie in the garden, picking insects off leaves,
crushing them between finger and thumb. She had loved the
garden in Washington; it had been her place of retreat, her
center of revitalization. He remembered the look of her sleeping face on the pillow, the weight of her breasts warm with
love; when his thoughts strayed to Ronnie it was with a start
of guilt that brought him awake. *Oh, hell,* he thought crankily,
chastising himself, and then the phone rang again and it was
Top Spode. "I'm at National Airport. Trumble's taking the
night plane to Tucson and he's got the goodies in his lap. You
going to be in town tomorrow?"

"I'll be at the ranch most of the day."

"All right, I'll reach you when there's something to report."

"Wrap it up as fast as you can, Top, because I've got another chore for you."

"Tucson or Washington?"

"Tucson. We're going to test the nation's security." Forrester said it dryly and his smile was one-sided.

"Now that sounds like fun," Top said, and rang off. Forrester rolled over on his shoulder and exhaustion lowered
him into a warm pool of sleep.

☆☆☆☆☆☆☆☆☆☆☆☆☆☆☆☆☆☆☆☆☆☆☆☆☆☆☆☆☆☆☆☆☆

Chapter Four

The great iron doors swung open slowly and the dark Chaika limousine rolled out of the courtyard of Lubianka Tiurma where Rykov had just completed his regular morning tour of inspection. Behind the limousine the iron doors swung closed with a solid noise that echoed the metallic clangings of the several underground levels of dungeons inside. The chauffeur was armed and a silent bodyguard shared the rear seat with Rykov; the interior curtains were half-drawn across the double thickness of bulletproof glass in the small windows. The route took them past the Bolshoi Theatre and Sverdlov Square and there was a very thin morning traffic of Moskviches, Pobedas and Volgas on the boulevard. Rykov's limousine kept to the center lane, reserved for official vehicles only, and he encountered no delays.

In Revolution Square a girl Intourist guide was lecturing to a thick-bundled coagulation of determined foreign tourists. The pavements were crowded with pedestrians on their way to work. Many of the men wore uniforms—civil servants, most of them; every Muscovite wanted to wear a uniform.

At Arbatskaya Square Rykov climbed out to walk the rest of the way. The slow-moving Chaika accompanied him. The possibility of assassination was one which Rykov accepted without qualms, but sensible precautions were not out of order and the bodyguard car stayed close.

Rykov's footsteps crunched the snowy cobblestones with an uneven rhythm broken by the thudding of his cane, for he had a bad leg now, the result of the unpublicized crash-landing of an Aeroflot jetliner six years before. The pronounced limp added a fine touch to his sinister appearance and by implying constant pain, enhanced his reputation for stoic fortitude. Now that he had worked his way up to a position where he gave more orders than he took it was gratifying to have members of the ruling troika inquire solicitously after his health.

He walked through the wide Arbat Boulevard past an elderly woman sweeping snow off the sidewalk. She wore a scarf over her head, not against the cold but because it was traditionally immodest for a peasant woman not to wear a scarf tied under her chin. The woman bowed with a gesture of obeisance; she did not smile, because she knew who Viktor Rykov was. So did at least ten million other Russians and several thousand foreign intelligence people.

He was a long way, not only in time and distance, from his birthplace in the Circassian mountains of Georgia.

When the October Revolution had stripped them of their lands his kulak parents had moved down to Tiflis, a city of mosques and bazaars, smugglers and vice, and Viktor Rykov had learned the devious texts of intrigue and deceit. In 1938 Beria's secret police had recruited him to spy on international black marketeers in the Crimea; Rykov had organized a cell of informants—an underground within the underworld—and his unique achievements had brought him to Moscow as a Control in 1940.

In 1941 at Smolensk he had been attached to the Fourth Bureau and posted out to the west to infiltrate the Abwehr.

At Moscow against Von Bock, and at Leningrad, he had done superb work: it had been one of his agents, in a Wehrmacht uniform, who had walked into Guderian's Panzer headquarters and brought out the detailed plans for the siege of Moscow.

Rykov had shown a genius for training Russians to look and act and think like Germans. There had been decorations and promotions and the transfer to the Far East: in August 1945 Rykov's deep-cover seedlings in Hirohito's crumbling empire had paralyzed Japanese matériel transport during the brief and bitter Soviet blitzkrieg of northeast Asia. From 1946 to 1953 Rykov had controlled Soviet networks in China, both in the Kuomintang and in the People's Republic. By 1953 he had completed the construction of the Amergrad camp at Kolkhoz Tselino and within eighteen months its graduates had begun seeding into America. Then Khrushchev had cemented his authority, Tolubchev had been retired, and Rykov had stepped into power in the Arbat.

Winter gray misted the city. A youth passed Rykov, one of the new upstart generation in peasant *valenki* boots and a sulky frown and a cotton-padded jacket. The young ones wanted everything given to them and it was not pleasant to speculate what would become of the world when these young nihilists took it over.

In time history always upstaged the hard-handed pioneers, found them redundant and superseded them with suave men of greater finesse and sophistication but lesser gut courage— the squeamish, effete, decadent ones.

Pioneers became forgotten men and these young soft ones listened to revanchist Nazism on the Voice of America and read the *samizdat* drivel that circulated underground: they had memories even shorter than their years, they had not lived through the war, they had never suffered, and now they found it all dull—the Revolution was almost sixty years ago and to them it was history, boring. There was no longer excitement or danger in being a Communist. They did the proper things but they did them dutifully with the knowledge that fathers were responsible for the politics of their sons. They joined the

October Society at seven and the Young Communist League of Komsomol at fourteen and learned to pay lip service to the goal of perfecting the working people's socialist alliance. They wrote drably for *Komsomolskaya Pravda* and massed their voices in uninspired rhetoric against those who challenged the national virtue and virility but all the time they wanted soft bourgeois comforts and they thought of their elders with contempt as the "uncles."

Rykov had no children and he was glad of it.

He limped past the Lenin Library and turned into the wide side street. A suite of offices in one of the Kremlin towers had been assigned to him for official purposes but he rarely set foot in it because he had no taste for bootlicking and here in this huge gray unmarked building in the Arbat district a kilometer west of Red Square no one's boots but Rykov's own were licked.

It was a graceless mausoleum, drab and cold. It housed the nerve center of the Soviet intelligence system; to neighbor agencies it was known as the Organs. A small sign in plain Russian characters hung inside the entrance hall:

K   omitet
G   osudarstvennoi
B   esopastnosti

The hall guards were big men, well armed and fully trained in unarmed-combat techniques. Rykov returned their salutes perfunctorily and went back through the building with his cane tapping disrhythmically. He waited at the lifts and heard the building's quiet thrummings.

These lower floors were filled with code and cipher rooms and the offices of Control officers commanding subsidiary networks of field agents. KGB was modern and efficient and heavy-budgeted, and it was huge: for each of the 200,000 employees of the American CIA there were twenty KGB agents; most of them were paid or blackmailed informants, not full staff members, but still the cadre of professionals was more than a million in number. In these offices their activities were coordinated and analyzed by banks of Minsk-32 computers, and the distillations of millions of words of daily reports were delivered each day to the desk of Viktor Rykov because Rykov was the supreme commander of this greatest secret army in the world. In his sixty-second year Rykov was heir to the mantle of Lavrenti Beria.

Rykov's office was imposing, the result of baroque and melodramatic whims on the part of a predecessor. It was a long trip across a series of Oriental carpets to the desk. The huge windows, arched and crenellated, looked out across the vast sprawl of Moscow's ancient low rooftops with their clustered chimney pots. The spire of Moscow University was a lean landmark against the gray sky. Here and there sprouted the dreary Stalin Wedding Cakes, sterile gray apartment towers with icings of snow.

Rykov hung his things on the coat rack and, as always, lit a Pamir before he sat down and reached under the orange silk lampshade to switch on his work light. He thumbed through the stack of reports and memos on his desk and turned to his bank of telephones to begin the morning round of calls to district commanders and Controls. It took nearly an hour and left him waspishly frustrated; he had the weight of organization on him and he despised it. At times he also feared it: the temptation to surrender to it was great—to become lulled by routine.

He pressed the button to summon his aide and almost immediately Andrei Bizenkev appeared. "Good morning, Comrade General." It was his little joke: Rykov was a general by rank and pay but he disdained the title and preferred to be addressed as Comrade Minister. Andrei had always enjoyed needling him and Rykov had always enjoyed being needled because there was a part of him that recognized the grave danger in taking himself too seriously.

The years had put a layer of fat on Andrei and pushed his hairline back so that he had become bookish and gentle in appearance. It was a deceit: in Rykov's view Andrei was the second best Intelligence expert in the Soviet Union.

Rykov separated out the Chinese signals and tossed the rest

of the papers across the desk. "None of that requires our attention. Have the assistants answer the ones that need answering."

"Very good." Andrei picked them up. "And the China dispatches?"

"I'll want to study them."

Andrei left without further talk. Rykov hardly heard the door close. He opened a drawer and picked out a pocket box of Drazhe candy drops, selected a lozenge and popped it into his cheek and spread the China decodes out on the desk. His mind picked up a word here and a phrase there and fitted them into a pattern while another part of him reviewed the meeting yesterday.

They had met in Comrade Secretary Fyodor Yashin's extravagant Kremlin office, each wall paneled in a different rare wood, an Imperial Russian Samovar tea service gleaming on a side tray.

The room was huge and the chandeliers pushed at the gloom. String tendons held Yashin's starched collar away from his neck but the lean hawked face was alert and hard. Yashin removed his rimless glasses. "Good day, Comrade." His voice had become scratchy with age. He pointed the stem of his meerschaum toward the two men in wing chairs, Marshal Oleg Grigorenko and Alexai Strygin, who was Vice-Chairman of the Presidium and personal representative of Party boss Kazakov.

They both stood up to greet Rykov.

Grigorenko had gone tub-bellied and his face had put on so much flesh that all planes and angles had disappeared and it was hard to visualize any bone structure underneath. He spoke politely in his rumbling deep voice and there was a faint click as he brought his heels together.

Alexai Strygin extended his hand and Rykov shook it quickly and firmly. One of the few modern changes of which Rykov approved was the substitution of the western handshake for the traditional bear hug. He and Strygin had known each other since boyhood: not enemies, but too cautious to be friends. Strygin was a small man with a Lenin beard and a half-bald head on which hair made a bushy line across the top from ear to ear. To some extent Strygin was a comfortable man, ambitious but secure in his position, and Rykov disliked comfortable men.

Not since Khrushchev's had a single pair of hands held all the reins of Soviet power. The policies of all the Russias were dictated by the twelve-man Presidium (Politburo) and in turn the Presidium was commanded by a troika of its members. Of those three men the best known was Marshal I. G. Tsvetnoy, Chairman of the Supreme Soviet and ostensible chief of state of the Soviet Union. Tsvetnoy was Zhukov's heir and in the reshuffling that followed the Brezhnev-Kosygin regime the Army, always a key force in Russian politics, had showed enough muscle to elevate one of its own to the top position in Russian government. But the Stalin and Khrushchev years had taught the necessity of checks and balances and Tsvetnoy's strength was delimited by the other two members. One of them, represented here by Strygin, was First Secretary of the Communist Party Mikhail Kazakov. The other, Secretary General of the Presidium and Premier of the Council of Ministers, was Yashin.

Yashin's was the least known face: he was not a public celebrity in Moscow and in Western countries very little was known about him. Yashin had seen to this because in spite of his vanities he disliked spotlights and always worked best behind the scenes . . .

Yashin never could resist dipping in a spoon. "The situation only grows more perilous with time, because every day increases the chance the Americans will break your system. How can you be sure they haven't broken it already? How do we know they're not poised to sweep all your people into a net?"

Rykov was patient. "If one agent's cover is blown it won't lead to others. That's always the first rule when you set these things up."

"They've had nearly twenty years to break it."

"And they haven't broken it, have they."

"We don't know that, Comrade."

"I'd know it. Do you think I'm without sources in American Intelligence?"

"Do you think they're without sources in yours?"

"They are where the Amergrad program is concerned. The Americans are adolescents when it comes to this sort of thing."

"I don't share your confidence. The risk of discovery is greater than the potential benefit. I suggest again that you draw up a plan for the withdrawal of the network."

Rykov let the silence grow. Grigorenko was watching him keenly. Rykov had got the job he wanted; Grigorenko was Commanding General, GRU (combined Military Intelligence Services) but that to KGB was as provincial ballet was to Bolshoi. Only because of his close ties to Yashin and Premier Tsvetnoy was Grigorenko on the Presidium at all. And by infiltrating the American military complex, Rykov's deep-cover team was encroaching on Grigorenko's territory.

Rykov said, "I grant it isn't foolproof. Nothing is foolproof. But our people are in a position to hamstring the enemy's nuclear capacity if it comes to war. Can you say the same for any substitute you're prepared to offer? No. As long as I'm capable of influencing decisions, my network will hold its position."

As long as I'm capable of influencing decisions—the gauntlet had been dropped and Yashin sat there looking at it, deciding whether now was the time to pick it up, but knowing in the end that it wasn't.

Yashin tugged at the flap of dry skin that sagged beneath his sharp jaw, and a wisp of smoke drifted free from the bowl of his pipe. The expressionless slits of eyes, the thin lips and very slightly shriveled face—behind the mask, Rykov was aware of the hatred. But Yashin wasn't ready to expose it. He had the patience of a Russian peasant—and the deviousness. He would wait.

Yashin said finally, "We'll keep the question under advisement. Let's get to the reports. Marshal Grigorenko—has there been any change in the Mediterranean?"

"None to speak of. Benghazi wants to blackmail us into

building an aviation-petrol refinery in Libya. Evidently the Libyan Army thinks it's going to withhold commitment of those two Derna divisions to Cairo if we don't agree to put in the refinery. We'll get the official demand in due course."

Alexai Strygin snorted. His voice gritted with sudden sarcasm. "Benghazi puts a high value on two divisions."

Rykov let his mind drift while Grigorenko made his reports on the Hanoi situation and the Tanzanian dispute; in response to each, Strygin delivered himself of cliché-ridden dissertations to which Rykov paid little attention. He was thinking of the sight he had passed on his way here: the tomb where Colonel Yuri Gagarin was buried in the Kremlin wall.

The brief years of the Cosmonauts had been a kind of golden age and in the decade since, Russia had lost her lead in space because Russian leadership had knuckled under to popular demands for individual effete comforts at the expense of collective technological advances: the Russian middle class had clamored for refrigerators and central heating. History, forgetting those who had starved, would not forget those who dominated the world, nor those who put the first man on Mars. Russia's revisionists had abandoned technological supremacy in exchange for slavish imitations of the gratifications of a dying capitalist society, and that very capitalism now threatened to destroy the Soviet Union. Rykov's agents had reported hints of a new American multiple-warhead system which might deploy within eighteen months— did that suggest war was becoming remote from the American mind? And the American danger was remote by comparison with the two others: the decay of Russian vigor and the immediate and present threat from just beyond Russia's own eastern underbelly. . . .

Strygin's voice ran down and Yashin turned toward Rykov, whose face became attentive. Rykov wore the filter stub of his cigarette on his lower lip; he peeled it free and put it out. He spoke softly, without heat, delivering the routine analysis of the week's developments, and he left one subject deliberately for the last. "Now I draw your attention to the reports we've submitted regularly on the China question." He leaned forward in the chair and draped both hands over the handle of his erect cane.

Marshal Grigorenko leaned to one side in his chair to break wind slyly against the cushion. Strygin watched Rykov, his face rigid with suppressed feelings, knowing what was coming and disliking it. Yashin only waited politely.

"Every evidence leads to the same conclusion," Rykov said. "The Maoists think we've gone soft, lost the determination to resist."

Grigorenko sighed. "The paper tiger again. China can be swatted like a fly. They know that. They'll make noise forever but there won't be war, Viktor. You know there won't be war."

"On the contrary. To the Chinese, war is the inevitable historical necessity. It's only a question of which of us will start it and when it will begin. On the answers to that question will depend the outcome of the war."

Alexai Strygin said, "As always you overstate the case."

"No."

Strygin turned to Yashin. "Every week he comes to us with some new wives' tale of Chinese perfidy which upon analysis becomes no more than a bee sting. But every time Comrade Rykov is stung by the bee he rushes to beat the hive with a club. The stings do no real harm but our friend wants to capitalize on them. He wants to make war on China and he will use any flimsy excuse to encourage it."

Yashin did not interrupt and so Strygin continued: "I spent two years in China. I know their problems, and they are too many and too difficult for China to waste time and resources in a war she cannot win. We have more than enough Warsaw Pact troops along the border to discourage any serious challenge. Our nuclear capacity is incomparably greater than theirs. The Chinese have offered far more verbs than violence, and with good reason—if nothing else deters them, the Chinese must always know that any attack by them upon us would merely give the Americans the excuse they've been looking for to bury China."

Drawing breath, Strygin glanced at Rykov and added in a harder voice, "As for the rest of Rykov's debating points, I can only suggest he's become the victim of the solipsism of his profession. His intellect craves to discover more information than espionage can supply. Spies will always guess at what they do not know, and the tendency is strong to use one's brain not to arrive at the truth but to support the prejudices one began with. Remember it was the KGB which embarrassed us all by assuming the Arabs could defeat Israel in the 1967 six-day war."

Rykov said mildly, "I was not the chief of KGB in 1967."

"It would have been the same," Strygin said. He went back to Yashin: "Rykov has a Stalinist's view of the world. I suppose it's inevitable, in his profession, but it is for precisely that reason that he must keep his political notions to himself. We can no longer afford to have the KGB dictate national foreign policy. I suggest Comrade Rykov ought to concentrate on the gathering of information and leave the fighting of wars to the Army."

Rykov flicked a cigarette against the back of his hand. After the echo of Strygin's anger had subsided he glanced at Yashin. "I should like to reply to that."

"Of course," Yashin replied with the attitude of a man offering another enough rope to hang himself.

"In 1945," Rykov said, looking from face to face, "Eisenhower asked Zhukov how the Russians cleared mine fields and Zhukov replied, 'We march over them.' Now that is the attitude of the Chinese today, and I don't believe we are capable of as much."

Grigorenko snapped, "The Russian soldier is no coward."

"The spirit of collective sacrifice requires more than courage, I think. It requires a national will."

"Stalinist claptrap," Strygin said.

"Evidently," Rykov murmured, "I have made the mistake of fragmenting the evidence. Each week I come to you with bits and pieces, and each week you point out to me that they are merely bits and pieces. Quite so. Let me rectify the mistake: let's look at the total picture.

"Six hundred years ago the Mongols invaded Russia without warning. Since the 1600's we have been fighting skirmishes with the Chinese along the Amur River. Until a hundred and fifty years ago the Mongols were still in possession of the Volga and Crimea regions and their rule imposed such oppression and ignorant backwardness on our people that today we still struggle to get out from under the memory and experience. Because of those little yellow bastards we're two centuries behind and we simply sit here waiting for them to do the same thing again because Peking calls itself a Communist regime and we all tend to follow the stupid idea that the enemy of one's enemies is perforce one's friend."

Strygin sat upright. "That's absurd. You're confusing Chinese with Mongols."

"They're all the same."

"No. Genghiz conquered Russia but the Chinese never have. Russia has never once made the kowtow of obeisance to China since Baikov's mission to Peking three hundred years ago—but forget that. History's always a good hiding place; it won't argue back. Let's talk about *now*."

"All right." Rykov's words fell heavily, dropped like shoes, spaced out: "Consider the evidence. The Chinese have enlarged their satellite-tracking station near Nanking, they've installed huge electronic complexes in the mountains in the Khentei, and they're constantly expanding the nuclear facilities at Lop Nor, Paotow, and Lanchow. According to the figures I submitted last week they've stockpiled at least eight hundred hydrogen warheads of all sizes. Their missile program has grown faster than we anticipated and as you know they have an initial ICBM capability now sufficient to destroy almost half the major cities in the Soviet Union."

"Yes," Strygin said, "but at what cost to themselves?"

Rykov's head turned. "They can sacrifice four hundred million men—more than our entire population—and still win. And they've no reluctance to do that, as long as the loyal Maoist elite survives. China has one billion people and they face a famine—in less than thirty years she'll have two billion; today if there's a bad crop year millions of them starve, and tomorrow even if it's a *good* crop year millions of them will starve. Look at it, then: China has got to expand into new

agricultural lands. Where's she going to find them? In Japan
or India or Indochina? Those areas are even more over-
crowded than she is. No, she's *got* to move into our under-
populated frontier regions.

"To do that," he finished in a different voice altogether,
"the Maoists are willing to risk a nuclear exchange—precisely
because they believe *we* are *not* willing to."

He spread his hands in the universally expressive gesture.

"Rubbish," Alexai Strygin said.

"Perhaps. But each year we spend debating the point gives
the Chinese another year to close the gap in military
strength."

Yashin said, "You're saying we had better crush them while
we still can."

"I'm saying that one day I'm going to report to you that the
Chinese will start to push buttons within twenty-four hours
and you are going to have to be ready to react instantly and
without any more of this idiotic debating."

Strygin muttered, "As always Viktor ignores the political
actualities."

"If we were justified in intervening in Czech affairs in 1968,
there's no reason we can't apply the same doctrine to China."

Strygin uncrossed his legs. "He talks reasonably," he said
to Yashin, "but the premises aren't reasonable. All this talk
of preparedness is a smoke screen. We're quite ready to repel
any Chinese attack, nuclear or otherwise, and Viktor knows it
and Peking knows it. No. He's saying we ought to get ourselves in a frame of mind to hit them before they can hit us.
He wants a Soviet blitzkrieg. Viktor and his friends carefully
avoid mentioning the obvious critical factor that negates their
whole position—the Americans are on the fence right now,
maintaining *detente* with us and putting out feelers to China in
the Warsaw talks, but if we attack China they'll have their
excuse to destroy us. Don't forget the Pentagon is in the
hands of generals who can't tell one Communist from another; as far as they're concerned Russia is stronger than
China, therefore Russia ought to be whipped. We're strong,
but we're not strong enough to fight China and America together." And Strygin smiled like a schoolmaster.

Yashin leveled his palms on the desk, pushed his chair back and stood. "Alexai is quite right. Our eastern defenses are on a constant alert and our missiles are pointed down Peking's throat. If there is to be war let the Chinese start it, because only then will the Americans ally themselves with us. Let's have no more talk of preemptive strikes. The KGB will spend more time providing information and less time trying to alter the policies of the Soviet Government. Now you must excuse me, I have an appointment."

That had been yesterday. Now Rykov sat in his office in the Arbat, pushing the China reports around on the desk and reflecting on the meeting. He had listened to Strygin's appeasing whine and Yashin's careful chastisements before; emotionally immune to them, he was neither angry nor dismayed. But the clarity of his own vision made him impatient with them. Yashin had the distraction of his personal vanity and Strygin had his comfortable ambition and his large family of artists and intellectuals. Rykov had none of those dilutions; he was a superior servant of the State because his whole and only dedication was to the State. He had been widowed eight years ago; there were no children; he had no weaknesses for material things, no wish for personal aggrandizement.

It was a time of great trial for the Soviet Union—perils within and without. Russia was encircled by external enemies and these had their allies within the Soviet Union—forces of decadence, flaccid muscles, sagging purpose, the aged weariness of a revolution running down. Viktor Rykov, childless, clear-headed, unsentimental, uncorrupted by bourgeois prejudices, had to protect the nation from all its enemies— that was his duty and that was what his talents best equipped him to do, and he thought dispassionately that the Soviet Union was fortunate to have such a man as Viktor Rykov in these tragic times.

With red ink he underlined items in the China dispatches and scribbled a number beside each underlining and leaned forward to study the result. The decodes had come up from the cipher rooms within the past twenty-four hours; they represented the sum of one day's intelligence activity by KGB agents and affiliates. Even in clandestine operations the vastness of bureaucracy had to be obliged and everything had to be committed to paper. Some were radio-code receptions, some were dispatches carried openly on paper in diplomatic pouches, some were blowups of films and microdots carried by courier agents, some were clippings and tear sheets from the world press, government publications, transcripts of radio broadcasts by government figures, advance copies of prepared political speeches—espionage relied heavily on the gathering *en masse* of nonsecret, openly available material. From enough of it came signs of trends, shifts in momentum, changes in attitudes. The first thing a police detective did to find a man was to look him up in the local directory. In intelligence it was the same: the cinematic exploits of cloak-and-dagger spies were the least part of espionage.

Rykov's red-underlined selections were brief:

1. Peking University. Chan Po-ku has been absent four days and has not appeared at his home during that time. His classes have been taken over by an assistant.

2. Peking. Meeting of State Cabinet scheduled for next week. Scheduled to attend: Chou; Chug Po; Fei Yunt-tse; Shen Yang; Jiou Ssu-kuan; An Tu; Lo Kai-teh; Yuan Tung; Sun Shih. *Not* scheduled to attend: Hsin Chaohua; Pu She-cheng; Tien Yat; Wu Tse-chao. (Peking Control notation: Those to attend are anti-Soviet; those uninvited are moderates. Fei, Shen, and Jiou are strongly anti-Soviet strategists and have never been invited to a top-level conference before.)

3. Hulun. 17th Chinese People's Army Hq. Commanding General Lu Tse-shek relieved of his command and retired, age 61, replaced by General Chi Thian, 63.

4. Mongolia. Unidentified important visitor arrived Ulan Bator by plane from Peking. Spirited away incognito by motorcar into the mountains to the east.

5. Peking newspaper, *Jenmin Jih Pao.* Two-page 12-column biography of General Li Tu-fen, 48, Chinese People's Air Force commanding nuclear and ICBM complexes along the Mongolian frontier.

6. Reference note from KGB File C-S-PRC-NM 647529710. *Dr. Chan Po-ku.* Born Chungking 1916, grad Univ. Peking, postgrad work M.I.T., junior staff Peenemünde, staff Dubna, has been instrumental in development of Chinese ICBM program. Now full professor Peking University.

7. Reference note from KGB File C-M-PRC-PA 49786119. *Chi Thian.* Born Shanghai 1911, joined Communist Party in China in 1927, attended Sixth Congress (1928), survived Long March (1935) and promoted to Major, fought Japanese in Manchukuo, promoted Lt. Col. & Col. (1939, 1944), assumed command of 7th Div. 4th C.P. Army as Lt. Gen. (1953, Korea), promoted to General 1961. (File note from Hanoi Control: General Chi was principally responsible for the Chinese hijacking of Soviet aid to Hanoi in 1967–68 which forced USSR to abandon trans-China rail deliveries, and ship military aid by sea from Vladivostok to Haiphong. Chi is known as a violently partisan anti-Soviet.)

8. Lop Nor. Rail-yard watch: arrivals this week, 16 goods trains, total of 2,317 goods wagons. (File note from review officer: *Cf.* last week, 11 trains, 1,428 goods wagons.)

9. Siberia regional summary: Chinese espionage in and around installations of the Soviet Far Eastern Armies appears to have increased.

10. Warsaw. Chinese–U.S. talks canceled this week because Ambassador Tai En-yi has been recalled to Peking for instructions.

11. Lanchow. Arrivals by air: three lieutenant-generals, People's Air Force (biog. summaries attached), with staffs. Arrivals by rail: 2nd, 3rd, 5th Antiaircraft Batteries (surface-to-air missiles), 4th Brigade, 17th CPA Division; support units and infantry; two sealed goods trains; four

extended-flatcar trains carrying estimated 240 SAM missiles and 16 large missiles, possibly ICBMs. Departure by rail: 386 civilian engineers and workers, destination Shanghai redeployment depot.

He summoned his aide and Andrei came in chewing on something. Andrei snacked constantly and his waistline showed it.

Rykov said, "Come around here and look over my shoulder."

"The red markings?"

"Yes. Do you believe in coincidences?"

"Not often."

"Then tell me what you see."

"One might suppose the disappearance of the rocket scientist from Peking University and the arrival of the unidentified high-level visitor at Ulan Bator are connected."

"Why?"

"Just last week we had confirmation they're beefing up the electronics and ICBM stations in the mountains there."

"Which leads you to what, Andrei?"

Andrei stepped back and brooded. "I see."

"Exactly. If they were preparing to launch their nuclear missiles they would want to have the best scientific adviser on hand at the launch site. Hence the apparent movement of Dr. Chan to Mongolia."

"If the unidentified visitor is Chan."

"Consider the rest. The Chinese State Cabinet has met twice in the past five months—unprecedented, when you recall the last two times the Cabinet met were in 1966 and 1970. If Peking plans to employ a first-strike ICBM force against us there would be a Cabinet reshuffling to dispense with the moderates, *n'est-ce pas?* We appear to be witnessing that. There would be a shift of popular emphasis from infantry and armor to air and ICBMs—we see that with the publication of a popular biography of General Li. There would be a shift of frontier commanders, drawing moderates back to the interior and replacing them with rabid anti-Russians, and we see that here with the arrival of Chi Thian at Hulun on the Siberian border. There would be a general increase in movement around nuclear and ICBM installations and we see evidence of that here—items eight and eleven. The recall of Peking's ambassador to Warsaw could mean any number of things but it's always possible they mean to prepare him the way the Japanese prepared their ambassador to Washington in December of 1941."

Andrei said, "Of course there are other possible explanations for all these things."

"Yes. We need to know more—and quickly." Rykov swept the dispatches together and stacked them. "Have copies of my underlinings typed up and sent to Secretary Kazakov with a note of explanation."

"Kazakov?"

"Yashin is a disbeliever and Marshal Tsvetnoy believes that in his old age he must act the part of the mellow statesman. If we're going to persuade the troika the danger is imminent, it has to be done through Kazakov. He's the only one whose eyes are open."

"He doesn't like you very much."

"I'm not asking him to like me," Rykov said. He watched Andrei pick up the sheaf of documents and then he said, "Where's Leon Belsky?"

"Prague, I think. Why?"

"Find him and make contact. Tell him he's detached from his duties. I want him here as soon as possible. By that I mean not more than twelve hours from now."

Andrei gave him a look of brooding speculation. "Belsky. What's he to do with China?"

"Nothing. I'm sending him to America."

Andrei took a breath. "To Tucson?"

"Yes."

"You're not activating the Illegals?"

"We'll see. For the moment I only intend to alert them. My intuition tells me we may need them without delay; I can't have half of them off on holiday in Mexico. They've been rusting a long time and they'll need stiffening. Belsky's the best man for that, and anyhow I'll want a line opened to Tucson, it's a nuisance having to work through the Los Angeles *rezidentsia* and the FBI probably has the thing covered anyway."

Andrei said, "If the Chinese attack the Soviet Union you'll want the Illegals to spike America's guns, is that it?"

"Not exactly," Rykov said. "You forget your place, Andrei —don't ask so many questions."

Before dawn Rykov and Leon Belsky checked through OVIR military control at Moscow's Sheremetevo Airport and walked out through the passenger gate into the biting wind. They had to duck their fur-hatted heads against it and lean forward as they walked. By the time they climbed the ramp of the jet Rykov's cheeks and nose were numb with cold and his bad leg was giving him trouble.

They had no luggage other than Rykov's attaché case. Rykov would be returning to Moscow directly from Siberia and KGB Control in Vladivostok would supply Belsky with his needs for the remainder of his journey.

Belsky made a bundle of his coat and shoved it under the seat. His face had the masked expressionlessness of a *mouzhik* peasant; he was a study in monochrome—brown suit, brown hair, brown eyes, brown skin. He had a slightly blurred face, the kind people seldom remembered; he reminded everyone of someone met somewhere before. In his own circle he was known as a *Hundertpassler*—a man of a hundred passports, his origins lost. He was a thoroughgoing professional and in many respects the best man Rykov had: he combined a vividly inventive mind with a totally responsive loyalty to Rykov. You seldom found that combination in a single individual; the imaginative ones were usually the erratic ones, and the dependable ones usually lacked sufficient inventiveness to deal with unanticipated crises. Belsky was a prize—who knew his own worth.

The plane was a regular Aeroflot jetliner but Rykov had

commandeered it and they were the only passengers. Snow made streaks along the windows when it took off into the freezing gale and the air turbulence was extreme.

"Of course I want a direct line opened," Rykov said, "that's your first job. You'll find plenty of technical help on the scene; that's one advantage of having a team this big. It all has to be set up very quickly because we don't know how soon we'll need activation. You'll be talking to most of them—certainly all the cell leaders—separately. Short of an emergency at this end you'll have to maintain security."

Belsky studied the list Rykov had taken out of the attaché case, reviewing the litany of photographic ID portraits and introduction procedures and the instructions Rykov had given him on the way to the airport.

Even at eleven thousand meters the plane encountered high jetstream turbulence and Rykov was vaguely aware of it when the pilot banked to starboard and angled south to detour around the weather. After a while, with Belsky still buried in the documents, Rykov dozed off.

He awoke drowsily with daylight and recognized through thin cirrus below the outlines of the Aral Sea. The launch complex of the Baikonur Cosmodrome—it meant the old Amergrad *kolkhoz* was an hour or two behind them. Rykov thought of the place without emotion.

Belsky said, "Clarification, please. In the event of activation they will have to move fast and there's a good chance of discovery. If cover is blown, do we continue operations or go to ground?"

"If you're ordered into activation you'll have to continue the operation right through to completion no matter what happens."

"In other words you're prepared to sacrifice the deep-cover network."

"It's not exactly a matter of sacrificing them. We didn't seed them there to remain in deep cover until they die of old age. They're to be used, they understand that."

"I hope they do. They've had twenty years to change their minds."

"That option has never been open to them," Rykov said. "You may have to stiffen a few spines, of course."

"And if I have to set an example or two?"

Rykov answered, "Do it."

They crossed high over the Irtysh River with Mongolia somewhere beyond the clouds to starboard and at noon the liner set down at Tomsk to refuel. When they took off again the weather was clearing and the flight followed the snowy ribbon of the Siberian Railway east across Irkutsk and the frozen surface of Lake Baikal, across the white tangle of the Yablonoi Mountains toward the drifted wastes of far-east Siberia.

Rykov said, "You'll have to keep the direct line open at all times once you've been ordered to activate. It's always possible a countermand will come down, even up to the last minute."

"Of course. You sound as if you seriously expect activation."

"It depends on the Chinese, doesn't it."

Belsky said, "We've never had a network this big that's been in place nearly this long. Most of them have children—adolescent and fully grown. It's going to be sticky."

"That's your job, Leon. You know I rely on you."

The expressionless brown eyes moved vaguely toward him and away again. "Those children are American children, not Russian. They are of no objective importance to us one way or the other, of course, but they are of considerable importance in that their existence has to have a bearing on any decisions made by the parents."

"The Illegals are there to execute instructions and they know it perfectly well—they know what happens otherwise: to them, to their children, to the relations they left behind in the Soviet Union." Rykov moved his hand in a gesture of dismissal. "I know it isn't simple, cut-and-dried, but you'll handle it. I chose you for this because you're the one man who can be relied on to carry out this assignment without being programmed step by step. Are you worried?"

"Of course I am." There was no visible sign of it.

"If you weren't, I'd think less of you."

It was dark when the jet made its descent at Khabarovsk, seven hundred kilometers due north of the port of Vladivostok. Rykov stood up and shouldered into his ankle-length greatcoat and tugged the earflaps of his hat down snug. "Good-bye, then."

Belsky kept his seat, only nodding his acknowledgment, and Rykov went out and down the ramp. The tarmac was bitter cold, windswept; the ice surface splintered under his boot soles like eggshells. He followed the lights of the terminal building, a corrugated-metal quonset-type structure. Behind him the big jet turned ponderously on its undercarriage and taxied out to the runway to take off again; it would deposit Belsky at Vladivostok and return in less than two hours to collect Rykov and take him back to Moscow.

He limped forward against the wind, bracing a crooked arm before his face. Siberia. How many thousands had been exiled to these wastes by his signature? The thought distressed him because he was not, after all, inhuman; but the requirements of the people as a whole always took precedence over the requirements of individuals, and Rykov—jailer, extortionist, executioner—was above all the instrument of the State.

But not unwitting. He had devoted his life to protecting the Russian people from their enemies. He seldom agreed with the Presidium line. He frequently used his power to block foolishness from above. He was instrument, but not puppet —never puppet. The survival of a nation was at stake and Rykov had no time to waste on slavish obeisance to those whom circumstances placed in positions superior to his own: his loyalty was to the Soviet Union, not to its rulers of the moment.

. . . The warmth inside the terminal was sudden and welcome. He checked in at OVIR and went through the turnstile looking for his contact. A small man, myopic and large-headed, came away from the coffee counter and smiled nervously. "Comrade Ivankovitch? Come with me, please?" The small man turned and led him toward a door with a KEEP OUT sign. "My name is Berdachev."

Rykov grunted.

The door gave way to a corridor—lino floor, yellow-brown government paint, office doors along both walls. The hallway was not heated and the air temperature was well below freezing. Berdachev led him down half the length of the corridor, around a corner into a side hall and into a small office occupied by filing cabinets, a long table, two unshaded lights suspended from the low corrugated ceiling, and two Oriental women. One was stunning; the other was enormously fat.

The fat woman growled, "Shut the door, Berdi, before we all freeze. Hello, Ivan."

Rykov removed his coat and threw it on a chair. "You don't look well, Valentia."

"It's the winter, I suppose one needs more sun."

"I want you to lose weight."

"Fat protects the blood from the cold."

"You're too conspicuous," he said, and glanced at the lithe young woman in yellow silk. Then he turned to face Berdachev at the door and said, "This will be private if you please."

The fat woman said, "I have complete trust in him."

"That's fine. You may have tested his trust. I have not. Do you mind?"

The huge formless shoulders moved. "Go, then, Berdi."

Berdachev blinked owlishly, nodded, and backed out of the room. Rykov watched until he disappeared around the corridor bend, then he closed the door and returned to the chair. The fat woman laughed. All of her.

In the gray building in the Arbat were cabinets filled with dossiers on every agent, and Valentia's was a thick file because her sexual proclivities had on occasion created risks. She was a voyeur and that was why the myopic young Berdachev had been with them—to couple with the stunning Anya for Valentia's amusement. But Valentia was an agent without peer and Anya was her eyes and ears.

Valentia was wedged into an armchair with her hips squeezing out under its arms. She had waxy yellow skin and the flat-cheeked, eye-folded face of her Chinese ancestors. It was no longer possible to detect any similarity between her features and Anya's but the lovely Anya was in fact her daughter.

"I want you both to go to Peking," Rykov said.

The fat face stirred. "Must we?"

He made no answer and she said, "It is such a distressing town, Peking. I despise it."

"Is it so much worse than this?"

"At least here we are among friends. I'm getting old—I no longer take the pleasure I once did from adventures."

"Your mission will be suitably sedentary. If acrobatics are required Anya can execute them."

"Is there no one else who could be sent? There must be others."

"There are no others."

"Nonsense."

"You're disagreeable and you don't want the job. That's precisely why it must be your job, Valentia. You will not be eager to please me and therefore you won't tell me lies that you think will please me. You are the only agent I can trust not to color things subjectively—not to ask the wrong questions and thus get answers different from what is before you." He added, "You have a choice, of course. You can refuse the mission and be shot. Or you can bungle the mission and be shot."

"Yes, of course, there's always that choice."

"Papers for both of you are waiting in Ussuriysk. You'll go in by the Chinese Eastern Railway, change at Harbin and entrain for Yingkow. From there you'll find your own transportation to Peking. You've done it before, you know the ropes. You're a Chinese from Mukden trying to drum up machinery for a voluntary farm-labor project and Anya is your daughter whom you have brought with you to charm the proper officials into parting with the necessary machinery. Her function in life is to be thrust at men by her domineering mother. I trust you won't find the role too hard to play."

"Your sarcasm is always entertaining, Ivan."

"If you cross paths with any of our people tell them that you're swimming to avoid an illness. That's your legend, don't deviate from it; we don't want our people knowing what you're doing. You understand? Particularly you're to avoid contact with neighbor GRU and Fourth Bureau agents. Your mission is private and you will report to no one except me, directly."

"Report how? And on what?"

"Patience, Valentia. You will collect your things from the cobbler in Ussuriysk, and when you reach Peking you will make contact with Chug Li and obtain from him a music box." A music box was a microwave wireless transceiver; a cobbler was a provider of false documentation.

He added, "Chug will complain, he'll try to find out what you're up to. Don't let him learn anything."

"Isn't he trusted?"

"As much as anyone out there is trusted. Nothing is certain."

"Not even Anya and me." She smiled slightly and the little eyes disappeared into folds. "Go on, then."

"Behind the Amergrad *dascha* there is an incinerator for human bodies. You may recall it."

"Yes."

"Then be trustworthy, Valentia. There's a lot of meat on you and it would stink a great deal. Let's have no more complaining."

"I complain to pass the time, dear Ivan, until you see fit to tell us what it is we are to do in Peking."

"You're vexing tonight."

"Such flattery," she said.

"About the music box. Chug has instructions to equip you with a high-speed recorder-player and a transmitter of sufficient power to reach Moscow at night. You know the frequency. You'll code your reports according to the command manual, not the field manual, and you'll put them on tape and broadcast them in ultra-high-speed bursts at thirteen minutes past the hour and thirty-seven minutes past the hour. Are you getting all this?"

"I shall memorize it all and throw my head away."

"Long-range direct communication is a risk but I must have

it. The China data coming from the field pass through channels and intermediaries before reaching me. At each step it is reinterpreted and abridged. An error at any point can be magnified enormously before it gets to me and I can't have any more of that, things are too taut now."

"What things?"

She was bemused; a little smile hovered on the bloated lips.

He shocked her out of it: "I think they're ready to attack us with their missiles."

With the corner of his eye he saw Anya sit up straighter. Valentia watched him from the depths of her clever eyes and said, "I should have known you wouldn't have flown all this way for anything trivial."

"Now I have your attention, do I?"

"Go on, Ivan."

"Everything points to it. They've whipped up a war psychosis and they're planning in terms of a preemptive first strike. They may be ready to launch it at any time. I need confirmation or denial and, in the case of confirmation, date and time and primary targets."

The huge engorged body lifted and fell with breath.

He said, "The reports I've been receiving have filtered through intermediaries who know my feelings about the Maoists—it's possible the intermediaries have been telling me what they think I want to hear, not what is actually true. Obviously I must be certain. That's your job."

"To get this kind of information I will have to take many risks."

"You mean Anya will."

"It's the same thing."

"Our profession isn't noted for its longevity." He made an impatient gesture, like a short judo chop against the air. "Valentia, don't spar with me, there's no time for it. You must be on your way. I came here personally to impress on you the gravity of this thing. The lives of millions of Russians may depend on you."

"Rhetoric doesn't impress me, Ivan, you know that. Tell me precisely what you want so that we can get on with it."

"I want you to bug them, of course."

"Them?"

"Fei, Shen, Jiou, Chug Po, An Tu, Lo Kai-teh, Yuan, Sun Shih—the Cabinet delegates to the Congress in Peking. They're already gathering now. The meeting was called hastily which means there should be larger gaps in security than usual. Your specialty is electronic surveillance and that's what you're going into Peking for. I want their quarters bugged, their aides, their meeting places, their persons—I want every word from every pair of lips monitored twenty-four hours a day until further notice."

"You know that's impossible. They'll equip the meetings with radio jammers and tape demagnetizers. But we'll do what we can. They can't install jammers everywhere. Trouser buttons can be replaced with micro-transmitters, bugs can be implanted in bedposts and telephones and toilets. We'll get what we can get, that's all. How much of a team will I have?"

"Every deep-cover agent in Peking has been alerted to put himself under your orders. Naturally we've excluded all of our agents who are known by the Chinese. Your work crew will be big enough but you will have to monitor everything yourself."

"Then I shan't get much sleep, shall I?"

"Jiou Ssu-kuan will be Anya's primary target. He has a weakness for anything that wiggles and as Defense Minister he warrants the highest priority."

"He'll be wired, then."

"Get every word," he said. He got up and put his arm into the sleeve of his coat.

Valentia put both hands on the arms of her chair and levered herself upright. Immediately she dwarfed the room. "If you intended to stun me you've succeeded. But if we assume you're right and they do plan to attack—what then?"

"Then let's hope we shall react in time."

"You'll forgive my impertinence, Ivan, but what if the Kremlin refuses to act?"

"Your job," he replied, "is to supply me with such evidence as will make it impossible for them to refuse."

"If the evidence is there we'll find it."

He buttoned up his coat and picked up the hat. "That's right. You will." He pulled out his snap-lid pocket watch. "My plane returns shortly. You'll get further details from the cobbler; he has coded instructions waiting for you. Anya?" He took the stunning girl's hand; she bowed slightly; Rykov nodded without changing expression and turned and opened the door.

Valentia said, *"Do svidaniya,* Ivan."

The corridor was freezing cold. Up at the corner the young Berdachev stood with his breath steaming gently from his nostrils. Rykov walked past him without remark and went half a dozen paces down the main hall before he stopped and retraced his steps silently to the corner.

Berdachev's voice: "Does he never relax?"

"Not in public," the woman said. "I stood watch with him once when we were breaking down a Japanese agent in Shimizu. Five days, and I saw him sleep two hours the entire time."

"Who is he, anyway?"

"The Kremlin's hatchet man."

There was more; Rykov did not stay to listen. He went back toward the terminal.

The Moskvitch needed valve work. It met Leon Belsky at the Vladivostok airport, driven by a hulking flat-faced Manchurian, and transported him to the waterfront. The car chugged and coughed the whole way. Belsky left the car without a word and the Manchurian drove away. A cold salt wind swept across the docks. It was almost midnight. Belsky plodded through the snow toward the lights of the crew shack on the landward end of a small industrial dock. The lights of the city vaguely outlined the big harbor and foghorns hooted continuously while lighthouse beacons stabbed the dark. Vladivostok was a closed city and there were no pedestrians or vehicles abroad except official ones.

Migachev was waiting for him in the crew shack. The room was overheated by a large coal stove and Migachev was stripped down to the trousers, no shoes, no shirt. His chest and shoulders were covered with a thick black pelt. "You belong behind a butcher's counter," Belsky told him.

"Well, I hate the cold. I was born in Sochi where it's warm. I wish I was there now."

"I know where you were born," Belsky said. "Get your clothes on—I'm in a hurry, we want to make landfall before daylight."

"Daylight tomorrow, you mean. Not today, unless you want my boat to sprout wings. If you're in such a hurry why don't you fly?"

"Too many people watch the incoming flights over there. Japan Defense Agency, CIA, Chinese—the whole world lives in Japanese airports. In this part of the world there are too many people who'd recognize me."

"Yet you're going over *there.*"

"Japan's the hot spot. A Caucasian like me sticks out. In America I'm just another middle-aged businessman. Come on, hurry up."

Migachev sat down to lace his boots. "We've plenty of time. Help yourself to the food."

Belsky ate standing up—black bread, herring, a cup of *koumiss.* "Aren't you ready yet?"

"I'm ready. Let's go." Migachev had put on a heavy turtleneck sweater over his undershirt, a topcoat over that, a heavy greatcoat over that, and a flowing oilskin slicker on top. He wore fleece-lined gloves inside his mittens and three pairs of socks inside his oversize waterproof boots.

"We're not going to the North Pole," Belsky said.

"The bridge on my boat is open."

Belsky grunted. "Let's go. Are my things aboard?"

"Yes, of course." Migachev warmed his mittens over the stove and turned off the lamp. Belsky followed him through the door by ear until he was beyond the end of the dockhouse and could orient himself by the city lights. Migachev's boots crunched the snow with loud hollow whacks. It was low tide; the water was six meters below, and Belsky moved with care —it would have been easy to slip off the dock. Migachev went down the ladder first and lighted a kerosene lamp on the boat.

Belsky climbed down, testing each rung before he put his weight on it. The boat was a twenty-meter fisherman—*sixty-five-footer,* he corrected himself doggedly. It had twin diesels, too much engine for such a boat, specially installed for Migachev's clandestine runs across the Sea of Japan. In outward appearance she was clumsy, disreputable, an old-fashioned fishing boat in need of paint, but beneath the waterline her hull was sleek over a deep-ocean keel, shaped for speed.

They went out of harbor on one engine. It growled sonorously; the boat's movement was sluggish until they cleared the last channel buoy and moved beyond earshot of land. Then Migachev cut in the second engine and opened them up. The fisherman jumped forward, riding high on her keel, making twenty-seven knots. The linesman came astern from his lookout post in the bow and took the wheel from Migachev, who turned and said, "We can go below now."

Belsky was enjoying the cold salt wind but Migachev was wet and miserable and went below without waiting an answer. Belsky followed him into the cramped cabin. He had to stoop to clear the transom when he entered. There was a tart chop to the sea and he had to keep hold of the bulkhead to avoid being pitched off his feet.

Migachev sat down on the lower bunk, nearest the heat of the engines. "Those are your things." Migachev pointed to the suitcase and the objects laid out on the opposite bunk. The suitcase was Samsonite, the clothing American with San Francisco and Fresno shop labels. Belsky already had with him the English tweed suit and overcoat he would wear on the Japanese leg of the journey.

Migachev said, "It will take about twenty-six hours to Komatsu. We should arrive about three o'clock tomorrow morning. You can catch a bus into Fukui, it's only seventy kilometers, and the train to Kyoto arriving at eight-fifteen. You have a reservation on the ten-o'clock flight out of Kyoto for Honolulu and Los Angeles."

Belsky examined the documents. There were three passports, all bearing different names. Two were American, the third Swiss. The Swiss passport in the name of Heinrich

Wiedemann, textile merchant, he would use to board the JAL plane at Kyoto and to clear American customs and immigration at Los Angeles—because, curiously, the Americans tended to inspect foreign visitors from friendly European countries with less care than they exercised in inspecting their own people.

Belsky had a look at the rest—visa, Social Security card, Fresno voter's registration, California driver's license, birth and baptismal certificates, school and university diplomas, an Air Force discharge, the lot—and then he climbed into the upper bunk and went promptly to sleep.

By the local calendar and clock it was early Tuesday afternoon by the time Belsky cleared Customs at Los Angeles International Airport and made his way to a telephone booth. Migachev had given him the number.

"Westlake Publishers, may I help you?"

"My name is Dangerfield," Belsky said. "I believe you have a message for me."

"Hold on a moment, please?"

The girl's voice was replaced by a man's. "Mr. Dangerfield? Right on schedule, sir. Have a good trip?"

"I think you've got something for me."

"Where are you calling from, Mr. Dangerfield?"

"Los Angeles airport."

"Then it's an open line. We might meet for lunch—do you know Flagg's? The taxi driver can find it, near the Beverly Wilshire. I'll meet you there in half an hour. There'll be a table in my name—Tucker Stark. Satisfactory?"

"No. Meet me at American Airlines here at the airport. The front entrance."

"Ah, that's somewhat irregular, Mr. Dangerfield. I'd prefer not to—"

"I have a plane to catch, Mr. Stark." Belsky hung up and went outside.

He confirmed his ticket and checked his bag and by the time he was finished standing in lines the contact was there at the front door. Belsky recognized the man from the photos in his dossier: Tidsov, cover name Tucker Stark, chief of the Los Angeles *rezidentsia*. As soon as he knew he had been spotted Tidsov walked into the building and turned toward the concession area carrying a leather suitcase, one of those squat soft bags designed to fit under an airplane seat. Tidsov put it into a twenty-four-hour storage locker, deposited a coin and locked it, and came away with the key in his pocket. Belsky watched him without actually looking at him more than once; he followed with the corners of his vision while Tidsov went into a telephone booth and closed the door. Three minutes later a blond man wandered past the phone booth and Tidsov stepped out of it and left the building without glancing at Belsky; meanwhile the blond man stepped into the phone booth Tidsov had just vacated, emerged momentarily, walked directly to the bank of lockers, inserted a key and withdrew the leather flight bag from the locker. The blond man carried the bag out through the glass-doored entrance and Belsky turned to watch covertly while the blond man exchanged glances with Tidsov. Then the two men separated and walked away in opposite directions.

A simple charade, probably unnecessary. The *rezidentsia* had a safe line but there was no telling who had a tap on the airport public phones; it wasn't as if Los Angeles International were an obscure filling station. The FBI might have had a routine tap and the phone call from Belsky just might have stirred up enough interest for them to send someone to observe the meeting place. If so, they would have witnessed, to all observable intents, a drop. If the FBI followed the blond man and grabbed the suitcase to find out what was in it, they would probably find old clothes.

Belsky waited near the paperback stand and then took off his topcoat and stood looking mildly exasperated, a man who didn't want his arm burdened. Finally his eye settled on the lockers and he allowed his expression to change, and he walked resolutely toward the lockers, found an open one—the one the suitcase had occupied—put his coat inside and spent a quarter and pocketed the key.

He had forty-five minutes before his flight; he looked at

camera displays and magazines and bought an *Examiner* and had a beer in the bar. When his flight was called he walked right past the lockers and then snapped his fingers with sudden obvious realization and went back to claim his coat. When he unlocked the door and reached inside he peeled away the envelope that Tidsov had taped under the locker ceiling; he concealed it in the folds of the coat and walked to his plane.

It was an hour's flight to Tucson. When the FASTEN SEAT BELT sign was extinguished Belsky went back to the lavatory and locked himself in. The envelope and its single sheet of paper were made of phosphor-treated flashpaper; he committed the message to memory in the time it took to read it, held it over the aluminum toilet bowl and set fire to it. By the time it had fallen into the bowl it had been consumed and he flushed the ash residue down and went back to his seat. The stewardess was passing out snacks, and Belsky smiled at her.

PRIORITY UTMOST
DANGERFIELD LA IA 2APR 1435 PST PANAM 363
VIA WESTLAKE PUBLISHER
KGB 1
CYPHER 1528 SG
SENT 2115 GMT WP ACKNOWLEDGE
MESSAGE BEGINS X TENTATIVE CONFIRMATION TARTAR IN-
TENT X DATE UNCERTAIN BUT NOT LESS THAN 7 DAYS NOR
MORE THAN 30 DAYS X TARTAR POLITBURO STILL UNDECIDED
AS TO FINAL COMMITMENT BUT ASSUME TARTAR ATTACK X IN
VIEW OF SHORT TIME AVAILABLE DISCARD PLAN Z X EXECUTE
PLAN B X ACCELERATE IMMEDIATE ACTIVATION OF PLAYERS
X STAND BY TO EXECUTE PLAN B3 ON SIGNAL POSSIBLY
WITHIN 120 HOURS X VR X MESSAGE ENDS 17639 42 2474

Chapter Five

Lieutenant Colonel Fred Winslow picked a ball-point pen out of the desk caddy and began to scrawl his OK and initials across the mimeographed duty roster but the pen wouldn't write and he had to scratch it savagely across the corner of an envelope to get the ink flowing. He made a noise and took off his reading glasses and wiped them, and scowled abstractedly across the small office at the place in the far wall where a window ought to be. There were only photographs: the Commander in Chief, the Chairman of the Joint Chiefs, the Secretary of the Air Force, the Air Force Chief of Staff. No window. The office was sixty feet underground and the light came from recessed fluorescent fixtures in the ceiling and there was only one way to tell whether it was day or night—the twenty-four-hour clock above the door. Now and then Winslow entertained the fantasy of installing a sixty-foot periscope and a four-by-five window to go with it.

According to the clock it was getting on to six o'clock and time to go home. He wandered into his tiny lavatory, buttoned his collar, hoisted his tie up from half-mast and inserted it neatly between the second and third buttons of his uniform shirt. The face in the mirror was round and mild, the eyes large and timid, the loose thatch of hair across his high forehead getting distressingly gray. He really looked as if he must have been middle-aged since birth: the kind of man who had been given a briefcase for his eleventh birthday and a book of crossword puzzles for his forty-third. Celia always laughed: *It's the perfect image for you, darling, why change it?* But Winslow remembered the adventuresome anticipations of his youth.

Nick Conrad put his head into the office. "Fred? Colonel Ryan's up in the Wing Commander's HQ, wants a word with you before you go off."

Winslow took his blue jacket down from the hanger. "What's the flap?"

"No flap." Conrad had sharp points on all his bones. A narrow feral face and waxy brown hair that came to a widow's peak, and a major's gold leaves on his neat uniform. He lit a cigarette and blew smoke out his nose. "Christ what a week."

"Why?"

"The whole load. Yesterday I had to pull OD and tonight I'll be here till midnight distributing the new codes." The doomsday codes were changed every four days—next week it would be Saturday, the week after that Wednesday. The envelopes came down from Colorado by plane under guard and wherever they went there had to be two officers in attendance —the courier from NORAD and the ICBM wing's Electronics Warfare Officer, Conrad. There were forty-two code envelopes and each had to be hand-delivered to its station by the two officers: two to each of the eighteen silos and the rest to command personnel. At the same time last week's envelopes had to be picked up and destroyed under supervision. It made for a long dreary evening.

Conrad was still holding the door and Winslow headed for

it but the phone rang and he had to turn back. It was Celia. "Darling, I know it's short notice, but Ramsey Douglass happened to phone just now and said he has to see us. I invited him for dinner—I hope you don't mind?"

Winslow closed his eyes. "All right."

"There's a letter from Barbara."

"Fine."

"She seems to have a boyfriend."

"A boyfriend. For Christ's sake she's fourteen years old."

"Never too early." Celia chuckled.

"I'm on my way out, but Colonel Ryan wants to see me. I may be a few minutes late."

"That's all right, Ramsey's not coming till eight. Bye, darling."

He hung up and walked past Conrad into the corridor. "We appear to have a dinner guest."

"Bon appétit."

"Ramsey Douglass."

Conrad lifted his eyebrows and scratched his angular nose. "I hope it's just social."

Winslow sensed anger in the Wing Commander's office when he entered. Colonel Bill Ryan, the base commander, sat rumpled in a steel-and-plastic armchair and only waved wearily by way of greeting. Major Pete Chandler, big and crew-cut and hiding behind enormous mirrored sunglasses, was on his feet at one side of the room and only grunted at Winslow. Pete Chandler was chief Security Officer for the complex.

Wing Commander Colonel Clarence "Bud" Sims was behind his desk with both elbows on the blotter, his glasses perched on top of his head. They had left dents on the sides of his nose and he was rubbing it wearily with thumb and forefinger. Sims was heavy-handed, direct, unsophisticated, painfully sincere. He said, "Thanks for dropping by, Fred. We'll only keep you a minute. Colonel Ryan's got a problem."

"I wouldn't call it a problem," Ryan said quickly, and Winslow noticed the way Pete Chandler's face turned with an irritable snap.

Bill Ryan added, "I didn't mean to make waves—it appears Major Chandler doesn't like this but we're going to have to arrange a guided tour of the complex for a VIP party and I'd like you to handle it."

"We've done it plenty of times. Why not?"

Pete Chandler growled, "Because this time it's Senator Forrester."

Winslow kept looking at Ryan. "I see."

Ryan didn't look comfortable at all. "Look, he's being frank about this, he's looking for ammunition against us—he thinks he can find holes in our security and naturally Major Chandler resents that. But we can't turn Senator Forrester away at the gate."

Wing Commander Sims said, "He's got every right to inspect the installation. He's a member of the Committee, and he's cleared for Top Secret. We've got no choice. Besides we wouldn't be doing ourselves any good by giving him the idea we're reluctant to have him here. We've got to give him the idea we welcome his inspection, because if he can find any gaps in our security we want to be the first ones to know about it."

Chandler made an exasperated sound. "He won't find any gaps. We all know that and Forrester knows it too—he's just grandstanding and I don't see why we should be accomplices in it." The motorcycle glasses had slipped down on his nose and he thumbed them back. "With all due respect, sir, Colonel Ryan's a friend of the Senator's and maybe we're getting wires crossed here. There's no—"

"That'll be enough of that, Major," Bill Ryan said. "Let's keep personalities out of it."

"Yes, sir. Permission to finish, sir?" Chandler was full of acid and Fred Winslow moved off a bit to the side to get out of the crossfire.

"Go on," Ryan said and flapped his hand vaguely.

Pete Chandler said, "Security's my responsibility, Colonel." He was facing a point somewhere between Sims and Ryan, and since they were both colonels it was hard to tell whom he was addressing; his eyes were invisible behind the dark lenses. "He's welcome to have a tour of the usual operational systems but if we let him zero in on our security arrangements he'll have access to information that not even our ranking officers have. We've got eighteen thousand men in uniform around here and outside of this room there aren't a dozen of them who know the whole security setup. And those dozen are men we can control. We've got no way of keeping the lid on a United States Senator once he gets hold of the information. For all we know he'll publish the whole thing in *The New York Times* and the Soviet attaché in New York will airmail a copy direct to the Kremlin—then where'll we be?"

Ryan snapped, "Give him a little more credit for brains than that, Pete. Whatever ax you may think he's grinding, the Senator's not about to give away the whole show out of spite. Besides, Title Eighteen's just as binding on him as it is on you and me."

"He wants to bring two other people along with him, doesn't he? A scientist and a spook of some kind? Suppose one of them decides he's willing to sacrifice a few years of his time in Leavenworth on the Senator's behalf?"

Ryan said, "You're clutching at straws." He turned to the Wing Commander. "He's your subordinate, Bud, not mine, but if I have to I'll request you make it a direct order in writing."

Sims was embarrassed. "Major Chandler, your exception has been noted. Anything you want to add?"

"I guess not."

"Then let's get on with it—unless you want to lodge a formal protest."

Chandler remained mute and the Wing Commander leaned back wearily in his tilt chair. "We don't need to have it on paper, do we? You'll show the Senator's party anything they want to see."

"Yes, sir. Do I have to volunteer things, or confine it to what they ask for specifically?"

Sims glanced at Ryan and Ryan shrugged. "Stick to what they ask for."

If Chandler was mollified he gave no sign of it.

The Wing Commander said to Fred Winslow, "All right then, Fred. They'll be here Friday morning at eight. Colonel Ryan will meet them at his headquarters and turn them over to you. From there on it's up to you."

Major Chandler said, "I'd like to keep them company."

Ryan looked at him. "As long as you keep a civil tongue in your head, Pete."

Chandler showed his teeth. "I'll mind my manners."

"Fine. I'm sorry if I jumped at you."

"Forget it, Colonel." Chandler turned toward the door. "Fred? You and I will have to map out some kind of itinerary."

Winslow nodded and looked questioningly at the Wing Commander and Sims sat up and felt the knot of his tie. "I guess that's all, Fred. Thanks for dropping by."

Winslow left the office. The floor vibrated gently with the thrumming of machinery. Pete Chandler walked along with him and when they were out of earshot of the Wing Commander's office Chandler said, "Christ."

"They won't find anything, Pete."

"Maybe." Chandler turned and buttonholed him. "We did, didn't we? If we could find it, why can't somebody else?"

"It took us years. What can they find in one day?"

"I just don't like it."

"Sure. Look, if it comes to the worst and they find the holes we'll just have to plug them and look for other holes. We did it before, we can do it again."

When Winslow got in the car he rubbed his paunch absently and felt the sweat begin under his uniform. He drove through the main gate and saw the little group of long-haired kids camped off to one side with their peace posters and NO PHAE-TON! picket signs; he drove slowly and looked for Alec's face among them, but his son wasn't there and Winslow felt remotely relieved.

Along Alvernon going north the traffic was clotted and slow. It took him three lights to make the left turn at Fifth and when he had executed the maneuver he heard the raucous hoot of a car horn; he looked around in irritation to find Nicole Lawrence beside him in her little foreign car, gesticulating with imperious jerks of her head. Winslow made a face and pulled off into the Elcon shopping-center lot.

The dying sun struck painful flashes off the rooftops of a thousand cars. Nicole pulled in a few slots away and Winslow walked over to her car. "What's the matter?"

"Come sit in the car."

He went around the back of it and got in. Nicole had a caustic look. She was tiny, she had a neat trim figure and good bones but some unhappy trick of genetic fate had kneaded and creased the skin of her face until at forty-five she looked as if she must have slept with her face pressed against a rabbit-wire screen.

The windshield of her car had a sign in it, *PRESS*—KARZ-TV. He looked at his watch and Nicole made the inevitable sour remark: "She's timing you now."

"We've got company for dinner."

"You sound ecstatic."

"Ramsey Douglass."

It made her grin fiercely. "Then I'm just a prelim bout to warm you up for him. Be a dear, Fred, open the glove compartment and hand me the tiger sweat."

It was eight-year-old bourbon, a flat pint. She drank from the bottle and said, "I'm glad I saw you going by—I was going to call you tonight. I need to know when Senator Forrester's going to visit the base."

"Where'd you hear that?"

"When he stepped off the plane last Saturday he told us at the press conference he meant to get to the bottom of things. Reading between the lines that means a junket to Davis Monthan AFB."

"And you want to collar him at the gate with a microphone and a TV camera."

"In the movies they call it a scoop," she said dryly. "Give."

"Why should I?"

"Friendship. Auld lang syne. Birds of a feather."

"I'll think about it."

"This could turn out to be important, Fred."

"If it does I'll let you know."

"What's come over you? You never talk back to me, Fred. You always try to make me feel as if I'm persecuting you. Now all of a sudden you're making with flip remarks."

"It's the moon. I'm having my period. Why all the sudden interest in the Senator?"

"He's news, isn't he?" She tossed her head back to drink from the pint and after a while she said, "Look at those billboards. Constant appeal to envy and fear and greed—a whole population dedicated to making the world safe for time-release antiperspirants. It's about time we started tearing the whole thing down so we can build something decent, isn't it?"

"You sound like my son."

"Then you've got a bright son."

"Alec? Clever sometimes; not bright. I had hopes for him once, but he had endless sieges of asthma and mononucleosis —he's twenty-two and he's only a sophomore; you can hardly call that bright."

"Will you all now turn to page seventy-two in the hymnal."

"I'm sorry. You got me off on it."

"You're upset, aren't you? What's on your mind, Fred? Lie down on the couch and tell me all about it."

He looked at her. "It's a stinking trap we're in, isn't it?"

"I hope this is just a mood, Fred. Just a stage."

"Why?"

"Because it's a little late for you to think about going back and changing anything."

"Did I say I wanted to?"

"The signs are showing. You're having second thoughts. Male menopause. I don't suppose you've mentioned it to Celia."

"No."

"Naturally. If you had she'd have rammed something up your ass to stiffen your backbone. Celia can get more militant than that hairy son of yours."

He thought of Alec, hands always in his pockets, his un-

breakable facial apathy, his scorn for the adult world which he
somehow intended to reject and enter all at the same time.

She said, "It's my job, Fred, you know that. I'm obliged to
remind you of certain things whenever I see signs of—uncer-
tainty—among us. I've been entrusted with this duty and that
means I can't let any of you spoil things because it would
reflect on me if you did. Now you've got Celia and you've got
Alec and Barbara and somewhere a long way from here you've
got a mother and two sisters and three brothers, and all of
them can be reached."

"You don't have to shout warnings at me, Nicole."

"You can go now, Fred. If anybody saw us together and
happens to ask, tell them I asked you about Forrester's tour
of inspection. Incidentally, you never did tell me when he's
coming."

"I didn't, did I?" He got out of her car and walked over to
his own.

He drove west into a tired old residential district. Big trees,
leafless, arched the street and threw patterns of spindly shade
that fell long and surreal in the late-afternoon sunlight, and
the stately old houses clung to a decaying dignity.

The houses on Stewart were small and the lawns parched.
Celia had the lawn sprinklers going and Alec's bright yellow
car squatted at the curb on its bald tires. Winslow drove into
the dirt alley behind the house and parked in the open because they had converted the garage into a party room last
year.

He found Celia cold-creaming her skin against the dry air.
She glanced in the mirror and said, "I do look a fright."

"You look fine." He kissed her cheek and picked up the
glass of whiskey and ice that stood beaded on the dressing
table. "You look gorgeous." He took a sip and went into the
bathroom stripping off his uniform as he went, showered and
shaved and lay on the bed in his underwear, waiting for the
after-shower sweat to dry.

"Should I wear this dress?"

"Why not?"

"Fred, you haven't even looked at it."

She stood by the open closet holding a loosely pleated yellow dress on a hanger, spreading it out over her forearm and giving it the uncertain appraisal of a shopper in a department store. She had always been lean and she had become a little bony the past few years—there was folded flesh at her elbows—but her posture was very good, she didn't have the caved-in slump of underweight middle age. She was in her bra and slip and her breasts looked full and round in the thin pink hammocks. Her face was chiseled and lovely but strong rather than warm. She had the power to attract men's second looks, and she did not look like the mother of a twenty-two-year-old son. Winslow said, "The dress is fine. Come here."

"No. You'd muss my hair, I'd leak all night, and anyway we haven't time."

"So damned practical." He rolled his feet to the floor and started to dress. "I saw the yellow car outside. Alec in his room?"

"He's writing a paper for one of his courses." She pushed the straight brown hair back from her eyes and gave him a smile that was distant and distracted; she presented her back to him and he zipped her up and she waited without moving until he gave her rump the ritual hand pat.

She went to the closet to get her sandals. She had the legs of a fashion model and he thought, *I'm lucky; why can't I just think about that?* But he was profoundly depressed. What was survival worth if it meant the need for endless caution? Mere existence wasn't enough: there had to be the promise of freedom from terror, there had to be hope.

She said, "Barbara's letter is on the table next to you."

He read it with a creeping sense of guilt. He rarely thought of Barbara except when her letters arrived, punctually every week, and when the headmaster mailed her monthly report card.

Her letter was full of the impatient strugglings of a nonverbal teen-ager to find something to say. Last Christmas she had come home for two weeks and shocked him—her skirt as high as her fanny, coping with adult bras and her first pair of false

eyelashes. He was too concerned to be amused: she was fourteen and he wondered how soon she would be experimenting
with grass and pills and vaginal foam and her first orgasm, if
she hadn't done already. In a few years' time would she be
freaked out in a pad somewhere with walls papered with posters of Fidel and Mao and the Panthers? *The orthodontist says my
braces can come off in May.* At least she could spell. He remembered the ridiculous silver-frosted paint she had put on her
fingernails. *Oh, Daddy, I mean, it's only sort of, like, you know,
everybody wears nail polish, hey?*

He put a clean shirt on. "I've told them and told them and
told them no starch in the collars. Christ."

"What's come over you?"

"Nothing."

"Rubbish."

"Forget it."

"Fred."

"Do we have to talk it to death? All right, look, we've somehow turned into middle-aged, middle-class Americans.
Doesn't that frighten you? With a slightly retarded son in
college and a disgustingly typical fourteen-year-old daughter.
We—"

"He's not retarded! For God's sake."

"All right, he's dumb."

"He's as bright as you are. It isn't his fault he's a couple of
years behind the rest of them; he was *ill.* But he's perfectly—"

"Fine," he conceded. "Let's not argue the point. Whatever
they are, they're ordinary American kids—doesn't that scare
you?"

"Why ever should it?"

"What on earth is going to happen when Alec and Barbara
find out?"

"Fred."

Her tone was different and he straightened from his shoe-
laces to look at her.

She said, "Do you know the risk we take just having this
conversation?"

"We have to trust each other, don't we?" But he knew what

she meant. When they had serious things to discuss privately they always went outdoors.

He rammed his shirt tails into his trousers and started into the hall. "Want a drink?"

"Yes."

He went to the little portable bar in the living room. From the back of the house he heard the muted racket of the radio, a hard-rock beat that meant Alex had opened his door. In a moment his son appeared in sandals, tight chino pants and a fatigue shirt. Alec mumbled something by way of greeting and Winslow said, "Taking five?"

"I, uh, figured I'd go out for a little while, finish up later."

"Then at least you could turn that radio off."

"Uh." Alec scuffed back down the hall and after a moment the noise stopped.

Celia arrived and gave her husband her wry smile and when Alec reappeared Winslow said, "You kids deplore the mechanization and dehumanization of technological life and you love this music that's nothing but electronics and mechanical noise. It's the least humanized music in the history of mankind. How can you explain that?"

"You always have to make sense out of things, don't you?"

"Doesn't everybody?"

"Sometimes you need to just put it in the groove and let it wail. Anyhow why ask me about it? You've got plenty of straights full of fifty-dollar-an-hour reasons for everything everybody does."

Winslow watched him. The boy shifted from foot to foot with his hands in his pockets and Winslow said, "Are you on something, Alec?"

"No."

Winslow's silence argued with him and Alec's head lifted. "I know I'm stupid but I do know the difference between freaky kicks and getting hung. I've seen them ride and I've seen them fall. Nobody comes down easy. I don't even try."

Winslow followed it, more or less. "I believe you; does that make me a typical straight fool parent who believes everything his kid tells him?"

"I don't know what it makes you." Alec moved two steps sideways, like a crab. "It's true, that's all. I don't use anything except maybe grass now and then, and I don't keep that at home."

"I'm grateful for that."

"Because you won't get raided?"

"Because I can't stand the smell of the stuff. Is there something on your mind, Alec? Something you want to talk to me about?"

"Uh, I was going to ask you, what are you going to do about Senator Forrester?"

It startled him. "What?"

"He's a heavy guy, Dad."

"And?"

"Everybody figures he wants to inspect the base, and a lot of people are waiting to see, uh, what you guys are going to do about it. I mean, if you guys try to shoot down Senator Forrester it could make a lot of noise."

"What kind of noise?"

"Look, there's walking around the air-base gate with picket signs like they're doing now, and then there's going out on that jet runway and having a sit-in on the pavement."

"To stop the planes?"

"It's been mentioned."

"Did those kids tell you to put it to me that I'd better help Senator Forrester or else?"

"Or else what, Dad?"

"I do a job. My job isn't going to be influenced by any crazy attempts at extortion."

"No extortion. The people are just waiting to see what happens, that's all." Alec's expression changed briefly, more a tic than a smile; he lunged toward the door.

Celia appeared in the kitchen door. "Dinner's going to be on the table soon."

"Save me a slice cold. I got to go."

Winslow said, "You might have told your mother before."

"Okay, I forgot. Is that a misdemeanor or something?"

Celia said, "Go to your meeting. I'll keep your plate warm for you."

Alec took a hand out of his pocket to open the front door and went out without saying good-bye.

Winslow said, "That kid doesn't even know how to *spell* discipline."

When he heard Alec's car start away with a guttural belch of noise he crossed the room and propped his shoulder in the kitchen doorway. "I hope they're just blowing off steam. They wouldn't get as far as the runway of course but if they did they might get hurt—a dose of jet exhaust wouldn't leave much of them."

She looked up from the stove but there was no time for a reply. The doorbell rang.

Ramsey Douglass was narrow as a plank and clothed in a slim sharkskin suit that gave him an air of slick elegance. He was a little sickly with his conspiratorial mannerisms; there was something silken and rustling about him. Middle age had settled his eyebrows into arches of perpetual irony. He sat on the small of his back, filled with sleepy sardonic arrogance. All through dinner he had filled the air with tart bitter commentaries: he had a ruthless and superficial felicity with words.

Winslow had eaten very little and consumed the lion's portion of the Beaujolais.

Douglass was Matthewson-Ward's SATAF coordinator and that put him at home both in the hardware industry and in Air Force circles; he was also deep in local politics and had been Congressman Trumble's chief campaign-speech writer.

Douglass sipped cognac and chain-smoked and held forth in his wintry caustic voice. "You cradle them in comforts, you sell yourselves on the curious notion that they're the most dedicated and principled and magnificent generation ever born, you accept without argument the proposition that they alone recognize the maladies of the world and have the wisdom to chart a new course for us all. What the hell do you expect them to do when you hand them carte blanche?"

Winslow made a noncommittal sound to indicate he was listening.

"You parents let them overrun you. You let them overrun their teachers and their school administrators. You're refusing to defend civilized values against these barbarian kids— you're handing them the world and telling them it's theirs to play with. I promise you I'm not nearly as afraid of the warmongers and capitalists and polluters and overpopulaters as I am of these babies. What's going to happen to the civilizations we know when this generation of ugly self-indulgent brats grows old enough to take over? What have any of them accomplished that earns them the right to be held up as the sages of our age?"

Celia laughed at him. She had that strength. Winslow had known him half his lifetime but had never developed nerve enough to laugh at Douglass. Celia said, "They started with sensible ideals, Rams. It wasn't until they saw that nobody was listening to them that they started to get raucous."

"Nobody was listening? Christ we were listening. We listened to them tell us that Mao was the only real Communist, that the Panthers are just peace-loving folks at heart, that there's no choice between the USSR and the USA because they're both fascist dictatorships, that the kids have the right to destroy the universities because they don't like the color of the wall paint. We listened, Celia. We just didn't believe it. These kids talk peace and make guerrilla war with terrorist tactics. They reject materialism and they embrace Daddy's credit card. They claim the establishment won't budge from its unyielding position but they offer nothing but nonnegotiable demands. They tell us to open our eyes and they glaze their own with drugs. They—"

"All right," Celia said. "We get the point. You're turning into an archconservative, Rams."

"Hell, I'm the only one in this room who hasn't sold out to bourgeois values. These babies aren't leftists. They're babies, playing with toys because you gave them the toys to play with."

"But don't you find something gallant about them? At least

they're willing to question the bourgeois values. They may be the first generation in history that's dared to challenge the contradiction between ideals and realities."

"Crap. Infantile romanticism. They're a kept generation—no sense of humor, they can't communicate with each other without sex because nobody ever gave them an incentive to learn basic English. They're experts at hooting down speakers and breaking up meetings—they'll defend to the death your right to agree with them but if you argue rationally their only answer is to shout you down and throw bombs. It makes me think of Hitler's brownshirts. Did you ever hear one of these kids stand up and insist that the *kids* should be expected to live up to their own demands? They make great high moral demands on everybody but themselves. Disagree with them and right away you're pigeonholed: another brainwashed member of the mindless fascist mass. Including you and me, which is pretty damn funny, you know. In Russia these kids would be put away until they learned the meaning of loyalty."

Celia crossed her fine long legs and smiled, and Winslow found himself staring stupidly at his own wife's discreet décolletage. He had learned long ago he was no match for Douglass' devious rhetoric and Celia's stubborn ripostes; he did not intrude.

Celia said, "Don't you think they're having the same problems in Russia?"

"They'll never let it get out of hand this way."

"What will they do, then? Purge a whole generation? Destroy the nation's youth?"

"If they have to. It's been done before. Stalin killed far more Russians than non-Russians but you notice the Soviet Union has survived and that's the important thing."

Celia said, "You'd have a different slant if you had children of your own."

"Thankfully I haven't."

"You really should have got married a long time ago." She was teasing him and Winslow resented her complacency because she was impervious to Douglass' abrasiveness and he was not.

"Why get married?" Douglass said. "It only means you'll probably get divorced." His eyebrows stirred. "Actually I suppose it all shouldn't come as a surprise—the kids are uninspired because they've got uninspired parents. Wouldn't you say, Fred?"

"What?" The skin on Winslow's face tightened.

"Look at you—soft around the middle, living in this plastic air-conditioned bourgeois paradise, going through life like a puppy that keeps wagging its tail hoping it'll persuade people not to kick it again. That's what that kid of yours sees—a tired middle-aged guy who goes through life being sold by the last person who spoke to him."

Winslow looked down to see that his hand had formed itself into a fist. Douglass laughed. "And never darken my door again, eh? You cut a rather ridiculous figure for a would-be pugilist, Fred."

Winslow opened his hand and heard Celia say, "That's enough, Rams." Her voice was cool.

"I suppose it is. I meant nothing personal by it. You do understand, Fred?"

Winslow made a sound of dismissal and pushed back the red haze of anger. Douglass uncoiled himself and stood up. "I suppose it's time to go. Oh by the way," he added, enjoying it, "a gentleman by the name of Dangerfield arrived in town this afternoon and I imagine we'll be getting together with him and some of our mutual friends very shortly—perhaps tomorrow. It gives pause for thought, doesn't it, after all this time?"

"What is it?" Winslow asked. "An inspection?"

"More than that this time, I think."

Celia said, "It doesn't mean anything," but not as if she believed it.

Douglass laughed. "You'd hate for anything to upset the applecart now, wouldn't you?"

"And you'd love it."

"It isn't a question of what I'd love. Let's not forget what we're here for. Celia, have you got any engagements planned for tomorrow and Thursday? If so cancel them—I'll want you available instantly. The same goes for you, Fred. Maybe you'd better call in sick tomorrow and stay home."

"I can't. We've got a Senatorial investigation coming on the base Friday morning."

"Forrester? Yes. Awkward timing, but we'll see what we can do. If worse comes to worst we'll meet without you and Celia will bring you up to date." Douglass turned away and went toward the door and added over his shoulder, "Let me recommend you prepare yourselves for whatever may be required. It may be time for us to take things out of mothballs and if so we don't want to find any moth holes in them, do we?"

Having given himself the curtain line he walked out.

Winslow watched the red tail lights of Douglass' Volkswagen disappear down the street and then he slammed the door and tramped back through the house. Celia was already outside in the yard. They walked silently down the dusty alley the length of the block and turned right on the gravel sidewalk. There was a chill and he wished he'd brought a sweater.

"He was only trying to throw a scare into us."

"He wouldn't lie about a thing like that, Fred."

"I wouldn't put it past him. I wouldn't put anything past him. Thanks for sticking up for me."

"Did I?"

"When you told him to shut up. I wanted to smash a few of his teeth."

"That wouldn't have been too bright, would it."

" 'Whatever may be required,' " he said. "What did he mean by that?"

"I don't think he knows, himself."

"He knows something we don't know. How can you take it so calmly?"

"What can we do except wait?"

They crossed a street and Winslow said, "Suppose we have to do something that ruins everything we've got here?"

"We've lived with that for years."

"Is that all there is to it? What about the kids? What do we tell them?"

"We don't tell them a thing, Fred."

"Sure. It'll be lovely if they have to find out from someone else."

"Who else is going to tell them?"

"For all we know we'll be in the headlines."

"For all we know we won't." She stopped and turned and faced him. "Fred, it's what we are here for."

"How can they expect us to be the same people we were then? Just because they've banked double pay for us and told us we could come home to early retirement as soon as we're finished here? Do they think that's really what we want after all this time? Go home to what? No friends left over there— God, we'd even have to learn the language all over again. A miniature apartment with a tiny refrigerator and if we're lucky central heating to get through those God damned winters— spend half a day standing in line to buy your clothes, maybe use half our savings to buy an unreliable little excuse for a car so we can go to the country on a few weekends in the summer when it's not snowed in. That's no good for us any more— you know it and they must know it; it's too late for all that. We've changed too much."

"Fred—"

"Please don't remind me I ought to be glad of a chance to serve my country. It isn't my country any more."

"I won't. We're a little too mature for all that. I won't even tell you we've been seduced by decadent bourgeois values— leave all that to Rams, he's the only one who still believes in slogans even if he's the one who puts them down. I'm sure we've been seduced by it all but I'm sure they never expected otherwise. They only expected one thing of us—that we never forget who they are, or what they're capable of. We're never out of their reach. Your brothers and sisters and mother, and my parents and nieces and nephews. Even Alec and Barbara."

"That's what Nicole said. I wonder if she knew about Dangerfield."

"Nicole?"

"She gave me a peptalk this afternoon."

"Then she probably knows. Rams would have told her

before he told us. They're two of a kind." She turned and began walking again. "They've got us on a leash. They wouldn't have sent us if they couldn't be sure of controlling us for our whole lifetimes—they wouldn't have taken the chance of one of us defecting. How many times have we walked up this street and had this conversation before? There aren't any loopholes. All we can do is to be thankful we've had the past twenty years."

"And Alec and Barbara?"

"Whatever happens they'll survive it or they won't."

"Do you get any real comfort from that kind of asinine fatalism?"

"Fred, what's the point of agonizing over things that are beyond our power to decide?"

There were clouds over the moon and between street lights it was quite dark; Winslow took his wife's arm. She said, "I was the one who was full of idealism when we volunteered to come over here. Sometimes I thought you came simply to be with me. I couldn't tell if it was what you wanted for yourself or not. But then I told myself I was flattering myself—no woman could force you to do a thing you didn't really want to do."

He stopped. His grip on her arm turned her and he felt heat in his cheeks; he said in an odd voice, "It could have been a lot worse, after all, couldn't it?"

"We've had twenty-three years together and we didn't end up hating each other. That's a great deal."

"We're both talking as if it's over."

A car came into the street preceded by its lights. They turned and began to walk home. Winslow said, "What are they going to want us to do? What are we going to have to do?"

She gripped his hand; it was the only answer she gave.

☆☆☆☆☆☆☆☆☆☆☆☆☆☆☆☆☆☆☆☆☆☆☆☆☆☆☆☆☆☆☆☆☆☆☆

Chapter Six

Early Wednesday morning Alan Forrester drove down from the ranch and racked the 200SL in a FOR OFFICIAL USE ONLY parking slot beside the courthouse. He walked by the open door of a Superior Court room where people were lined up in rows of chairs waiting to be heard—prostitutes with cheap wigs and rickety legs and the absurdly fur-dressed pimps who had come to ransom them.

The Pima County Courthouse had been built in the Moorish style, hollowed out with a square central courtyard and a veranda-covered balcony in lieu of a hallway. The balcony teemed with civil servants in shirtsleeves and cotton dresses, complacent as eunuchs. Forrester, towering and striking, made a center of attention as he progressed. He shook hands and spoke greetings by name and signed a few autographs, and took note of the number of passersby who made a point

of pretending not to see him. The battle lines of public opinion were being drawn up.

He went into his private office by the side door and found
Jaime Spode asprawl on the couch. A babble of voices came
through the closed door of the outer office and a newspaper
lay on the desk, TORNADOES KILL 17 IN TEXAS PANHANDLE.
There was a small two-column head halfway down the page:

SOVIET DENIES AIM TO SURPASS U.S. IN MIRVS.

Washington, *April 2* (UPI)—The Soviet press agency Tass
issued the first official statement on the growing tempest
over the alleged U.S. plan to deploy the Phaeton MIRV
system of missile warheads. The Soviet Union asserted it
was not seeking to add a further spiral to the arms race
by seeking nuclear MIRV superiority over the United
States.

The Soviet report seemed clearly a reaction to the
disclosures last week by Senator Alan Forrester (R-Ariz)
that combined Pentagon-House forces planned to rush
official authorization of Phaeton Three through both
houses of Congress before the issue could be debated
in public. The Phaeton Three multiple-warhead system is
(*Cont. on p. 7*)

Forrester opened the paper to read the continuation and
when he glanced up he caught Spode watching him. "With
friends like the Reds, who needs enemies in Congress?"

Forrester grunted.

"Old man Shattuck still avoiding you?"

"Yes."

"I don't wonder. I checked around and it seems Shattuck
Industries gave a hundred-thousand-dollar check to Congressman Webb Breckenyear's campaign fund two years
ago."

"I might have expected that." Forrester reached for the
intercom switch. "Ronnie?"

The speaker crackled. "Yes, Mr. Spode?"

It was a clear enough signal: there was someone in the outer
office who wasn't to know Forrester was in.

"Come in when you're free, will you?"

On the speaker behind Ronnie's "Yes, sir," he heard a woman's harsh acrimony: "Every seven puking seconds another puking mouth to feed with six tons of meat and five tons of wheat and twenty-six million tons of water and God knows what-all—I am going to camp in this puking chair until hell freezes over or I get in to see the puking Senator, whichever comes first. If I don't get his signature we'll all get crowded off the God damn puking planet."

Ronnie had left the intercom turned up long enough for them to hear what she was up against and it made Spode laugh with a hard bray. "Out to save the puking world all by herself—what'll you bet if I go out there and tell her to fuck off she'll be horrified?"

"I don't mean to seem rude but what are you doing here, Top?"

"Resting my feet."

"Is that your gentle way of telling me you can't crack Ross Trumble's nut?"

"No, it's my gentle way of telling you my feet are sore because I've been standing in doorways for forty-eight hours keeping a tail on him. Every place he goes he takes that fucking briefcase with him. I think he sleeps with it under his pillow. But I've got a girl down here today from Orozco's agency and maybe she'll be able to pry him loose of it."

"I need those figures, Top. I postponed the inspection tour of the base as long as I could but we've got to go through with it Friday morning and I've got to have those figures before that. You've got less than forty-eight hours."

"Yeah, I know." Spode stretched. "Listen, it's all right this time because I just spent an hour checking this room out, but you really ought to be more careful what you say to me. Breckenyear and Trumble have got FBI buddies and you want to look out for bugs."

Forrester was impatient with it but it was true enough. The ones who saw Communists under every rock were capable of doing almost anything in the name of national security and that included spying on a United States Senator.

He said, "I haven't time to fool with that woman now, but I need Ronnie in here. You'd better do it—be as gentle as you can."

"I'll just wave my tommyhawk." Spode squeezed through the door and disappeared.

Forrester finished reading the newspaper item. There was a quote attributed to Senator Woodrow Guest: "Our liberal brethren seem to be looking for a scapegoat. First it was the draft, then Dow Chemical, then white racists. Now it's the defense industry." It was easy to hear the tone of biting scorn in Guest's silver voice.

Ronnie came in miming exhaustion. "I thought that woman was going to shout my ears off."

Spode trailed in and ambled back to the couch. "On her way out she was still talking to herself—heading for the Mayor's puking office." He sat down and clasped his hands on top of his head, spread-eagling his elbows.

Ronnie had her notebook. "Senator Guest's office phoned. He's flying into Phoenix tonight and he asked if you'll be available for a conference Thursday morning—tomorrow—at ten. Congressman Trumble will be there. And Ramsey Douglass of Matthewson-Ward."

"Where?"

"Senator Guest's house. Scottsdale."

Spode said, "If Woody Guest's willing to fly all the way out here to meet you maybe it means he's ready to knuckle under and hold hearings."

"I think he is," Forrester said. "He's got quite a few enemies panting around for a crack at his throne and some of them are up for reelection this year. If he refused to hold public hearings it would be an unpopular move and some of the moderate conservatives in the Senate would feel forced to dissociate themselves from him—especially in an election year. No, he'll come out foursquare in favor of open hearings, but when they're held he'll do his best to cloud the issues. So we've still got to whip up public concern and work on the swing voters in the Senate. For openers, that Shattuck Industries contribution to Breckenyear's campaign will do— Shattuck doesn't even have a plant in Breckenyear's state. I want to make that contribution public. Can you document it?"

"That's what you pay me for."

"Fine. It'll cast a shadow over Breckenyear and maybe even his redneck supporters will be embarrassed by it. But if I'm going to put pressure on the Senate we're going to need more ammunition like that. I want to know every campaign contribution that came out of the defense industry's checkbook, because when my friends get up to make speeches supporting their good American buddies in the hardware industry I want to show facts and figures that will discredit their motives."

Ronnie sucked in her breath and the sound couldn't be mistaken for anything but disapproval. He looked at her. "You don't like it, do you?"

"It has a smell of blackmail—extortion. You're playing dirty pool."

"Do you think this is a game? The hardware lobby has too many of my honorable colleagues in its pocket—bought and paid for. I can't outbid the giants but I've got to equalize the pressure somehow. The Pentagon has a hundred billion dollars a year to sling around and how many Congressmen are going to bite a hand that feeds them that well? Don't you think I have a right to offset that pressure? We've got one hundred Senators and fourteen of them are officers in the military reserves; we've got more than five hundred Congressmen and almost a hundred and thirty of them are reservists. Including Webb Breckenyear and Ross Trumble and two dozen other key members of Congressional committees that handle foreign policy and appropriations and defense."

Spode said to Ronnie, "I hope you took that down, it's a nice campaign speech."

She said, "I still don't like it, Alan."

It was the first time she had done that in the office and he noticed Spode's quick glance of interest. A spot of color showed at Ronnie's cheek and she hurried on: "Have you thought about what will happen if it backfires? They'll resent being exposed."

"Let them. I want the public stirred up—I want the Senate flooded with mail. That's what pressure's for."

Spode said, "You'll likely get just as much mail against as for."

"Doesn't matter, Top. The pressure on Lyndon Johnson didn't come from the majority but it was enough to reverse his Vietnam policy and that happened only because the peace movement drove everything else off the front pages. I want to make Phaeton the number-one headline issue—the point where we draw the line on this hardware cancer. If we have to drag a few skeletons out of closets then let's drag them out."

Spode pulled the side of his mouth back with a click as if he were dislodging something from his back teeth. "You're a lot more politician than you look." It wasn't clear whether he meant it as compliment or rebuke.

"Just get me the Phaeton figures from Trumble's file, Top. Let me make the policy decisions."

"I always do, don't I?"

He took Ronnie to dinner at Cliff House and they sat at a corner-window table with Tucson on the plain below them, three hundred square miles of incandescent lights. Half a dozen tablehoppers made ritual pilgrimages to their table and Forrester gave them all a smile and a handshake and a few words, and when the last of them departed Ronnie said, "Do you have to put up with that all the time?"

"You have to tolerate them—it's no job for an introvert."

"You must get sick of it."

"I usually have Les Suffield around to remind me I need their votes."

She searched his face with an odd intensity. "How important is it to you?"

"Let me quote Grover Cleveland: 'What's the use of being elected unless you stand for something?' I'd turn it around: 'What's the use of standing for something unless you can get elected?' "

"You meant it the first way around. You're a poor liar."

A piece of a smile shaped his mouth. "You're a hard girl to lie to."

"Then why try? If you meant that cynical-sounding remark

you wouldn't have involved yourself in this Phaeton mess. It's
likely to destroy your political career."

"Evidently you don't believe my opponents when they
claim I'm trying to feather my political nest."

"Don't you stand to lose more votes than you could possibly gain? The whole state of Arizona lives on Pentagon
money. But then that column in *Time* did accuse you of turning your back on your own constituents to woo the votes of
the big liberal states and I haven't heard you deny that. Are
you really running for the Presidency, Alan?"

"If I can jump from Cleveland to John Kennedy, every
woman wants her man to become President but no woman
wants her man to become a politician in the process. Or in the
words of our good friend Woody Guest, that's a bridge I'll
double-cross when I get to it."

"What about speaking for yourself?"

"What'll you have for dessert, Ronnie?"

"In other words, let's change the subject."

She was cross with him. She buried herself in the menu—
he watched the way her dark hair swayed with silken weight
when she tipped her head down to read, and swung back
when she straightened. "You know what really annoys me?
You're trying so desperately hard to be a nasty ruthless son
of a bitch. It just doesn't fit you."

She was so earnest he had to laugh at her and his laugh was
the kind that demanded one in return, but afterward Ronnie
said, "I'm serious—you've got so much going for you, why
throw it over? You're everybody's picture of the American
political messiah—big, good-looking, sincere, involved with
people's problems. . . . Am I making you blush? It's true, you
know—you're genuine, under all that grade-B tough talk
you've been spouting. Don't you see you're only going to hurt
yourself if you try to make yourself over into an ordinary
conniving politician, using people, greasing squeaky axles,
making cheap deals? Why degrade yourself?"

"Aren't you asking me when I stopped beating my wife?"

"It wasn't a loaded question and you know it."

He had to organize it in his mind and when he spoke it was
slowly and in a low tone to make her see it was important. "I

suppose I've been all those things, Ronnie. Big, dumb, honest, painfully sincere. And immature and totally useless. Following the trends and beating the right dead horses and plodding dutifully along in the tracks of the groundbreakers. God knows I'm no hysterical revolutionary, but a little while ago I woke up to the fact that I've been elected to a position that calls for responsible leadership and all I've done is to be a follower."

"And when did this great revelation come to you?"

"Don't be sarcastic, it doesn't suit you."

"I'm sorry. I didn't mean it to come out that way. I just wondered if your wife's death had anything to do with the change in your thinking."

He thought about that. "I suppose it did. I'm not sure. It's true I made up my mind after Angie died—you always go through a stage of introspection and reappraisal when something changes your whole life in a moment that way. But I'm not sure you could trace it to cause and effect. To tell the truth I never knew how insanely trivial death could be until I lost Angie—all the stupefying casual life-must-go-on business, the petty everyday details of funeral arrangements and insurance and that whole mountain of impersonal rubbish, it's all so stupid and irrelevant but in a way it's exactly what you need at a time like that because it gives you things to do and worry about. I didn't just sit down and bawl and think everything out deliberately and decide to change the course of my life then and there. There was never any time for that kind of thing. But you must know all this—you lost your husband."

"That was a long time ago and you've changed the subject again. It's taken me all day to work up the nerve to talk to you this way and I want to finish before I run out of steam. I'm worried because I think possibly this Phaeton thing popped up at just the right time for you to clutch it to your breast. Something to occupy your attention—you're compulsive that way, you need an obsession, you're not the kind of man who can be at loose ends for long. It might just as well have been a woman—it happens to everybody, doesn't it? Don't you think it's possible you dived into this Phaeton fight without even stopping to see if there was water in the pool? And when you found out what a desperate chance you were taking you panicked and decided you had to use every dirty weapon you could lay your hands on because if you can't have Angie maybe you'll take the Presidency of the United States as a consolation prize?"

It was a long speech breathlessly delivered and when she had finished she lifted her shoulders and chin.

He said, "You're tough."

"I don't like what I see you doing. What you're changing yourself into."

"Your concern means a lot to me, you know."

She avoided his eyes.

He said, "You've got it wrong, Ronnie. I don't really lust after the dreary delegate-wooing and all the greasy lubrication of party machinery you have to go through to get into the White House. My ambition is to accomplish something, not to be something—you see the difference? For the first time in my life I've got a cause, a reason to step out front and act like a leader, and because I believe in this fight I believe it's my fight to lead. Let the rest of them get on the bandwagon for a change."

"Fine. Then get in there and steer the fight on the floor. But don't make it dirty."

"I can't stick to sentimental notions if it means forfeiting a victory on an issue this vital. We're dealing with an insane competition in ultimate weapons that can produce the ultimate end."

"In other words if you lose this fight the world will end—do you honestly believe that?"

"I believe it's possible."

Over coffee Ronnie turned businesslike. "There were a few calls while you were in conference with Professor Moskowitz. I'd better bring you up to date."

Her smoky voice had become brisk. "Les Suffield called to check in—nothing terribly important, the Secretary of Defense has called a news conference for Friday afternoon and the Secretary of State will be on *Meet the Press* Sunday, and Les thought you ought to know because undoubtedly they'll both discuss you. I tried Frank Shattuck again but of course he's out, to us, and—"

"Top tells me Shattuck's in cahoots with Webb Breckenyear. You may as well cross him off. No point wasting more time trying to set up appointments that he'll keep breaking."

"All right." She made a note. "Now, about yesterday, I had a rather long talk with one of the personnel officers out at the Shattuck plant. It was educational—let me give you the gist of it. I asked him what the reaction had been among the employees and he surprised me—he said it hadn't caused much stir. Most of them know Shattuck Industries intends to bid on the lion's share of the Phaeton component systems, and Shattuck's likely to end up winning a good many of the contracts, but they don't seem to care terribly whether it all comes through or not. A few of their contracts are due to run out soon, but according to Mr. Karakian about a thousand people leave the plant labor force voluntarily each year and that would just about coincide with the attrition from the completion of current contracts. They don't visualize having to lay off very many people even if they don't get any Phaeton contracts. There's no union representation at Shattuck, of course —right-to-work—and men are laid off on the basis of job elimination, employment record, and seniority, in that order. Karakian said the men are quite aware that as long as they do good work they haven't got much to worry about—the company always lets the goldbricks go first. He was frank about it, said not many people go to work in aerospace-defense who can't live with this kind of insecurity. They've been through cutbacks before and they expect them again. When I asked him about his own job he just laughed and said he'd just bought a new Dodge and made the first payment and he wouldn't have done that if he was worried."

Forrester's eyes were wide. "So much for the specter of wholesale catastrophic unemployment if I kill the Phaeton program."

"I thought you'd like it. Now let's see—I briefed you on the conference tomorrow in Scottsdale—Senator Guest, Congressman Trumble, Ramsey Douglass. I've never been quite clear on exactly what Douglass does, but Trumble wants him there so I have to assume he's important enough to be included. He works for Matthewson-Ward but I don't really understand where he fits in."

"He's their SATAF coordinator—Site Aerospace Test Activation Facility. When Matthewson-Ward delivers a missile to the Air Force Douglass has to see that it's set up properly and tested out before he turns it over to the Government. It's a job that requires a good deal of political maneuvering— Douglass got it because he's both a first-class engineer and an active Republican. He moonlighted as Trumble's chief speech writer in the last campaign and I suppose he'll do it again this year. He's worked his way up in the party on the local level and I understand he pretty much tells the County Supervisor what to do. But he stays pretty much behind the scenes because he hasn't exactly got the kind of personality it takes to get up in front of crowds and charm people."

"I'll say. He's such a bitter little man. I can't stand him."

"Nobody can. But he's got a brain like a scalpel."

"Let's talk about someone else." She reached for her coffee with a theatrical shudder.

"That must have got cold by now." He turned to signal the waiter.

"Never mind," she said, "it would only keep me awake. I really shouldn't drink coffee after five." When she looked at her watch he followed her glance and found himself attentively studying the fine pale hairs on her slim forearm.

"Almost ten," she said. "My goodness. I'd better take the body home and put it to bed."

He parked at the curb outside the palm-fringed apartment court where she lived. It was the third time he'd driven her home but she hadn't invited him in and he had not pressed her to. Still he felt challenged by her odd admixture of warm personal concern and guarded, almost hostile reserve.

He walked around the car and helped her step out over the high sill of the old Mercedes; he walked her along the flower-bordered walk to the far corner of the court and when she found her key she hesitated and then with an impulsive gesture thrust it toward him.

He unlocked the door and stood back. "Well, then," he began, with the awkward feeling that neither of them knew how to break off the evening.

She reached inside to switch on a light. "Would you . . . like a nightcap?" Her eyes were very wide.

"Only if—"

"I do. Come in before I change my mind." A quick smile fled across her face and she went ahead of him with her lovely high-hipped stride; when she turned, waiting for him, her lips parted and she followed him with her eyes when he extracted the key and shut the door and tossed the key on the small telephone table.

The apartment was small and untidy, sparsely furnished and cluttered with easel and paint stand and stacks of stretched canvases. The walls were crowded with oils which he knew immediately to be her own work—bold colorful landscapes, bright with the primary hues of the desert, filled with a fascination for the high craggy tors and multitiered serrates of the rugged uplands. The paintings filled the room with a fury of color.

She was nervous. "You like them, don't you? I feel ridiculously pleased. Do you know that's why I was afraid to let you come in? I had to steel myself—I was desperately afraid you'd laugh at them." She tossed her head as if released; her hair tumbled loosely over one shoulder.

He turned a slow circle on his heels and then walked around to view them separately. "I love them."

A cloth concealed the work on the easel and he reached for the corner of it but she spoke instantly: "Don't. Not yet—please?"

He let it fall back, the painting undisclosed, and turned. She bustled toward the tiny kitchenette. "Sit down anywhere. It's Chivas Regal with a splash of water, isn't it?"

There was a silver-framed snapshot on the coffee table and he was studying it when she brought his drink. The man in the picture was young, a Midwestern sort, dark blond hair, neat ears, a rugged blocky sort of face without much nose but a good big jaw. A face full of easygoing openness and healthy self-confidence. He put it back where he had found it and said, "Your husband."

"Yes."

"You've never told me about him."

She was silent long enough for him to think she wasn't going to answer. She sat opposite him, drawing her legs up under her. Finally she said, "I suppose he wasn't exceptional. I mean, you wouldn't have singled him out in a crowd. But we loved each other and when he died . . ."

When she trailed off he reached for her wrist. "What is it?"

"I really don't like to talk about it."

"Maybe it needs talking about."

"Now you're trying to get revenge for the way I pinned you to the wall at dinner tonight."

"Fair enough," he said. "What was he like?"

She brooded toward the photograph. "He was alive. Vital —enthusiastic. He came from Topeka—his father worked for the railroad. Phil was an engineer and his whole face would light up when he thought about building things. He was really a very straightforward guy—no hidden corners. He was working on his Ph.D. at the university here when he died. I had a secretarial job with a phone-company executive and Phil had a fellowship, and we were living in a horrible little house trailer in one of those miserable camps on Miracle Mile. Sometimes Phil used to go across the street to bowl a few lines on afternoons when he didn't have classes. One day he didn't come home and we went to tell him it was dinnertime—a girl friend and I—and we found . . ."

After a while Forrester said, "You may as well finish it, Ronnie."

Her eyes were barely open. "In the weeds behind the bowling alley. He'd been clubbed and his wallet and class ring were gone. The police never found the muggers who'd done it."

"Was he dead when you found him?"

She gave a start. "I—I don't know."

"You don't know?"

She withdrew her hand and twisted her face away from him. "I don't remember it very well."

"That's natural. Sometimes—"

"No. It wasn't just a minor thing. I feel ashamed of it—you see the truth is I had a pretty severe blackout and it lasted quite a while. I spent several months in a sanatorium, Alan. I came out of it, of course. All kinds of therapy. Insulin, hypnosis—the doctors put the pieces back together, more or less, but there are things that still haven't come back to me. I'm sure it's just as well. I don't know, I've never been able to work it out in words. It seemed to burn something out of me and I've never wanted to work up the strength . . . Perhaps there just isn't enough of me left over to offer anyone again. Phil and I gave each other everything we had."

She seemed willing to let the conversation die but Forrester revived it deliberately: "That was eleven years ago."

"I know what you're trying to make me admit. It's true enough but it's not as easy as it seems. Maybe there's something wrong with me—a wire down, inside."

"That's ridiculous. Possibly you let yourself brood your way into an obsession but it's time you came out of it."

"Now who's being tough?"

"An eye for an eye," he said in a mausoleum tone, and it made her laugh and suddenly she was on her feet moving gaily toward the easel. She lifted the covering cloth and threw it back and stood aside proudly. "Do you like it, Alan? Please like it."

The painting was incomplete around the edges but the subject was unmistakable—the great pink mesa that towered at the corner of the ranch. She had caught it in late-afternoon sunlight, all magenta shadows and cruel incisions. Her bold brushstrokes had dispensed with trivial distractions and left only the great looming rock against a cobalt sky and he heard her say with an embarrassed little laugh, "That's how I really see you, you know. But don't take that in a trite Freudian way. I want to finish it by the weekend."

"Why?"

She moved around the room, suddenly shy. "Because you're probably going back to Washington soon and I want you to take it with you."

She was trying very hard to keep it casual but the strain in her face proved the deceit of it. He turned his back to her, ostensibly to look at the painting again but actually to hide his face from her because his throat was thickening and his eyes felt tight and he didn't want her to watch him do combat with the sudden confusions inside himself. This was what he had not only wanted but subconsciously planned, but now he felt a sense of panic because he wasn't ready for it just yet. His inner defenses were up; his mind, with stubborn refusal, simply didn't want to face it and he found himself thinking wildly about everything except the question at hand.

He had meant to break down Ronnie's hostile barriers and he had succeeded but suddenly he was afraid and wanted to withdraw: did that mean the same thing might happen if after a carefully plotted campaign he won the White House? Would he discover he really didn't want it and was terrified by it? Was there something inside him that made him fear success, like an athlete who suddenly and inexplicably ran out of steam when victory was in sight? He remembered Les Suffield railing at him just before the end of the last campaign when during a television speech he'd blurted something ad lib that had shocked the audience—*For Christ's sake are you trying deliberately to blow it, Alan? You had them in the palm of your hand but now* . . . And in the end the election had been much too close; he had barely squeaked through with a five-thousand-vote plurality. He couldn't even remember what it was that he had said. But there had been other times: in high school he had fudged his senior exams and blown the valedictorian's chair; in the summer of his twenty-third year he had all but failed the bar exam; in court prosecuting a murder case he had forgotten to ask a key witness a key question and had watched the defendant walk out of court free; in Congress he had steered the writers' tax bill all the way to the floor but neglected to sew up three votes that would have made the difference between passage and failure. . . .

The sudden insight stunned him and he stood filled with frightened wonder, face and hands stilled, hearing Ronnie move forward behind him—the whisper of nylon thighs, the catch in her breath when she spoke: "Alan? What's wrong? What is it?"

He felt her weight behind him and he turned quickly and drew her close to him so that she wouldn't see his face; he tipped his head to get the noses out of the way and kissed her with crushing violence but she kept her lips tightly compressed and hard.

She pulled herself away from him and touched her mouth. "What's the matter?"

"I don't know. I don't know, Ronnie."

She stared. "What are we getting ourselves into?"

"Are you frightened?"

"I feel rocked—and I don't want to."

"Ronnie, I—"

"I've never been any good at the casual oh-hell-after-all-we're-both-adults game, Alan."

"Neither have I. It's nothing to do with that."

"Then what is it?" She was pleading to know.

He was shaking his head as if to clear it and her face came into sharp focus before him. Suddenly he realized what had been wrong before: he had been looking at her only in relation to himself, seeing her only as a part of his own difficulties and the possible instrument of a cure for them, but not as herself, a complete and separate being with difficulties and a unique identity of her own. In his mind she had been an antidote to the memory of Angie: he had kept thinking of her as a means of deliverance—a departure rather than an arrival.

"It isn't like that now," he said.

It startled her. "It isn't like what?"

He smiled. "I'm not making sense, am I? I've been standing here making discoveries. It's hard to explain."

He stood quite still and put his hands on her arms; after a while her mouth lost its nervous smile and began to soften and when she lifted her glance to his face her whole body suddenly was in her eyes. She brought her hands up under his elbows and slipped her arms around him as if they had been designed to fit exactly there and she said, "I think I'm falling in love with you. You were right, I am frightened."

"Of me?"

"No. Of myself. I didn't want this to happen."

"Why?"

"Because I didn't want anything intense—I can't play games of ships that go bump in the night, but I can't do it the other way either." She shook her head with abrupt impatience. "Now I'm the one who's not making sense—but there are things I just can't put into words."

"It's all right." He was smiling gently and he slid his hand slowly and lightly up her arm and felt her shudder; her lids became drowsily heavy, a humid lowering that seemed to express both desire and regret, and when she spoke his name her voice underwent a subtle thickening modulation. He embraced her, gathering her hair in his hand at the back of her neck, feeling her tremors and the warmth of her legs and breasts. They kissed slowly and this time her mouth opened against his, luxurious, and he tasted the flick of her tongue.

"Maybe I had better go."

"No." Her answer was very grave. "Please stay? Please?"

They made love on the bed with long languor. She was warm and lovely and he had a vivid sense of _déjà vu_, as if it were a union of long custom between them, as if they had already known the intimate secrets of each other's bodies. There was no awkwardness and no urgency but only the gentle pleasures of caress and coupling that led without haste to the high rigid pain of ecstatic climax. But afterward when they lay close together, so close her two eyes blended into one, she seemed afraid again and when he tasted her lips he felt the startling salt dampness of her tears.

☆☆☆☆☆☆☆☆☆☆☆☆☆☆☆☆☆☆☆☆☆☆☆☆☆☆☆☆☆☆☆☆☆☆

Chapter Seven

Leon Belsky had picked the motel for escape routes rather than comfort. He had taken a room in the rear with several exits close at hand—the rear windows of bathroom and bed-room gave access to a tree-tangled trailer court that was flanked by auto junk yards into which a man could easily fade.

He had rented the beige Ford under the name of Meldon Kemp and checked into the motel under the same name. Then he had left it to make his contacts.

The room was spacious and cold with cheap blond furni-ture. Belsky absorbed it with a single glance when he returned to it at midnight. He opened the suitcase on the luggage stand to appraise the telltales he had left—documents lying in slight disarray with the corner of the top sheet touching the middle letter of the word "finance" on the sheet below. The letterhead was that of an industrial-relations concern in San Francisco. The two-page letter was addressed to Meldon Kemp in Los Angeles and was full of names and figures. It looked like the kind of commercial code of instructions and information marketed in the intercompany espionage game. Actually the message was spurious, but they would always go for documents immediately and if they had time they would take photos, which meant disturbing the arrangement of the papers.

No one had been at them; the room had not been searched. Outside he could hear the big trucks roar by on the freeway and the lament of a distant siren. He dialed nine for an outside line and then a seven-digit number; it was answered on the first ring and Belsky said, "Hello, this is Dangerfield."

"Sorry, I think you must have the wrong number." It was Douglass' voice, feigning impatience. Belsky said, "I'm at the New Executive, Room Twelve. Call me back within ten minutes."

"That's okay."

Belsky took the multiband transistor radio out of his suitcase and opened the back of it to expose the high-speed cassette recorder and the telegrapher's key. He took out a notepad and coded a brief message in dots and dashes. Before he was finished the phone rang.

"Dangerfield?" It was Douglass again.

"Yes. We're on an open line."

"I know."

"How are we set?"

"Two of them can't make it tomorrow. One's in Washington and one's in Phoenix and they'll both be tied up. The rest can make it."

"When do you go on duty?"

"Eight."

"Anyone in your group go to work earlier than that?"

"No."

"We'd better meet at five in the morning, then."

"That early?" Douglass didn't bother to keep the irritation out of his voice.

"You people have gone soft, haven't you?" Belsky said.

"What did you expect?"

"It's the only time I can give you. Get them there." Belsky hung up and resumed coding the report in his notepad. He knew how Douglass would handle it; it was standard operating procedure: dial each number, let it ring once, hang up. For the recipients the single ring was a signal to look at their watches. Five minutes later Douglass would dial the same series of numbers again, and again let each ring once. It was a simple code: the five-minute interval between rings indicated a five-o'clock meeting; the place was pre-arranged.

When he finished coding the report to Moscow he connected the telegrapher's key to the cassette recorder's input terminals and tapped out the cipher onto a slow tape. He hooked the radio's transmission antenna into the room's television-aerial socket and connected the output terminals of the tape deck to the microphone jack of the transmitter, checked the transmission frequency setting and turned his wrist to look at his watch. Twenty-two minutes past the hour he pressed the send key and switched on the cassette recorder. It had been rigged to a high playback speed, so that the signal went out in an instantaneous pulse, a burst far above audible range.

He repeated the impulse twice within thirty seconds and then began to dismantle the equipment. A Red submarine lying off the coast of Baja California would have picked up the signal and relayed it to a trawler in the North Pacific, from which the signal would again be amplified and rebroadcast to a KGB receiving station in Kamchatka. None of the relay stations possessed copies of the master code and therefore the content of the message would be known to no one but sender and final recipient.

Belsky ripped the top four sheets off his notepad to make sure there were no indentations on the pages below. He burned the loose sheets over the toilet and flushed the ashes down.

After he bathed he lay on the bed, reviewed the day's events and made his evaluations. He had to activate the teams as quickly as possible and that left no time for the retraining they required; he would have to reassert discipline immediately and the best tools for that purpose were fear and humiliation.

When he was satisfied with his plan, he allowed himself to catnap.

At three o'clock he dressed and drove into the city and found a curbside telephone booth under the overhanging illuminated sign of a savings-and-loan office; he chose the spot because neon lights would jam most electronic bugs.

When Hathaway answered Belsky said, "I'm at 989-2612. Get to a pay phone and call me." He hung up and stood beside the booth waiting for the telephone to ring and watched insects swarm under the intersection's hard blue mercury lights. He was moved to remark the contrast between this desert springtime and the dark Asian winter which still gripped the steppes at home.

A passenger in a passing car threw out an empty paper cup and the wind scudded it to the curb and the telephone rang.

"Mr. Dangerfield? Hathaway."

Belsky said, "They'll start arriving at five o'clock. Have you got everything ready?"

"Yes, sir. We've spent three hours going over the place and it's clean."

"All right," Belsky said. "Keep your people alert. I'll get there before five but if any of them arrive ahead of me hold them in the front room until I come in. I'll want a complete search of every arrival, down to the skin. Explain that to your team."

"Yes, sir. Looking for anything in particular?"

"Weapons and bugs."

Belsky rang off and drove down the avenue to an all-night diner with a bright neon American flag above its massive Fat Boy sign. The place had been invaded by a crowd of motorcyclists and the plastic tabletops were thick with crash helmets. But the late hour seemed to have subdued even these predators, and Belsky was undisturbed at his counter place except for a plump girl who took the stool beside him and ate four doughnuts with single-minded concentration. The motor-cycle toughs trooped out after a few minutes and he heard the arrogant thundering of their bikes. Belsky felt that a society so decadent as to permit the continued existence of anarchic bands of killer-terrorists was doomed to self-destruction. He was not given to political introspection but certain things were self-evident and one of them was the abiding need for discipline within groups of any size. That was true of the Illegals especially.

He checked the hour again but there was ample time; he allowed himself an extra cup of coffee, pouring cream from a glass syrup pitcher with a steel spring-loaded thumb lid— a peculiarly American device that fascinated him.

Down the block from the house one of Hathaway's people was sitting in a parked car. Belsky parked some distance away and let the man have a good look at him under the street light when he got out of his car and walked by. The man nodded almost imperceptibly.

The bungalow was obscured from neighbors' view by tall oleander hedges. Belsky went up the cracked flagstone walk and Hathaway emerged from the shadows on the porch and spoke a low greeting. Hathaway was forty, crew-cut and dark, paunch beginning to swell. He wore a T-shirt that showed off his thick arms and husky muscled shoulders; wire-hard hairs on his chest and back burst through its fabric. He held the door for Belsky.

Douglass had picked the place years ago as his cell's meet-ing place because the woman who owned it lived alone and her habits of odd hours and odd company made it unlikely that gatherings here would attract attention. The living room was crowded with flowers and ferns planted in old phar-maceutical jars. The repulsive plants writhed everywhere and for a moment Belsky felt as if he couldn't breathe.

Hathaway's Air Force Tech Sergeant tunic was hanging on the back of a chair. A uniformed Airman Second Class named Torrio was fooling with the controls of a portable metal detector. Torrio was a short man with a thin pocked face and a stiff curry brush of brown hair that added two inches to his height. He nodded with reserve. Belsky had assembled them six hours ago with no advance warning and told them precisely what they were to do and no more; now Torrio and Hathaway stood awkwardly, trying to look like typical Government-Issue bureaucrats, but with fear and curiosity on their faces.

Belsky said, "You want to ask questions, don't you? Forget them. Torrio, go back and get the woman."

After Torrio left the room Belsky said to Hathaway, "How is it arranged?"

"I've got a man outside in a car. He'll screen them as they arrive. They'll come into this room and I'll hold them here. I'll send them one at a time into the bedroom, back that way, and Torrio will go over them for metal. Then they'll go out the back door from the bedroom and you'll talk to them out there. It's a screened-in porch—patio, if you want to call it that."

"I don't like that. Voices carry outdoors."

"There's a high hedge around the back of the place and both neighbors have got cinder-block walls around their backyards. There's nothing behind this house but an empty lot."

Belsky still didn't like it but this little living room wasn't big enough and it was too late to change the location now; he wished he'd had time to inspect the place beforehand. Douglass was a fool for recommending it.

Belsky said, "We'll be done with the first group in forty-five minutes, no more. You and Torrio will make sure they get on their way. You and your men will leave before six o'clock and you'll take the woman with you."

"Isn't there another meeting at six-fifteen?"

Belsky, removing a thick envelope from his inside breast pocket, only glanced at him. Hathaway said, "I get it. You're changing the security shift for each bunch so none of us will be able to identify anybody outside of the people we already know from our own cells."

"Just do your job. I'll tell you everything you need to

know." But Belsky was impressed; the man was brighter than he looked and might prove useful.

It was a requisite never to break security by allowing subordinates to communicate directly with their superior: any one of them might be tailed to the superior. But Rykov's message had made it necessary to break many such rules. By midnight he would have met with almost one hundred Illegals, representing sixteen cells, and tomorrow there would be more meetings. He was exposing himself to great personal risk, but only because nobody was going to be able to trace back beyond Belsky himself: he would not lead anyone to his own superior and if he should be trapped there was always the death pill inside the hollowed tooth. Belsky was quite prepared to make use of it if cornered. Nevertheless on those infrequent occasions when his nerves acted up he found his tongue experimenting tentatively with the loose tooth; years ago he had reached the sensible compromise of removing the pill from his mouth whenever he went to sleep. He always kept it near at hand but there remained the chance he might be caught asleep and prevented from reaching it; but that risk was preferable to the risk of swallowing it by accident.

Torrio came in with the woman. She wet her lips with the sharp pink tip of her tongue and said, "So you're the prince who's come to wake Sleeping Beauty."

He made no immediate answer. His silence was calculated to unsettle her. He wanted to use this opportunity to appraise her as he appraised them all, to judge their excellences and weaknesses and to determine the extent to which they had been affected by the cultural shock that penetrated all Communist agents exposed to Western societies.

"You're a pretty drab-looking prince," she said, trying to needle him into response. He didn't rise to it and she began to show she was unnerved.

Her name was Nikola Lavrentyeva; in America she was Nicole Lawrence. A little crepe dress clung to the curved surfaces of her small spider-waisted body. When she moved, her breasts stirred with braless insouciance. Her toes, in open sandals, were a bit dirty. Cynical dark onyx eyes in a pinched simian face; a vague sullen smile, nervous, discontented, suggestive of stormy passions. The ugly wizened face was at odds with the lean thrusting body and he got the feeling her looks had faded faster than her appetites. Her hair was pulled back from her scalp so tightly that it looked as if it must ache: a sign of things repressed, emotions held precariously in check. She looked susceptible to the kind of incendiary emotions that could make a shambles of surface loyalties and rationalizations. Dangerous, then; to be watched.

He said, "Leave us," and waited until Hathaway and Torrio had gone away into the back of the house. Then, finally, he spoke to the woman. "Nikola Lavrentyeva, daughter of Nikolai Lavrentyev and Ella Galharova Lavrentyeva."

Her dour smile showed tiny teeth. Her eyes were overhung by thick droopy lashes—cunning eyes. "What if I don't play the game with you, Comrade?"

"Do you want me to answer that question?"

Her face changed; she saw he had no patience with coquetry. She said in a harder voice, "My grandparents—Anastas Lavrentyev, Valentia Lavrentyeva, Josef Galharov, Nikola Blokhova Galharova." She tilted her face away from him. "I'm surprised I still remember them."

"Your parents are quite well. Your sister Marya is a successful physician, you know."

"Little Marya. That's hard to picture, Comrade—ah?"

"You'll know me as Dangerfield."

"That's not quite fair. You know my name."

He said, "Come with me," and went toward the hallway. "Is that the bedroom?"

"Yes."

Torrio and Hathaway were inside the cluttered room and Belsky sent Hathaway back to the front of the house. "They'll start arriving soon." When Hathaway had left he said to Torrio, "This one first."

Torrio showed his surprise. "Her too?"

"Get on with it." Belsky backed up against the door to push it shut and stood with his shoulderblades against it.

Torrio said, "I got to search you. Better take off your watch and rings. You got any metal teeth?"

"No." She turned toward Belsky; her mouth was sucked in with a tight look of disapproval. "It so happens this is my house."

"You're rather defensive, aren't you?" he said mildly.

Her eyelids dropped, covering her thoughts. "All right, Torrio, get it done."

Torrio ran the nozzle of the metal detector over her as if it were a vacuum cleaner. Belsky said, "Finish it, Torrio," and Torrio's face became suffused with color when he put down the metal detector and spread his hands in a gesture of apology to the woman. "You'll have to strip."

She hated it but she pretended indifference. She lifted the dress off over her head and dropped it carelessly on the bed and stood quivering in translucent panties. Torrio made his face blank. "Them, too."

She stripped them off without remark. Torrio glanced toward Belsky and found no reprieve there; he went forward breathing shallowly and examined her armpits and the soles of her feet and went into all the orifices of her body with a doctor's rubber finger-glove. When Torrio was done and had turned to the bed to inspect her clothes, the woman stood up straight and faced Belsky. She had the body of a ripe young girl—rigid high breasts like pink rubber, soft curve of waist and thighs. She faced him with her breasts thrust forward, arms akimbo, feet apart, challenging him to remain unperturbed, and she scored her point; Belsky did not take his eyes off her when she put her clothes on and smoothed down her dress.

Torrio's face was covered with a light oily sheen. Belsky said, "Do that with all of them."

"You really think you need to—"

"Be quiet," Belsky said. "Do as you're told." He went through the back door and found himself on a concrete patio surrounded by screens. Evidently it had once been an open carport. It ran the width of the house, about twenty-five feet by fifteen. The furniture was bamboo and rattan with print-fabric cushions. Reptilian potted plants hung from the roof on wrought-iron chains. He said, "There's another room I haven't seen."

Nicole's reply was hostile. "You haven't seen the kitchen or the bathroom or my office. Which one did you have in mind? Or were you thinking of another bed?"

Of course she had an office. Probably she did most of her work at home. She was a political reporter for one of the television stations, he recalled. "Don't spar with me, I haven't got time."

"What's the matter? You're not a fag, are you?"

"You haven't got meat on you like a good Russian woman."

"If you like cows." She showed her teeth. "I think you're kinky. You get your kicks out of pushing people around. I know a couple of cops like you."

He put his lazy stare on her and after a moment it made her step back; she waved a hand around in front of her and said in a different tone, "Look, I keep forgetting you're not local product. The average red-blooded American loudmouth is a whining coward inside. You're not like that but it takes some getting used to—don't forget I've been out of touch for twenty years."

"I haven't forgotten it," he said.

Five of them arrived shortly before five o'clock. They emerged from the bedroom one by one, adjusting their clothes; they were all on edge. Ramsey Douglass was last to arrive. Belsky was displeased. At sight of Douglass, Nicole stirred and lifted her hand quickly to her hair as if to reassure herself nothing had given way. A curious and revealing reaction: Belsky watched them now as a pair.

Ramsey Douglass was handsome in a weak Byronic way; he wore his hair in sleek fingerwaves and a comma of it fell across his forehead. He had the look of one who was recovering from a fashionable illness. (Belsky's mind made the automatic memorized connections: Ramsey Douglass = Dmitri Smolny, born Leningrad 1931, trained at Dubna, commissioned ensign in Red Air Force 1952, degrees in aeronautical engineering and physics, linguistic aptitude high, political rating adequate; married 1952, widowed 1953, son Fyodor Dmitrovich now 22 and employed by Intourist in Moscow.)

There was very little time to study the others because he had a great deal to tell them and they would have to be on their way within forty-five minutes to make room for the next batch. He made a kind of shorthand inventory compounded of what he knew from their dossiers and what he got from quick scrutiny:

Nick Conrad, Major USAF, electronics warfare AOS (Nikolai Konrad, forty-two, recruited into KGB from Red Army in 1952 and trained in languages and electronics).

Adele Conrad, Grade 9 civil servant, senior clerk-typist Eareckson Wing personnel department, DMAFB (Alla Konrada, forty-one, recruited into KGB while a modern-language student at Moscow University, met and married Nikolai Konrad at Amergrad, 1953). Three children, all of whom had been born in America—ages 19, 18, 15.

Fred Winslow, Lieutenant Colonel USAF, Deputy ICBM Wing Commander, Eareckson Wing, DMAFB (Vladimir Vozshin, forty-four, recruited into KGB from Aeroflot pilot-training program and trained in military administration and languages).

Celia Winslow, housewife, active in community affairs— League of Women Voters, Pima County Democratic Party organization, Parent-Teacher Association (Kassia Vozshina, forty-three, recruited into KGB with her husband and trained in languages). The Winslows had a twenty-two-year-old son born in Russia and a fourteen-year-old daughter born in West Germany where Winslow had served a two-year tour of duty as a major with a ground-to-air missile squadron.

Two others were not present. Ilya Zinenev, in Washington, D.C., had been recruited out of Leningrad University and seeded into Tucson as a university mathematics instructor but as requirements had changed he had been shifted into the political sphere. Boris Dolinski, today in Scottsdale, had been assistant to a Ukrainian commissar when recruited, and had been trained in American political science by KGB at Amergrad. The absence of these two didn't matter since the mission would be military rather than political.

The Rykov plan had allowed for the fact that the American armed forces tended to rotate their personnel from base to base. About one-fifth of the Amergrad agents were posted away from Tucson at any given time: Winslow, for example, had served tours of duty in West Germany, Alaska, South Vietnam, New Jersey and California. But Winslow's predecessor as Deputy Wing Commander had been another Amergrad agent and his successor would be yet another. This was ensured by the placement of Amergrad personnel administrators in key Pentagon and NORAD offices so that control was maintained over transfers and reassignments. The preponderance of Amergrad agents remained in Tucson at all times but the scheme allowed for sufficient rotation to avert suspicion. By the same token local officials like Adele Conrad had been seeded into positions from which they could direct the placement of lower-echelon agents like Hathaway to units where they could exercise maximum leverage from within.

The scheme had been worked out to maintain cell-to-cell security. The system was analogous to a cargo ship's watertight bulkheads, which were designed to seal off any compartment that leaked, to preserve the seaworthy integrity of the vessel as a whole. Of the nearly three hundred Amergrad agents, there wasn't one who could identify more than eleven of his comrades. Most of them could identify only four or five. In the entire Western Hemisphere there was only one man alive who could name all 287 Amergrad agents: that man was Leon Belsky, and each time he thought of it his tongue twitched against the hollowed molar near the back of his lower jaw.

He sat them down and told them what they were to do. He delivered his address in a pitchless voice, without animation, as if it were a ritual incantation. While he spoke he watched them. They were filled with nervous anxiety, that much was evident—all except Ramsey Douglass who appeared bemused.

"The objective is the missiles themselves rather than the command hierarchy. You have to work out the details in terms of a one-shot coup, not a continuing operation. Moscow wants these ICBMs fired at targets of Moscow's choice. That's all you have to do, shoot the missiles—not take over the air base or the state of Arizona. In a way this makes it easier but remember you won't know the precise day or hour until the last minute and when it comes you've got to be prepared to move instantly and simultaneously. It'll require faultless timing.

"I'm meeting with you before the others because your cell is the key to the whole job. Winslow will execute the command to fire the missiles. Conrad has to see to it that our own code envelopes are substituted for the NORAD ones at the proper time. Douglass will draw up the details of target reprogramming. Douglass and Conrad together will have to blueprint the severing of the fail-safe communications links within the missile groups themselves so that when the group commanders double-check for confirmation they'll receive the replies we'll be substituting for NORAD signals."

Ramsey Douglass showed a double row of white teeth. He spoke in a drawl. "You'd have to interdict the security system and the communications hookup at every level from Colorado Springs and Washington on down. How am I supposed to handle that?"

"You're not. Everybody has his own job to do—just worry about yours. When the time comes we'll have control of every communications relay and all signals to and from the silo complexes will go through us. No messages will be allowed in or out except those we initiate. The group commanders won't know they're receiving fake messages and the higher commands outside the base won't know anything unusual is going on here until it's too late for them to do anything about it. Of course they'll see the missiles on radar after they've been launched but they'll have no way to stop them."

A throbbing vein stood out in Nick Conrad's forehead. Fred Winslow was twisting his knuckles. Adele Conrad's eyes were

moist and blinking fast like semaphores; Celia Winslow's stare
was fixed against the knot of Belsky's necktie and she kept
rubbing her thumb across the pads of her fingers. Nicole
Lawrence stared astringently at Ramsey Douglass as if it were
up to Douglass to remedy the situation. The five of them
made a studied mute tableau; only Douglass seemed capable
of rational speech.

Douglass of course was the cell leader and he had had more
advance warning of the meeting than the others, but he hadn't
been told the purpose of it. Either he was a man who adapted
quickly or he was bright enough to have guessed it had to be
something like this. In either case it made him valuable. But
Belsky didn't like this screened porch as a meeting place and
it was Douglass who had suggested it. The man was erratic;
there were signs he was too easily prepared to choose the
paths of least resistance without asking enough preliminary
questions.

Still, it was Douglass who asked the obvious question: "Just
who are we supposed to shoot at? I assume that information's
on a need-to-know basis but you've got to realize we have to
know the general nature of the targets if not the specific
locations. Before you tell me it's none of our business you'd
better know this. These missiles have been fueled and installed with the expectation that if they're ever used, the targets will be Russian or Chinese. Now if Moscow wants us to
shoot them at Washington or Western Europe or Tel Aviv,
you're going to have to tell us pretty far in advance. It's not
just a question of reprogramming the target coordinates—it's
a question of adding or draining fuel and programming new
data cards for the computers and all sorts of preparations that
you simply can't do at the last minute. These birds weren't
installed with the idea in mind that they'd ever have to be used
against targets in Colorado Springs or the District of Co-
lumbia. Do you understand what I'm saying?"

"Perfectly. Take my word for it that we've taken that problem into account in our planning. You'll be given the target
information in time to make all necessary adjustments and
preparations. For the moment we're withholding it because
we're entering a critical stage of activation and that means the

risk of some of you being blown is greater than it's been at any time since you were seeded in. If you're blown and cornered you'll be questioned, and you can't reveal what you don't know."

Douglass said, "That's okay, as long as you know the full extent of the technical side of it. If that's going to be my responsibility I've got to be given time enough to do the job. On a thing like this you can't just get nine women pregnant and expect a baby in one month."

The kitchen door squeaked open and Belsky's head whipped around. Hathaway stopped in the doorway and said, "I'm sorry to bust in. It's important." He lifted his chin in beckoning signal and stepped back into the house.

Belsky strode inside and pulled the door shut. "What is it?"

Without speaking Hathaway turned on his heel and led him past the closed bedroom door to the room beyond the kitchen, Nicole's office.

Hathaway pushed the door open and stood to one side and when Belsky stepped into the doorway he saw Torrio in the room holding a stranger at gunpoint. The stranger's face was rigid with alarm.

Hathaway said, "Torrio found this guy out back of the house with a shotgun mike and a tape recorder. Bugging your meeting."

The stranger winced when the door slammed. He had his hands behind his head and his shoulderblades against the wall. Torrio was sitting on a corner of the desk, on one hip, training a .25 Browning automatic pistol on him from eight feet away. The surveillance equipment lay on the desk blotter —a small battery tape recorder and a high-resolution microphone with a nine-inch cone and disk sound reflector, one of those ultrasensitive long-range microphones adapted from missile-tracking antennae. It had a shoulder stock like a light carbine and there were stethoscopic earphones. The device was familiar enough to Belsky. With it you could hear ordinary conversation four blocks away.

Belsky said, "Do you know him?"

"I've seen him around," Hathaway said.

Torrio reached under his elbow with his left hand. Belsky
saw a wallet in it. He took three steps forward and emptied
the wallet on the desk.

Driver's license, Social Security card, private-investigator's
license, Police Auxiliary membership card, miscellany. August R. Craig (the Police Auxiliary card listed him as "Gus
Craig"), 357 South Kavanagh Ave., Tucson, Arizona 85716.
Driver's license: ht 5′ 10″, wt 150 lbs, date of birth Aug 1
1933, place of birth Peoria, eyes brown, hair brown, identifying marks left earlobe missing, ½-in. scar on lower lip.

Belsky could hear the man's breath rasp in and out. Hathaway swung toward him. "Who're you working for, Craig?"

Craig's only reply was a nervous hostile grin.

Hathaway made a fist and moved forward on the balls of his
feet. Belsky said, "No. Come out here with me." He went into
the hall and nodded through the doorway to Torrio, who
stayed put and kept his gun leveled. Hathaway emerged from
the room and pulled the door to. Belsky said, "I have to finish
with these people. I'll attend to him later."

"You want me to soften him?"

"No. Let him sweat a while—leave him alone until I'm
ready for him. It'll shake him up."

"He ain't the only one that's shaken up."

"I want you to comb the place to make sure he hasn't got
a partner," Belsky said, and returned to the patio.

He pulled the chair forward and sat down. The interruption
had given them time to absorb the impact of what he had told
them. They were in the first stages of digestion now. Winslow
and his wife had slid their rattan chairs close together and,
remarkably, they were holding hands. Adele Conrad watched
Belsky with a curiously impassive face and he couldn't tell if
she had really accepted it all and made peace with herself or
was simply in a mild stage of shock. Major Conrad was nodding his head rhythmically as if he had said something to
himself and was agreeing with it. Ramsey Douglass was staring down the plunge of Nicole's neckline where her unsup-
ported breasts quivered when she turned to face Belsky.

He had reduced them initially by forcing them to submit to a degrading bodily search. Naked, his mouth and anus probed, a man lost some of his defiance. Belsky had rocked them with the blunt announcement of their mission and had made them feel smaller by refusing to divulge answers to their questions. Now they had had time to regain some of their balance but they were still unsettled and it was time to hit them hard so that there would be no question of their obedience henceforth. It was a simple problem of discipline: the cruelty which he now inflicted was of no emotional consequence to Belsky.

He removed the thick manila envelope from his pocket and placed the stack of postcard-size photos on the wicker table by his chair. He gave the group time to speculate about the photos while he spoke to them:

"When you came here you'd spent an exhaustive year learning the lessons of protective coloration—you were taught how to be Americans. But at the same time you were, and you are, Russians. You signed an oath in which you pledged secrecy and eternal obedience. You were advised that every year you spent outside the Soviet Union in KGB employ would count as two years toward your retirement and of course that means you are eligible for retirement now at any time when you return to the Soviet Union. You'll be eligible for all the benefits of consumer priorities, respected status, preferential housing selection.

"I mention all this simply to remind you that there are worse things than returning to the Soviet Union and the privileges that will accrue to you in recompense for the loyal service you have done Mother Russia."

Ramsey Douglass spoke without bothering to pry his lips apart. "We're a little old for a recruiter's pep talk, don't you think?"

Belsky's face hardened. "What we require of each of you now is a total sense of loyal duty. There'll be no time for you to stop and debate whether what you are doing is right or wrong. What you must live by is a fundamental obedience.

"I'll remind you that Moscow keeps hostages on each of

you to discourage your defection. We can always imprison
these hostages in the interests of national security. I suggest
the possibility of seven years' coal mining on a penal squad
in a *taiga*, or ten years in the Potma labor camp. But we also
recognize that hostages are not always effective levers of persuasion. After twenty years we can't be certain all of you still
hold your Russian families in such close regard that you'd do
anything to avoid jeopardizing them. After all, you haven't
seen or heard from these people for half your lifetimes. Douglass has a son he hasn't seen since the boy was eight months
old—how much can he mean to you now, Douglass?"

"He's my son." Douglass' expression was hot and unforgiv-
ing and again he spoke without moving his lips. "If you're
suggesting I don't care about him—"

"I'm saying it's possible. You understand why I can't depend on your assurances.

"Perhaps some of you feel you don't need to be bound by
any oath you signed half a lifetime ago. Perhaps you feel
you're out of our reach. We understand that. We understand
the superficial attractiveness of the decadent bourgeois life
and we don't expect you to realize you may have become
unwitting tools of a system in which men exploit other men
and the workers have been conditioned to lick the boot that
kicks them.

"You all know in a general sense that the penalty for devia-
tionist crimes is severe. But we're not interested in penalizing
the guilty. We're interested in making sure no one is tempted
toward guilt. The only fish that get caught are the ones that
have their mouths open. You people will keep your mouths
shut, and I'm going to show you why."

He pointed to Nick Conrad and beckoned with his finger
and when Conrad dragged himself out of his chair Belsky
handed him the packet of photographs. "Examine those
closely if you will and pass them around."

The blood drained from Conrad's face when he looked at
the first picture; he backed toward his chair, moving like a
mechanism. Adele took part of the stack from him and passed
them out, and Belsky spoke abruptly—this time in Russian:

"The remains you are looking at are those of the members of a cell of Illegals who were seeded into Bonn in 1962. Three years ago they formed a secret compact and resolved to refuse activation. In the event of pressure they agreed to defect to the Allied authorities rather than submit to recall to Russia. They considered themselves safe since West Germany is the most anti-Communist and well-policed state in Europe. They counted on the efficiency of German security to protect them.

"KGB has a number of mobile disciplinary squads, one of which is commanded by a Mongolian known as Tircar whose work you see in these photographs. As you see most of them have been systematically dismembered beginning with the digital extremities. The punishment was inflicted gradually over a period of ten or twelve days—perhaps you can see the evidence of that in the profuse extent of the bleeding. If they had been killed first and then hacked up there wouldn't have been so much blood away from the remains—once the heart stops pumping the blood stops spurting. The order of events has been worked out by Tircar and his people. First the children of the Illegals are assembled within view of their parents. The female children are impaled with bottles which are then smashed. The male children's genitals are removed and stuffed into their mouths. Adolescent girls are raped with spiked dildos until they shriek for death. The parents are forced to watch this and when the children die Tircar turns his attentions upon the elders."

He stood up and walked from place to place collecting the photographs. He put the pictures away without looking at them. "You find this inconceivable but I remind you that all acts which further history and socialism are moral acts. In Moscow we have great confidence in you; we're quite sure this kind of measure won't be required in your case. But if it proves necessary Tircar and his Mongolians can be brought into this city within forty-eight hours. I won't belabor it any further."

Nicole said very dryly, "You ought to apologize to the Party for your negative thinking, Comrade."

"I hope you're right," he answered gravely; he was demonstrating the seriousness of his purposeful melodrama.

He turned to Douglass. "You're the cell leader. I don't need to know every step you take in carrying out your mission, but you'll have to inform me of all details which require the cooperation of people outside your own cell. You'll have to work out the rest of the details among yourselves and I don't need to remind you we haven't time for endless mental masturbation and debate. You know how to reach me. That's all for the moment—you'll leave by twos, at intervals."

Gus Craig sat tensely with one shoulder raised. When Belsky entered the room Craig stirred, ready to bounce out of the chair, but Belsky's eyes jammed him back down in his seat.

Craig's upper jaw poked forward so that his mouth had a gopher appearance; his undershot chin receded to the skinny neck and made his Adam's apple look like a second chin. His eyes kept dancing from spot to spot as if to make a moving target that would be hard to hit. Belsky judged he had probably been hit hard and often.

"All right," Belsky said. "Push him."

Torrio pocketed his gun and went around behind the prisoner's chair and held him down by the arms while Hathaway struck him with a scientifically wielded blackjack. Hathaway worked with a nice precision on that exact spot at the point of the shoulder where the nerves run shallowly over the bone. Hathaway paralyzed Craig's main joints effortlessly, and Craig exhaled with a long slumping sag of disappointment and disillusion. Belsky heard him utter a monosyllabic curse. Torrio lifted him to his feet and Hathaway searched him brutally, jabbing with knees and elbows and the heels of his palms. Agony pulled at Craig's mouth; he thrust his jaw forward to bite at his upper lip in order to keep from crying out. Hathaway, imbecilically calm, grabbed the front of his shirt and pulled his face down onto the desk. Craig's teeth clicked; his jaw sagged; his eyes rolled up. Belsky could see him going under, losing focus; he made a signal and Hathaway stepped back; Craig slipped to the floor in a slow ungainly pirouette and lay on his back, belly rising and falling with his breath.

Belsky stepped forward and stood looking down at Craig and when the eyes blinked and stayed open he said, "Who are you working for?"

"You ain't going to make me talk."

"They always say that. You know you're going to talk, Craig. Don't make us crack you."

"You bloodless bastard. Stick it up your ass."

Torrio held Craig's hand out on the floor and Hathaway stepped on the fingers with methodical brutality. "I can break every bone in your hand. That what you want?"

Craig's eyes showed his distress. "No. Let me up."

They picked him up and put him in the chair. Trembling violently, he sat hunched, the hurt hand pinched between his squeezed-together knees. His mouth worked.

"The name," Hathaway said. "Who you're working for."

"The CIA."

Hathaway made an exasperated sound.

"That's the truth."

Belsky said, "I rather doubt you'd recognize the truth if it kicked you in the teeth."

Hathaway said, "Now you want to try again or do we put you back on the floor and step on that hand again?"

Craig rubbed his knuckles. His whole body was unsteady. Hathaway said, "Get it done or get off the pot, Craig."

Belsky said, "He takes a mulish delight in prolonging this. If he had any courage at least he'd have the dignity to be willing to die without wasting anyone's time."

Craig simpered. "You ain't going to kill anybody."

Hathaway was indifferent. "Why not? It'd be just another funeral nobody'd go to."

"It'll just be an entry in a file someplace," Torrio said. "Where they make out the compensation check to your widow."

"He's not married," Hathaway said.

"Then he ain't got anybody at all to grieve for him."

Belsky said, "Aleksandr Bakst. Forty-one years old, born in

the Tadzhik SSR. Recruited into KGB from the Polotsk petro-
chemical plant where you were a security guard. You finished
training at Amergrad in 1955 and came here the same year."

Hathaway said, "I knew him from back there but he's not
in our cell and we're not supposed to recognize them out
loud."

"In this case it hardly matters since he won't leave this
house alive," Belsky said. "I suggest we walk him into the
bathroom and see how well he breathes under water. Drown
him in the toilet bowl but space it properly so that he goes up
and down for a long time, choking, wanting air."

There was always a weak point and he had found Craig's—
water. Craig took it badly. He dragged his uninjured left hand
down across his face and began to shake. His eyes became
lacquered with horror and Belsky gave him ample time to
construct a vivid picture before they walked Craig into the
bathroom. Only then did Craig break the ugly silence, in a
high-pitched voice that twanged. "What do I get out of it if
I do tell you?"

"Of course we can't let you go. You see that."

Craig swallowed. Belsky said, "If we have to dig for it you
go into the toilet. If you turn the bag up and shake it out for
us we'll make it fast and easy and you won't feel it."

"I guess that just ain't good enough," Craig said. Aimlessly
his left hand stirred toward his shirt pocket and plucked out
a pack of cigarettes. Hathaway batted the pack out of his hand
and then gave him one of his own cigarettes.

Craig said resentfully, "My cigarettes ain't poisoned. I can't
stand these menthol things."

"Yeah," Torrio said gravely. "They might give you cancer." He cupped his fingers to examine his nails.

Belsky said, "You're a licensed private detective and you
were hired to make a tape of our meeting. The people who
set it up had to know about the meeting. I can think of only
two men who knew about it and didn't attend. Therefore all
I need to do is kill both of them to insure our safety—so you
see we don't need your information vitally. It will only be
corroboration and it might save one man's life."

Hathaway was bouncing the heavy leather-covered black-jack in his open palm. Craig looked at that and at the lidded toilet bowl. Saliva ran out of the corner of his mouth and he said, "All right."

Hathaway said, "That's more like it."

"He called you Aleksandr Bakst," Belsky said, "and he spoke the names of your parents by way of identifying himself. He said he had orders from Moscow and you had to tape these proceedings for him."

Now the hate shone through Craig's fear. "If you already know the answers why push me around?"

"Because I want to know which one called you."

"Maybe I didn't catch his name."

"Put him in the toilet," Belsky said and began to turn away.

"Jesus H. Christ. It was Trumble. Congressman Trumble. He called me from Phoenix about one o'clock this morning and he said he couldn't get to the meeting but he had orders to cover it so he had to have a record of it." Craig gripped the edge of the sink; he looked faint. "I swear that's the truth. That's all he told me."

"I heard you say that before."

"I'm not holding out on you."

"How do you know it was Trumble?"

"You can't mistake that voice. Christ, I know the man. It was him."

"All right." Belsky nodded to Hathaway and Hathaway bludgeoned Craig behind the ear. Torrio caught him and held him up against the sink but Craig was unconscious. Belsky said, "Have you got a place to keep him?"

"Alive?" Hathaway showed his surprise.

"Yes. I may need to question him again."

"You think he was lying?"

Belsky said, "I'm not going to stand in this damned bathroom and argue the point. You understand simple orders, don't you?"

Torrio said, "We'll put him on ice. Don't worry about it."

"I won't," Belsky said, and looked at his watch and left.

☆☆☆☆☆☆☆☆☆☆☆☆☆☆☆☆☆☆☆☆☆☆☆☆☆☆☆☆☆☆☆☆☆☆☆☆☆

Chapter Eight

"We've got a war against Communism, gentlemen—pretty soon every man is going to have to stand up and be counted. We've got to keep stopping them every place they try to move in. Fight them on their own ground because if we don't do that now we'll be fighting them in Alaska and Hawaii and then in Chicago and New York. And it's too late when you have to do that."

Senator Woodrow Guest continued, "Some people among us would like to disarm us and show the world what nice friendly peace-loving pacifists we are. Look, there's nothing in the book that says they can't lick us or won't. We can be defeated. But some of our well-meaning crypto-socialists have blinded themselves because they want to think the Soviets are as peace-loving as they are. The left wing has an

167

endless capacity for giving the Commies the benefit of the doubt. It refuses to admit the danger of Communist aggression even when the Reds overrun Tibet and Soviet tanks invade Hungary and Czechoslovakia. This kind of thinking sold us out in Vietnam by caricaturing our military commanders as feebleminded neofascists. This kind of thinking has brainwashed our youth into a wish to believe we've got no need for armaments and national security. This kind of thinking makes no distinction between war and the deterrents of war. My Lord, gentlemen, is there no one left in our halls of government who owns a sense of honest outrage?"

When he paused he smiled a little and lifted the lid of his humidor, selected a cigar and held it like a moustache under his nose. His wise elegant face was averted, but Forrester recognized its expression—the look of a poker player trying to decide whether he has impressed his opponent with the strength of his bluff.

Guest stirred in his chair and broadened his grin. "I won't bore you with the rest of it but it's a pretty good speech, don't you think?"

"If you like saber-rattling. I fail to see how it's relevant to the subject at hand."

He saw color rise in Guest's cheeks. And Congressman Ross Trumble scowled silently at his dusty shoes.

They were gathered in the study. There were to have been six but when Ramsey Douglass phoned to say he couldn't attend, Guest and Forrester dismissed their own seconds and it was just the three of them now.

The Scottsdale slopes had been bulldozed into a terraced suburb of expensive châteaux inhabited by new merchant princes and young bosses of aggressive corporations. Woody Guest did not fit in with the rest of them but that didn't matter; he lived on the mountain in the splendor of his Moroccan villa because from these heights he could see the city that had made him. The Guest family had owned half the real estate in downtown Phoenix from territorial days forward.

Beyond the landscaped resort hotels Camelback Road was a broad spear with its palm trees converging into the shimmering hover of turbulent heat. In the blinding sunshine a half-million panes of glass shot painful reflections back from the flats and every shadow was black with a sharp edge. The study's glass wall commanded that view; inside, the room was spacious enough to enclose what Guest maintained was the biggest Navajo rug in existence. They sat in deep soft leather chairs, and the oak walls were lined with books and a few masculine paintings and the autographed photographs of seven Presidents.

Forrester had been met at the door by Guest's wife Myra. She was frail and never without a cigarette; she had shown him into the study in her faraway fashion, eyelids drooping—he suspected she had been addicted to some tranquilizing drug for a long time.

He had found Woody Guest taking his ease, clad in weekend slacks and sport shirt. Guest's eyes were set in deep weathered folds and there was authority in the poise of his handsome head. For three hundred years the Guest clan had spread its branches west from Georgia plantations and everywhere a Guest settled, his back porch became headquarters and fountainhead of local political power. When Woody Guest said, "Don't label me a right-wing reactionary just because I believe in the traditional American values," he believed exactly that. But the values he lived by included a three-hundred-year legacy of back-porch shrewdness, the ingrained understanding of the uses of power. Woody Guest was the complete political chameleon: he could wear a justfolks drawl as effortlessly as he wore the more characteristic aristocratic manner that kept people at a respectful distance.

Ross Trumble had arrived shortly after ten and squeezed his bloated hulk into the room with a disturbing absence of his usual affability. He seemed strangely subdued, his heavily lidded eyes more guarded and secretive than usual. His dewlappy face and oddly prim mouth made him look as if he had intimate knowledge of too many sybaritic vices. He had walked into the room carrying his black attaché case, spoken his greetings with a smoker's wheeze, accepted a glass of iced tea, and then spent the next five minutes sitting and squinting through the glass at the sunshine.

During that time Woody Guest had trotted out a copy of the speech he intended to deliver before the State Republican Committee.

"It's saber-rattling," Forrester said again. "You always were a man whose oratory could bring tears to his own eyes."

Guest laughed comfortably; he was a hard man to rile. "Young friend, I'm only trying to save you grief. No one can look quite so foolish as a man who gets wrapped up in his private crusade. A zealot quickly becomes a bore. I'm only trying to give you the kind of advice your father would have given you if he'd been here. He was one of our great Senators —I learned a fair passel from him and I want to pass a bit of it on to you by way of returning the favor. Your dad would have warned you against the folly of taking a stand on anything just before a reelection campaign—anything, let alone an issue as volatile and complex as this one. Now I'm telling you out of my heartfelt love for you, son, you're going to have to pull in your horns right now and behave yourself or you're going to get dumped on your ear by the party."

"The first time I ran for office my father said to me, 'Alan, you want to watch out for old Woody Guest, he talks real good —you could spread it on toast.'"

He heard Ross Trumble's laugh—a long voiceless wheeze —and Guest laughed too, and Forrester said, "I take it you support the same line, Ross?"

"Senator, look at it this way. Man has always lived with elements that could destroy him but we've learned to control them. It may turn out to be the same way with wars—but only as long as we can maintain the balance of power in responsible hands. We invented war and we'll just have to invent some substitute for it, but until we can do that we need deterrents."

Forrester turned quickly and surprised a look of fascination in Woody Guest's eyes. "Well don't that beat all," Guest said.

A crimson flush suffused Trumble's big face. "We're not animals," he said inaccurately. "But we've got to buy time and we can do that only by convincing the other big powers they can't afford to monkey with us on a nuclear scale. You disarmament advocates just don't take that into account: you just don't see that the idea of massive retaliation is a temporary stopgap, not a permanent solution."

"A malignant stopgap," Forrester argued. "The idea's fundamentally unstable. Whether it's permanent or temporary, it can still incinerate the world. Let's use short words: we're building hardware for a war we know will be our doom. To hell with deterrents—the idea's obsolete. Our ten-thousandth Phaeton won't offset their two-thousandth in any real strategic sense.

"You both know I've never disputed that we need enough weapons to defend ourselves. But one-twelfth of the productive output of the *world* goes into military expenses—one-twelfth of the work output of every human being on earth, dedicated to our own mutual slaughter. Half our budget goes into a military stockpile that's already big enough to overkill Russia and China forty times—we're past any legitimate defense requirements, we're just feeding a cancer. Of all people, why should the military be beyond criticism and accountability? Since when is the existence of an insatiable appetite an excuse to feed it? Senator, the more weapons you've got, the easier it is to think about using them, and the more thinkable it becomes the more inevitable that they'll be used."

Guest showed his teeth around his cigar. "I suppose you've discussed all this with the Soviet Union."

"I'm not arguing foreign policy. I don't care what the Russians do. We can destroy them regardless, and they know it. But in the meantime we've created a monster with a vested interest in its own perpetuation. To justify its existence we let it come up with estimates of the enemy threat. These estimates are always based on the worst possible threat the enemy could pose. And then on the basis of that imaginary threat we let the researchers develop deadly weapons and deploy the damn things. Naturally the other side panics and starts a crash program to beef up their own systems, and of course that provokes our side into building another new system. . . . I'm not talking blue sky, Senator. You may recall the Safeguard program was designed to protect our ICBMs against something like four thousand warheads the Russians were supposed to be capable of deploying. So we built four thousand of our own. It turned out the Russians had built only sixty but in the end they had to expand their own program to keep up with ours. When you overestimate a threat you make it real. Now you want to escalate the whole thing again—it's like winding a watch spring one notch tighter; one day the whole thing snaps and you get pieces of clockwork all over the floor. It's time to break the whole sorry cycle.

"Now I'll grant you've got a product with a lot of sales appeal because you're selling defense of home territory. But the Phaeton can't do us any good and it could well do a great deal of harm. The only tangible benefit will be the contracts the aerospace companies fatten on. Don't think I can't bring that home to the voters."

Senator Guest removed the cigar from his mouth. "We're talking in circles. Brass tacks now: exactly what do you want, Alan?"

"I want permanent cancellation of the Phaeton Three program."

"Even at the expense of your own reelection?"

"If that's the choice, yes. I don't believe it is."

"You realize you could easily get reelected and then start this fight?"

"False. If these hardware systems aren't controlled before they're built they can't be controlled at all."

Guest went from patient attentiveness to hard anger in the blink of an eye. It was a pose but it usually worked. "You're a gold-plated fool, Alan. You're on the party's shit list and we're offering you an olive branch and you're slapping me across the face with it. Now you've had plenty of time to look at the ramifications and you can't pretend you're ignorant of them. You know the score but I'll mention one or two of them again just so there's no mistake. First we're in an election year and in the Senate we've got fourteen incumbents up and the Democrats have got twenty-one seats up. Twelve of our fourteen are shoo-ins or at least reasonably safe, while the opposition has got maybe eight, maybe ten vulnerable seats. Now if we can hang on to twelve of our fourteen contested seats and pick up just four out of the ten the Democrats control now, we'll have a majority in the Senate for the first time in twenty-odd years. That's why it's important that the party hang on to your seat, and that's why we're having this little talk today. The party doesn't want to dump you, young friend. We need your seat. But if you force it we'll run Trumble here against you in the primary and believe me we'll wipe up the floor with you, son."

Forrester felt strangely bored: he had known everything Guest was going to say before he said it. But Ross Trumble's teeth formed a sudden accidental smile and Forrester realized this was the first Trumble had heard of the possibility of his being elevated. But it didn't last long. Trumble lapsed again into brooding indifference; he was attending his own private thoughts and clearly was not listening when Guest resumed: "You may not want to believe this but it's still true that whoever owns the means of production governs our lives. That's true in Communist Russia and it's true here."

"Praise Matthewson-Ward, from whom all blessings flow," Forrester said.

"If it pleases you to jeer. Our defense contractors pay more than ninety million in taxes into Arizona school districts and state and county and municipal governments. If you people get hairs up your asses and cut off those contracts and those plants have to close down, whose pockets do you think that tax money will have to come out of?"

"I'm sure you intend to make sure the voters get that message."

"Then you understand me. We'll have your guts for guitar strings, son." He said it mildly.

"Possibly," Forrester conceded. It was his serve and he drew breath and glanced at Trumble. The fat man turned to stare back at him and the hanging wattle shifted under his round chin. Forrester was startled to see the expression behind those buried eyes—they seemed to be pleading—but then the eyes closed up and Trumble didn't say a word.

Forrester addressed himself to Woody Guest. "Ross is welcome to run against me. But if he does I'll ask whether his campaign contribution from Matthewson-Ward two years ago influenced his votes on the House Military Appropriations Committee, and I might throw in a few TV speeches explaining how I find it hard to imagine Shattuck Industries giving a fifty-thousand-dollar check to Senator Woodrow Guest's last campaign without expecting anything in return. Maybe we'll start calling Ross the Congressman from Matthewson-Ward—has a nice ring to it, don't you think?"

Trumble did another strange thing: he threw his head back and uttered his long wheezing laugh. It had a touch of hysteria to it.

Guest was grinning wickedly because this was the kind of fight he enjoyed. Forrester told him, "I can document it down to photocopies of the canceled checks, if you like."

"And you're willing to let that hit the fan?"

"Did you think I'd come in here alone like a tame sheep with no ammunition of my own?"

"To tell you the truth I'm not sure what I thought, young friend. For a while there I thought maybe you'd gone around the bend." Guest chuckled and his eyes glittered when he added, "Do you want to sling verbs around or do you want to do a little horse-trading now, son? Because if it's the latter I suggest you sit down and quit looming over us."

When Forrester settled into the chair he turned it slightly to bring Ross Trumble into the scope of his view. Trumble sat with the attaché case on his lap and his eyes on the toes of his brown-and-white wingtips.

Guest said, "Now let's talk. Or are we dealing with what the kids call nonnegotiable demands?"

Forrester smiled. Woody Guest was an old wheeler-dealer politician with moss growing down his north side and Forrester liked him immensely.

"You told us what you wanted," Guest continued. "We'll go on the assumption that's your asking price but now let's get down to what you're willing to settle for."

"Fine. Do you want to swap horses for a while or do you want to get right down to the truth?"

"The truth usually saves time, son."

"But it doesn't leave much room for dickering and that might take some of the fun out of it."

Guest twinkled back at him. "If you take the fun out of politics what's the sense of doing it? But let's get down to it. You're not going to get party backing for your fight against the powers that be. So what'll you settle for?"

"Anything I can get," Forrester said simply. "I'm in this fight to the finish. With or without backing from the machine. Any help I get, that's just gravy."

"I think we understand each other, then."

"I'll tell you what I'd *like* to settle for."

"The moon with parsley."

Forrester grinned at him. "A little short of that, Senator. I'd like to have a look inside that attaché case on Ross's lap, for openers."

Trumble stirred; he had not been listening to them but his ears had picked up the last few words. Guest said, "Why? What's in it?"

"I expect he's got Webb Breckenyear's breakdown of the Phaeton Three appropriation figures."

"Why the hell would a man lug that around with him to a meeting like this?"

"I understand he never lets it out of his sight."

"That's ridiculous," Trumble growled. "The subject of this meeting was Phaeton. I brought facts in case the discussion turned that way."

"Then you're prepared to show them to us?" Forrester asked.

"No. Only to refresh my own memory. Look, Senator, these are private documents and they're the property of the House Military Appropriations Committee. The Committee's got a Democratic majority—how would it look if I opened up this file to a couple of Republican Senators?"

Guest said, "Then you won't let Alan have access to them?"

"Under the proper circumstances and at the proper time. Before the bill comes to a vote the facts will be made public —otherwise how could the House vote on it? But it's still in the preparation stage now. Nobody in any line of business releases tentative estimates before the details are finalized."

Forrester said dryly, "Knowing Webb Breckenyear, those figures will be made public about forty-five minutes before it comes to a vote."

Guest was grinning at him. "I keep telling you, son. That's the way the game's played. It's Webb Breckenyear's committee, not yours."

"Webb Breckenyear's a fossilized reactionary fool and we all know it."

Guest's trim shoulders lifted and fell. He said in an idle tone, "He won't live forever. In the meantime we can put up with him. He's done a great many fine services for this country in his time. But I might suggest you do look a bit ridiculous carrying that thing around, Ross, if what Alan says is true. It's not the crown jewels."

Trumble grunted. But he took the case off his lap and set it down on the carpet beside his chair. "Just don't let me forget it when I leave."

Guest laughed.

Forrester said, "There's another thing I'll settle for. I accept the fact that I won't get Republican backing in the primary. But I'm going to run. Maybe you'll put up Ross against me and maybe you'll put up somebody else—it doesn't matter. The point is, suppose I win the primary?"

Guest saw what Forrester was getting at and he seemed to appreciate it. He started nodding his head before Forrester finished the rest of the statement: "If I win the primary against the machine's hand-picked candidate I'd like to have your assurances the Republican Party will give me its wholehearted backing in the election campaign this fall."

"You seem pretty sure of yourself, young friend. Of course that's the essential blindness of any politician—if he didn't think he was going to win, he wouldn't jump into the race in the first place. But you're dismissing our strength pretty lightly, don't you think?"

"Not at all. I just think I can lick you."

They were both smiling and the smiles were not false.

Guest said, "You're talking about going way out on a limb and then asking the Party to come reel you in."

"Not at all. I'm saying if I can demonstrate the power to attract a majority of registered Republican votes in the primary I want to know the Party will back me afterward."

"Probably it will. But you're going to have to deal with Bill Borad's Senate Republican Campaign Committee. It's his largesse that's going to help determine the makeup of the next Congress and maybe Borad won't be too keen on throwing a lot of money into a campaign for a young maverick Senator who doesn't want to stand for what the national party stands for."

"I'm not talking about money and I'm not talking about the national party, Senator. And you know it. I'm asking if I'm going to have your endorsement and Ross Trumble's endorsement and every other Arizona Republican's endorsement if I turn out to be the Republican candidate for the United States Senate this November. And I'm not just talking about lip-service endorsements, I'm talking about active support and campaigning."

"Well, of course I can't speak for everybody." Guest's head swiveled. "What about it, Ross?"

"You don't have to worry about me," Trumble said. The secretive eyes blinked. "If I'm still around you'll have my support. If you win the primary."

If I'm still around. Forrester watched him with closer focus.

Guest said quickly, "Are you all right, Ross?" So the same thought had struck him too: Trumble was talking like a man whose doctor had just told him he had six months to live.

"I'm fine. I gave up smoking last month and it's made me irritable, that's all. Or maybe it's the diet pills. I'm trying to take off fifty pounds before the campaign—voters don't like fat politicians much any more. You've got to consider the television image." The prim mouth settled into a twisted smile. "What do you suppose would've happened if Charles Steinmetz had had to go through a television interview to get a job at G.E.?"

"You're sure there's nothing wrong?"

"I've never been in better health."

Guest leaned back in the leather chair and tucked his square jaw in. "All right, Alan. You've got our assurances. My personal word on it, you'll have my support and Ross's if you win the primary. Of course the primary itself is another story. We'll fight like tigers and I suspect we'll beat the shit out of you." Then the grin flashed again. "Of course a politician's word is worthless; you ought to know that."

"Not yours. This isn't a campaign promise, Senator, it's your word to me as a friend."

"Yes. And I'll honor it if the circumstances arise. Frankly I don't think they will. If I were a bookie I wouldn't even bother laying off bets on you."

"Then you'd stand to lose your shirt," Forrester said amiably.

Guest shook his head with weary avuncular goodwill. "Ever watch a dog come yapping out into the street and go chasing after a fast-moving car? Do something for me, son—stop and think about what would happen if the dog ever managed to catch the car."

When Forrester walked down to his car he found Ross Trumble beside him.

"I've got to talk to you. Not here—not now. Can I call you?"

"Of course. Any time."

"I'm not sure exactly when we can meet. As soon as I— anyhow I'll call you. Thanks, it's—important."

Forrester couldn't remember having seen the man so nervous. "What's wrong, Ross?"

Trumble's head jerked back and forth in negation—almost a spasm. "Later. I'll call you later."

"I still want a look inside that attaché case."

"Maybe that too."

Trumble turned abruptly and waddled to his car. Forrester watched him drive away down the hill.

When he jackknifed himself into the low bucket seat and looked back at the house Woody Guest was in the doorway's shadow, his white hair like a beacon. Guest waved lazily and Forrester answered in kind before he drove down the curving asphalt drive in the thin haze of dust left hanging in Ross Trumble's wake.

The interior of the old Mercedes had been designed to approximate a millionaire's conception of the cockpit of a pursuit airplane. They had discontinued the model a decade ago and not replaced it with a newer design. Parts were getting hard to come by, but Forrester was determined to keep it until it became a vintage antique. It carried him blithely along Interstate 10 with hardly a ripple at seventy-five miles an hour. He had picked up a sandwich and a can of lemon-lime soda in Casa Grande and he ate in the car, sprinkling his shirt with crumbs and grinning because he hadn't done this in years.

It was a hundred and twenty miles to Tucson and on the road he reviewed the conference and felt satisfied if not elated. He had the insight to realize that on this particular day he wouldn't have been crushed even by a flat turndown by Woody Guest and Trumble. Shards of hard sunlight reflected off the long hood of the Mercedes and he squinted along the highway through his sunglasses; he nudged the heavy car up to an effortless eighty-five and checked the mirror for patrol cars. He was in a hurry because Ronnie was at the other end of the road.

Last night he had watched her sleeping face and felt a slight edge of guilt, as if he were eavesdropping. Her eyes had opened with a mischievous smile; the night was full with her pleasure and she had snuggled close like a warm furry inquisitive pet and refused to let him out of bed until he was almost late for the drive to Phoenix—no time to stop by the hotel, he had shaved with her Lady Electric razor and brushed his teeth and kissed her deeply and gone on the road breakfastless.

Six hours ago. Now he pulled off the freeway and got sucked into the flow of traffic across the bridge into the old Spanish center of Tucson, parked and walked toward the courthouse. The flag whipped in the desert wind and an empty beer can clattered across the terrazzo; it was probably eighty degrees officially, more on this sun-blasted concrete.

He took the courtyard steps two at a time and went into his office smiling. Ronnie wasn't there.

Les Suffield was asprawl on the couch reading the morning paper. He had a look at Forrester's face and said, "Let me guess. You just won the Irish Sweepstakes."

"Not quite. Where's Ronnie?"

"What the hell kind of greeting is that for your long-lost executive assistant that you haven't even seen in a whole week? Where's Ronnie? What about *me*?" Suffield sat up grinning. "Jaime was right, then. You been bit."

"All right, since you obviously want me to ask. What are you doing down here?"

"Uncle of mine took sick. He's in St. Mary's, nothing serious—gall bladder. Gave me an excuse to fly out. I thought I'd better talk to you."

"That sounds ominous," Forrester said. He went behind his desk and pulled the chair out and sat down.

"As for Ronnie, I told her she could take the afternoon off. I'm holding the fort, standing by to repel boarders and whatnot. She said to tell you she's gone out to the ranch and you're expected there for dinner." Suffield's eyes were round with innocent mockery and his wide mouth grinned. "The way she said it sounded downright proprietary."

There was a stack of correspondence on the desk bound up in a heavy rubber band. Forrester glanced at it and Suffield said, "Your first bundle of hate mail. I thumbed through it. Mostly unsigned, of course. When they get that blasphemous they don't like to put their names on it."

"To hell with them then." Forrester swept the stack into the wastebasket.

"Sure. But maybe you ought to keep count. Give you a rough tally of sentiment."

"So far the mail's been running eight to one."

"For you?"

"Yes."

"How about that?" Suffield said. "There have been a few columnists' blind items in the Washington papers over the past week. I don't know if you saw them."

"No. Blind items? What about?"

"You know the kind of thing. Not mentioning names but thick with insinuation. Young Republican white knight gets tarnished armor, will be dumped by party machine for insubordination. You know the drift. A lot of people including the Secretary of Defense and several Senators have agreed to appear on panel TV news shows to shoot your position full of holes. I might remind you at least thirty-two Congressmen own interests in television stations and most of them by some odd coincidence are pretty far over to the right."

"What's that got to do with anything?"

"Just that it may make it kind of hard for you to get your message across to the Great Unwashed. Unless you want to shell out the price of an aircraft carrier to buy your own television time."

"You mean national television time? Why would I spend money on that? This is Arizona, Les."

"I didn't get the impression you wanted to run for President of Arizona."

Forrester only smiled. Suffield said, "The point is the networks are lining up a lot of big guns. I've heard rumors about rumors to the effect that the President himself may throw a few needles your way at his next TV press conference."

"I always welcome publicity."

"Not that kind you don't. Believe me. But I think you don't recognize that the parent companies of all three TV networks are deeply committed in aerospace contract work. Ordinarily the network bias runs toward the liberal side of things, as Mr. Agnew pointed out a few years ago, but when you start tromping on aerospace you're stepping on a very sore corn."

"I take it this is Lesson Number Four in Suffield's Elementary Politics."

"Like I said, I'm just staying aboard ship to point out the shoals. I still think you've tackled an elephant with a flyswatter, but if that's your game I'll help out all I can, right up to the funeral." Suffield ran strong fingers through his shaggy pelt of gray hair. "How'd it go with Guest and Trumble?"

"I've been ditched as far as the primary's concerned. Trumble may run against me, but I've got a pledge from both of them that if I win the primary in spite of their opposition I'll get the full backing of the party in the election campaign."

"That's better than nothing, then."

"Frankly it's more than I expected to get."

"Nuts. You like to undersell yourself—I've pointed it out before. They need you almost as much as you need them, when you come right down to it. Neither party has very many hotshots around with your brand of vote-getting charisma. Aside from Lindsay, who's left besides you? All the rest of them are tired. No—Woody Guest will go pretty far off his usual base if that's what it takes to keep you from switching over to the Democratic Party. You may get more Republican support than you think."

"Maybe. Maybe not. Don't forget they ditched Lindsay in the primaries when he ran for reelection."

"And then he won in spite of it and they welcomed him back into the fold because if they hadn't he could have made hell for them."

"Maybe," Forrester said again, not at all convinced. "Anyhow I think we've got to assume I'm not going to be the fair-haired Republican boy for a while. I've got to run an independent campaign without clubhouse support and we've got to plan accordingly."

"Yeah. A paper clip, a Band-Aid, a rubber band, a wad of chewing gum and a shoestring."

"A pretty thick shoestring. I expect it'll take half a million dollars to beat the machine in the primaries and if I have to I'm prepared to put it up myself."

"Jesus. You really are serious about this. You'd have to mortage the ranch."

"No. Old James Hayden Forrester socked away a pretty good pile of real estate and invested capital and I'm good for a few million without dipping into the cookie jar at home."

"But if you spend it and lose you won't have a thing to show for it."

"If Defense spends thirty billion dollars on Phaeton Three and one of the damned things blows up in its silo what do you think we'll have to show for that?"

"Okay, okay."

"Have you seen Top Spode?"

"Today? No. He called and talked to Ronnie but she didn't tell me what it was all about."

"He's on a job for me and I think I want to call him off. If he calls after I leave, tell him to get me at the ranch."

"All right. But I think maybe I'd better spend the rest of the afternoon making the rounds, seeing what kind of support we can drum up for you in the primary. You must have a few friends left and I want to reach them before the opposition gets to them."

"Good idea."

"I'll use the phone in the front office, then." Suffield uncoiled himself and strolled to the connecting door. He paused there and turned and spoke after an interval. "Listen, about Ronnie—"

"What about her?"

"Just—well, this might not be a good time to let it ripen into something. You know?"

"What the devil are you talking about?"

"I mean, it's not so long since Angie died, is it? You've got the voters to think about."

"For God's sake, Les!"

Suffield showed his discomfiture. "What would it look like, right now? Rich prominent widowed Senator gets hot pants for his dewy-eyed secretary. I mean, you'd be laying yourself open to all kinds of locker-room snickers, and you don't need that kind of gossip right now—things are tough enough without it."

"Let's just leave my personal life and Ronnie's out of this."

"In politics that ain't so easy, amigo." Suffield turned through the door and pulled it shut behind him.

Forrester stared at the closed door for a long time before he reached toward the In box.

Tucson was a prime example of how boulevards and superhighways created a centrifugal force that flung vital energies out of the downtown area. The stores had moved out to glittering suburban shopping centers and the old-town decay was particularly depressing in the hard sunshine: the abandoned business sites seemed singularly out of place under the vast cobalt sky. A traffic light halted Forrester between a cut-rate furniture store, peeling yellow stucco, and a rancid little hotel with its doors wide open and its sagging chairs inhabited by girls in thin dresses who would come out on parade after dark. A theater marquee advertised "mature adult films" and the titles were in Spanish.

He let in the clutch and the Mercedes growled up the ramp and out into the left lane. He went southeast at a good clip, driving too fast for the traffic, darting from lane to lane to pass daydreamers and trucks. Past the VA Hospital towers and the municipal airport and the dusty end of Davis Monthan Air Force Base; past the Truckers' One Stops and dreary motels, out into the uninhabited cactus flats with distant mountains on all the horizons. Dinosaur-shaped billboards flashed by— *SEE Colossal Cave! 1 Mi.*

He left the Interstate at Mountain View Junction and sped south into the hills on the blacktop county road, tires whistling on the sharp turns. He had all the windows open and the wind roared in his ears and tangled his hair.

The arid plain gave way to brush hills and now he was coming into the grass country with scrub timber on the higher slopes; he made the acute turn into the secondary road and the Mercedes leaped forward toward home.

The Forrester ranch had been carved out of the old Spanish Baca Float grant; it was the size of a small European nation. He passed herds of browsing Angus cattle and saw a jeep bouncing across a distant pasture; dust raveled high in the Mercedes' wake. Beyond the low ridge to the southeast he could see the big red-rock landmark Ronnie had painted: it rode along with him.

He passed the manager's big house and half a mile of workings: crew quarters, outbuildings, feedlots, corrals, smithy, gasoline pumps, the grass landing strip. The gravel drive took him up the long curve through great heavy trees to the hilltop from which the hacienda commanded twenty miles of Forrester grass in any direction. His grandfather's *vaqueros* had dubbed it the hacienda; in fact it was an Edwardian architect's idea of a Georgian manor and the front was a white colonnade two stories high. Angie hadn't liked it very much: it was too much house, she had felt diminished by it. It had been built in an era when servants were more plentiful than masters.

Ronnie had heard the snarl of the Mercedes and she was on the porch when he walked out of the garage. He watched for her quick slanting smile, teeth white against her tan face. She wore a light sweater with the sleeves pushed up casually above the elbows. The wind spun her hair around her face; she combed it away with her fingers and tossed it back with a shake of her head. When he started up the steps her mouth softened and parted and her breasts lifted; when he reached the top step and lifted his hands she came obediently into his arms. Her nails dug into him and her voice was thick and sweet in his ear: "Welcome home."

The falling six-o'clock sun burst through the windows of the big front room. Mrs. Gutiérrez tried to keep everything shut up when he was gone—she hated the sun, it faded everything. Ronnie said, "I know it lets the dust in but it's too glorious a day. I'm afraid I've opened every door and window I passed."

"Good."

"How did it go?"

"Scottsdale? Better than I'd hoped." He told her about it while he made drinks.

They sat down on the huge divan with their hips and shoulders touching. With the sun in her face she was squinting and wrinkles had gathered at her temples and forehead. She had confessed she would be forty next month, and that was both unbelievable and irrelevant: with her bone structure and health she would still be lovely and ageless twenty years from now.

When he had told her about the conference she wriggled loosely and gave him a serene unhurried kiss; then she left him momentarily, flowing toward the kitchen. When she returned she was tasting an index finger. "To prove I'm not a total failure at domestic science I've cooked dinner for us. I hope you like roast lamb."

"I love it."

She came forward in relief. "When I think of all the things I want to learn about you the mind boggles."

"I don't like seafood much. The occasional swordfish steak, that's about it. I hate shellfish. But it doesn't really matter, does it, Ronnie?"

She was biting her lip in feigned alarm. "But I adore seafood. Don't you see we're completely incompatible?" And laughed at him and kissed him again. "I just can't keep my hands off you—isn't that a terrible thing to say?"

"You're so beautiful tonight," he murmured, and wrapped his arms around her.

"Absolutely delicious," he said and patted his mouth with a napkin. "Perfection."

"I'm not a bad cook, really. I was nervous and the asparagus got overdone." She smiled quickly. "Actually I'm sort of a cozy quiet girl, you know. I like to cook for you."

They cleared the table together and went into the front room holding hands like children. The setting sun veined the clouds like pink-white marble and the rich warm light was soft against her face. She sat on the floor at his feet. The coffee made a good smell; he seared his mouth with the first sip and set the cup down. She rested her head against his knee and smiled up at him; her hand crept toward his and she said, "Darling."

"What?"

"Nothing. I was tasting the word. Darling. It has a good sound."

"It does to me." He touched the tip of her nose with a forefinger and she wrinkled her nose at him.

"You have strange gold flecks in your eyes. It makes you look as if you've got little incandescent lights inside."

"Top used to swear I could see in the dark."

She sat up. "Oh damn. Now that does it. I really am going to pieces over you. What would Amy Spencer's Secretarial School think of me? He called you this afternoon."

"Who?"

"Jaime Spode. He said to tell you he'd engaged a female operative from Orozco's agency, whatever that means, and that he expected to deliver the goods tonight. And he said he'd had Orozco put a tail on the subject in Scottsdale, and the subject had driven straight from the meeting to a filling station on Camelback Road and of all things put in a phone call from the pay booth to Orozco himself. Does that make sense to you? There's more."

"The subject is Ross Trumble. Top's been trying to get something from him. Go on."

"Well Orozco told Jaime he'd had a call from Trumble trying to locate a man called Gus Craig—one of Orozco's operatives. Trumble seemed terribly upset about him. Orozco made some phone calls but he couldn't find Craig either. Jaime explained to me that Orozco ordinarily won't tell one client anything about another client, but Trumble isn't an agency client so if Craig had any private deals with him that was no concern of the agency's.

"I'm trying to report this the way Jaime told it to me, but it doesn't make too much sense to me. Orozco's people trailed the subject into Phoenix. Trumble parked on a side street and walked into a small hotel in a state of great agitation. He made several calls from the telephone booth in the lobby and he spent two hours writing a letter on hotel stationery. He bought stamps at the desk. Orozco's man got close enough to read Trumble's handwriting and Jaime said this might be important because Orozco's operative saw the address Trumble wrote on the envelope. It was yours. The ranch here."

"Here?"

"That's what Jaime said. Why would Trumble write a letter to you? He'd just been with you."

"I have no idea."

"Anyhow Jaime said Trumble mailed the letter and spent a few hours hobnobbing with his political cronies in Phoenix and got on the road toward Tucson around four-thirty. Jamie called here about five and told me to tell you all this. He said he'd be in touch with you later tonight or in the morning."

"Did he say where I could reach him in the meantime?"

"No. I assume he'll be following Trumble, so he probably doesn't know where he's going to be."

Forrester said, "I was going to call him off. But maybe it's just as well to let him go ahead. Writing to me—it's curious."

"So am I."

"Not much point worrying about it until we have more to go on."

She lifted her hair loosely, high above her head, and let go and shook it out. "Coffee's getting cold."

"Let it wait." He took her hand and stood up and lifted her to her feet. She smiled again; her hands touched his shirt, shyly, and slid up the back of his neck.

"Odd how you find love only when you're not looking for it."

"Just let this go on forever," she whispered, and covered his mouth with hers.

She stood taut in her skin and Forrester rolled over on the bed and said drowsily, "You cried again."

"I know. I'm foolish—it's silly. Every time we make love I'm terrified—what if this is the last time?"

"You're thinking of him again. It's a mistake to hang on to the past too tightly."

"It's not that. Not the way you think, darling."

"Then what?"

"I can't explain it. There are things it's better not to know about the people you love."

When she blinked her eyes were moist again and he stood up and held her against him. "Never mind," she said. Her voice was muffled against his chest. "Let's just think about here and now. That's all there really is."

"Tell me what's wrong."

She only shook her head and went ahead of him into the bathroom.

They showered together and afterward he took the phone off the hook.

☆☆☆☆☆☆☆☆☆☆☆☆☆☆☆☆☆☆☆☆☆☆☆☆☆☆☆☆☆☆☆☆

Chapter Nine

"He'll be along any time now. You'd better get over there."

The girl shifted her buttocks in the car seat and kissed Spode with moist warmth and suction. She reached for him and smiled. "He's a fat slob. If I had my druthers—"

"Git," he said good-naturedly. He reached across and patted the far side of her rump. "I'm doing my best to act like a stoical stony-faced Innun and I wish you'd quit waving it at me or I'm likely to lose my cool."

She was a sleepy girl with pale blond skin and the vaguely pretty face of a plastic mannequin, sewed into a tight skirt that showed little signs of strain at the seams and a blouse that revealed more than a small area of creamy breasts with a sweat-shine in the cleft between them.

Spode had parked at the curb in the middle of the block,

farthest from the street lights. Across the street the house was dark, a big low ranch-style on a landscaped hundred-foot lot. When the girl opened the door to get out she blew Spode a regretful kiss. Spode said, "He can drink you under the table. He may be a fat slob with a bad case of lechery but he used to be an FBI agent. Don't sell him short. Keep your head."

"I get sixty dollars a day from Orozco—what do you think he pays me for, my virginal innocence?"

"Just don't get cocky, Jill."

"How long am I supposed to keep him occupied?"

"Midnight at the earliest. Preferably one o'clock."

"Where will you be at two o'clock, then?"

Spode grinned.

She stood there fitting into her clothes like a girl facing a seventy-mile-an-hour wind, breasts and buttocks swelling. Spode said, "Bet your ass."

"I'll see you then." She walked away swiveling and Spode's eyes followed her hungrily; she reached the far curb and stepped back into the shadows beside the hedge. Spode shifted his attention to the rear-view mirror and kept it there, waiting for headlights.

The first car was a false alarm. The lights came along the street slowly and at first Spode thought it was their man because the car slowed to a crawl fifty feet behind him. But evidently the driver didn't know the neighborhood and was looking for house numbers on mailboxes. The car drew level with Spode's and the driver was looking the other way, looking at Trumble's house; the driver studied the dark house for ten seconds and then drove forward. Spode had only a glimpse of the face in the reflection of dashboard light and there was nothing remarkable about it—a brown bland middle-aged face. The car moved away picking up speed, a pale Ford sedan. Insurance salesman, probably.

A breeze blew through the car and Spode hunched to light a cigarette, cupping his hands together against the wind. A gust of laughter carried across lawns from a house down the street. Someone's TV or stereo was turned up, a girl hoarsely singing "Have I Stayed Too Long at the Fair?"

He hadn't heard that song in years and it took him back to the early days with the Agency.

He was still in the Army then. In a bar in Highland Park, New Jersey, sitting at the curve of the bar listening to the bouncer tell the kids to keep their glasses off the jukebox; he was taking another drink and knowing his mouth would taste rancid by midnight. Trying to decide whether to re-up. His enlistment was about to expire and he really didn't know what he could do outside the Army, and just then two guys in neat gray suits walked in and took the stools on either side of him and started talking. They had an easy jocularity and a casual way of getting right down to friendly first names—"I'm Donald Coe, just call me Don."

They had signed him up that night.

When his enlistment expired he took four weeks off in New York and screwed everything that would hold still long enough and at the end of the month reported to the huge building in the Virginia woods outside Washington. They had kept him busy for fifteen years but in the end he had quit because he couldn't stand their brand of incestuous paranoia: he hated being watched constantly by security officers who even peeped on men's rooms. Anyhow toward the end they'd had him at a desk where all he did was disburse vouchers for confidential "Class A" funds that came out of hiding places in Congressional budgets. In the beginning the recruiters had looked up from the clipboards and warned him, "You may find yourself in some pretty tight places. Do you still want the job?" But they hadn't scared him out; they'd bored him out.

And then Trumble drove up and began to turn into the driveway and Jill, timing it nicely, came striding out of the shadows as if she'd been walking down the sidewalk and let Trumble's car clip her.

From where Spode sat it looked just right, very convincing. She jumped back after she'd slapped the fender loudly and her little cry was just startled enough without being theatrical. Trumble's car jerked to a halt, tail whipping up in the air, and Trumble climbed out shaking and hurried around to the far side of the car. The girl was picking herself up and Spode heard Trumble's apologies falling all over themselves. "Are you hurt? My God. Are you all right? I'm so terribly sorry— I just didn't see you there at all. . . ."

Jill dusted herself off and smoothed down her skirt. As soon as it was evident she hadn't been maimed Trumble's attitude changed; in the glow of the headlights he stood back and stared at Jill. Spode chuckled privately. He heard Jill say, "Christ, these freeways are murder, aren't they?"

"I'm really sorry, Miss—?"

"Do you live here?"

"Yes—I, ah, if there's anything I can do?"

"You can damn well buy me a drink," she said, and shuddered dramatically. "Christ. What a night. First Chuck walks out on me for some cheap chippie and now you come along and knock me on my ass. I should've stayed in bed."

Trumble said eagerly, "Well by all means come inside, we'll fix you right up with a nice big drink to settle those nerves, Miss—?"

"Have you got bourbon? That's what I need, a good triple slug of Ancient Age. Christ." Jill bent over to pick up her handbag and Trumble was staring down the deep plunge of her neckline.

"Bourbon, Scotch, gin, whatever you wish. My God, it's the least I can do. I might have killed you!"

"I wish you had." She rubbed her hip and winced. "I'm going to be black and blue, I just know it."

"Well come inside, come inside. One triple bourbon coming right up, Miss—?"

Spode watched him park the car and and go to the door with the attaché case in one hand and his house keys in the other. Jill waited by the door rubbing her hip and Trumble was so eager he almost dropped the keys.

They were inside three or four minutes. Then they came out onto the front step and Trumble was saying, "I can't understand what happened to it. I'm sure there were at least two quarts of bourbon on that shelf. I just can't understand it."

Spode glanced over his shoulder at the dull gleam of the two bottles on the back seat of his car.

"Anyhow I doubt it was Ancient Age," the girl said. "I just have this thing for Ancient Age, you know?"

"But that's just it. One was Bellows and I'm positive the other one *was* Ancient Age. I just can't understand it."

"Well anyway it's very nice of you to offer to take me out. Are you sure I'm not intruding on your time? I really didn't know you were a Congressman and all. I mean that probably sounds stupid but I actually don't pay much attention to politics and things like that. My—Chuck always used to say, 'Don't vote because it only encourages the bastards.' I mean, no offense, I didn't mean it personally—you're really a nice guy, you know that? But I don't want to intrude, you're probably frightfully busy. . . ."

"Nonsense. We're both shaken up—it's exactly what we need to quiet our nerves. I know a nice cozy little place on Grant Road." Trumble was maneuvering her toward the car.

"It really is awfully nice of you, Congressman Trumble. Do I call you Congressman or Representative or Your Honor or what?"

"Call me Ross." Trumble put his hand on her rump and smiled. He was wearing a rumpled suit and a five-o'clock shadow and a ridiculous pair of half-glasses low on his bulbous nose but the girl gave him an intimate smile. Spode watched the car drive away and straightened his face. He smoked another cigarette to give Trumble time enough to come back if he decided to ditch the girl after all, but there wasn't much chance of that. After ten minutes Spode got out of the car and walked across the street carrying his camera equipment and tools.

He had never crossed paths with Trumble in the old days but he knew a little of Trumble's background. Sometime after the Korean war he had turned up in Tucson with a law degree, passed the state bar exam and hired on as junior trial deputy with the County Attorney's staff. He hadn't been fat then. For some reason he had quit that post in 1956 and joined the FBI as a recruit. After a few years he'd started to gain weight and according to the gossip Spode had heard, Trumble's determined satyriasis had come to the attention of the Bureau's district director, whereupon Trumble had been called on the carpet and asked if he would stand in the way of a replacement. Trumble had returned to Arizona and taken a job with Shattuck Industries doing some kind of legal work which amounted essentially to lobbying in Phoenix on the company's behalf. The work had brought him into close contact with politicians and before long he was working his way up in the Republican machine, and when the last Second District Congressman had opted to run (unsuccessfully) for Governor, Trumble had stepped into the vacated position. He had been in Congress four years now but his FBI background was evident in the security devices that protected his house. Spode had had the devil's own time breaking in an hour before to steal Trumble's whisky.

As a matter of course Spode went equipped with screwdriver and malleable wire and a small variety of burglar's tools, not excluding a few celluloid credit cards which were enough to break into most homes in five seconds. Sometimes it was necessary to open a door chain with a thumbtack and a rubber band and sometimes a lock actually had to be picked, but usually that was the extent of the difficulty. But in Trumble's case the burglar alarm was connected to every door and to strips of metallic tape around every windowpane. Undoubtedly there was some kind of auxiliary battery system indoors so that if the house current were cut off the auxiliary would take over immediately. In the past Spode had overcome such systems by going in with a glass cutter—making a hole in the center of a window rather than at the edges where he would interrupt the alarm tape. But here he couldn't afford to leave evidence that he had broken in.

There was still a way. But it had been tedious. Like most ranch-style houses in Tucson, Trumble's had a slightly peaked roof shingled with asbestos. The low attic contained ceiling insulation and aluminum ductwork systems that fed

air-conditioned and heated air into wall vents in all the rooms.
The ducts were less than a foot square in cross-section but the
attics through which they ran had to be designed big enough
for servicemen to crawl in alongside the ducts. There was a
large metal grating at one end of the house under the eaved
roofpeak, giving access to the electric exhaust fan that ven-
tilated the attic space, and at the other end was another grating which provided a place for air to come in so it could
circulate through the exhaust fan. Spode had tackled the second grating. He had had Jill's help; she had stood on his
shoulders and unscrewed the grating and then jumped down
and given him a boost. He had crawled in, twisting his shoulders to fit through, and found himself buried in an itching
mess of excelsior-style insulation. He'd found the service
crawlway and climbed up on it and spent quite a while picking insulation out of his hair and clothes because he couldn't
very well leave a spoor of the stuff all over the house. Then
he'd crawled from rafter to rafter with the pencil flashlight
and eventually found the plywood trapdoor that gave access
to the house below. He'd spent a good while examining it
for magnetic leads but so far as he could tell it wasn't
wired. It was sunk in the ceiling of a clothes closet. When he
opened it he climbed down onto the hat shelf and then
dropped to the floor through a thick row of Trumble's jack-
ets and coats; the closet had the vaguely decaying smell of
dried sweat.

This time he had to jump to reach the grating. He chinned
himself inside. He knew the route now so this second intru-
sion was easier. He pried the trapdoor up and went down
into the house and walked through it looking for the attaché
case.

The black case wasn't wired with explosives, though it
wouldn't have surprised him. He picked the locks and set up
his camera on a C-clamp mounting which he screwed to the
lid of the toilet. He put the documents on the tile floor to
make the pictures; he had chosen the bathroom because it had
no window, only an exhaust fan, and the neighbors wouldn't

see the light. When he had what he had come for he put the papers back in the case, locked the case and put it back on the living-room desk where he'd found it. He wiped everything for fingerprints and looked at his watch, and because there was plenty of time he took the little voice-activated bugs out of his pockets and began planting them in various places around the house, particularly near the three extension tele-phones. They were button-sized micro-transmitters with a maximum range of about three hundred yards but that was more than sufficient for Spode's purposes. He pasted them under the telephone stand and under a lamp base and behind the bed's headboard and under the frame of the living-room couch.

Traffic was a faint distant mutter in the room. He had one bug left and he was trying to decide where to put it when he heard a car stop just outside, a door thud shut, shoes come up the walk with authoritative stride. Spode's hair rose.

He waited for the doorbell to ring because if it rang then this wasn't Trumble coming home. But it didn't ring and when he heard the key go into the lock he wheeled and went back through the house.

Before he reached the closet he heard the front door open. Footsteps came inside and he knew he couldn't climb up into the attic without making noise. He would have to sneak out after Trumble went to bed. He spoke a silent oath and darted across the hall into the guest bathroom; closed the door and flicked the pencil torch around to orient himself so he wouldn't go banging into anything. When his eyes had memo-rized the room he switched off the light and stood breathing shallowly through his mouth, listening.

Footfalls moved around but there was something odd here. The feet went from room to room, pausing now and then but never settling down. Somebody was searching the house and it wasn't Trumble because Trumble would have turned lights on.

Spode felt the stir of his blood. If the man was armed and surprised him here it could be trouble.

He wrinkled his brain trying to remember whether he'd

seen anything here that might make a weapon. A faucet dripped relentlessly.

Somebody—one of Trumble's endless string of women—had left a jar of cold cream on the shelf above the sink. Spode wrapped it in a guest towel and twisted the towel ends to make a handle.

The intruder was looking for something big because he wasn't opening drawers and cabinets. Maybe he had been keeping surveillance on the house, had seen Spode and was now searching for him. But Spode had been trained to spot that kind of thing and there hadn't been any sign of watchers on the street or in the shrubbery. A neighbor from another house? But he'd arrived in a car.

Shoes came down the hall and stopped. Spode tensed, knowing the man was just beyond the door and listening with the same taut apprehension.

He heard the doorknob turn. A crack of light appeared—a pencil torch like his own, masked and reddened by fingers. The door came open a little wider and Spode saw the hard black oily gleam of an automatic pistol with a perforated silencer screwed to the barrel.

He brought the wadded jar down on the gun wrist hard enough to paralyze the tensor muscles which otherwise would have pulled the trigger involuntarily.

The gun dropped and clattered but the man had presence of mind to yank the door shut. The gun got caught on the floor between the door and jamb and the door bounced open again. One certainty: it wasn't a chance burglar. Sneak thieves seldom carried guns and never stayed to fight. But this one did: came in and slammed the door back hard enough to shatter the mottled glass of the shower stall. A shard cut the back of Spode's hand but Spode was in motion. The penlight made an arc and there was enought light: he smashed the blade of his hand into the man's larynx.

The intruder had only one good hand now. It brought the penlight up to the injured throat and Spode went for the solar plexus with board-stiff fingertips. He folded the man but the wild-swinging right hand smashed against the side of Spode's jaw. It was going to hurt to chew for a day or two. Spode cracked him across the back of the neck and the man went down.

The first thing Spode went for was the automatic pistol. He checked the safety as he turned. The penlight was on the floor under the sink, still burning, rolling slowly. The man was blinking. Spode switched on the ceiling light and had a look at him.

Now Spode recognized him—the man he'd seen drive past the house slowly a little while ago. An ordinary round face, brown hair, unexceptional eyes. Middle-aged and on the burly side. He looked like a civil servant, a faceless assistant to an assistant. But the side-vented brown suit had been tailored to accommodate the belt holster.

"Who are you?"

"I guess it's my turn to ask that question. Got a wallet? Let's see it."

"Stop waving that gun at me. You're not going to use it until you've found out what you want to know from me."

Spode said, "Let's have your ID."

"May I get up?"

"Stay put a while."

The man moved with the kind of care a professional used when he knew he was dealing with another professional. There was no chance of misinterpreting any of his moves. He produced a flat wallet; Spode stepped back out of reach before he opened it. His heels crunched broken glass.

There was a blue-gray identification card with official seals that said the man was Meldon R. Kemp, Grade G7, assistant research director for the World War II Division of the National Archives in Alexandria, Virginia. The driver's license and other cards had been issued in California and there were two blank checks on the First National Bank of Fresno. A California concealed-weapon permit and a Federal Government handgun license. The man was well papered with documentation.

Spode showed his teeth and his disbelief. He tossed the wallet back and Kemp put it in his pocket. When Spode made gestures Kemp got up and sat on the closed toilet lid. "And who are you?"

"Call me Sitting Bull. The ID card says NARS but it's the wrong color. The FBI uses those colors; you're not FBI."

"Are *you?*"

Spode grinned. "I'm just a tourist." He threw it out casually to see what reaction he'd get; the word could have a particular meaning.

He got the reaction. Kemp smiled a little. "That's all right then, we've just got our wires crossed. Look, Area code 703, 306-8585. Ask for Extension 520 and describe me to the man who answers."

Now that was interesting. It was one of the Agency's numbers. It made Spode doubly suspicious because Kemp had given him a little too much in answer to a simple question. Agency people weren't supposed to go around giving out their phone numbers at the drop of a hat. Kemp had to be working on two alternate assumptions: that Spode was a colleague or that he wasn't. If Spode was in fact an agent and called the number, the Agency would deny Kemp's existence irrespective of the truth and Spode would be expected to believe Kemp was on a top-secret assignment. On the other hand if Spode was not a colleague then Spode wouldn't take the risk of calling himself to the attention of a government agency because Kemp had surprised him burglarizing a house and if Spode wasn't an agent himself he'd be questioned about it. Conclusion: in giving Spode an answer Kemp had actually posed a question, and it would be answered for him by Spode's response. If Spode called the number, Spode was an agent. If not, he wasn't.

It was rather neat but Spode punctured it. "It's easy to sling out vague hints that you're a G-man. It's a handy cover and it would take me a long time to prove you're not what you pretend to be. If I call that number they'll just tell me they never heard of you."

Spode got out his camera. It was a pocket Minox loaded with Tri-X film for document work under poor light; it would be a bit grainy for a portrait blowup.

Kemp didn't like it but Spode had the gun and Kemp couldn't play games. "Keep still a minute," Spode drawled, and took five or six snaps of his face. He pocketed the camera and let the gun droop in his fist. "Now we're going to talk. I haven't got the patience to wait you out while you bring out a few yards of standard evasions and cut them to fit. Either I take you somewhere and work on you or we can get it done here—but if we do it here let's forget about the S.O.P. preambles."

He could see Kemp was mildly amused. The idea of interrogation didn't intimidate him a bit. It was only to be expected; whoever Kemp was working for, he was a pro.

Kemp was a curious one. Opaque eyes, neutral American accent, elusive, characterless, neither large nor small: an unobtrusive shadow.

Kemp said, "Let's not take it anywhere else. I'd only keep looking for a chance to jump you and violence attracts too much attention, don't you think?"

"Suit yourself. You can start talking, then."

"I guess not. If the tables were turned how much would you tell me?"

"That'd depend on how much I had to lose."

"You're in an awkward bind, you know. You could break a few of the bones I need the most but there's no guarantee that would make me open up. You don't know what kind of repercussions would come back at you, because you're not sure who's back of me."

"You're just not going to budge, are you?"

"Not an inch," Kemp agreed amiably. "We might as well call it a draw and part company."

Spode had to smile. The guy was good. Too smug, maybe, but nonetheless very good. Spode was pretty sure he could break him down, but if he did and Kemp turned out to be an Agency man it would put Spode between a rock and a hard place, and nothing about this incident seemed important enough to justify that sort of risk. Of course that was exactly the reaction Kemp was counting on, but you didn't make trouble solely because the other fellow expected you not to.

So Kemp was right; it was a standoff. Spode circled him cautiously and got down on one knee to get a light grip on the edges of a glass shard Kemp had pushed out of his way on the floor. It would have fingerprints on it. Spode wrapped it in his handkerchief and put it in his pocket with the Minox. Kemp watched drowsily and massaged the back of his neck; his control of his emotions was superb.

Spode took his time wiping his own prints off the cold-cream jar and the surfaces he might have touched in the scuffle. Kemp said, "It's a shame about that busted shower stall. Maybe your people can arrange to have it replaced and get the mess cleaned up before the owner of the house comes back."

Again the statement concealed questions: Did Spode work for an organization big enough to handle that kind of chore quickly? Did Spode know how soon the occupant would return?

Spode gave him no satisfaction but took what he could from Kemp's statement: Kemp didn't know where Trumble was or how long he would be away.

It was all shadowboxing and Spode could do better away from here. It was time to clear out. He said, "I'll go out first. You can lock up when you leave. When I'm gone give me a few minutes to get clear—I might get trigger happy if you're too tight on my ass."

"Sure you might. I can see you're the type who'd just go all to pieces."

"Why take the chance?"

"I'll give you five minutes. Do I get my gun back? If I lose the thing I not only have to pay for a replacement but I've got to explain how I lost it. You understand."

"I understand, but I'll keep it. Next time you'll know better." Spode backed out into the hallway.

"You've probably left prints on some more of that glass. Was I you I'd wipe them off before I left."

"I guess I'll have time for that."

"I guess you will." Spode turned and walked toward the front of the house, not hurrying.

In a hedge across the street Spode concealed the battery tape recorder that would pick up signals from the bugs he had planted in Trumble's house. The bugs were voice-activated and the tape would run only when there was sound, but just the same there was only two hours' tape on the machine and that meant someone would have to retrieve the tape once or twice a day and replace it. Spode didn't know what good it would do to monitor Trumble but sometimes a blind shot paid off.

He spent two minutes going through Kemp's car. He had left the house ahead of Kemp for two reasons: to see what was in the Ford, and to see what Kemp might bring out of the house with him. He was sure that Kemp had been searching for something too large to hide under his jacket.

Spode made it look as if he was planting a bug in Kemp's car. It was what he would have done if he'd had a bleeper on him, but that wasn't the kind of thing he carried around. Anyhow it would take Kemp quite a while to make sure the car was clean.

By the same token there was no reason to believe Kemp hadn't planted a directional bleeper on Spode's own car before he'd gone into the house. It was unlikely because Kemp probably thought the car belonged to a neighbor, but it was always possible. Still, Spode didn't have time to hunt for it now. He just got in the car and drove away. His headlights swept the trees when he turned the corner; he made a circuit around three sides of the block and extinguished the lights and waited near the corner, doubting Kemp would fall for it but always willing to try the elementary things first. He could see Kemp's car through a ranch house's corner windows. Kemp hadn't appeared yet and Spode used the time to review the clues Kemp had dropped.

When five minutes had elapsed he was satisfied he had milked Kemp's hints for all he was going to get out of them.

But the interval began to disturb him. Kemp had had plenty of time to get on the phone and summon reinforcements and if Spode was still hanging around when they arrived he might find himself in trouble. He began to think about giving it up.

Then Kemp came out of the house and walked casually to the Ford. He was clearly emptyhanded. The Ford backed into a driveway to turn around, and came forward; and Spode let him go. No point tailing a professional: the man would know how to ditch a tail and there was no way on earth to keep single-handed surveillance on a man who didn't want to be followed and knew how to shake pursuit.

Spode switched on his lights and drove away.

He pulled into the lot behind the Tropical Inn on Speedway Boulevard and went inside to use the pay phone. It had been a long time since he had last dialed this long-distance number but his fingers worked without hesitation. It was nearly midnight and that meant in Virginia it was almost two in the morning, but that didn't matter to the Agency; the Agency worked a twenty four-hour day.

A girl's plastic voice chirped in his ear. "Good morning, six-eight-seven-nyun."

"Extension three, please."

He heard the whistles and buzzes of the automatic switchboard. A man's voice came on the line: "Extension three." It was a voice Spode knew well and he was relieved it was still there.

"Howdy, George. This is Jaime Spode."

"Well for Christ's sake. Where the hell you been keeping yourself? Still working for that politician?"

"Aeah. Too dumb to quit. How's everything back at the old stand?"

"Situation normal all screwed up. Where you calling from, Jaime?"

"Arizona. Listen, do you boys happen to have a tourist taking in the scenery down here in Tucson?"

"Why?"

"Because I just ran into a fellow who dropped a few hints."

"Describe him."

"He's pushing fifty, all brown—hair, eyes, clothes. Maybe five-foot-ten, hundred and seventy-five, round face, no visible marks, small earlobes, square hands with small fingernails. I took him for an insurance salesman the first time I saw him. He knows all the tricks, he's a pro. Standard American speech pattern, light baritone. He was carrying an S & W nine-millimeter with a Swiss-cheese silencer, hip holster. I took a few snapshots and I think I've got some fingerprints but that takes time and I wondered if the description would ring a bell."

"Not offhand it doesn't, but then with fifty thousand field agents kicking around the world—"

"Look, George, the guy gave me Colonel Cecil's phone number and told me to check him out there. He didn't say whose number it was and I guess he was waiting to see if I knew. I didn't call Cecil for obvious reasons. All I want to know at this point is whether I should lay off this guy or not."

"What's your phone number there?"

Spode read it off to him.

"Pay phone?"

"Sure."

"Okay, stay put, I'll call you back."

Spode hung up and stood in the airless booth with the door slightly open so that the dome light in the ceiling was off. A plump girl got off a bar stool and came over to buy cigarettes from the machine; she gave him a speculative look and Spode grinned at her but shook his head. The girl shrugged and went back to the bar.

Something was needling Spode's mental corners. He scowled and tried to focus on it but it was elusive. He still didn't have it when the phone rang.

"Jaime?"

"Still here."

"Look, where'd you run into this guy?"

So it was like that. Spode stiffened and pulled the booth door shut. "Who is he, George?" His voice had an edge now.

"I don't think we want to talk about that on an open line, Jaime."

"Then we don't want to talk about where I saw him either, do we?" Spode was horse-trading. Evidently George had run the verbal description through the massive computerized R & I and a card had popped up.

"Look, Jaime, this is kind of touchy because you're not an employee any more. But we all know you're no security risk so I'm going to play this a bit looser than the regulations call for. I want you to deliver those fingerprints and negatives to Art Miller right now. Can do?"

"Maybe. There'll be a price tag."

"I thought there would but that's okay. This may turn out to be big enough for all of us."

"Does Miller have a safe line?"

"Yes."

"Then you phone him and tell him to cooperate with me. Will you do that?"

"Of course. He'll tell you what you want to know. But you're going to have to play this one strictly by our rules, Jaime. As far as this one goes you're back on our team again."

"Up to a point. I still work for the Senator."

"We'll talk about that later. I'll call you at Art's. How long will it take you to get there?"

"Fifteen minutes."

"I'll talk to you. Get going and make sure you're alone."

Spode hung up and went out to the car. Drove out through the alley and made the right turn on Speedway and spent five minutes going through the standard maneuvers to disclose a tail. When he was satisfied he cut south across the city toward Broadway. Street lights made pale pools along the empty streets and at the Broadway corner a traffic light blinked red, on and off. Spode's nostrils dilated; he was keyed up now, sensing the scope of things.

For three minutes he sat in the darkened car a block from Miller's house and looked out the long empty street toward the desert. Nothing showed up, in front or in the mirror, and when he was sure he got out of the car carrying the camera and Kemp's gun.

The lights were on and the drapes were drawn. Miller

opened the door, looked past him in all directions and let him in. Miller was bald and slow-moving, but his big round gut was hard as a truck tire. He was only thirty-three or so. He edited a little regional monthly magazine; that was his cover. His editorial office was in the house and that made it handy. He had been divorced five years ago and lived alone. Spode hadn't seen him in several years but they didn't take time to cover the amenities; Spode put the camera and the gun on Miller's desk and said, "Okay, so who is he?"

"We'll have to make sure. George said you had prints too. On the gun?"

"Maybe, but they'd be mixed with mine. This'll do better." Spode dumped the broken piece of shower-stall glass out of his handkerchief onto the desk.

Miller picked up the camera and handled the glass carefully by its edges. "Let me set these up back in the darkroom—I've got a dusting-kit back there too. You want to wait or you want to come with me?"

"Hell, I want to talk. I'm coming with you."

Miller took him through to the back of the house into a small windowless room that smelled of photographic chemicals. "What film you got in here?"

"Tri-X. Most of it's documents and I'll thank you not to read them—it's for my boss. The mug shots will be the last five toward the end. I didn't use up the whole roll."

"Okay. I've got to turn off the light to transfer it into the tank. Stay put so I don't go crashing into you."

The room went dark and Spode stood still. "You still didn't say who he is."

"We're not sure, of course. But it could be Leon Belsky."

Spode blinked in the darkness. His lips went dry and he licked them. His whisper was hoarse: "Sweet Jesus."

When the film was in the lightproof development canister Miller switched the light on and dusted the glass shard with powder. "Too bad it's mottled glass. It may not come up as clear." But it was coming up; Spode could see the whorls and ridges held by skin oil when Miller blew the excess dust away. "But these don't look half-bad." Miller placed it carefully upside-down on the glass carrier of his Xerox machine and ran off three paper prints of it until he had a clear one. "A lot faster than photography," he explained. "Now we'll shoot this off to Virginia."

They went across the hall into the office. It was a maddening clutter of papers and glossy color photos and scattered books. The telephone had a document transmitter attached to it. Miller dialed and got through to Extension Three. "George? Art Miller. Jaime's here and I've got a Xerox of some fingerprints. I'm going to put them on the phone. You hooked up? . . . Okay, here goes."

Miller put the telephone receiver down on the transmitter cradle and fed the Xerox sheet into the machine. It would take the scanner a few minutes to cover the whole sheet. Miller said to Spode, "Anything else, Jaime?"

"I got the license number of his car of course, but it was a new Ford and he probably got it from Hertz. He's going under the cover of Meldon R. Kemp. NARS researcher ID card with FBI colors. Various gun permits and the like from Fresno. I can write it all down if you want but I doubt it'll lead us to anything."

"How much did you give him?"

"Nothing much. But he'll have to act on the hypothesis that I'm U.S. Government and that I'll find out who he is."

"So he's probably clearing out right now. It's a shame, but there you are. How'd you come up against him?"

"I think I'd better talk to George about that first."

"Okay," Miller said without rancor. The transmitter was finished and Miller picked up the telephone. "Got it, George? . . . Okay, I've got high-speed chemicals in the darkroom and we'll probably have mug proofs for you by the time you've run those prints through the file. I'll call you back. But meantime Jaime wants to talk to you."

Miller handed him the phone and Spode said, "If it's Belsky then we've got a strange situation here, George, because I ran into him in Congressman Ross Trumble's house."

He had made the decision in the car driving over here. If the Agency was going to be involved in this at all they were going to have to know the whole truth, or at least as much of it as Spode knew himself. There was no point manufacturing expedient half-truths because they would only backfire. The Agency wasn't interested in Senator Forrester's need for the Phaeton figures; there was no reason for any of this to affect Forrester's activities. How much Spode would tell Forrester would depend on whether he came up with information of use to Forrester's case. It was possible this had nothing to do with Forrester and in that event Spode didn't intend to mention it at all.

So he gave George the whole thing on the telephone and Art Miller was standing across the hall in the darkroom, within earshot, taking it in.

George asked, "What did he seem to be looking for?"

"I don't know. Maybe he was looking for Trumble."

"In a dark house? With a flashlight and a gun?"

"I don't know anything I didn't tell you, George. I'm not holding anything back."

"Then let's mull it for twenty minutes and get back to each other when these paper returns are in."

Spode cradled the phone and sat down in Miller's office chair and tried to pull the threads together.

He went out to the living room to get on the extension so they could have a three-cornered conference. The photos and fingerprints had turned up positive: it was Leon Belsky, no mistake. It wasn't the first time Belsky had been in the States but it was the first time they'd spotted him here; the other times he'd stayed ahead and they hadn't caught up with him until he'd returned to his favorite East European haunts—Prague, Bucharest, Odessa. Belsky was a Control, not a field agent. Wherever he went there was something important.

Spode said, "Look at it. He circles the house, maybe he's been driving by for hours waiting for Trumble to show up. He sees there's nobody home. Finally he lets himself in—I assumed he had keys but maybe he's a good lock man. He had to unlock the alarm system as well as the door. Anyhow he

gets in. Assume he's waiting to jump Trumble. He figures
nobody's home, but he's a pro and he's supposedly got his
mind in working order, so naturally he goes through the
house to make sure it's secure before he settles down to wait
for Trumble to show up. He's not really expecting to find
anybody, so he's a shade less alert than he might be otherwise,
and I manage to get the jump on him. Now we have a little
tête-à-tête and I leave. Possibly he's gone back there to wait
for Trumble, but I doubt it—he's got to assume I've reported
him, so right about now he's probably going across the border
into Mexico. But we know one thing. He wasn't there looking
for the same thing I was looking for. I was after documents.
Belsky was after something man-size. We have to assume
Trumble. Anyway whatever Belsky was up to, you'll probably
have to find out at Trumble's end."

George's voice said, "Don't be so quick to assume he'll pull
in his horns and run for it. He hasn't finished whatever he
came here for. Moscow had something important in mind or
they wouldn't have picked a heavyweight in his class. He
knows we've spotted him but he's got a lot of room to hide
in. He knows we haven't got the slightest idea where to start
looking for him. We have to go on the assumption that he
hasn't completed his assignment yet and that he'll try to go
through with it; he's taken risks before, he's not easy to scare
off. So there's still a chance we can flush him."

Spode knew what was coming. "I don't work for you guys
any more, George."

"Cut that out. This is big and you know it."

"Nobody's paying me to stick my neck out. I'm on the
Senator's payroll, not yours. He's got things he wants me to
do—I can't just cop out on him."

"Lose a little sleep—work two shifts."

"I've got a girl waiting on my front porch right now wondering where the hell I am. If I don't get home soon it's going
to be a cold night."

There was a stretch without talk and he heard Art Miller
breathing. George said, "You mind hanging up, Art?"

"Not at all. Talk to you later." There was a click and shortly afterward Spode heard the darkroom door latch shut.

Spode talked quickly, trying to forestall the grey-faced Virginian at the other end of the line. "I'm going home, George. It's not my war any more."

"It never was, was it."

"What's that supposed to mean?"

"Jaime, you never got a commission in the Army and you never worked your way above the subaltern level in the Agency."

"So I ain't got a whole lot of ambition. So what?"

"You don't need ambition, Jaime. You just need to get yourself together. You want to figure out where your loyalties are. You've never wanted responsibilities and you've never wanted to take initiative. You always had to have somebody hand out the assignments—tell you what to do."

"Okay, there's chiefs and Innuns. Everybody can't be a chief."

"You could. Any time you decided to get off the fence."

"George, I haven't got time for a fifty-dollar-an-hour consultation."

"This is for free. Belsky's dropped a responsibility in your lap and you've got to decide whether or not you're going to accept it. And you've got to think about something bigger than yourself when you weigh it out."

"Oh Jesus. Now you're waving the fucking flag at me."

"You're the only one who can get to him."

"I didn't ask for it."

"Jaime, you didn't ask to be born."

"The answer's still no. It ain't my job."

"Then think about this. Belsky knows your face. He's got some connection with Ross Trumble and you're also involved in something that Trumble's involved in—the Phaeton project. It's not unlikely you'll cross Belsky's path again. But in the meantime he's not going to ignore the meeting you had. He won't be able to let it alone, he'll pick at it until he finds out what you were doing at the house and who you are and who you work for. He'll find out you're on Senator Forrester's staff and he'll decide there's a chance you didn't report the meeting to anybody else. You see what that could lead to? He'll want to cover his tracks and he may decide he can do it by silencing you."

"I've been shot at before."

"What about Senator Forrester? You want him shot at too?"

"You bastard," Spode said wearily.

"Belsky will look for you, Jaime. It's not my fault, it's just a fact. He's going to look for you anyway so you may as well let him find you, because that's the best way for us to find him."

Spode sagged into the chair with the phone against his ear. "All right, George. Let's have all of it."

"We'll put people on Trumble to try to find out what connection he's got with Belsky. I'll keep you up to date. We'll put some men on Forrester to cover him. Is there any intermediary you usually report to on the staff or do you work direct with Forrester?"

"I work with him. Sometimes Lester Suffield's in on it—the Senator's aide."

"All right. We'll do the legwork. Maybe Belsky's registered somewhere under the Meldon Kemp name—we'll cover that. I'll have Art put one or two people on you so you won't have to feel too exposed."

"Tell them not to get in my way. I hate tripping over eager beavers."

"I wouldn't use second-string people on this, Jaime. You know better than that."

"Just keep them out of my hair," Spode said with a good deal of force. "Tell them to stay out of my goddamn bathroom. I don't like being spied on when I crap."

"Look, we've been over all that before and I've apologized to you before. It was a mixup with the FBI, some crank anonymous accusation, and it shouldn't have happened."

"You're damn right it shouldn't." Somebody had written a letter saying he was a fag and all the departments from FBI to the Agency were paranoid on that subject. Spode tightened his dark face into a savage grin. "Suppose I *was* a faggot, George?"

"Shut up and get to work."

"Yeah." He hung up and glanced at Belsky's automatic pistol on the table and called back through the house. When Art Miller appeared Spode said, "I'll see you. You may as well hang on to that iron. Might find out who it was registered to."

"You back on the team, Jaime?"

"Let's just say I'm free-lancing on a one-shot contract. The day I sign onto you guys' payroll again is the day you better have me inspected for rabies." He turned to the door. "You know my phone number," he said morosely by way of parting, and went.

☆☆☆☆☆☆☆☆☆☆☆☆☆☆☆☆☆☆☆☆☆☆☆☆☆☆☆☆☆☆☆☆☆☆☆☆☆☆

Chapter Ten

Friday in Moscow the snow was falling as if dumped out of shovels and scattered by big-bladed fans. The Chaika moved along the Official Cars Only lanes with its wipers thumping, snow building into little cakes in the lower corners of the windshield. Inside the car Rykov felt overheated, partly because of his overcoat and partly because of the big meal he had put under his belt at the Aragvi.

He had stuffed himself to the belching point with *canakhi* and *shashlik* and Georgian tea and watched Yashin pick at his *chakhokhbili;* the sword dancer had whirled by, fast pirouettes with the sword pointed at his own body, and the music had been high and frantic, and through it all Yashin had maintained his ascetic detachment and infuriated Rykov. Men without passions were abominations.

At the height of the featured dance Yashin had removed his rimless glasses to polish them. "My dear Viktor, surely you know the old Japanese proverb, 'You can see another's arse but not your own.' " The wintry glance, never quite a smile. "What you propose is a Carthaginian peace. Annihilation of peoples. Really I think you need a rest."

"Comrade First Secretary, the news from China—"

"I have seen all your evidences and I am not impressed. Xenophobia is the root of the Chinese character, but there's no reason for us to have it—it is not a communicable disease. Viktor, you suffer from messianic fantasies, you wish to think of yourself as the supreme player in an immense global chess game, you are obsessed by the notion that if power is disused it may atrophy and therefore it must be exercised—and since we are not at war with anyone at the moment we must *go* to war with someone."

But the dark winter of Asia was ending; the Chinese war machine stirred with rumbling vibration; there were no responsible leaders to halt it: China was a country which boasted of its ancient civilization yet remained politically adolescent, full of immature ambitions to achieve rule over all of Asia. Yashin had rested his case on the supremacy of the Soviet retaliatory plan and that was that. In the Kremlin they made a Plan and the Plan was all, the Plan was always right and invincible, only people could be mistaken, and if people made mistakes they were punished. Yashin's plan was the wrong plan and when it proved wrong Yashin would be punished—but that was no satisfaction: that would be too late.

Well, then, I too have a plan.

The Chaika crawled past the Moskva Hotel. Rykov sat drawn into himself with his fist locked over the clubbed handle of his walking stick. His scowl was filled with *weltschmerz.* They were never going to get a full and clear-cut revelation of precise plans from the Chinese, a people whose politics had been steeped in secrecy and intrigue and prestidigitatious misdirection for thousands of years.

Rykov was chief of KGB for the excellent reason that he had not only a brilliant mind but also the peculiar intuitive genius it took to bridge the rational gap between two separate clues that could appear to have no logical connection. And he was getting his clues every day from his mother-daughter team in Peking. In Beria's day one word from the KGB would have been enough to galvanize the Soviet Far Eastern forces into intensive war preparations. But today there was no one with initiative enough to commit the nation to an attitude of preemptive self-defense. The ruling troika contained three men none of whom dared move before the others, and as a result there was no capability for instant reaction or decisive policy-making. They blundered into situations and they lacked a clear and single will.

He had thrashed it out with them singly and by twos and in group, and it was always the same. They were afraid of one another. They were afraid of making a mistake. They were above all afraid of the United States: "If we attack China the United States will come into it against us, on China's side. We can't afford that." Over and over again. In the first place it was a dubious supposition: Washington, forewarned but not given enough time to react, might stay out of it altogether. But assuming it was true (and it probably was): there was still a way to forestall it.

Last night he had asked Kazakov, "Suppose I could guarantee that in the event of a war between China and the USSR the United States will come in as our ally. Regardless of who started the war. In that event what would you say?"

But Kazakov like the others had berated him for his primitive militarism: "You are living in the past, Viktor. Can you not comprehend the devastation of a nuclear exchange? Wars must be confined to limited conventional scope and total war must be avoided at whatever cost."

"Suppose the United States were to initiate a preemptive nuclear strike against China. What then?"

"You talk impossibilities, Viktor."

At ten minutes to three the Chaika reached the big gray building and Rykov walked across the curb and entered his kingdom with a dusting of snow on his hat and shoulders. It matted itself and melted slowly as he limped along the corridor taking the uneasy salutes of subordinates. A major wearing stars on his red epaulets stopped him in the hall to talk about the reemergence of the *samizdat* magazine *Novy Mir* and Rykov brushed him aside. The *samizdat* publications were vile and seditious and it was KGB's job to suppress them but in recent years it had become like trying to stamp out armies of ants with a boot heel. *Samizdat,* the underground press, mimeographed and circulated surreptitiously from hand to hand, denigrated the nation and the Party. Some of them had Western assistance. They promulgated the kind of dissidence that had weakened the Russian will and threatened to crumble Russia's inner strengths. Some of the writers whose work appeared anonymously in *samizdat* were clever young intellectuals whom the state had feted as cultural heroes—ingrates, traitors, dupes. Rykov was catching up with them one by one but the flood seemed endless. The big Minsk-32 computers analyzed *samizdat* texts for frequency-of-words and rhythm-of-style to pinpoint the identity of the anonymous authors and in time Rykov always ran them down, but the monster had infinite heads; it was impossible to decapitate it.

It was a grave issue but today he had no time for it—he left the major standing flatfooted in the corridor and limped on toward the lifts. In the bullpens paper tapes writhed on the floors, spilled by automatic typing recorders and decoders. The lift took him up to his own floor; it was quiet here. He went into the great office, hung up his things, sat down at his desk and punched Andrei's intercom line. "Has the Marshal arrived yet?"

"No. He's due in five minutes."

"Bring him straight in." Rykov switched the machine off and closed his eyes, the better to concentrate his thoughts.

Marshal Grigorenko's flat beefy face was closed up tight: he distrusted Rykov always.

Andrei ushered Grigorenko into the office and Rykov, as he got up to greet the Marshal, motioned to Andrei to stay.

He got right down to it. "Even at the top of one's profession there are always men who can destroy you and subordinates who can plot intrigues against you. We're none of us beyond accountability."

"Just so," Grigorenko said.

Rykov said, "You have your own agents in the Chinese People's Army. What do they tell you?"

"Is KGB now begging the help of GRU?"

"If your information is the same as mine then we must act, Oleg. You must see that."

"Act how? It isn't our place to make policy."

"Please don't avoid the question. Is your information as alarming as mine?"

"I haven't seen yours, Comrade."

"You've seen what I've presented to Kazakov and Yashin and Tsvetnoy and Strygin. Chug Po and Lo Kai-teh are already fighting between themselves to decide which of them will become chief of state for the new Chinese republic of Mongolia. Fei Yung-tse has already staked out eastern Siberia for himself. The Chinese Cabinet ministers are dividing up the spoils before a shot has been fired; surely you can't believe they're only playing hypothetical war games as Comrade Strygin insists? Yuan Tung actually sought to employ one of my own agents to obtain the latest defense charts of Vladivostock —you've seen that report. The Seventeenth Chinese Army has been moving into underground shelters a battalion at a time at Hulun. Practice exercises? Strygin is blind because he wants not to see—but you and I can't afford that luxury. Oleg, it is you and I who will be purged when the war is over and the troika seeks scapegoats to punish."

"Go on."

At least he had the big oaf's attention. "In the mountains east of Ulan Bator six of China's most senior and experienced missile scientists have surfaced with full-scale staffs. Rail shipments into all those forward offensive-missile-site areas have quadrupled in the past week. They've moved two hundred long-range heavy bombers into the Lop Nor area. General Chi Thian has stockpiled enough food and matériel in underground lead-lined bunkers to keep his army fed and equipped in their bomb shelters for two months without resupply. You've seen it all."

"And what is it you want of me?"

"There's going to be a war. Is GRU ready for it?"

Grigorenko sat with hands on knees, the weight of his belly sagging against his thighs. "You can be sure we are ready. Three-quarters of a million men, seventy Warsaw Pact divisions deployed along the border."

"And three million Chinese facing them."

"We have ten missiles for their one."

"Russia has been defeated by the Tartar hordes of Genghiz Khan, the Swedes, the Poles, the Japanese—beaten by everyone, because we've always been too slow to react, always been too backward."

"Comrade, they haven't made a single move toward breaking off diplomatic relations. They're only shaking a fist at us, hoping we'll back away from the contested frontier areas rather than risk war. If they seriously intended to bomb us, surely they wouldn't be so obvious about it."

It was the troika line, straight out of Agitprop and *Pravda* and *Izvestia*. They were all desperately anxious to believe it was only a Chinese bluff. If you wanted badly enough to believe a thing, you did believe it.

Rykov said, "But let's assume that they are in fact ready to attack us. Assume further that they do attack. Take an arbitrary date—Sunday the seventh of April. Two days from today. GRU carries a heavy responsibility for defense. Are you ready for that?"

The Marshal rubbed his chin. "You're talking foolishness," he said disagreeably.

"It's only a hypothetical question. Answer it."

"You know full well our nuclear bases are ready at all times to retaliate instantly."

"Yes. To rain nuclear missiles on China's major cities and missile bases—but suppose China's missiles have already been fired and the central Maoist elite has fled the cities and is holed up in bombproof shelters under the mountains of Lushan in central China. So our retaliation does nothing more than kill off a few hundred million of the little yellow bastards, which does no great injury since they're over-populated anyhow. And when both sides have exhausted their nuclear arsenals the Chinese ultimate weapon comes into play —the individual footsoldier. Chinese tanks roll into Mongolia and Siberia. Chinese troops invade Soviet territory and over-run our bases. They have three times our manpower—ten times our manpower if we restrict the discussion to our forces in the Far East. Now I'm asking you, are we prepared for *that?*"

"You're saying footsoldiers will be able to fight effectively over territory that has been devastated by nuclear weapons."

"Not necessarily. The missiles of both sides are aimed primarily at cities and military concentrations."

"You forget fallout."

"One has to assume that life goes on. You're evading me, Comrade Marshal. Why?"

"Because I think your hypothesis is untenable."

"Just for one moment assume it isn't. Then what is your answer?"

"You're trying to goad me into admitting we're in an unsatisfactory state of war preparation. It isn't true. Our troops are better equipped than theirs, better trained, better led."

"That's not the issue. The issue is their level of alertness. The speed with which they can be mobilized. In the event the Chinese launch a full-scale invasion forty-eight hours from now, will our forces be able to respond swiftly enough to stop the Chinese in their tracks and fling them back into China? That's the only question I'm asking you, and it's the only question you haven't answered."

"I can only answer it by saying that if war comes, it won't come in the way you postulate."

"In other words our troops are prepared to counteract any small-scale exploratory probes the Chinese may send into the disputed territories, but if it came to an all-out invasion we would not be ready to repel it."

"That's not what I mean either."

"Then say what you mean."

Grigorenko leaned forward. "You're trying to trap me. If China rains nuclear missiles on us they will not follow it up by invading Soviet territory with ground troops. They will wait for us to invade them, because that's the way they have always fought. China swallows all its invaders. China has never invaded alien territory."

"I submit Tibet."

"A triviality, and beside the point. My information confirms that in the unlikely event of wholesale war between our countries the Chinese will simply wait to ensnare us in their net. On their own home ground they can defeat us. On our ground they can't. They know that. They won't invade. Now on those terms I can answer your question: yes, we are prepared for it. We are prepared for the Chinese to invite us to penetrate their frontiers with mass armies. Our preparation is in the nature of rejecting the Chinese invitation. If war comes we will not make the mistake of marching our armies into China's rural countryside. We will not allow them to draw us into their brand of fighting where every Chinese farmer becomes a guerrilla resistance soldier. We will spearhead directly into their centers of industrial production and military communications. We will destroy their productivity and smash their industry and then we will withdraw to our own borders and wait for them to sign a peace."

Rykov murmured, "And what if they roll into Mongolia and Siberia in spite of your projections to the contrary?"

"They won't."

"I only suggest you prepare contingency plans to deal with the situation."

"You know perfectly well such contingency plans have been drawn up for years and periodically updated."

"Then let me suggest you dust them off and supply your field commanders with copies of them. What harm can it do to be prepared?"

Grigorenko was studying him with renewed care. Perhaps Rykov knew something Rykov wasn't telling him.

Rykov added, "Recall the proverb. 'The road to Siberia is

wide; the way back is narrow.' The penalty for unprepared-
ness can be severe."

Marshal Grigorenko left, walking heavily on his heels. Andrei
escorted him out and returned, shutting the door. "He's got
something to think about."

"The question is, will he act? And will he act in time?"

Andrei stood in front of the desk with his hands clasped
behind him. His round bookish face was tipped to one side in
the pose that meant he had something to say.

Rykov sat back. "Let us hear what's on your mind."

"Only this. What if they are right and we are wrong? They
have seen all the evidence we've seen. They've reached a
different conclusion."

Rykov regarded him thoughtfully, lips pushing out, eyes
squinting. "They're frightened. They believe what is most
comfortable to believe. They're products of the assembly line
of government we have here in which every functionary has
a limited area of responsibility and therefore feels immunized
from overall accountability. They have no policy but to remain in power. They are riding a bicycle—they don't seem to
realize that when it stops rolling along it falls down. They
seem to think as long as things can be kept the same, nothing
bad can happen to them."

"Yet it is still possible they are correct in this instance. The
facts are open to more than one interpretation. It's possible
the Chinese are getting ready to attack us. But it's also possible they're only trying to frighten us into making border
concessions."

"No. That's what they want us to think."

"I am not sure of that, Viktor Ilyich."

"When has my intuition been wrong?"

"Never," Andrei conceded, and added, "up to now."

"I regret deeply your lack of confidence in me."

"I only wish I could be as certain as you are. Probably it is
my weakness." Andrei came forward and put his hands on the
front of the desk. His face hovered close to Rykov's. "I think
I know your plans."

"Then perhaps you'd better tell me what you think they are."

"I think you're going to order the Amergrad group to launch American missiles on Chinese targets."

"Go on, then," Rykov breathed.

"It has to be so. The Chinese will believe they've been attacked by the Americans. Naturally China will retaliate with its own ICBMs against the United States. There won't be time for the Americans to convince the Chinese it was a mistake. The Americans will see the Chinese missiles coming in and of course they'll react—they'll launch their missiles against China in force.

"In the meantime their President will be on the hot-line telephone to us, but Premier Kazakov will know nothing. Whether their President will believe him is open to question, but as long as we do not join in the Chinese attack the Americans will be obliged to concentrate their counterattack on China. Quite certainly Comrades Kazakov and Yashin would not be inclined to join the Chinese in such a conflict; we would either remain neutral or even perhaps join forces with the United States to crush the perfidious yellow enemy for all time. American missiles will destroy China; Chinese missiles will cripple the United States; the blame for the initial attack will rest on the United States; and the Soviet Union will emerge unscathed, untouched by nuclear craters—the single surviving great power."

Andrei's jaw crept forward. "It's a brilliant plan, Viktor."

Rykov was sitting back and his eyes were almost shut. "But."

"But. Yes. I have reservations."

Rykov's heavy lips parted. "You have a superb mind, Andrei."

"Then I am correct in my conclusions?"

Rykov's answer was some time in coming. But finally he opened his eyes and spoke in his hard Georgian voice. "You are correct."

☆☆☆☆☆☆☆☆☆☆☆☆☆☆☆☆☆☆☆☆☆☆☆☆☆☆☆☆☆☆☆☆

Chapter Eleven

"Spode," Hathaway announced, coming in the side door. "His name's Jaime Spode. He's a Navajo Indian."

Belsky was irritable, maddened by the hours of hiding. He turned his head balefully. "Is he federal?"

"No. He used to be. Nowadays he's on Senator Forrester's staff." Hathaway sat down on the bed. It was the spare room in Ramsey Douglass' little house on Water Street. Hathaway's uniform was starched and the iron had pinched a hard crease into the sergeant's chevrons on his sleeves.

Belsky said, "It could be a cover."

"I doubt it. He appears to be independent as a hog on ice."

"Spode?"

"Yes."

"He struck me as a professional."

"Sure. He dates back to military counterintelligence—Korean war. He cracked a few North Korean POWs, I hear. Forrester was his CO out there; they're old buddies." Hathaway looked at his watch. "Torrio ought to be along with the package pretty quick now."

Belsky grunted. "But Spode may have contacted the federal people."

"Why should he? He didn't know who you were."

"We don't know that."

"If he'd made you, the Trumble place would've been crawling with Federal cops by now."

"Possibly not. They may be being clever."

"If Spode reported back to anybody it was to Forrester. Don't forget you caught him breaking and entering. He wouldn't take his story to the FBI because he'd have to admit that."

"There are agencies other than the FBI."

"The FBI's charged with internal security."

"Was Spode an FBI agent?"

"No. Trumble was."

"I know that," Belsky snapped. "At least we've got sources on Senator Forrester's staff. We can find out how much Spode told Forrester and whether or not it went any further than Forrester."

"Yeah. Maybe we'll have to get both of them, what do you think?"

"I'll let you know." Belsky went to the window and peered out through the curtain. The sun was less than an hour high and the mesquite in the vacant lot threw a long shadow; a big gray bird was hopping along with a lizard in its beak.

Belsky said, "I take it there was no trouble at Torrio's end."

"Worked fine. Torrio and Corrigan kept testing the phone until Trumble got home and answered. About forty-five minutes ago. They told him they'd just taken Ramsey Douglass into St. Joseph's with some kind of attack, and Douglass was on the critical list and wanted to see Trumble right away. It ought to have gotten him out of the house like he had a burr up his ass.

"We couldn't just go in after him because for all we know Spode's got people watching the place. But Torrio was going to wait for him to drive by and then tail him to the hospital and collect him at the hospital parking lot. If it all went on schedule they ought to show up here in a few minutes."

"I'd like to know where he was all night," Belsky said.

"Ask him, then." Hathaway opened the side door and tossed the butt of his cigarette out.

Trumble waddled in full of outraged dignity. Torrio entered behind him with the gun, walking in sideways, looking back, and kicked the door shut. Hathaway was on his feet; Belsky stayed seated by the window.

"What the devil is the meaning of this? Do you people have any idea who I am?" Trumble demanded.

Belsky said to Torrio, "How much did you tell him?"

"Nothing. Just got him and brought him."

Hathaway said, "No trouble?"

"Clockwork. We pulled in right beside him in the hospital lot and showed him the guns and he got in the car."

"Anybody see you?"

"No. Only guy around was a doctor parking his car a good distance away. He didn't pay us no more attention than he'd pay a no-parking sign."

"This is absurd," Trumble said. "Do you people know the penalty for kidnapping?"

"Come off it." Hathaway gave him a pained look.

"Abducting a United States Representative at gunpoint in broad daylight—you people are in grave trouble."

"Yeah," Torrio said, and grinned at him.

Belsky spoke mildly. "Call you Boris Dolinski. Son of Josef Andreivich Dolinski and Natasha Khruscha."

Trumble's mask of authority sagged; he shifted his stance in confusion. Hathaway made a gesture with his head and eyes and Torrio backed out of the room the way he had entered. Trumble stood splayed with his head swinging like a worn-out boxer having trouble trying to locate his opponent in the ring.

"Sit down, please," Belsky said. "The bed will do."

Trumble hesitated. Hathaway made to move forward and Trumble sat down slowly on the edge of the bed.

Belsky said, "You seemed to feel the need to monitor our meetings yesterday. Why?"

"Who gave you that idea?"

"A fellow called Craig if it matters."

"I never heard of him. He must be lying."

Hathaway laughed unpleasantly and lit a cigarette. Belsky acted bored. "We don't want to force you to undergo rehabilitation, Comrade."

"I suppose that's a euphemism for torture?"

"If you like. We don't want to hurt you—it degrades us too." Belsky reached over and lifted the half-glasses off Trumble's nose, dropped them on the rug and crushed them under his heel until the lenses broke. Belsky had once known a prisoner who had crushed the lenses of his glasses and swallowed them to prevent himself from talking.

Trumble said, "I don't suppose you'll allow me to confront this man Craig and demonstrate that he's lying."

"I'm afraid that isn't possible. You'll have to refer to Craig in the past tense."

Trumble laughed—a dry cackle. He sat with his elbows on his knees, face hunched into his hands. Hathaway said, "Look at him. Soft as a number-four pencil. Won't take me no time at all to crack him."

"Perhaps it won't be necessary." Belsky touched Trumble's shoulder. "Your courage does you no credit, Comrade. It comes from ignorance."

Trumble looked straight ahead, not at Belsky.

Hathaway said, "One thing that usually works. You pour boiling water into his ear through a funnel."

No response.

Belsky said, "You wanted a record of the meeting. Why?"

"I couldn't be here myself. I wanted to know, that's all."

"You were going to sell the tape or give it away. The only questions are, to whom and why?"

Ashes dripped off Hathaway's cigarette. Belsky turned to him. "Put a dose of scopolamine in a glass of water for him."

Hathaway nodded and went out the hall door but before it closed Trumble said, "All right—all right." Hathaway came back inside.

Trumble said, "You had two questions. First, to whom was I going to deliver the tape. It's immaterial—I hadn't made up my mind yet. *Time* Magazine, NBC, the FBI, anybody—what difference does it make? I wanted to expose you. Your second question—why. Because I'm an American now and it's just that simple." Trumble's thick head lifted and he squinted myopically; he spread his hands. "Just that simple."

"Of course you realize what you will have brought on your father and your sisters."

"Three inconsequential people. They mean no more to me than a schoolteacher or a girl friend I might have had twenty-five years ago. Anyhow nothing you can do to my family will undo my betrayal now, will it?"

"It will set an example for others," Belsky said.

"I understood that. Of course I didn't expect to get caught before I'd finished."

"Finished exposing us to *Time* Magazine?"

"Something like that."

"Do you expect me to believe this?"

"Suit yourself. I've told you the truth."

"It's quite a neat explanation."

"You just can't comprehend that a man could transfer his loyalty to an adopted country?"

"Oh, I'm sure you've got an honorable cause. They always do."

"But you still think I'm lying."

"Yes."

"That's too bad. I don't know what to tell you."

Belsky made another signal to Hathaway and Hathaway left the room. Trumble said, "Now you'll administer the scopolamine. It won't do any good, you know. I've told you everything. Perhaps you'll get a few details out of me, but since I didn't get a chance to act they won't make any difference."

"We'll see."

"Scopolamine brings on a talking jag, doesn't it?"

"And a bad hangover."

"Was it you who smashed my shower stall? What the hell were you looking for?"

"You. Where were you?"

"Enjoying myself," Trumble said, "for the last time in my life."

A man who knew he was going to be killed regardless of what he said was under no inducement to tell the truth. That was the main reason for Belsky's disbelief—that and the fact that Trumble had trotted out his explanation too readily.

Trumble said, "I've got to go to the bathroom."

"Later."

"You know what fear does to a man's stomach. Do you want this room to stink?"

"Take off your belt and leave it on the bed. Let me see what's in your pockets."

Trumble emptied his pockets onto the bedspread. There was a penknife with which he might have done some damage. Belsky took him across the hall into the bathroom and removed Douglass' safety razor and all the medicines and razorblades from the medicine closet. There were still the tiny glazed window and the bathroom mirror, but he would hear the noise if Trumble tried to smash them.

He left the bathroom door open. Beyond the tub enclosure he could see Trumble's knees and the trousers bunched down around his ankles. He kept an eye on the knees. If Trumble had a cyanide tooth like his own it would be all over, but the possibility was remote; besides, if Trumble had possessed a death pill he could have used it without going to the bathroom.

Trumble grunted now and then with effort: fear could have that effect on the bowels, as he'd said.

Hathaway returned with the drug in a glass and set it on the bedside table and joined Belsky by the door. "He's stalling."

"Of course. But the longer he evades it the more time the fear has to work on him."

The knees sagged outward like the splayed legs of a seated drunk. Hathaway made a face. "Hurry it up."

"I'm coming." Trumble's voice was high-pitched, tremulous.

Torrio came into the bedroom by the outside door. "Douglass."

Hathaway's face snapped from Torrio to Belsky. "Want me to keep him out?"

"No, I've got to talk to him. Let him in."

"I guess," Torrio said. "It's his house."

Hathaway said, "Get back on guard."

"Take it easy, Sarge, Corrigan's out there." Torrio backed out and shut the door.

Belsky heard Trumble grunt in the lavatory. The front door sounded and footsteps came through the house—Ramsey Douglass in a sweat-damp shirt. "What's all this?"

"Never mind," Belsky said. "I've got a chore for you."

"Christ, I was about to turn on the air-conditioner and have a cold drink."

"Some other time. There's an Indian named Spode who works for Senator Forrester. Do you know him?"

"I know who he is. He's expected at the base this morning with the Senator's inspection party."

"I had an encounter with Spode last night. It's imperative that we find out whether he identified me."

"I'll see what I can do."

"Another thing. Our job will be hard enough without having to deal with meddling outsiders on the Air Force Base. See if you can find a way to discourage the Senator from hanging around the place."

"What do you suggest I do, take a potshot at him?"

"Your sarcasm can be annoying, Comrade. You'll think of something, I'm sure. We don't want him in our hair."

"Anything else?" That too was sarcastic. "You realize I'm only Matthewson-Ward's SATAF man, I'm not a Government employee. I haven't got the run of Davis Monthan."

"Your people have. Do I have to tell you how to delegate authority? Do you want a blueprint?"

"Now who's sarcastic?"

In the bathroom one of Trumble's feet stirred and just then the radio in the bedroom made a noise. Belsky wheeled to the writing desk and switched on the recorder, pressed the record button and started the high-speed tape. The incoming message was pitched above audible range but after the tape ran out in forty seconds he rewound it and set the playback speed at 1⅞ IPS and hooked the output connectors into the radio's small speaker. He stood over the notebook with a pencil and flicked the fast-forward dial until he reached the point on the tape where the message had been recorded, reversed to the beginning of the signal and wrote down the dots and dashes as they clicked out of the speaker. Then he erased the tape and straightened to face the others. "Are you still here?"

Douglass said, "I wasn't sure you were through with me."

"You've got things to do. Do them."

"Isn't there a chance the Federal types will pick up that signal? It's on the normal radio frequencies."

"It's gibberish to them and besides they don't know who's receiving it. Stop asking questions—go."

Douglass gave his uneven smile and went. Belsky heard the front door slam and Hathaway swung to yell into the bathroom. "Time's up. For Christ's sake you've had time to lay a ton of bricks."

Trumble's knees didn't stir. Hathaway stiffened . . . and Belsky went past him into the bathroom and found Trumble slumped back against the toilet tank with both arms down in the bowl between his legs. The bowl was crimson with blood.

Hathaway said over his shoulder, "The bastard chewed through the arteries in both his wrists. He's bled himself to death."

"You and Torrio get rid of him. Spread some blood on the broken glass in the shower stall in Trumble's house. Leave the body there—make it look like suicide."

"Which it was."

"Suicide because he didn't want to talk. He knew something that we don't know."

Hathaway's scowl lifted. "Maybe he's already blown the whistle on us. You think you better shift your base of operations again? I know a place."

"All right. As soon as you've finished with this. Now move."

When Hathaway went outside to get the others Belsky went back into the bathroom and stood above the bloated corpse and tried to think it out. But Trumble kept getting in the way of his thinking. It had been a long time since anyone had got the better of him. His strength had always been his attention to detail, his resourcefulness in covering all possibilities. Trumble had upset everything. *A gutsy son of a bitch:* yes. He'd had to bite great chunks out of his own wrists to make the blood pour out fast. But he'd died knowing something, hiding something, and Belsky had to know what it was.

In the absence of certainty he had to assume Trumble had made preparations to expose the Amergrad network—in the event of his death or disappearance. All he had to do was to call a contact daily with the understanding that if he ever didn't call, the contact should deliver information into certain hands. That would explain why there hadn't been any sign up to now that the network's cover had been broken. If vibrations had already reached Washington Belsky would have been informed: Rykov had ample sources in Washington. So the cover was still intact, as of *this moment,* but if Belsky's reasoning was correct it was only a matter of hours, or at most a few days if Trumble's system had depended on postal delivery of information.

Under scopolamine Trumble might have disclosed his arrangements and Belsky might have reached the contact before the contact had time to release the information. So knowing he was to die anyway, Trumble had killed himself to safeguard the information.

It might not be the truth but the probability was good. On the other hand it might be a massive and ultimate bluff—just a desperate attempt to persuade Belsky the network's cover was about to be blown, so that Belsky would abort and withdraw.

Belsky left the bathroom and sat down on the bed to decode the signal from Moscow. While he was working he heard

Torrio and Corrigan grunting with the effort of removing the
fat corpse from the bathroom. Hathaway waited in respectful
silence with his big shoulders filling the bedroom doorway,
keeping his distance while Belsky worked his ciphers. The
message took shape and Belsky's face contracted.

PRIORITY UTMOST

DANGERFIELD TUC

VIA NUCSUB 4

KGB 1

CIPHER 1541 SG

SENT 1308 GMT D ACKNOWLEDGE

MESSAGE BEGINS X EXECUTE PLAN B3 DATE 7 APR IGNITION
TIME 1830 X REPEAT X EXECUTE PLAN B3 DATE 7 APR IGNI-
TION TIME 1830 X VR X MESSAGE ENDS 17652 42 5474

About fifty-five hours from now, Sunday at 6:30 P.M., Belsky
had to fire the missiles.

By the time Belsky taped a quick acknowledgment and
broadcast it, Hathaway's men had driven their car around into
the alley behind the house and wrapped the corpse in a plastic
cover and stowed it in the trunk compartment of the car.
Belsky stood in the back door of the house and said, "Do it
fast and get back here."

"Something up?"

"Everything's up. Where's the nearest public phone?"

"Booth by that gas station on Elm just the other side of
North Park. Three, four blocks." Hathaway pointed west-
southwest.

In the bedroom Belsky tested the radio batteries and
packed the apparatus into its compact case. Folded up and
closed, it looked like a large but ordinary portable transistor
radio. Essentially that was what it was, with the addition of the
miniature recorder and the shortwave transmitter. At one
corner of the case was the socket which enclosed the telescop-
ing aerial and at the other corner was a small red globe which
would wink with a bright rapid flash when an incoming signal
activated the receiver to self-start automatically and record
the signal on high-speed tape. The Japanese toy's low output
signals had to be relayed and amplified by intermediate sta-

tions but nevertheless it took hardly twenty minutes for a message to travel the distance between Belsky and Rykov.

He drove down to the filling station and filled the tank of his rented car, took his change in dimes and carried the transceiver into the curbside booth and set it on the seat by his elbow where he would see the red flasher if it began to blink: from now on, he'd have to watch the radio at all times; if a countermand came he had to be prepared to abort the mission he was now starting.

His first call was to Lieutenant Colonel Fred Winslow at Davis Monthan; it took five minutes for the switchboard to find him for "Colonel Dangerfield" and when he came on the line Belsky barked at him: "Henceforth leave word where you can be reached. They've been tracking you down for five minutes. What if this had been a no-notice ORI?"

"I'm sorry, sir. I did leave word but it must have got tangled up."

Belsky had to talk like an Air Force colonel: there was no reason not to assume there were other ears on the line besides his own and Winslow's. The enlisted people on the switchboards wouldn't know there was no Colonel Dangerfield in the chain of command but they would recognize it instantly if Dangerfield didn't sound right.

He said, "I understand the Wing Commander will be absent from the base for the next seventy-two hours and that means you'll have command. You'd better keep on your toes, Fred."

It was meant to sound like a tip-off that the brass was planning to spring a no-notice Operational Readiness Inspection. In actuality it was an instruction: Winslow had to get rid of the Wing Commander for seventy-two hours and take over the wing himself. It was up to Winslow to work out the details.

Winslow said, "I, ah, haven't been informed yet as to how soon Colonel Sims will be leaving for the, ah, weekend."

Winslow was unnerved; that was bad.

Belsky said, "Well, I hear he'll be up in Colorado Springs tonight for a conference with General DeGraff at twenty-two hundred. I guess he'd have to leave there by eight o'clock tonight if he's flying up to NORAD."

"Yes, Bud mentioned something about it but it slipped my mind," Winslow lied. He was doing better now, getting the hang of it.

Belsky said, "It's too bad you'll miss the party. It ought to be quite a bash. Half-past six Sunday night. Maybe Colonel Sims will be back by then and you'll be able to come. We'll save some Scotch in case you show up late."

"Yes, I'd hate to miss it, sir. Been a long time since the old gang got together. Christ, do you remember that blowout we had in Darmstadt?" Now Winslow was winging it; the sudden shock had induced a talking jag and Belsky had to cut him off.

"Yeah, that was sure a lulu, Fred. And I wouldn't be surprised to see a few ICBMs go off right in my living room at this one. Some of the boys can really put it away. I hope you'll be able to make it."

"Six-thirty Sunday evening, huh? I'll sure try, Colonel, and thanks for inviting me."

"Won't be the same without you."

"I'll find out when Bud Sims plans to get back here."

"Do that. And don't forget to bring that gorgeous wife of yours, Fred. You know where the place is."

"No. That is, it's been a long time, Colonel. As I recall it's kind of hard to find."

"I'll get a little map of the roads over to you, Fred."

"That'd be mighty kind, sir. I mean I'd feel like a fool if I got all dressed up and didn't know where to go."

"Okay, Fred, I'll shoot it over to you." They were talking about the identity of the targets and those could hardly be given by telephone.

"See you, Colonel. And thanks again."

"Sure enough, Fred." Belsky broke the connection. Now Winslow knew he had to activate the final firing sequence at half-past six Sunday evening.

Belsky plugged another coin into the phone and made the second of the dozen calls he would have to make. He felt nerveless and unhurried. His only concern was tidiness: the operation had to be performed exactly as ordered.

☆☆☆☆☆☆☆☆☆☆☆☆☆☆☆☆☆☆☆☆☆☆☆☆☆☆☆☆☆☆☆☆☆☆

Chapter Twelve

The broadcast studios of KARZ-TV occupied a low cinder-block building on Drachman Street about a mile north of downtown Tucson. Ramsey Douglass felt edgy and irritable when he parked at the curb and walked to the heavy glass doors. The waiting room inside was freezing cold; the air-conditioning had been built for 120-degree summers and nobody had adjusted it for the 85-degree outside temperature of early April.

The skinny man at the reception desk sat with a telephone against one ear and a finger stuck in the other to block out the piped music that flooded the room like an oil spill. An American flag hung limp on a standard in the corner and above it, suspended from the ceiling, an animated color cartoon flickered on the screen of a television monitor, without sound.

Douglass waited for the receptionist's attention; finally the man at the desk hung up the telephone.

"My name is Douglass, to see Miss Lawrence. It's important."

"I'll see if I can locate her." The bow tie bobbed up and down at his throat.

Douglass said, "You could hang meat in here."

"I know. Mr. Burgess likes it cold."

"Look, it's on the urgent side."

"Yeah. You wanted Nicole Lawrence?" The man picked up his telephone and pushed buttons. "Hi, Gene. Nicole back there? . . . Well did she come in yet? . . . Guy out here wants to talk to her, says it's real important. Okay, if she isn't, then she isn't." He hung up and tipped his head back. "She came in a little while ago but she's not here just now. You want to wait?"

"Not particularly. No idea where she went?"

"You might try the coffee shop around the corner on Stone."

Douglass left without thanking him and walked down to the corner. There was a motel coffee shop down the block, the only one in sight; he found Nicole at the counter brooding over a glass of tea full of crushed ice. When she saw him in the mirror she made a face and spoke without turning her head. "One if by land and two if by sea."

"Let's go."

"My if we aren't manly and domineering this morning. I'm busy."

"Come on, we've got things to do."

Nicole sighed and turned her small creased face toward him. Since when has anything had any importance for you before eleven o'clock in the morning? Whence cometh thy serious mien?"

Douglass dropped a quarter on the counter and took her elbow. When he had steered her outside she laughed aloud. "The waitress must have taken that for a lovers' quarrel."

"My car's around the corner," he said and took her up the

walk, still gripping her arm. "We've got a little disciplinary problem and that's supposed to be your department."

"Has Fred Winslow been wetting his bed or what?"

"We'll talk about it in the car." They turned the corner and he went around to the driver's side without opening the curbside door for her. When Nicole got into the Volkswagen she said, "Someday you really should take a few lessons in elementary etiquette."

"I always adjust my manners to the company I'm in." He turned the key and the engine started with a pop and a hum.

"Where are we going?"

"To the courthouse."

She nodded. "I thought we'd get around to that—it's time we straightened her out. You'd have thought she'd have learned her lesson the first time."

"Apparently not."

"And those who do not learn from history," Nicole drawled, "are doomed to repeat it. But this time we could hardly leave him behind a bowling alley with his head crushed in."

He circled the block and made the left turn into Stone Avenue. "Actually it's a little late in the day for her personal entanglements to matter. If it were just that I'd let it ride. But somebody's got to get to Forrester and persuade him to quit meddling at Davis Monthan for a while."

"She doesn't know about the activation yet, does she?"

"No, I tried to reach her but she was at Forrester's ranch and they must have taken the phone off the hook."

They went through the railroad underpass and got caught in the coagulation of morning traffic between Main and Pennington. Nicole said, "I wish to hell this Dangerfield bastard had stayed home."

"So do I. But we can't do anything about it."

"Do you think they'll really go through with it? Or is it just part of some international bluff they're trying to pull off?"

"I have no idea. You're supposed to be the political expert —what do you think?"

"I think we're in a son of a bitch of a mess," she said. She stretched indolently on the seat and adjusted herself with her legs loosely apart. "I guess we asked for it. You can't stand in the middle of the freeway and not expect to get hit by a truck."

He fished out a cigarette. "We'll just have to do the job and get out."

"You make it sound easy."

"They'll have to get us out afterward. It would be too embarrassing for them if we were left behind and discovered and forced to talk."

"I thought of that," she said, "but let's face it, if they want us to start pushing buttons it's got to mean the big war and by the time it's over with I can't seriously believe there'll be much left of Tucson but a big hot hole in the ground."

"No. That's what I thought at first but it doesn't make sense that way. Figure it out. The targets have to be one of two kinds —Western or Communist. If the targets are in the Soviet bloc it could only be for one reason—Moscow wants the United States to start shooting first, so that Moscow has an excuse to 'retaliate.' But I don't buy that because it'd be just too high a price to pay. We've got fifty-four warheads in this complex of silos and even if all of them landed on reasonably uninhabited areas the fallout would wipe out half the population of the Soviet Union. No, I think we eliminate that."

"What about Europe? West Germany?"

"I can't conceive of any reason to bomb Europe, can you? And the prevailing winds are westerly so you'd have the same problem—fallout over Russia. What's left? The third-world countries? Israel? None of them's big enough to justify using nuclear ICBMs."

"You've just about ruled out everything."

"It narrows down to home base. They're going to have to shoot at targets in the United States. NORAD, maybe, the big SAC bases, the Pentagon, that kind of thing. It'll leave the nuclear subs and a good deal of other firepower but it'll damage this country's military strength enough to discourage the United States from shooting at Russia, because the United States would lose. Besides, NORAD will see the missiles coming in, they'll know where they were launched from—they'll know they're not Russian missiles. They'll be confused; they won't know who to hit back at. What can they do? Bombard Tucson with hydrogen warheads?"

"Why not?"

"Once these missiles are fired Tucson's arsenal will be exhausted. Why bomb it then? No, all they can do is pick up the pieces and start an investigation to find out what happened down here. By that time we'll all have to be out of the country —probably in Mexico on our way back to Russia. It's either that or kill all of us and Dangerfield's only one man, he can't wipe out three hundred of us."

"Once they get us all out of the country and in one group they can kill us easily enough."

"But once we're that far they'd have no reason to. As soon as we're beyond the reach of the American authorities we're no longer a threat to Moscow."

"You've got it all worked out, haven't you? But I still don't see it the way you do. I still feel like a punchcard that's been programmed to do a job without knowing why. We're supposed to think it's necessary just because a stranger comes in and says it's necessary."

"It's not a hoax. I checked with Moscow—Dangerfield's legitimate."

"I never thought he wasn't. That's not the point."

They had crawled two blocks in the traffic and a truck in front of them was gnashing its gears; they got stuck at the light.

In a different tone Nicole said, "I'm frightened out of my wits." She turned and reached across the seat and put her hand on his thigh. "Ramsey?"

"Stop it. Christ you've got a one-track mind."

The light changed and he put the car in gear and whipped it brutally out into the left-hand lane, nearly clipping the tailgate of the stalled truck. The car behind him screeched and he heard the angry yelp of its horn. When he was clear of the traffic snarl he floored the accelerator and took the Pennington Avenue turn too fast, clipping the curb and rocking the car violently on its springs. Nicole was laughing unpleasantly and when he pulled into the courthouse parking area he slapped her viciously across the face.

She stopped laughing but her mouth was still twisted with mockery; it turned itself inward now; she was bitter with herself. "Of all the impotent bastards in the world I had to pick you to fall for."

"One of these days I'll ream you out," he said in a weary mutter. "You God damned supercilious bitch."

Her face didn't change but after a while she said, "Look at us. We're both insane, you know we are. We're utterly mad."

"Aagh," he said, disbelieving it, dismissing it.

"We are. You can deny it to me but you can't deny it to yourself, can you? We've been living lies for twenty years, and they've eaten us away like acid. How can we be expected to tell the difference between lies and truth after all that? We're examples of the legal definition of insanity: we simply do not know right from wrong."

"Get a grip on yourself. You can't afford to fall apart now. Do you know what Dangerfield would do if he heard you talking like this?"

"I'm not sure I really care. We've been falling apart for twenty years. But up to now we could hold ourselves together with the hope that they'd never decide to activate us. Now they've removed that and we haven't got a damn thing left."

"You're talking treason," he said, not as if it mattered.

"Of course. Whatever we do it's treason—treason to one side or the other."

"Don't worry about sides for Christ's sake. Worry about your own skin."

"That's all you've ever worried about, isn't it?"

He said, "Don't tell me you're any different."

"I suppose I'm not. I won't martyr myself to save the world. But I don't want to die."

"Then just do what they tell us to do." He got out of the car and slammed the door.

She caught up with him halfway to the courthouse. "We are, you know," she said. "We're both quite mad."

☆☆☆☆☆☆☆☆☆☆☆☆☆☆☆☆☆☆☆☆☆☆☆☆☆☆☆☆☆☆☆☆

Chapter Thirteen

She was sitting at the desk absently sorting the letters that had come in the morning's delivery. A few of them required the Senator's personal attention and those she put in his In box. The rest were letters from citizens, many of them from states other than Arizona, most of them concerning Phaeton Three. She stacked them in pro and con piles; someone in the Washington office would be doing the same thing with the mail there.

It didn't require her concentrated attention; her thoughts were adrift, stirring with drowsy eroticism. Even when she was not with him now she was thinking of him. He had become all too important to her and it was no good; she didn't belong to herself. For his sake she had to break it off. For the past hour she had tried to put up reasons she could give him for

241

ending it but her mind kept twisting them and she kept finding reasons why she should not break it off.

When other men had approached her she had sized them up coolly and only dated them when she felt sure they had nothing permanent in mind; the others she had chilled quickly and effectively. But now she didn't know what to do.

She didn't want to work, to speak with anyone else. She didn't want to do anything except be with him, to watch him wash and shave and dress and eat—and to sleep with him. She had caught herself thinking: *He is my world and I want to be his.* Her breasts ached; she felt light-headed; she looked at the clock and then she closed her eyes and said very softly and without great conviction, "No."

When Douglass and Nicole came into the office she was startled but she knew immediately why they had come before either of them spoke a word.

Douglass said, "Are you alone here?"

"Yes."

"Where is everybody?"

"I don't know where Les Suffield is. The Senator and Jaime Spode went out to the base a little while ago."

"We want to talk to you about that," Nicole said.

"Yes. About Senator Forrester," Ronnie said.

"About his inspection tour of Davis Monthan," Ramsey Douglass said, and that did surprise her. She looked at him more closely. His silken glance was intended to inspire fear; his eyes saw everything, knew everything. Douglass closed the outer door softly, like an alderman. Nicole said in her abrasive matter-of-fact voice, "Is this place bugged?"

"I have no idea," Ronnie said. "I wouldn't know where to look."

"I would," Douglass said, and went around the room looking behind things and under things.

Nicole pulled a chair out and sat down near the desk. "You really light up for the good Senator, don't you?"

Ronnie didn't answer but kept her eyes on Douglass. He put the floorlamp down and came to the desk and unscrewed the mouthpiece and earpiece of the telephone receiver to look at its insides. Ronnie felt tiny drops of sweat burst out, beading her hairline and prickling the roots.

Nicole spoke as if Ronnie weren't in the room. "She's always been independent and proud, stuffed full of romantic sentimentality. When that type falls in love with a man she really falls."

Douglass said abstractedly, "You don't often find a woman with more sense than temperament." He pried back an edge of the felt bottom-cover of the desk lamp and peered inside.

Of course they were trying to unnerve her; it was a ritual with them. But even knowing what they were doing wasn't enough to immunize her. The words they spoke were banal and trite and she had said them all to herself anyway; she was angry now because it was enough to have to suffer this self-inflicted agony, it was too much to have to discuss it.

Douglass said, "Shove back a minute."

She pushed her chair back on its casters and Douglass crouched to take the drawers out of the desk and investigate its insides and undersurfaces.

Nicole said, "You can't offer him anything, love, and you can't ask him to wait. The only thing you can do is walk nobly out of his life. Why make it hard for yourself?"

"I know all this," Ronnie said. "I'd already decided to break it off."

"Isn't that ducky." Douglass' voice was muffled because his head was under the kneehole of the desk.

Ronnie said, "Look, you don't need rubber hoses. I'll behave." She felt washed out but there was a kind of relief: she had needed this confrontation, she hadn't had the strength to make the decision alone. "I'll end it today."

Nicole said, "No you won't."

"Come again?"

"You'll string him along a while."

"But it will be easier to cut it off clean—I'll just clear out my desk and go. I'll telephone him and tell him it was no good, I'm leaving Tucson and going somewhere else to get a job."

"That's just what you won't do," Douglass said, straightening up and dusting his hands. "I think it's clean."

Nicole said, "How about the walls? Through-the-wall listening devices?"

"It's an old building. These walls are thick. Anyhow you've got the County Supervisor's anteroom on one side and the license-issuing office on the other—too much traffic in and out, nobody'd fix anything to those walls. It could be spotted too easily."

"If you're satisfied, then."

Ronnie said, "I wish you'd explain yourselves. You sound as if you don't want me to break it off at all. I don't understand."

"You'll break it off," Ramsey Douglass said, "when we tell you to break it off. I'd have thought by now you'd have learned to obey orders."

She didn't need reminding and of course they knew that. She had fallen in love with an outsider and she had married him against orders; she had been young and her defiance had been strengthened by passion. Phil had been a native-born American; he'd known nothing of Amergrad. She had told him nothing, given him no clues, he'd never suspected a thing. But possibly they had been right; there was always the possibility of a slip of the tongue. Still, didn't all of them run that risk? But they had forced her to watch while they slowly beat him to death with bludgeons behind the bowling alley.

Douglass said, "The cells have been activated. The man has come from Moscow."

She sat erect. "What?"

"We've been ordered up. To do the job we're here for." Douglass' lips had been upturned in his sour smile but now they went flat and lifeless. "So you see in any case you'll be leaving soon enough. They'll have to evacuate us when the job's been done."

It was beyond her capacity to absorb; she drooped in the chair like a loose sack of laundry and sweat trickled down between her breasts. Her face crumpled and collapsed slowly into defeat and she covered it with her hands. She was beyond tears but when Nicole spoke her rigid body jerked galvanically.

"Pull yourself together. We haven't got time for you to have another breakdown." Nicole's voice was gentler than usual. The wizened face turned toward Douglass and when Ronnie looked up she saw on Nicole's features an expression of black fury. It did not seem personally directed against Douglass: it was simply an unreasoning rage and Ronnie realized in that moment that they were all caught by the knowledge that everything had been ended for them by the whim of a faceless man twenty thousand miles away.

The fact that they were all in the same trap somehow made it possible to bear. She said, "All right. You have instructions for me."

Douglass and Nicole exchanged glances. Nicole nodded as if thoroughly fatigued.

Douglass said, "We haven't been told when it's to take place. I suppose they think it's none of our business, our job's just to swing the hammers, we don't have to know what the building's going to be. But we're supposed to isolate the base. It'll be a very tricky caper and we're going to have our hands full enough without your Senator crawling all over the base tripping over us. He's got clearance to go everywhere in the complexes with his hand-picked scientist and his Navajo detective and if any of them spots our preliminary maneuvers it could blow the whole thing open. So that's your job: distract him, discourage him, pressure him to lay off. He's got to be kept away until it's over and done with. I can't tell you how long that'll be but they wouldn't set this up too far in advance; there'd be too much risk of leakage. A week, maybe only a few days."

"I don't see how I can do that. He makes his own decisions —I can't tell him what to do."

Nicole turned. Her simian face picked up the light from the window and seemed at once bitter and amazed. "Don't be a fool. Seduce him—drag him away on a white-hot orgy. A woman like you could put everything else out of his mind."

Color suffused Ronnie's cheeks. "I'm not the type. I wouldn't know how."

It elicited Nicole's harsh bark of laughter. "With your looks? Christ if I had your looks I could make the President of the United States forget he ever saw the White House."

"He knows me too well. I can't just change overnight into a sex maniac. He'd know something was wrong—he's not a fool."

"Every man's a fool where women are concerned."

Douglass said, "No, she's right. If you'd air out your mind once in a while you'd see there are problems sex doesn't solve."

"You ought to know about that," Nicole snapped.

Douglass disregarded her. "Look, Ronnie, you're his center of communications, you make his appointments and screen his incoming calls and whatnot. You can rearrange his schedule and he'll never be the wiser."

"How?"

"He's at Davis Monthan this morning with his two hired snoops but it's only a preliminary survey, he's planning to go back four or five times more, isn't that right?"

"Yes."

"We can't have that. When he comes back to the office today I want you to tell him Colonel Sims called and asked if he'd postpone his next visit till Tuesday or Wednesday because the base has been alerted for a no-notice Operational Readiness Inspection and they'll be closing the base until the alert's ended; they'll be too busy to conduct his party around. Got that?"

"Yes, but what if he calls them to confirm it?"

"He won't if you're convincing enough. Now tomorrow you can call Colonel Ryan and tell him the Senator's been called into an emergency conference—something political—and won't be able to resume his inspection tour until Tuesday or Wednesday. And if Tuesday comes and we still need to keep him out we'll think of some other herring. Now you can take care of that, can't you?"

"I suppose so. But he's a friend of Colonel Ryan's—suppose he happens to call him and finds out I lied?"

"Then you'll just have to bluff your way out of it, won't you?"

Nicole said, "Just bat your eyelashes and wiggle at him."

Ronnie said uncertainly, "I don't—" But the telephone interrupted her and she picked up. "Senator Forrester's office."

"Hello, is Mr. Spode there, please?"

"Not at the moment. May I take a message?"

"It's rather urgent that I reach him." The man's voice was calm, filled with authority; she didn't recognize it.

"Who's calling, please?"

"My name is John Warren Block. It's important that I get in touch with Mr. Spode as quickly as possible. Do you have any idea where I might reach him?" There was enough interference on the line to suggest it was a long-distance call.

She said, "Right now he's out at Davis Monthan Air Force Base with Senator Forrester. You might try there, but I'm not sure they'll be able to find him right away. Would you care to leave your phone number?"

"He knows the number. John Warren Block. Thank you, I'll try the base." *Click.*

Douglass said, "Who was that?"

"Someone trying to reach Jaime Spode."

"What was his name?"

"John Warren Block."

"Ever heard of him?"

"No."

"Well it's probably nothing. But did Spode say anything to you about anything that happened last night?"

"No. I only saw him for a few minutes this morning. He and Alan—Senator Forrester—went out together to collect Professor Moskowitz and drive out to the base."

Douglass nodded. "All right, when you talk to Forrester

you've got to find out what Spode told him about last night. Particularly about a man he met last night."

"I don't understand—what am I supposed to be looking for?"

"Find out if Spode recognized the man and whether he notified any officials about him."

Nicole said, "What's this all about?"

"Our man from Moscow had a run-in with Spode last night. We've got to find out whether Spode carried it any farther. If Dangerfield's under suspicion we've got to know about it."

The implications ran rapidly through Ronnie's mind and Nicole said to Douglass, "She's very quick—you can see she understands what it could mean." Nicole came forward to the desk and put her palms flat on its surface, her face close before Ronnie's eyes. "You're right, of course. If Spode saw too much and communicated it to the Senator it may be necessary for us to take steps to make sure the information goes no farther. We can't afford to have the place crawling with FBI. On the other hand we'd be idiots to take any unnecessary action against a United States Senator—think of the furor that would cause. We don't want to touch him if we can help it, but if he knows too much we'll have to do something."

Douglass said, "He might have to suffer a sudden illness and retire to his ranch for a few days accompanied by a doctor and one or two nurses and of course his confidential secretary. You'd have to go with him and handle the phone calls and inquiries from reporters."

Ronnie said, "He wouldn't be—"

"Hurt? No. We couldn't afford that, could we? Besides, once we're finished here it won't matter what he tells the authorities. The job will be done and we'll be gone. In the meantime if he doesn't know anything we'll leave him alone. But if he does know something we'll just have to keep him incommunicado—perhaps under sedation—until we're ready to leave."

"As long as he won't be harmed."

Nicole said, "We wouldn't touch a hair on his handsome head. On the other hand nobody's going to pay much attention if a few Russian professors and nurses and ballerinas happen to be arrested and sent to a torture camp."

The reference was to members of Ronnie's family and she said, "I know—I know."

"And your beloved brother," Douglass said, and that took her aback.

She said, "But my brother's right here—you wouldn't harm one of our own group!"

"Under the circumstances we need your services more than his," Douglass said. "He's expendable. He's got nothing to do with the military base. So you see his life is in your hands."

"Just in case you think about changing sides," Nicole drawled.

Ronnie said, "Nobody in this country even knows I'm his sister."

"You know it and he knows it. That's all that really matters, isn't it?" Douglass turned to go. "You know what you're to do. Come on, Nicole."

When they were gone she sat with no more expression than a plastic mannequin's but her right hand slowly closed into a small fist and the knuckles turned white.

☆☆☆☆☆☆☆☆☆☆☆☆☆☆☆☆☆☆☆☆☆☆☆☆☆☆☆☆☆☆

Chapter Fourteen

Forrester stood with one hand on the iron balustrade looking out across the heaped-up distance toward the approaching airplane. On the tower above him the radar dishes turned steadily, without sound, and out toward the hangars crewmen with big sound suppressors clamped over their ears stood clear of intakes and exhausts while airplane engines, tuning up, sucked the thin dry air by the ton. Wind ruffled Forrester's hair and whipped away whatever Bill Ryan was saying. The others—Spode, Colonel Sims, Professor Moskowitz, Major Pete Chandler—stood in a knot a few feet away, watching the distant F-111 extend its wings and turn final on the range with a tearing sigh of sound.

The plane sank toward the desert and lined itself up on the runway. It grew big as it rocketed forward, sun racing along its wings in fragmented reflections, and Ryan yelled something about its performance supremacy while the F-111 hit the pavement a mile away and rumbled forward at high speed past crash crews. When it stopped at the maintenance hangar its crewmen climbed out in their hooded moon suits and the three uniformed men on the platform with Forrester all gave him a gung-ho show of teeth as if they were very proud of the fact that the six-million-dollar airplane had managed to land without breaking up.

An airman came out of the tower onto the concrete apron and saluted and spoke to Colonel Sims. The wing commander nodded and followed the airman inside. Forrester listened to Bill Ryan's idle talk with half his mind and flicked his eyes over the others. Top Spode had something on his mind and that was disturbing because Forrester needed Top alert today. Moskowitz beside him was dwarfed—neat, gray, small, pot-bellied; the Professor had been awarded the Medal of Freedom for his work on the Titan missile program but he looked as if he'd be at home in a quarter-half poker game or in a bar with a schooner of draft beer. He had the knobby knuckles of a longshoreman.

Bill Ryan was saying, "You'll have to go the rest of the way without me. I've got to stick around the admin block. This job keeps me strapped to a watch and I get the feeling we're overdue for a surprise alert inspection. They spring them on us all the time to test our reaction time—we don't want to get caught with our planes down, do we?" Ryan smiled without pleasure; he seemed irritable.

Forrester said, "We'll try to keep out of your hair."

"Sure. Bud Sims will take you around—the birds are really his bailiwick. I'm just the landlord. Major Chandler here has authority to clear you into any area you want to see. Professor, good to meet you." Ryan shook hands with Moskowitz and Spode, batted Forrester's arm and went inside the tower. Colonel Sims was coming through and held the door for him and they exchanged a few words in the doorway, and when Sims came out onto the apron his face was screwed up into a mild perplexity.

"Gentlemen, I'm very sorry to cop out on you but I've just had a call from a hospital in Yuma—my wife was down there looking over some real estate and she's been taken ill. I'm sure it's nothing serious, but I'm going to fly down there."

"Of course," Forrester said. "I'm terribly sorry to hear that —I hope she'll be all right."

"I'm sure she will. But she'll want me there. My deputy will be taking over my duties until I get back. I'm afraid Colonel Winslow can't run the store and show you folks around at the same time but I've told him to cooperate with you to the best of his ability. Major Chandler here will guide you wherever you want to go. I'm sorry to duck out this way but they're warming up a plane for me down there right now. Gentlemen?"

There was a quick round of handshaking and Sims went, walking fast, a tall man who wore the uniform as if he'd been born to pose for a recruiting poster.

Jaime Spode's outdoor eyes were crinkled into suspicious slits. "They're dropping off like flies. If I didn't know better I'd think we had bad breath."

Major Chandler uttered an uneasy laugh. "It must look like that. But I'll do my best to fill in for the Colonel." Chandler's eyes were covered by huge curved mirror-lensed motorcycle sunglasses and he wore gray Air Force coveralls, cut very tight, with a dozen zipper pockets. Forrester thought he must have spit-shined his boots with lighter fluid and a nylon stocking: the toes had a wicked shine and altogether the meaty-shouldered chief of base security gave a sinister impression of latent violence. The polished ones were often the pathologically sadistic ones.

Standing rigidly with his chest out like an aquatic bird's, Chandler said, "At your service, gentlemen. Where to?"

"The launch complex, I think," Forrester said and Chandler took them downstairs through the admin tower and whistled up a gray USAF Chevrolet, For Official Use Only. Forrester got in back with Moskowitz; Spode slid into the middle of the front seat between the Major and the driver, and

Chandler turned with his left arm over the back of the seat and said, "We'll be bumping into a little more confusion than you'd normally find out there today. We've got a standardization-and-evaluation team down here from Z.I. Command to inspect our combat capability. I'd like to avoid getting underfoot—if they trip over us they'll score points against the base."

Moskowitz' eyes twinkled and Forrester nodded; Chandler was going by the book but he wasn't going to go out of his way to make things easy.

A B-52 bomber circled high overhead with vapor trails spreading from its eight jets and Major Chandler kept up a running monologue thick with jargon that both explained and obscured the installations they drove past. The road went through a guarded gate in the security fence and across absolutely empty desert—greasewood, cholla, manzanita, ocotillo, paloverde, sand. A narrow side road ran off to the right and Chandler said, "One of our ABM silos, about a mile over there."

"Sure," Moskowitz said, "to defend our investment."

"To defend our strike capability, Professor. We can't just leave the birds wide open for the Reds to knock out with their first strike."

"I know, but it's still a strange world in which people are defenseless and only strategic weapons can be protected."

"We could protect everybody"—Chandler's face twisted toward Forrester— "if Congress gave us the money to build a full-scale ABM system."

Forrester said, "I'm not the department of sympathetic ears, Major. That's over in Congressman Breckenyear's office."

Chandler's face made no visible change. Forrester wished the man would take off those infernal sunglasses. Chandler said, "War travels fast these days, Senator—we're just keeping up with the Ivans."

"Or are they the ones who're just keeping up with us?"

"You rather let them get ahead of us, Senator?"

"Ahead and behind are words that don't mean much when

you've already passed the finish line. I'm talking about over-kill now."

"I know. I read your speech in the paper."

"And you think I'm wrong."

"Senator, we don't keep moving, they'll move right ahead and figure out ways to neutralize our birds. Then it's not overkill any more, it's We Lose. God knows we don't want a thermonuclear war but maybe the real danger isn't in going to the brink of war but in shrinking from the brink of war."

It was a speech he'd heard Woody Guest make once and hearing it from Chandler's lips made him smile slightly. "You have a lot of faith in technology, don't you, Major?"

"Kept us alive this long, sir."

The door to the concrete dugout was marked simply WING HQ and it was guarded by armed sentries in white helmets and a KMS machine which compared the thumbprints on their ID cards with their own thumbs. Chandler said, "Be pretty tough for a saboteur to get in past this, Senator, if that was on your mind."

"I see you *have* seen my speeches." Forrester smiled his political smile.

"Yes, sir. It usually pays."

"Know your enemy."

Chandler slid his card into the machine and pressed his thumb to the scanner. "An unauthorized visitor would have an easier time getting into Fort Knox. The cards are magneti-cally coded like a printed circuit sealed inside the plastic. It took a direct order from the Secretary of Defense to get them for you and they'll be destroyed the minute you leave the base. Well then, in we go—after you, gentlemen?"

The nerve center reminded Forrester of an airport control-lers' console room: tiers of screens above a vast curved desk surface. Chandler kept up a running commentary: "If one of my inspectors spots any of these boys goofing off just once his ass is grass. . . . I guess you already know we've got all kinds of redundancies and duplications so it's impossible for a crazy to go off his nut and shoot off a bird. The President has to push the button. Nobody else. We've got double-check verification procedures and the whole procedure can be stopped at any point right up to ignition by a countermand from the President or NORAD. It's a whole lot easier to stop it than it is to start it."

Jaime Spode was looking at everything and Forrester knew the information was being absorbed into Spode's mental computer, sorted for weaknesses, filed for later recovery.

Professor Moskowitz watched with a detached expression and when he turned toward Chandler he said, "You're talking about a preignition countermand. On the old birds we had self-destruct mechanisms but I understand they've eliminated them on these. What if the missiles have already been launched? Can you still stop them?"

"No. Once they're in the air they're gone. Unless you can shoot them down and that's damned unlikely. If we had a radio signal to stop them the Reds could use it to neutralize our strike—you can't keep a radio code private forever. I mean, everything's got to be tested and the Reds watch us with everything they've got whenever we test a bird. If we used open radio transmission to control them they'd pick up the signals and work out the codes and frequencies. Can't be done, Professor."

Forrester said, "You've never tested the missiles with live warheads."

"No sir, but we've tested the warheads underground and we've tested the birds with dummy warheads. Everything works, Senator, honest to God, I give you my word."

They went through low tunnels, heels ringing on the echoing concrete; they wore hard hats and flashed their ID badges at the checkpoints. The low roar of ventilator blowers was an oppressive rumble. Chandler led them onto a circular balcony and when Forrester looked up and down all he could see was the massive polished skin of the ICBM and the confusion of machinery around it—pipes, cables, platforms, wheels, ladders, lights, joints, cylinders, gears, devices.

Chandler delivered himself of his set-piece speech: "This is one of our eighteen Minuteman Threes, a multiple-warhead three-stage missile with a tri-gyroscope guidance system like the ones that put the Apollo ships down on pinpoints on the moon. After she's launched the first and second stages burn out. They're decoupled by explosive connectors and they fall free. When the third stage ignites it accelerates the payload to orbital speed. She's up at a ballistic altitude zenith of about eight hundred miles and once she's up there above the atmosphere she sheds her ceramic heat shield to lighten weight. Then she coasts in orbit until her micro-circuit computer, which is programmed with the target information, fires the retro-rockets and brings her down toward the first target.

"You've got three warhead reentry vehicles—RV's—triggered by altitude fuses. If the target's a city they'll detonate high above the target to maximize the area of destruction. A twenty-megaton blast at altitude will destroy brick buildings in a circle maybe fifteen miles in diameter. But if your target's an enemy missile base your RV has to get in low to dig the enemy's missiles right out of their hard silos. That means impact inside four hundred yards of the silo. That kind of accuracy requires meticulous programming and that's why the ground-support systems for each one of these silos are as big and complicated as the inside of an aircraft carrier."

Forrester listened with half his mind; when Chandler stopped for breath Forrester changed the subject: "And what if you don't get your Phaetons, Major?"

"In other words why can't we make do with what we've already got here? Senator, how much do you know about the Russian SS-9?"

"Not very much."

"The SS-9's a lot bigger than this bird here: big enough to carry five times as many warheads as our bird. So far they've deployed about four hundred SS-9s, which is enough to target our whole deployment of one thousand Minutemen, assuming they've got a good enough delivery system to knock out our hard silos. Naturally we hope they don't—we hope they'll leave enough unhit for us to retaliate and cripple them. Our clout depends on convincing the Reds we can penetrate our warheads into their turf no matter what they do. The object of the game is to keep them convinced we can inflict unacceptable damage on them. If they line up enough SS-9s to kill our whole system they don't have to worry about that any more unless we're lining up something against them—like the Phaeton Three."

Moskowitz said, "It's funny the way you Air Force people ignore the Navy."

"Professor, there's a limit to the size and speed of a bird you can launch from a submarine. We've got maybe thirty nuclear submarines deployed on station at any given time, and they may have a few hundred missiles and warheads among them but all the Reds have to do is knock out those thirty submarines to destroy the whole Polaris-Poseidon system. The Navy puts a lot of store in mobility and concealment but I wouldn't bet my ass the Reds couldn't attack all our subs simultaneously—they've got a sophisticated sub-tracking system and you can be damn sure they know where every one of our subs is right now. Let's don't forget they don't need to make a direct hit to knock out a sub. Set off a nuke anywhere in the neighborhood and you make a shock wave that'll take any submarine out of action. But even supposing they did miss two or three of our subs we'd still be talking about thirty-ton missiles with a maximum range of maybe twenty-five hundred miles. A submarine-launched bird is a lot easier for their ABM defenses to handle.

"No," Chandler concluded, "the only real knockout punch we've got is this Minuteman Three and if they deploy enough SS-9s to cancel these birds out, then where's our deterrent against a preemptive first strike?"

Moskowitz wore a bemused little smile that implied he didn't believe a word of it. Forrester couldn't get away from the notion he was listening to a computer. Chandler's pronouncements were set pieces right out of the little propaganda booklets printed up for Public Information Officers. To Forrester's mind they were all infected with a tragic blindness: the generals talked only to other generals; they parroted 1950 slogans of deterrents, weapons gaps, the Communist monolith. The machinery had grown in sophistication; the commanders had not. *I have seen the future, and it does not work.* He ran his eyes up the dismal great column of the missile, gleaming dully in the antiseptic artificial light, and he heard Moskowitz begin to speak in his wry classroom voice.

"Of course your whole position goes into a cocked hat, Major, the minute you admit our early-warning system will give us enough time to launch these missiles before any incoming ICBMs have a chance to knock out the silos. The Russians haven't devised any methods yet of sneaking an SS-9 across twenty thousand miles of airspace without its being seen."

"They're working on it," Chandler said, and when Forrester looked at him he couldn't see any sign that the man was joking.

Top Spode had been wandering along the platform poking his brown beak into niches. When he came by Forrester he said, "Like to have another look at the ROG command post on our way back."

When they emerged from the ROG access tunnel a fat Tech Sergeant intercepted them, red-faced and out-of-breath as a volunteer fireman: there was a telephone call for Mr. Spode; would he mind taking it over here?

Major Chandler excused himself and went across the thrumming cavern to have a word with an officer at the far end of the Iconorama and Forrester said to Moskowitz, "Do you see how young these men are? We've given these things to children to play with."

"I don't know," Moskowitz said. "Did you ever read Poe's essay on simpletons and bluffing in 'The Purloined Letter'? It ought to be required reading in Washington. The thesis is, when you're trying to guess your opponent's next move your best chance is to identify your own reasoning intellect with your opponent's. If you value his intellect too high or too low, you'll guess wrong. Now it takes a high scale of intelligence to identify deliberately with an opponent's cunning, but the next best choice is to pick somebody whose intellect is the equivalent of the opponent's. Most likely to think the same way, you see?"

"Professor, you're way beyond my limits of subtlety."

"All I'm saying is, the intellectual level of Russian leadership is third-rate and we may actually have a better chance if our own leadership isn't vastly superior to theirs. Kennedy was a brainy man but he made the mistake of assuming Khrushchev was too intelligent to try planting missiles in Cuba: we almost had a war over that. But if they know our leadership is just as dumb and trigger-happy as theirs they won't try to run dangerous bluffs on us. Maybe we need to keep it on that level, because we know what happens if we don't.

"Put yourself five miles away from a one-megaton blast. The force would destroy most of the concrete and brick buildings inside that radius and earthquake-effect and the wind-drag pressures behind the blast would knock down most of what was left; anything left standing would probably be melted by the heat of the fireball. If you were still alive somehow, your clothes would burst into flame and you'd suffer flash burns and retinal burns—the kind that killed half the victims at Hiroshima and blinded thousands more. Your eardrums might burst, your lungs might be ruptured, you might be killed or maimed by flying bricks and glass. Everything around you might burst into flame and if you weren't burned to death, you might suffer heat stroke or carbon-monoxide poisoning. Oxygen depletion and extreme heat can cause respiratory damage from inhalation of radiated heat. Then there's the whole gamut of radiation-fallout effects on human biology—beta and gamma and X rays, always bearing in mind China and Russia use very dirty bombs. The effects aren't pretty. Quick death, slow death, permanent injuries of every degree—ulcerated cutaneous lesions, burns, internal destruction, blood and tissue deterioration, genetic mutation, cancer, fibrosis, disintegration of bone marrow. . . . Senator, you know what we're trying to fight. It's what Lapp called the technological imperative: if a weapon can be built it will be built. These gadgets have become a central object of worship in our time and you can't take a society's idols away from it. Sometimes I think you and I are just lying down on the tracks."

"No," Forrester said. "We're going to lick them this time. I'm not a bad in-fighter, Professor. And we're gathering support every day."

"But we've got this damned technological clock ticking away—maybe it's too late to stop it. Each side keeps goading the other into a first-strike psychosis; there's always the temptation to turn a so-called retaliatory weapon into a first-strike weapon. Remove the other side's deterrent by knocking out their missiles before they can be fired. Leave them helpless to hit back. It's the old Why-Not-Victory idea—feebleminded cretins. This Phaeton system—what'll they do with all the lethal radioactive wastes from the spent elements? It'll multiply the permanent storage problem out of sight. And the risk of accident? A radioactive leak, a chemical reaction, some stupid little component that got passed through quality control when the inspector was yawning? We've always had those risks but when you multiply them a thousandfold you go right off the crap table. Speaking purely as a mathematician I'd say the odds stink."

"Make a stab at a figure."

"I'd have to sit down and work it out."

"Will you do that?"

"Sure, why not?"

Chandler and Spode returned from their separate errands at almost the same moment and Top Spode's face was closed up tight. "Let's get out of here—something's come up."

Forrester asked the question with his eyebrows but Spode only shook his head, mute.

The Professor got into the back seat and on the sun-blasted concrete in front of the admin block Forrester saw Major Chandler, who had just bade them good-bye with cool civility, stop to remove his big sunglasses and polish them. Forrester was amazed to see that behind the great mirrored shields the eyes were little buttons, too small for the rest of Chandler's face.

Spode put the car in gear and pulled out of the parking slot. Forrester said, "All right, what's up?"

"Later."

They were in Spode's car because Forrester's two-seater wouldn't have accommodated them. Spode drove through the gate and accelerated past the ugly parasitical traps that had sprung up to milk the airmen: SALES & SERVICE, DISCOUNT, AIR-CONDITIONED, LOW DOWN PAYMENT TO SERVICEMEN, TOP VALUE, ALL CARDS HONORED. Past a hamburger stand and a beer joint and a retread tire shop, dust hanging in the unpaved parking lots. The sun was molten brass. Forrester said, "All right, Top, what'd you spot?"

"Hard to say right off. But I tried to case it as if those pushbuttons were the crown jewels. I think it could be done."

Moskowitz snorted. "Of course it could be done. Any group of crackpots with a little scientific training could think of a dozen ways to beat the fail-safe systems. All it takes is the instincts of a safecracker."

"And the organization of a Gestapo," Forrester said. "I still don't put too much credence in it—it's a far-fetched notion but it's worth exposing if there's any risk at all."

Spode said, "It would take more than a handful of crazies. You'd need fifty or a hundred people and they'd have to be in the right places with the right training and a hell of a lot of preparation. But there's no single security point I could see that's so foolproof it couldn't be breached. Take those KMS identification systems—those visitors' cards for the three of us got prepared fast enough, and that means they could be fixed up for anybody. All it takes is one insider. Maybe you could do it without an insider for that matter—pick an airman's pocket and make copies of his card, slip the original back into his wallet and nobody's the wiser. Just leave blanks for your own people's thumbprints to be filled in, and get uniforms for your people. I don't see how any of it's beyond the reach of some of these fascist outfits that have passwords and code

names and keep bazookas in their basements. Half of them
are Air Force people or retired Air Force people."

Spode crowded the 45-mile-an-hour speed limit down
Twenty-second Street. "You'd have to get your hands on
copies of the codes they use and that might be tricky; they
keep changing the codes. But it could still be done. Each one
of those blockhouses down there has a phone and a microwave radio—I had a look. That's the key point, communications. Every system has to have a bottleneck here and there
and if you can take over those bottlenecks you can control all
the incoming and outgoing messages. Once you do that the
rest's no problem. We'll need to tap a few sources and work
up a complete chart of the communications they'd use in case
of a nuclear attack."

Moskowitz said, "You sound like you're plotting to do it
yourself."

"Only way to figure it out, Professor. Put yourself in the
other guy's shoes and decide how you'd do it if you were
him."

Forrester said, "The point is, it can be done. That's what
terrifies me. Fifty or a hundred fanatics with Nazi minds—if
that's all it would take, it's fantastic."

Spode turned up Cherry Avenue past Bear Down football
stadium and north into the campus—stolid brick buildings on
incongruous palm-tree-studded lawns. Spode pulled up by
the administration building. Kids walked by in bunches and
Moskowitz' glance swiveled to follow girls' legs. "When will
you want me in Washington to testify?"

"Guest set the hearings for three weeks from Monday—the
twenty-fourth," Forrester said.

"I'll be there." Moskowitz extended his knobby hand across
the back of the seat to grip Forrester's. "The odds still stink,
but I've got a little hope—for the first time. Don't bail out on
me, Senator. Pleasure to've met you, Mr. Spode." Moskowitz
got out of the car and trailed after a trio of long-haired girls
as if attached to them by a leash. Spode's eyes didn't dally on
the girls at all; Forrester couldn't remember having seen
Spode this tense.

"All right, Top, what's the matter?"

"Not sure. Wait till I get to a phone. That call I had, it was important but we couldn't talk on that line."

Spode drove onto a gas-station apron and Forrester watched him put through his call in the glass booth. When Spode came back he said, "Okay, we've got to talk."

Spode handed him five photographs and talked while he drove. "His name's Leon Belsky. He's Russian KGB, one of their good ones. I took the pictures last night because I bumped into him at Trumble's—he was doing the same thing I was but he was looking for bigger game. I took the pictures and his gun to somebody last night to find out who he was."

"The Agency?"

"Aeah. Look, follow this because it all gets to a point. I left the gun and the negatives with Art Miller—he's the guy who developed them for me. I gave you the Phaeton specs this morning but I held out on the rest because at that point you didn't need to be involved in it. But now there's two dead guys and a third guy missing and they're all tied into it, and you need to know about it because I think they're after you and me now."

Forrester's scalp contracted. "Then you'd better spell it out. Who's dead and who's missing?"

"Ross Trumble's dead, for one."

Forrester stared at him.

Spode turned the wheel to take a corner. His jaw had crept forward to lie in a hard line. "In his bathroom on a pile of broken glass with his wrists cut open. They made it look like suicide, but it wasn't. I was the one who broke that glass and Trumble wasn't there at the time. So now we know what Belsky was looking for—he was looking for Trumble, to kill him. But we still don't know why. The letter Trumble wrote you from Phoenix—maybe that will have some answers."

It was a quiet street, cottonwoods and elms throwing pools of shade. Spode pulled to the curb and switched the engine off. "The other dead one's Art Miller. The guy who had your negatives and Belsky's gun. Remember I left the stuff with Miller last night. It was a stupid mistake and you see what it cost Miller. If you want to plant a bug on somebody a gun's a good place to put it—bug your gun and then let somebody take it away from you. There must have been a beeper in Belsky's Smith and Wesson, and Belsky must have followed the signal right to Miller's house. They found Miller dead a few hours ago. The gun and the negatives are gone so Belsky must have taken them with him.

"The missing guy is one of Orozco's private operatives— the one Trumble was trying to reach when he called Orozco's office, remember? Sawed-off guy called Craig. He had some hook-up with Trumble and now he's missing too and possibly dead. Whatever it is, it's big, and we're in it, you and me. Belsky traced back as far as Miller and if he was scared enough to kill Miller then he's scared enough to kill both of us if he gets a chance at us; he knows I can identify him, and he's got to assume I've told you all this since I work for you. He's got no way of knowing Miller was an Agency man—he'll assume Miller was just a pal with a darkroom who developed my pictures for me. So he may figure if he knocks off the two of us fast enough he's safe."

"I see." Forrester was pawing his big jaw; things were going by very fast and he was trying to keep focus. It was as if they had leaped back more than twenty years to Korea: military counterintelligence, all the training and the months of experience in the lines, drifted through his mind in flashes and he sorted out the useless questions and narrowed his attention like a cone toward the significances. In the end he said, "Then the question is why this man Belsky came here and killed Ross Trumble. I assume the Agency must be in high gear by now looking for him."

"Sure. Not that they've got much chance of finding him. He'd checked into a motel under the name of Meldon Kemp and they've got a man on the place but there's no chance at all he'll show up back there. Nobody even knows where to start looking because nobody knows what he's after. If he only came here to kill Trumble then he'd be halfway back to Moscow by now, but I don't think that was it. If they'd wanted an assassin they wouldn't have had to use a man as important as Belsky. Anyhow if it was hit-and-run why'd he go out of his way to trace his gun back to Miller and kill him? He'd have run for it instead. No, Belsky's still around here and he's still worrying about me. And you."

"It's hard to grasp, Top."

"It might be easier to understand if it made any sense." Spode looked at his watch. "They've put tracers on Ross Trumble to see if they can come up with something at that end. Right now we can't see any connection between him and Belsky outside of the Phaeton thing, and why the hell should Belsky kill him over that?"

Forrester shook his head.

Spode reached for the key. "They told me I could call back and find out if they've dug up anything that helps. I may as well try."

When Spode came back to the car from the telephone kiosk his eyes were busy—like an animal that knew it was being stalked. He started the car and headed into the back streets. "The Agency sent a man to cover my place in case Belsky showed up looking for me but it looks like Belsky beat them to it. The place has been searched—quick but thorough. Maybe looking to see if he could find any indications whether I'm still working for the Agency. He's got to be hoping like mad I'm free-lancing now and didn't call in the troops."

This Belsky was a professional but that wouldn't make him immune to the seductiveness of hope. He would tend to believe what he wanted to believe—that Spode was independent and that Washington wasn't onto him. It would make Belsky a little less careful but it would put Spode's life in jeopardy and Forrester found himself worrying about that at the expense of wider concerns. He was a man to whom friendships had always been as sparse and infrequent as they were profound. He had nothing much in common with Top Spode other than shared experiences that went back twenty-odd years but Top was one of the finest men he had ever known and in a personal sense Top's individual safety was of more importance to him than a truckload of state secrets.

Spode found a place to park where there was nothing in sight but a few houses and two sleepy mongrels on a lawn. "A few developments. I left voice-activated bugs at Trumble's house and the Agency retrieved the tapes a while ago when the cops were taking the body away. There were a couple of voices, just fragments, one guy calling another guy 'Sarge' and telling him to take it easy with the knife. My ex-boss figures they must have killed Trumble somewhere else and snuck the body back into the house, and one of them had to cut him to pour some blood over the floor and make it look like Trumble killed himself in the bathroom. Incidentally the local cops aren't in on this; they bought it as a suicide."

"But that's not the main point," Forrester said. His brain was beginning to work. "The main point is, Belsky isn't alone."

"Aeah. He's got at least two guys working for him."

"One of whom may be Police or Air Force. 'Sarge'—Sergeant."

"It could be a nickname too. But anyhow he's got local help." Spode locked his fists around the steering-wheel rim and stared at them. "Damn it I hate working blind. We're peeling back corners but we don't even know what to look for."

"What did they find out about Trumble?"

"They're still working on it. So far most of what they got checks out with what we know about him. County Attorney's staff, FBI stint, lobbyist for Shattuck, running for Congress—nothing new there. But the records on Trumble only go back about twenty years. Before that it's zero. Trumble had an Army discharge certificate but the military-records people in St. Louis have no record he was ever in the service. He had a bachelor's and a law diploma from Northwestern but Northwestern's never heard of him. He came to Arizona in fifty-five with an Illinois driver's license but the Illinois highway department doesn't show any license was ever issued to him. He had a birth certificate too and a lot of other documentation and so far none of it seems to check out."

Forrester stared at him. "That's insane."

"It doesn't prove anything about who he was but it proves who he wasn't. He wasn't Ross Trumble. There never was a Ross Trumble."

In the end Spode said, "I'm not holding out on you. That's all I know. You know the choices as well as I do and it's up to you."

"You never like to make decisions, do you, Top?"

"That's neither here nor there. It's your choice, not mine —I take your bread, I sing your songs."

"The Agency wants you to make a target out of yourself to draw Belsky into the open, is that it?"

"Aeah."

If Belsky had running dogs then he might not do it himself but that didn't matter in principle: if you could draw the running dogs into a trap it was the same as drawing Belsky into the trap since the running dogs would lead you back to him if you knew how to handle it.

"If you're going to be the bait in the Agency's trap you don't want to be too obvious about it, Top. If they think you're advertising for attention they'll pull back."

"Quit talking about me. Talk about you. I see the way you're thinking but this ain't Korea and it ain't 1953. You're a United States Senator, you've got no business playing cops and robbers. Belsky's got two goons we know about and he may have more—it could be a big organization for all we know."

"I've never subscribed to the conspiracy theory of history. I can't believe the Russians have recruited very many people here."

"Christ, you can hire thugs by the dozen for pay—all they care about is the money, they don't need to know who's giving the orders or why."

When Forrester made no immediate answer Spode turned to look at him. The dark strong face was troubled—a very personal concern. "It's getting too hairy. Not for me, maybe, but for you. I think you ought to dig a hole."

"Hide out?"

"Just until they run Belsky down."

"He can't hire very many thugs who'd be willing to risk harming a United States Senator."

"Nuts. All the thugs have to do is find you for him. Belsky can take care of the messy details himself."

Forrester said slowly, "It might take too much time, Top."

"It might. But you're a long time dead."

"We're just starting to get momentum. If I hole up now this Phaeton fight will lose steam and we may never get it rolling again."

"I didn't say it was easy. You could lose your crack at the White House too."

"You too, Top?"

"Hell I'm all for it. You'd find a slot for me and the Indians would have access to the President's ear for the first time since Teddy Roosevelt."

"You're getting off the subject."

"I talk a lot when I'm nervous. Listen, you've got to decide right now—if you decide to dig a hole you can't go back to the office from here."

"No, I suppose not."

"And you can't go to your hotel or the ranch and you can't communicate with Ronnie because if Belsky's serious about silencing us all those things may be watched."

Forrester's chin dipped toward his chest and he dragged a big hand down his face. Spode's head swiveled, indicating his wary interest in a passing car. Forrester said, "There's only one subject of interest to a Soviet agent here."

"The missiles."

"The missiles," Forrester agreed. "Trumble was involved with them, you and I are involved with them. Belsky must have some interest in them. I think we have to find out."

"And maybe blow your whole case. It could mean the Russians are scared to death of the Phaeton and right now anything that scares a Russian to death is something the public's likely to vote for."

"But we've still got to find out, haven't we?"

"You mean you feel a duty to find out, even if it does wreck your case. You know I think maybe you're the first honest politician I ever met? Here you're already way out on a limb and you want to try hanging from twigs. These people are killers."

"If I drop out of sight Belsky will know why."

"What difference does that make? If he can't find you he can't hurt you."

"I just can't afford to have my hands tied right now, Top. The balance is too delicate. Without a leader the whole fight will disintegrate. But I'm not inclined toward heroics; you know that. I'll take every precaution I can—I want a fair chance to survive it if Belsky comes after me."

Spode drew a breath into his wide chest and let it out slowly. "If you won't pull in your horns all the way at least let me check you into the Ramada under a phony name—one of those rooms in back where you can use the side entrance and not be seen going through the lobby."

"Fair enough. But I've got public appearances to make starting Monday, and I'm not going to cancel them."

"That gives us a couple of days. Maybe we'll run him to ground before then."

"There's one other thing," Forrester said. "You mentioned it yourself. They may try to reach me through Ronnie."

"Aeah. I didn't want to think that through out loud."

"We've got to. Suppose Belsky gets to her?"

"You mean suppose he forces her to toll you into a trap. They do work that way. If he knows enough about you and her. Maybe he doesn't—it hasn't made the papers."

"Don't we have to assume he's got good sources of information? I think we'd better arrange to get Ronnie out of the office." Concentration made brackets and creases in his face. "Les Suffield can hold down the office for the time being. I suppose we have to expect them to tap the phones. We'll have to make some arrangement with Les to report to me by outside phone. It had better be clean at both ends so they won't be able to get at me through Les."

"Easy. You prearrange it that you'll call Les at certain times of day at a pay phone. That way he doesn't have to know where you're calling from and if they get to him he can't tell them anything. But it puts Les in a tight spot."

"We're all going to have to rely on you to keep the heat off, Top. You're the Judas goat—you're the one Belsky's going to have to find."

"That's all right, I'll have plenty of cover."

"Be sure Belsky doesn't spot it."

"You're never sure of anything in this kind of business," Spode said, and reached for the ignition key.

☆☆☆☆☆☆☆☆☆☆☆☆☆☆☆☆☆☆☆☆☆☆☆☆☆☆☆☆☆☆☆☆☆

Chapter Fifteen

The Gaz military vehicle rolled to a quiet stop near the end of the runway and Andrei waited inside until he saw the plane's lights describe a low turn at the far end of the strip. Then he got out and stood in the night wind wrapped in a trench coat cluttered with pockets, flaps, buttons, epaulets. The khaki belt was cleated tight against his belly and he wore a brown trilby hat with the brim turned down both back and front. The jet's landing lights picked him up and his face had a gray tired look.

When the plane stopped Andrei walked out to meet it. The starboard jet had been left idling and it made a whistle and stench. The door near the tail swung open, hinged at the bottom, becoming stairs, and Andrei waited on the tarmac while the man in the raincoat made his way down the stairs.

271

The man in the raincoat stood on the bottommost step and the two of them spoke in Chinese.

After fifteen minutes' conversation the man in the raincoat climbed back into the airplane and by the time Andrei had walked to his vehicle the plane was already taxiing forward to make its takeoff run.

When it was airborne Andrei climbed into the Gaz and let in the clutch. The Gaz leaped spryly across the tarmac toward the service road.

On the way to the ring road he passed somnolent *daschas* nestled in stands of fir and birch. The countryside was carpeted with snow and it was temptingly easy to believe in the myth of the communal serenity of the peoples of the USSR but Andrei had memories of famines, peasants feeding roof thatch to the stock, cattle dying: Andrei was far away from his boyhood but his roots were in the land.

He played games on one of the cloverleaf intersections of the ring road until he was certain there was no one following him; drove past tall buildings under construction on the outskirts of Moscow, open steel frames festooned with cranes and scaffolds; drove into the city past a crowd of Old Believers gathered in front of a church for a midnight service; made his way along Tsvetnoy Boulevard into the Arbat and into the military garage where the dozing attendant nodded vaguely; and walked around the corner to the KGB building.

The night sentries cleared him up to the fifth floor and he sat down in his office with a bright light shining directly down on the top of his desk, the only light in the room. He picked up the phone and dialed slowly, his thick fingers hardly fitting into the holes in the dial, methodically picking out each digit —G3-92-01.

He leaned back in the chair and that was when he saw the shadowy figure in the open connecting doorway to Rykov's office. It was Rykov, leaning on his cane. Andrei showed his surprise but not his chagrin; he gave Rykov a smile and a hand gesture and when a voice answered the telephone Andrei said into the mouthpiece, "Yes, is this G2-71-08? . . . Forgive me, I must have dialed improperly." He cradled the telephone and Rykov came away from the doorway and approached one of the leather chairs near Andrei's desk. Rykov's limp seemed very pronounced.

Rykov settled into the chair before he spoke. "Go ahead, complete your call—I'm in no hurry." His voice was as thick as if he had been drinking.

"I can take care of it later. A matter of no importance."

Rykov nodded vaguely, dismissing it. "In *The Brothers Karamazov* Dostoyevsky has one brother say to another, 'Sometimes it is very unwise to be a Russian.' "

Andrei smiled.

"You don't need to humor me," Rykov said. "I am not senile."

"What sort of talk is this?"

"Only a fool without humility can get through hours like these without misgivings. I have set things in motion without the troika's permission. If I fail I'll be purged, liquidated, but that doesn't matter. What stings is the knowledge that I'll be charged with treason against the state when in fact I am a patriot if I am anything at all."

Andrei said nothing and after a moment Rykov mused, "The Japanese proverb has it that great villainy is often called loyalty. Of course any war is proper and just if you win it and get to write the history books." He lit one of his Pamirs and held it nervously, lifting it to his lips every few seconds with a jagged motion. "If Belsky fails, it will destroy me and there is nothing I can do about it."

"Belsky has never failed," Andrei said politely.

"The fate of us all has never rested on Belsky's shoulders before," Rykov replied.

Ticking silence, and then Rykov continued, "I spoke again with Yashin tonight."

Andrei started. "And?"

"The same. He accuses me of desiring a Wagnerian glory, a Pyrrhic victory. Once again I showed him our evidence and once again he shrugged it off—he has the audacity to quote Stalin to me: 'Paper will put up with anything printed on it.'

To him either the Chinese are too clever to risk war with us or they are stupid enough to be bluffing."

"That's only rhetoric," Andrei said. "It fails to take the facts into account."

"Exactly what I said to Yashin. But as always it is Grigorenko who has Yashin's ear and the GRU is persuaded it is all a Chinese bluff to make us give ground."

Andrei drew breath; he made his voice reluctant: "The GRU could be right."

"Right?" Rykov spat the word out as if it were an insect that had flown into his mouth. He stabbed his cigarette into the tray on the corner of the desk and immediately lit another. Andrei could not recall having seen him so angry; it was a bleak chill that came off Rykov like death and Andrei, who had been ready to speak, held his tongue.

"What does it matter if they are right or wrong? China has thrown down the gauntlet, bluff or not. We must accept the challenge or back away from it. The troika means to back away and we cannot have that. Khrushchev's regime was toppled in the end because Khrushchev backed away when Kennedy rattled a saber. And Cuba was far away across the world. What must happen if we give ground before the Chinese on our own borders? Is there any question? Another debacle on our part and there will be nothing left of Russian resolve, Russian will, Russian courage. Stalin sought to appease Hitler and we know what came of that, and still the troika carries on. To preserve the illusion of peace they will give away our Far Eastern lands and they will give away Russian dignity. 'We must hold up our heads among the civilized nations of the world,' Yashin says. As if the opinion of the rest of the world mattered more than Russia's opinion of herself."

Andrei spoke carefully. "Naturally I agree that peace is not the sole objective—not at the expense of Soviet territory or as you say Soviet dignity. But possibly war is not the only available alternative."

Rykov's thick lips rolled around the cigarette. "Strategy is not your strong point, Andrei. It is China, not the Soviet Union, which has offered the ultimatum. *N'est-ce pas?"*

"Yes, I think we all agree on that."

"And Yashin insists it is a bluff, and you are not certain but that Yashin is right."

"Intending no disloyalty, I must concede the truth of that."

Rykov continued the dialectic: "Whether it is a bluff or not China is shaking the mailed fist at us. What are the options? Only two. Accept the challenge and fight back—by hitting them before they hit us. It's elementary but the troika remains stubbornly blind to it and that is why we have had to take these extraordinary clandestine measures."

"It is a logic with a weakness," Andrei replied, willing to say it now because Rykov had calmed down. "The weakness is that yours are not the only alternatives."

"I see no others."

"But of course there is another," Andrei said mildly. "We simply ignore the challenge. Act as if we know nothing of their war preparations. Continue as before, giving no ground yet starting no hostilities. After a while the Chinese will have to recognize the foolishness of their fruitless threat and they'll dismantle it."

"An assumption of dubious validity, Andrei, unless we are prepared to admit at the outset that under no circumstances is China willing to risk war—that the entire structure is pure bluff."

"The GRU assumes it is."

"The GRU does not have our resources," Rykov said patiently.

"But with all our resources we have not received incontestable evidence that China actually intends to attack us. Clues, hints, possibilities yes. But no Chinese official is known to have stated unequivocally that they intend to make war on us."

"The bulk of the evidence is far too substantial to ignore."

"But it is not conclusive."

Rykov said, "It is to me."

Andrei dipped his head. "Your judgment has always been correct."

It was the proper thing to say. It earned Rykov's fatherly smile.

When Rykov left the office and went into his own, Andrei went downstairs two flights and entered one of the subsection Control offices. The sentry nodded and drew himself up because a visit from the Second Secretary was rare. Andrei closed the door behind him and made use of one of the safe-line phones. It took a little while to get through and when Yashin came on the line his first words were, "Wasn't that you before?"

"Yes. Viktor came in just as you picked up."

"I see." On the telephone Yashin's voice seemed particularly scratchy with age. "What has happened, then?"

"Yevtenko arrived from Peking and I spoke with him."

"Does his report coincide with those Viktor has been receiving from his people?"

"More or less. There were no remarkable differences—no one is lying to us. It's a question of emphasis. They might make the same moves either way; you can see that—if a bluff is to be convincing it must look like the real thing. But Yevtenko has been on the scene a long time and I should be inclined to rely rather heavily on his aptitude for scenting the difference between a real effort and a sham. That was why I wanted to meet with him personally instead of having him report by the usual channels—I wanted to gauge his feelings as well as his knowledge of the facts."

"And?"

"He believes they are bluffing."

"Why?"

"As I say, it's mostly intuition. He assumes the Chinese expect us to be spying on them—otherwise it couldn't be a bluff, you see. They must intend for us to know what they're doing. With that in mind a few lucky coincidences become less coincidental. For example, when Yuan Tung sought an agent to obtain up-to-date defense charts of Vladivostok he just happened to single out one of our own double agents for the assignment. Several things like that. One of Yevtenko's sub-agents had been in deep cover for three years until Yevtenko activated him on my orders a few days ago—the subagent has spent a year as a domestic on the staff of the Maoist elite retreat in the mountains of central China, the underground bunkers where the Maoist leadership will presumably safe-guard itself during a war. Viktor has had extensive reports of increased shipments into that retreat—indications that they are preparing the subterranean caverns for a long siege. But our subagent reports that the preparations inside the under-ground bunkers have not been nearly as comprehensive as those outside. For example bedding has been received but has not been unpacked. Many of the foodstuff shipments are of a perishable nature and they do not have sufficient freezer capacity to store them for any length of time. That sort of thing. What I'm getting at is that it looks as though they are making war preparations only in the places where they have reason to expect us to see the preparations."

Yashin said, "That sounds fairly conclusive to me."

"No. Not necessarily. It could all be explained—perhaps they expect to set up the bedding later; perhaps they still have freezers scheduled to arrive within the next forty-eight hours. It's all conjectural. But Yevtenko has a very keen nose and no matter how hard I pressed him he still insisted he smells a bluff, though it is not cut and dried by any means."

"But Viktor still plans to set off his private war in less than forty-eight hours?"

"Yes."

"Then we have reached the end."

"Comrade First Secretary, I must repeat what I said at the outset when I first came to you. There are times when it pays to sit still and do nothing—it is possible to win out that way if your opponent's position deteriorates faster than your own. I repeat that in your own interests. You know what happens to several key comrades if Viktor is deposed—they must go down with him. I have no access to the methods he has de-vised of destroying them in the event of his own downfall."

"The downfall of a handful of old men is a very small thing

by comparison with the downfall of the very planet, Andrei. It's not even worth discussing."

"But we still have time. I earnestly expect to obtain proof that the Chinese have mounted nothing more than a bluff. If I can obtain it within the next twenty-four hours I'm sure I can persuade Viktor to abort. He can give the countermand at any time up to half an hour before the assigned moment. But of course Viktor is the *only* one who can give that countermand —he alone knows the signal; he and Belsky agreed on it privately."

"Of course. If that weren't the case we could have put a stop to this nonsense the minute you brought word to me."

"There isn't time to break Viktor down and force the code out of him. He must be reasoned with and we need evidence to do that."

Yashin said bitterly, "I'm not sure it would do any good at this late point in the game. You and I and all the others have changed as the world has changed but Viktor is still living in Stalin's era and wishes to drag all of us back into it with him. He is at war with the inevitable and I'm not sure but what he'll continue his operation regardless of what evidence he gets to prove the Chinese don't really mean to go to war. Andrei, you are the only man in the world for whom he has affection. You must persuade him. You know what's at stake."

"I do. But he has always been the stronger of us. Always."

"To him you are like a son. There is a time when a son must step out of his father's shadow. You *must* prevail. Of course you recognize that once it is done you will take Viktor's place; it goes without saying."

"I don't want his place. I have been his second for almost thirty years. When Viktor goes there's nothing left that I want here. I'll retire to a farm somewhere."

"You are a good man, Andrei. I know how painful it is for you."

"I shall do everything in my power."

"Do more than that, Andrei."

☆☆☆☆☆☆☆☆☆☆☆☆☆☆☆☆☆☆☆☆☆☆☆☆☆☆☆☆☆☆☆☆☆☆☆☆

Chapter Sixteen

The garage behind Ludlum's house had been converted into a plywood-paneled room containing a large round poker table with green felt topping. It was getting dark outside and they were grouped around the table under a ceiling lamp; the light was harsh, with smoke wheeling through it. The linoleum floor was littered with shoe-crushed cigarette butts and Styrofoam coffee cups.

Belsky was saying, "The reason should be obvious. You can't have an effective committee if it numbers more than six or seven people; beyond that they always fragment into subgroups and the leader loses control. When circumstances force you to have a committee of fifteen or twenty, the best solution is to gather the six or seven top people into a sort of executive committee to make the basic decisions and pass them on to the others."

Ludlum said, "I see that. But we've got a hell of a lot of people to pass the word down to and not a hell of a lot of time to do it in. If I had a couple of my people here now, just to listen, it'd save a lot of time getting them aside to where I can talk to them."

"You'll just have to make the time, Captain."

Ludlum opened the snap-ring top of a beer can. It spewed with a hiss. Ludlum was in his uniform, Air Force blues with railroad-track insignia. A huge gorilla torso on strangely spindly feminine legs. A pugilist, and other things as well: communications officer for the missile wing, Amergrad cell leader, expert in electronics.

Belsky said, "It shouldn't be that bad. In theory the force numbers well over two hundred Illegals but in practice we've only got to work with about eighty-five—the people directly connected with the operation."

He was talking to fill silence; they had to wait, the group wasn't complete. Restive, Nick Conrad got up and stood by the edge of the window, watching for the latecomers. His fingers toyed with the venetian-blind cord, tying and untying knots in it. A little less than forty-eight hours to go.

They heard the car coming. Ludlum stood up and went outside. The screen door closed behind him with a hiss and a slap. Belsky pulled the light string and they waited in darkness. He could feel their heat around him—Conrad, Hathaway, Adele Conrad, Fred Winslow. With Ludlum outside and the two new arrivals it made an ungainly group, seven of them not including Belsky, but he couldn't pare it down any tighter.

Ludlum held the door for Nicole Lawrence and came in behind Ramsey Douglass. "Okay," and Belsky switched on the light.

Nicole said, "Where's the john, Leo?"

Ludlum said, "Christ. We haven't got time for you to powder your nose."

"If you don't want to get your shoes wet you'd better point the way for me."

"Over there." Ludlum pointed to a door; Nicole went

through it and closed it without even nodding at the rest of them.

Douglass pulled out a chair and sat down at the poker table and said dryly, "What are the stakes and who's dealing?" He reached into his pocket with thumb and forefinger and brought out a heart-shaped tablet which he popped into his mouth.

Belsky said, "Take care with those amphetamines."

"I've had no sleep in two days. I can handle them. I'm not a pill freak."

Belsky said to Fred Winslow, "Taking things in order. You're now in command of the missile wing?"

"Temporarily. Until they send in a replacement for Colonel Sims." Winslow looked full of bile; he wasn't meeting anyone's eyes.

Ramsey Douglass asked, "What happened to Colonel Sims?"

Winslow said very angrily, "His plane crashed on the way to Yuma. I understand they found indications that several sticks of explosive had been taped to the control cables of the plane. Altimeter-fused. I don't like that, Dangerfield. You told me to get him out of the way temporarily and I did: we put some nonlethal poison in his wife's coffee down in Yuma and he was on his way down there to hold her hand in the hospital. It wasn't necessary to have him killed."

"There was no way to be sure he wouldn't return at the wrong moment," Belsky said. "Don't fight me, Vozshin, we haven't time." He turned to Hathaway. "What about Spode and that Senator?"

"Spode's been seen here and there. The Senator hasn't. He dropped out of sight after he left Professor Moskowitz at the university gate this morning. It looks like he's gone to ground."

Ramsey Douglass said, "I talked to Forrester's girl friend and she hadn't seen him. When I called her back later she'd gone."

"Gone home?"

"Just gone. Maybe she's with him. In any case she's got

instructions to keep him out of our hair. I talked to her brother but he doesn't know much of anything, or didn't a few hours ago. I can check back if you want."

"Never mind," Belsky said.

Hathaway said, "If Spode persuaded the Senator to go to ground it's got to mean Spode made you, Dangerfield."

"I know. Our cover is wearing thin but it can't be helped."

"You want us to take Spode out?"

"For the moment we've more important concerns. It's just as well if the Senator has been scared off: he'll be sure to stay away from the Air Base for a few days and that's all we really require of him. As for Spode he can't possibly know enough to interfere. At the worst he's reported my presence to Washington and there are agents looking for me, but as long as I remain out of sight we're in no danger. They have no way of knowing about the rest of you or the operation we're executing. And if we ignore Spode they may begin to get the idea I've fled the area. No—leave them alone."

The toilet flushed and Nicole emerged from the lavatory. "You ought to clean up that loo sometime, Leo." She took the empty chair beside Ramsey Douglass, and Belsky saw Douglass move slightly away from her. It was one of the things that made Belsky uneasy, the relationship between Nicole and Douglass—uneasy because he had not been able to determine the nature of it. On the surface they gave the impression of a pair of mutually destructive organisms drawn together by some curious masochistic force—but there had to be some explanation for it. They were all needed, these people—he needed their faculties and it disturbed him whenever hints of neurotic weakness revealed themselves. Douglass appeared calm enough but there were signs that not far under the surface was a potential for violent hysteria; if the man was likely to come apart in a crisis it was no good.

"Eighteen-thirty hours. For those of you who don't go by the military clock that's half-past six P.M." Belsky looked at his watch. "It's now almost eight so we have forty-six and a half hours."

They reacted mainly with alarm; several of them blasphemed quietly and Fred Winslow's face took on the expression of a man about to burst into tears.

Ramsey Douglass said, "Then we'll need to know the targets. Right now. The cards have to be punched so we can reprogram the guidance consoles."

"I'm quite certain none of our targets has been overlooked by American planners. It won't be necessary to feed any new information into your computers: the targets are all in China."

He let them babble a moment before he cut them off. "It's no good asking me why. I don't make policy and it doesn't concern you. Now shut up and let me finish. You have eighteen missiles here, each containing three warheads—fifty-four nuclear devices. There will be forty-seven separate targets; the additional seven warheads will be used for secondary strikes on hard silos which need to be hit more than once. An hour ago I prepared this list—two copies." He took the handwritten sheets from his pocket and unfolded them on the felt table cover; passed one of them to Winslow and said, "Well?"

"I'm not sure. I'll have to check to be positive. But you're probably right—I'm sure we've got all these programmed already. They're logical targets in case of war. The nuclear installations, the big cities, some military bases. I see you've got more of a concentration on army bases along the Russian border than we'd probably figure on ordinarily, but I expect all these have been programmed."

"Memorize that list. You can't afford to be caught with it in your possession. The first thing you'll do when you return to the base is check the computer files to be sure there's a card for each of these targets."

"Yes," Winslow mumbled, staring at the sheet of Chinese words. Beads of sweat stood out on his forehead.

Belsky pushed the second copy across the table to Nick Conrad. "The same for you. It'll be your job to provide the proper coded commands for these targets. The codes are scheduled to be changed tomorrow evening, isn't that right?"

"Yes."

"Then you've got the better part of twenty-four hours. Substitute our codes for the real ones and distribute the bogus code envelopes to all stations. Then, prepare the proper code sequences for Captain Ludlum to use when he simulates the issuance of attack orders from NORAD and the President. You understand this perfectly? Are there any questions?"

Conrad brooded over the list. "The time factor's tight but I don't see why we can't do it. But you've got to be damned sure there's no way for a legitimate signal to leak in or out."

"That's not your job. Concentrate on your own assignment. Do you foresee any difficulty?"

"Difficulty? Sure. But nothing impossible."

"Then we can rely on you for that." Belsky turned to Nicole. "Your job is to assemble all Amergrad personnel at the municipal airport at precisely six o'clock Sunday evening —all personnel who are not directly involved in the final sequences of execution. The others will be Sergeant Hathaway's responsibility. But it's up to you to communicate with all our local personnel and get them here at the appointed hour. There are to be no exceptions; you understand that. If any member is unable to be present you will give me his name and location."

"So that he can be liquidated, Comrade?"

"Yes. You can see what the result would be if even one of us remained behind to reveal what had happened here."

"Makes sense," Hathaway said. "But how do we work the getaway?"

"Colonel Winslow will arrange for the presence of a C-141 Starlifter jet on one of the alternate runways of the municipal airport at the appropriate time." He turned to Winslow. "The plane must be fully fueled and manned by a flight crew drawn from our own numbers. You may call it a training flight or whatever you choose. I am correct in assuming the aircraft is capable of containing two hundred and four people including crew?"

"It'll be a hell of a squeeze. We'll be like sardines in there." Winslow's face was tight with strain. "The number you're

talking about is the number of Amergrad agents in Tucson,
isn't it? Agents alone—not their children."

"The number represents the surviving members, yes. Two
are dead."

Nicole said, "That makes two hundred and three. I take it
the two hundred and fourth passenger is yourself."

"Correct."

"I suppose that's meant to convince me you weren't planning to send us all crashing into a mountain."

Winslow interrupted. "What about our families? Our children? We have to know, Dangerfield. What happens to
them?"

"Nothing."

Hathaway said, "We have somebody tailing your son
around town, Colonel. Just to make sure you stay in line. But
nothing's going to happen to him unless you make it happen."

Winslow wasn't letting it go. "You mean we'll just leave
them behind. Never see them again."

Belsky said, "Can you think of another way to handle it?
The children are Americans. They know nothing of the truth.
In Russia they'd represent a threat to us all. Here they offer
no threat to anyone since they know nothing of value. Their
parents simply disappear without warning. They'll be upset,
naturally; they'll go to the police, hire private detectives,
what-have-you, all of this assuming such institutions are still
in operation following the nuclear disruption. The children
will survive your disappearance if they survive the war."

"The war," Winslow murmured. "It'll be that, won't it? I
mean, there'll be retaliation."

"To some extent. Once these missiles have exploded over
China there won't be a great deal of retaliatory capacity left
in China."

"But Russia will come to China's aid."

Belsky said, "I can tell you this much. Russia will not come
to China's aid. I have been authorized to disclose that much
to you so that you won't be unduly concerned about the
likelihood of your children being killed in a nuclear holocaust.

Russia will not bombard the United States unless the United States attacks Russia first, and that is most unlikely. There is a certain risk from Chinese counterattack, yes, but your children stand a good chance of escaping harm since the Chinese retaliation will most likely be directed at American bases in the Pacific and along the West Coast—their ICBMs haven't the range to reach too far inland."

Winslow said, "My daughter is in school in California."

"I'm sorry, Comrade. But that's no proof she'll be hurt."

Douglass said, "This jet plane. Where's it going to take us? Cuba?"

"Of course," Belsky said. "And from there to the Soviet Union on board an Aeroflot plane."

Winslow, clearly, still had his mind on his family, but by evident effort he wrenched it away and said uncertainly, "There's one thing we haven't covered that bothers me. Our whole system is geared to a second-strike premise. That is, we're set up to fire these missiles only in the event of enemy attack."

"The enemy attack will be simulated. Your wing headquarters will receive all the signals it would receive in the event of a real red alert. That's Captain Ludlum's field of operation."

"I understand that," Winslow said. "But the missile squadrons aren't the only units that get activated under a red alert. The Pentagon goes on DefCon One—Defense Condition One—highest alert status, like when JFK was assassinated. The DefCon One signal alerts not only the ICBM wing but also the rest of the base. The SAC planes get a 'Batter Up' order to get them airborne so they won't be caught on the ground—all that kind of thing. Is that going to happen here?"

"Obviously not. Airplanes have radios. We couldn't very well have a wing of SAC bombers take to the air and then request confirmation from NORAD on the open airwaves which we can't control. To do that we'd have to take over the whole of NORAD and we can't possibly do anything like that."

"But then what happens when the ICBMs go on red alert

and the rest of the Air Base remains on normal status? It won't make sense to anybody."

"There won't be any contact between the two groups. Pay attention now because I haven't time to repeat myself. The essential mechanical and electronic preparations will have to be done tomorrow night under cover of darkness. Mrs. Conrad, it's your job to see that the sentries who are assigned to guard duty at the key points both inside and outside the missile silos are members of our group. That applies to the twenty-four-hour period beginning at six tomorrow evening. You have that?"

"It'll take some reshuffling of assignments," Adele Conrad said, "but I suppose the ones who suddenly find themselves with a weekend off duty won't complain. I'll have to get together with the officers in charge of these assignments."

"Never mind the details now. But Captain Ludlum's people will be working in the open and the sentries who see them must be our own people. We can't have any alarms. You'll have to see that the members of Captain Ludlum's teams are off duty, or assigned to places where Captain Ludlum needs them."

"We'll take care of it." She might have been talking about the installation of a television set in a ranking officer's bedroom.

Belsky said, "The key to everything is to seal off communications. We've got to be certain there's no leakage in or out."

"It ought to work," Ludlum said. "We've had twenty years to work out the details, and Douglass here keeps us up to date on everything new they install by way of equipment."

"Your plan is satisfactory, but there's one vital thing it doesn't take into account. We may get orders to abort from Moscow at any time—we've got to be prepared to react exactly as you would react if an actual countermand came down from the President."

Ludlum said, "You've got to be above ground with your radio receiver, is that it?"

"Yes. So you've got to maintain one thread of contact with the outside—contact with me."

"Well, we're disconnecting the antenna systems. We can wire an independent receiver into one of them and hook it into one of Fred Winslow's scrambler phones. That'll give you direct voice contact with Colonel Winslow and he'll have his finger six inches from the countermand button." Ludlum's blunt head turned. "We can test it as soon as we've wired it up. I don't see any big flap about the technical end but Nick's got to get the codes to us in time. How soon can I have copies?"

Conrad said, "We'll start printing right away. Sometime tomorrow morning be all right?"

"It'll do."

Belsky shifted his seat on the hard chair. "About personnel —we don't have enough trained people to handle all the message traffic that will come through; after all we're throwing a red alert at them and they'll be firing back requests for clarification and verification. Unfortunately there's no way we can simulate incoming rockets on their radar screens and they'll want to know why they don't see anything on radar if there's an attack under way. We've got to convince the launch personnel that NORAD and the Pentagon and a few other sites are under attack by Chinese missiles. That will explain to them why they're being ordered to fire on China, and they'll attribute any foul-ups in communications to the confusion of the attack."

Ludlum said, "The easy way's to act as if the Chinese are dumping enough megatonnage on NORAD to dig Cheyenne Mountain right out of the ground. Then all orders will appear to come from Looking Glass—the airborne headquarters— and if a lot of it gets garbled by static the launch people won't get suspicious."

Nick Conrad stood up, looking at his watch and shooting his cuff. "Listen, I'd better get going—we've got to set up the codes and start printing."

Nicole said, "Yes, let's not keep the Kremlin waiting."

Belsky had left his rented Ford in a pay-parking lot and torn up the ticket; he was driving a dark Dodge hardtop that belonged to one of Hathaway's men. The car smelled of tobacco and there were big fuzzy dice hanging from the mirror. He drove up the Sabino Canyon road and made a left turn into a vague dirt track that ran back into the hills. On the tall weeds between the road's ruts the headlights picked up fresh dark grease that had rubbed off the bottom of a recent vehicle.

The place had been a farm. It had been abandoned for several years; the windows were smashed, the shingles cracked, the barnyard overgrown.

When Belsky stopped the car he blinked his headlights on and off twice before he got out. Culver appeared in the barn door and waved. "Hi there, Mr. Beldon. Right on time."

"Everything all right, Culver?" Belsky carried the transceiver in his left hand.

"Got everything you ordered. Come see for yourself." Tim Culver had the quick restless eyes and the mouth-corner speech of an ex-convict. He backed up to make room in the doorway and when Belsky came inside Culver slid the big door shut and switched on a big multicell flashlight. The beam played over the ton-and-a-half truck. It had U.S. Air Force blue paint and a variety of stenciled white identification markings. The barn smelled of old hay and fresh paint, and the glass and chrome of the truck were stripped with masking tape; the truck was still aglitter with wetness. Near the back of the steel-enclosed bed there was a patch of Army olive-drab paint that hadn't been covered yet.

"I just got a little left to spray," Culver said. "I took care of the stencils up front first because that white stuff's tricky; you got to dry it just right or it runs."

"Looks good, Culver."

Culver went back and got the spray canister and resumed work on the back of the truck. Its loading doors stood open; Belsky looked inside. The small steel tanks had been fitted carefully into soft-lined wooden frames to prevent their being jarred. Belsky made a quick count—twenty-four pressure tanks, each with valve and hose. They were smaller than aqualung tanks and looked vaguely like fire extinguishers.

Culver said, "I already took the plates off. You bring those Air Force plates?"

"In the trunk of my car."

"Okay. I'll put them on soon as I finish up here."

"Take your time," Belsky said. He looked at his watch in the reflected glow of Culver's big flashlight.

Squares of brown corrugated cardboard had been taped over the insides of the rear-door windows to make it appear from outside as if the truck were loaded with cartons.

Belsky said, "Did you have any trouble?"

"Naw. I waited down at Sierra Vista and when the truck came out the Fort Huachuca gate I tailed it out toward the highway and went by it on that narrow stretch above Tombstone—dumped out the spikes, and when it blew a tire I handled them easy with that rifle of yours. That's a sweet silencer."

"What did you do with the bodies?"

"Buried them out back of the barn here." Culver lowered the sprayer and stood back to shine the torch along the truck and study his handiwork. "Let that dry overnight it ought to look fine. I'll get those plates now."

Belsky waited while Culver screwed the Air Force plates onto the truck's license-plate brackets. Afterward Culver straightened up and said, "That first ten thousand was real sweet, Mr. Beldon. I hope you got the other ten thou with you."

"Right here, Tim. You've done a fine job." Belsky took an envelope from his pocket and when Culver came to take it from him, Belsky's single blow to the throat crushed Culver's windpipe.

He carried the body to the car and got the pint of whiskey from the dashboard glovebox. He poured the whiskey over the corpse, draped a canvas tarp over the passenger seat of the car, and then lifted Culver into the seat. He drove out to the canyon highway, turned left toward the mountains, accelerated the car to high speed and on a leftward curve threw Culver's body out. It was no easy maneuver but it was not the first time Belsky had performed it. The body bounced off the road and crashed into scrub brush. Leaning far over in the seat, Belsky pulled the passenger door shut and slowed before he reached the canyon park gate; he made a sedate U-turn and went back the way he had come. He noticed when he went by that the body was not visible from the road. That was all right. He returned to the farm, opened the barn door, drove the truck out and put the car inside the barn. He took the transceiver over to the truck and placed it on the seat, closed the loading doors and started the engine. He drove very slowly until he reached the paved highway because he didn't want to kick up dust that would adhere to the wet paint. Going into Tucson he bounced along high up in the cab, maneuvering the truck with professional ease.

He had obtained Culver's name from the Los Angeles *rezidentsia*—the name of a habitual criminal willing to do anything for pay. But he couldn't have let Culver run around loose afterward with the knowledge of what had happened to the truckload of GB3X nerve gas he had hijacked from the Army Proving Ground at Fort Huachuca.

The gas was colorless, odorless, designed to kill within seconds.

Belsky drove through Tucson on Wilmot Road and Fifth Street and Alvernon Way—main arteries—because he would attract less attention than by driving through back streets. When he reached Twenty-second Street he turned right and made all the green lights in the two-mile stretch to the railroad overpass. He turned right into the warehouse district that lined the Southern Pacific yards and drove the truck easily through the narrow clearance of the open doors of the corrugated-metal storage building Hathaway had rented two days before in the name of the Tanner-Kavanagh Packing Company.

He switched off the headlights and closed the building's overhead door before he climbed into the back of the truck with the flashlight and the can of aluminum spray paint and carefully obliterated the warnings and descriptive stencils on each of the twenty-four canisters. He was nearing the last of them when the blinker on the transceiver began to flash.

The apparatus was programmed to tape-record the incoming message automatically and so he took the time to finish spraying paint on the canisters before he opened the transceiver case and rewound the tape to play it back and write out the message. It took two or three minutes to decode and when he was done he had filled a notebook page in his crabbed hand.

> PRIORITY UTMOST
> DANGERFIELD TUC 6 APR
> VIA NUCSUB 4
> KGB 1
> CIPHER 1548 SG
> SENT 0527 GMT D ACKNOWLEDGMENT UNNECESSARY
> MESSAGE BEGINS X PREVIOUS INSTRUCTIONS CONFIRMED X
> EXECUTE PLAN B3 1830 7 APR CONFIRMED X HENCEFORTH
> BE ALERT FOR COUNTERFEIT INSTRUCTIONS THIS FRE-
> QUENCY X EXAMINE CIPHER REFERENCES WITH UTMOST CAU-
> TION X HENCEFORTH ALL LEGITIMATE INSTRUCTIONS FROM
> VR WILL CONTAIN PHRASE FROM FATHER CHRISTMAS X RE-
> PEAT X FROM FATHER CHRISTMAS X RELY ON YOU X VR X
> MESSAGE ENDS 17661 42 6474

It was nearly two o'clock in the morning when Hathaway arrived at the warehouse. He said, "I got a million things to do. I hope this ain't going to take long."

"Not long at all," Belsky assured him.

"Where'd you get that truck?"

"Have you got time to waste asking pointless questions?"

"Sorry." Hathaway's uniform was rumpled. He glanced into the truckbed.

Belsky said, "It's a nonlethal gas. I want you to have your men secrete some of these canisters in the ventilation and circulation systems to cover all occupied rooms of the launch complex. You're to rig the valves with electrical switches so that they can be opened by remote control from the exit you plan to use when you evacuate our people after the missiles have been fired. Do you understand?"

"I know what you're telling me but I don't get the point."

"When you and the others leave the launch complex we don't want you followed and we don't want people buttonholing any of you and asking hysterical questions. If you trigger these canisters when you leave, the gas will render everyone unconscious in the launch complex. They won't regain consciousness for at least two hours and that will give us ample time to get everyone into the aircraft and be on our way."

It was an expedient lie. Hathaway and his men had had twenty years to make friends with Air Force enlisted men, some of whom would be in the launch complex. There wasn't any point in burdening Hathaway's conscience with the knowledge he was going to murder them.

Belsky climbed into the back of the truck and carefully lifted four of the canisters out and left them on the floor of the warehouse. "I'll need these for another location," he said. "You may take the rest."

"Truck and all?"

"Of course. How else did you expect to smuggle them into an Air Force base?" Belsky picked up the transceiver and turned toward the door. "I'll use your car. I'll be at Ludlum's."

"What happened to the car we gave you?"

"It got mislaid," Belsky said, and went outside.

☆☆☆☆☆☆☆☆☆☆☆☆☆☆☆☆☆☆☆☆☆☆☆☆☆☆☆☆☆☆☆☆☆

Chapter Seventeen

It was four o'clock in the morning before Fred Winslow found a moment to make his way to the coin-operated public phone in one of the underground day rooms. He wasn't sure it wasn't tapped but he took the chance. He put through the call to Celia and exactly half an hour later he made a vague excuse and slipped up to the surface. She was waiting outside the fence and he eeled into the car past her. "I haven't got very long."

In the starlight the boniness of her face was accentuated; her eyes looked very large; her smile was fixed and meaningless. Winslow said, "They've put a tail on Alec."

"Well, we thought they might." She looked preternaturally tired—too tired to care about anything at all.

He said, "Tomorrow night. They've ordered us to shoot the missiles tomorrow night. Half-past six."

"Dear God," she whispered.

"At China. All the targets are in China." He had been doing that for hours—saying things twice. He shook his head violently, trying to clear it. "Dangerfield says the strike will wipe out most of China's retaliatory missiles and the Russians won't come into it at all unless the Americans start shooting at Russia first. He said they'd allowed him to tell us that much because they want to reassure us that our children have a good chance to escape being caught under an atomic blast."

"He'd have said that whether it was true or not."

"I know," he said. "I know. But it could be true, couldn't it?"

"Because you want it to be true? How can we believe anything that man says? Truth means nothing to them—why should it? They tell us what they want us to know."

He was carrying an executive call-up—a radio-activated pocket device that would emit a high-pitched whistle if he was needed down below. He kept waiting for it to sound.

He said, "No, it's not true. We're programming the missiles to hit sites in the north and west of China. We're not going to hit the sites on the Yellow Sea and those are the ones that are aimed at the United States. Dangerfield says they haven't got enough range to get much deeper into this country than the Pacific Coast but that isn't true either. If that really was the case he couldn't expect our launch people to believe the Pentagon was under attack by Chinese missiles, could he?"

"You've got to get a grip on yourself, Fred."

He gripped her forearm. The chilly sweat of fear streamed down his ribs. He pulled his head around toward her and said, "Have you thought about it? What we talked about?"

"How could I have thought about anything else?"

"I know. But what I meant was have you decided?"

"No. Not for myself. But I'll do whatever you decide, darling."

"Maybe this is one time I'd really rather have you make the decision."

"I can't."

He sat studying the backs of his hands and then turning them over and studying the palms. Finally he pressed them together until the knuckles cracked. She was watching him anxiously and he felt his face color under her stare. "We're grotesques," he muttered. "Twenty years leading double lives—twenty years is so long when you break it up into hours but it still isn't long enough. We've become middle-aged Americans. We chose to forsake everything Russian—the flavors and smells and sounds of Russia. You can't steal the results of the next election from the government safe. You don't wait for the tramp of police boots, the knock on the door, transportation to penal squads in a slave camp, legions of secret police. . . . I remember how we used to seal the windows in the wintertime and go to bed very early and sleep in all our clothes because we couldn't afford fuel. . . . God, stop me, Celia, I'm babbling."

She twisted in the seat to grip him on both shoulders. His face slumped forward and he turned unashamedly toward her; she printed warm gentle kisses on his tear-streaked face.

"I had my mind made up," he said. "I was ready to do it. And then they told me they had someone following Alec—just to keep me in line, they said. Oh Christ. Alec's just a boy. We can't make him share in our guilt."

"He's twenty-two years old, Fred, and he's going to suffer whatever happens. He's going to lose us whatever we do."

"Should we do it, then?"

"I can't—I don't know."

He thought of Alec, husky with young energy.

She said, "What do the rest of them think?"

"I haven't asked them. I can't speak for them. How could I ask them? They'd report me to Dangerfield and we'd both be killed."

She said nothing. He thought of Barbara, fourteen years old and away in California with her school chums and her silver fingernail polish. He tried to remember whether Sacramento was within fallout radius of the California defense bases. It must be; there were so many bases. Russian roulette: how many missiles did the Chinese have? How many would they launch at California targets? How many would penetrate the ABM defense screen? But all it took was one. He thought of the film lectures: *We project a fifty-mile destruction radius for the Chinese twenty-megaton warhead. . . .*

He said, "I'm going to do it," and the sound of his own voice electrified the skin of his spine. "I'm going to do it, Celia."

She was watching him; in the bad light he couldn't make out her expression. He asked softly, "What do you think, then?"

"No. First you decide you're going to do it and then you ask me what I think. No. If you were sure of yourself you wouldn't have asked me now—you see what you're doing, Fred? You want me to tell you you're wrong, because then you can get all worked up with self-righteousness and indignant rationalizations and you can get angry enough to convince yourself that you are right. But we can't play that game this time. It's too much—too much at stake. We can't decide out of anger."

He reached for her hand—blindly, timidly; he was looking the other way. "You're right. I always do that, don't I." He wanted the buzzer in his pocket to summon him away because down below, working, he could fix his mind on practical technical things. But it remained still.

"We still have a little time." He looked at his watch. "Thirty-seven hours and forty-five minutes, to be precise." His mouth twisted.

"Refusing to make a decision—that can be a decision in itself, you know."

He nodded. "The idea is we're all supposed to leave together when it's done."

"I know. Nicole talked to me. I'm to be at the airport at five-thirty tomorrow evening. The side gate, where the old entrance used to be."

"It's an older runway they don't use too much anymore. I

had to get clearance for a so-called training flight to use it tomorrow evening. I gave them some official-sounding gibberish and they yawned their way through it and gave us permission because they don't have much air traffic out there at that time of night anyway. They're flying us to Cuba, you know."

"Yes, she told me."

"What's the point of their keeping us alive after we've done the job here, Celia? That's what keeps nudging me to decide to do it. The feeling that no matter what assurances Dangerfield gives us it still makes sense for them to kill us all. He killed Bud Sims, you know. We'll all be together in that airplane—it wouldn't be any trouble at all for him."

"He'd be killing himself too."

"Maybe he's willing to do that. Maybe he's a good German —obeying all orders without question; maybe he's prepared a parachute for himself. Or maybe at the last minute he'll arrange to be left behind and the plane will blow up after takeoff. I keep thinking how easy it would be for him to do things like that—there are so many ways. As long as any of us remain alive, even in Russia, we're a danger to them. We're no danger dead."

"I've thought of those things too," she said, "but I can't put those pictures out of my mind. The ones he showed us—that Mongolian, Manchurian, whatever he is, Tircar. The children tortured and murdered while the parents watched."

He closed his eyes. That was all he had been able to think of—Alec and Barbara. "That's what Dangerfield wants us to do. Remember those pictures and obey orders."

"They're offering a trade. They've made a bargain with us. As long as we put ourselves in their hands our children will be left alone."

"I don't know. I keep thinking there must be a way to do it without condemning Alec."

"Perhaps there is. But I think we must be prepared to make the decision on the basis that we'd be sacrificing Alec's life if we went against them."

"I can't do it now," he said, and was ashamed when his

voice broke. He reached for the door handle. "I've got to think it out more clearly. I'll decide, but I just can't do it now."

"My poor darling," she murmured, and he squeezed her hand tight as if to draw a current of strength from her. When he got out of the car she stared at him with eyes that looked like two holes burned in a blanket.

☆☆☆☆☆☆☆☆☆☆☆☆☆☆☆☆☆☆☆☆☆☆☆☆☆☆☆☆☆☆☆☆☆☆☆☆☆☆☆

Chapter Eighteen

When Forrester pulled the door softly shut behind him it drew Top Spode's glance; Spode had been sitting by the window staring out, eyes narrowed in a thoughtful squint. "Morning."

"Haven't you been to bed at all?"

"No. You don't look like you slept much yourself."

"Not much." Forrester's dreams had left an aftertaste of fear, though all memory of them had gone.

"She all right?"

"I don't know." Ronnie had taken it badly; she had been ill half the night. "She won't see a doctor."

"Asleep now?"

"Yes."

"Then let her sleep," Spode said.

Forrester was dressing while they talked. "Have you been on the phone?"

"All night. Nobody knows anything. Belsky hasn't turned up. They found the car he rented on a parking lot. He'll never come back for it. I don't know if it fits into this but somebody hijacked a truckload of nerve gas from Fort Huachuca."

"Nerve gas," Forrester muttered, buttoning his cuffs. "God."

"Yeah." Spode picked up the phone and said, "Room service, please. . . . Hello, this is three twenty-seven, send up a pot of coffee and two cups and a plate of bacon and eggs, will you? Bacon fried crisp and two eggs over hard. . . . Yeah, thanks."

"Don't you want anything to eat?"

"I had a couple of doughnuts an hour ago where I made a few calls." Spode got out of the chair and stretched; Forrester heard the ligaments crackle. "I've been letting myself be seen around town but nobody's taken any potshots at me."

"He may be long gone, Top."

"Then why did he kill Art Miller? No, I can't buy it." Spode scowled outward—the sky was cloudy above the rooftops across the way. "My ex-boss and I kicked around a lot of things on the phone to see if anything rang any bells. The Agency's been picking up signs of a big Chinese flap along the Russian border—bigger than anything they've ever seen. The President's holding an emergency session of the National Security Council this morning. Since I'm not on the payroll there were certain things I couldn't be told on the record, but reading between the lines I gathered that one or two friendly KGB types have made overtures to their opposite numbers in the Agency to feel us out about taking sides in the event of an eruption over there."

"Between China and Russia?"

"Yes. Of course they've had these flaps before. Bluff and double-bluff—brinkmanship, Chinese style. They push until they meet too much resistance and then they squat down and wait for things to cool off before they start pushing again. Process of attrition—but the Russians have been getting fed up with it. You would too."

"But what's that got to do with Belsky?"

"God knows," Spode muttered. Knuckles rapped at the door and Forrester grimaced and stepped into the alcove out of sight until he heard Spode tip the waiter and close the door. Spode set the tray on the coffee table.

Forrester took the dome off the plate and sat down to eat. "I'm sick of hide and seek, Top, it's not my style."

"I know. But I'd like to find out what's really going on before we start taking any chances."

"We're not going to find out anything sitting here."

"It's not your job—you've got other fish to fry. Let the professionals handle Belsky."

"They don't seem to be getting anywhere, do they."

"And just how far do you think you could get? What did you have in mind, strapping on a six-shooter and spreading the word around town you'll be waiting for him on Stone Avenue at high noon?"

"Jaime's right, you know." Ronnie's voice drew Forrester's head around sharply. She stood in the bedroom doorway in last night's skirt and blouse, slightly rumpled; she had washed the sleep off her face but she wore no makeup. She was stunning.

Forrester stood up with his napkin in his hand. "Feeling any better?"

"I'm fine—I don't know why I went to pieces. I'm miserable because I kept you up with all that silliness. Forgive me?"

"As long as you're sure you're all right."

"Well, tired and a little jittery—and very ashamed of myself." Her smile was reticent.

He indicated the plate. "I've hardly started. Why don't you eat this while it's warm—I'll have some more sent up."

"I don't think I'd better do that yet. Please go ahead and finish." She waved him to his seat and went back into the bedroom. She left the door open and he saw her sit down at the dressing table to comb her hair. "Jaime, have you talked to Les Suffield?" There was something a bit taut behind the casual question and Forrester watched her with full attention.

"A little while ago," Spode said. "Why?"

"Oh—nothing."

But Forrester saw her shoulders stir, almost as if with relief. He pushed the plate away; abruptly he felt no hunger at all.

She had been like that last night too, even while she was alone with him: distant, polite. Like a relative on a visit. She had tried to explain last night: *It's all happened too fast, hasn't it, Alan? Don't we need a little more time to get our feelings about each other sorted out? I had my life neatly compartmentalized until just the other day and now overnight everything's changed—I need a chance to get my breath but I can't right now. You've sprung this horrible Russian murderer business on me and I know it's unreasonable, I know it's not your fault, but I just can't. . . .* She had cried out and shut herself into the bathroom.

She seemed to feel their eyes on her; she said by way of explanation, "I just thought Les might know something that would help."

She had always tended to lean on Les Suffield. It was Suffield who had first brought her into his organization. Forrester had always found it slightly odd; Ronnie in her way hated the devious mechanisms of politics and yet she seemed to have extraordinarily high regard for Suffield, who epitomized the back-room philosophy she deplored. It was possible she had had an affair with him but somehow Forrester found it hard to credit, for reasons he couldn't articulate.

He reached for the coffee and squeezed his eyes shut; he was tired, his mind was wandering. Spode had picked up a newspaper and it rustled like submachine-gun fire. Forrester said irritably, "It must be something to do with the missile factories; nothing else seems to explain Belsky's being here. If only Ross Trumble were alive to explain—"

The edge of the same fast-traveling thought struck them all and Forrester saw Spode sit bolt upright. Ronnie came into the sitting room again with her fingers at her throat and

Spode said with vast self-disgust, "Oh Christ. The damned letter."

Ronnie said something, not a word, and Spode got to his feet so fast his knees knocked the chair back against the radiator. "Orozco's man said it was addressed to you at the ranch."

"Then let's get it," Forrester said, on his way to the door.

Ronnie said, "Wait—don't go."

When he looked back she said quickly, "Suppose he's waiting for you to show yourself? The Russian."

"I can't spend the next week hidden away here—I'd start climbing the walls. And I have to know what's in that letter."

"But it's probably only a copy of the Phaeton specifications —the ones Jaime's already photographed. You asked him for them and he told you he might send them to you. Isn't that what you said?"

Spode said, "Whatever's in that letter it's not the Phaeton specs. Trumble wrote it out longhand in the hotel lobby. It was a letter—a long one."

Ronnie had crossed the space between them; she reached for Forrester's sleeve. "I just don't want you to risk being hurt. Why can't you stay here while Jaime and I drive down and get the letter?" She gave a sudden smile—tremble-lipped, pale.

"I don't understand you, Ronnie."

"Is it worth exposing yourself just for a letter that probably has nothing in it?"

"Nothing in it? The man wrote it less than twenty-four hours before he died. We've got to assume it's vitally important."

"But it may not even have arrived yet. It's only Saturday morning—he didn't mail it till Thursday afternoon, in Phoenix, and you know how slow rural deliveries are. . . ."

Spode said, "What time does the mail come in down there?"

"About one in the afternoon," Forrester answered.

"Then there's a good chance it'll show up today."

Ronnie was shaking her head. "I can't explain it, Alan, I just have a terrible feeling. I'm frightened for you—I keep having visions of that awful man waiting for you with a gun."

Spode said, "I expect he's got better things to do with his time than hang around out in the boondocks waiting to set up an ambush. We ought to be secure as soon as we get out of town. I can pull my car around back of the hotel in the alley here."

"But they might recognize your car." She flicked her eyes back and forth, and Forrester frowned with incomprehension. When she realized it was no good trying to dissuade him she turned to Spode and implored, "At least let's get help. Les Suffield has a pistol. Call him—ask him to come pick us up in his car. They won't be looking for his car. And they wouldn't attack four of us, would they?"

Spode shrugged. But Forrester said, "It might be a good idea, Top. Not necessarily for protection but I think Les ought to be in on this."

"If you say so. I'll call him."

The morning sky was misty with the promise of rain; a diaphanous halo surrounded the sun, and heavy clouds were building up over the Tucson Mountains west of town. The air itself seemed to have thickened and been stunned; even though the streets were filled with the usual noises of traffic there was a muted sense of great silence. Now and then in the distance thunder clattered like bowling alley pins.

When they reached the freeway Suffield buzzed up the electric windows and switched on the air-conditioner to diminish the roar of wind and make conversation possible. In the front seat with Suffield, Top Spode did the talking, giving it to Suffield in summary doses.

Suffield was dubious to the extent of glancing at Forrester in the mirror at one point and saying, "I cite Mark Twain— 'Reader, suppose you were an idiot. And suppose you were a member of Congress. But I repeat myself.' End of citation. You've got a talent for finding absurd situations."

Forrester made no reply and Top proceeded with his précis. Forrester sat uneasy in the corner and felt isolated, detached in the sealed car as it hurtled through the morning on the straight highway that four-laned toward the mountains. Beer cans and half-buried bottles glinted along the desert roadside. Ronnie sat far over on her side of the back seat, her lips parted amd heavy in repose; she had covered her eyes with dark harlequin glasses. She was looking out her window, tense as if she were waiting for something. She seemed consumed by irrational fears; he had never seen her like that before. Perhaps she had been right: perhaps they had let it all come together too fast, perhaps they needed to back away and learn each other. He was beginning to realize the scope of his ignorance about her.

Suffield stopped by the gate and Jaime Spode got out. They all watched him open the mailbox. Catching Les Suffield's profile, Forrester saw the jaw hinge bunch up and something struggle fiercely behind Suffield's eyes. But the voice was very controlled. "It appears the postman dallieth."

Spode slid into the car. "Not due yet anyhow—let's go up to the house and wait."

The banality of the exchange made it all seem unreal. Ronnie bit a thumbnail. Forrester was vexatiously alert to the tension in the car. He felt responsible for it but he did not understand it because they all seemed disproportionately apprehensive. When they reached the house Ronnie went up to the door with her marvelous flowing walk—nothing would change that—but once inside she began to flutter, opening blinds and putting coffee on to boil and plumping up cushions, never alighting, never looking directly at Forrester. Finally it was too much for him: "Will all of you just sit down for one minute? You're all acting as if I've committed some unforgivable faux pas and you're making a belabored point of ignoring it."

"Oh nonsense," Ronnie said crossly. "But you've made me so nervous I'm waiting for spies to come crawling out of the woodwork with great gleaming knives between their teeth."

Les Suffield was at the front window looking out and Spode said, "You can't see the mailbox from up here."

"I know. I was looking at those clouds. We're going to get some rain—any chance of the road getting washed out?"

Forrester walked to the window to have a look. The unrolling clouds had heavy black bellies and the shadow streaks of grey rain slanted toward the peaks along a wide front beyond the western perimeter of the valley. Tall lances of cloud shot forward from the crest. "Sometimes the arroyos fill up with flash floods—you may get eight feet of water in some of the dips in the road but it always dries up after a few hours, half a day at the most. You learn to accommodate yourself to those things down here."

"But if we don't beat that out of here we'll probably be stuck here overnight, won't we?"

"It's possible," Forrester said indifferently. "There's plenty here to feed us. Don't worry about it, Les."

Suffield shrugged his thick shoulders and turned, reaching around to adjust the hip-pocket gun under the tail of his jacket. "It's quite a story, Jaime. If I didn't know the source I'd take it for a fairy tale."

"I wish it was."

"How much do the Government agents know about this?"

Spode made a gesture. "Not much more than we know."

"There's got to be an explanation for it."

Forrester went back to the couch. "Maybe we'll find out when Ross Trumble's letter arrives. I think the coffee's boiling."

Ronnie bounced out of her chair and Suffield turned. "I'll help with that." He trailed her out toward the kitchen and the low run of their voices came back into the room but Forrester couldn't make out the words. It went on for some time until Spode said, "They seem to have gone into a huddle out there. I guess we did spring it on them kind of sudden."

Ronnie came in with a tray and distributed cups; the coffee made a good strong smell. "I'll throw something together for lunch in a little while." When she handed his coffee to Forrester the cup and saucer rattled in her hand.

Suffield came in, agitated, preceded by his voice: "I just tried the phone. It's dead."

Forrester flapped his big hand toward the window. "The line goes across to the Santa Cruz—it's already raining over there and the wire may be down."

"I don't like that."

Spode said, spuriously mild, "Les may be right. It could be somebody cut the wire." He carried his coffee to the window and took up a post there.

Suffield said, "Who else is around here?"

Forrester was still scowling at Spode; he turned to answer Suffield's question: "The crew will be out—with a storm coming in, they'll be bunching the herds."

"Haven't you got a house man?"

"Just the housekeeper, Mrs. Gutiérrez. She's my manager's wife—when I arrive with guests she always fades out of sight and waits at home until she's called."

"She live around here?"

"The white 'dobe down below. We passed it on the way. You've been here before, Les, what's the matter?"

"Just that we're pretty isolated here, aren't we? It could be an awkward time for friend Belsky to drop in."

"I hardly think it's likely."

Spode said, "I wouldn't exactly—" and then he stiffened at the window. "Dust out above the road. Your mailman drive a jeep down here?"

"Yes." Forrester put his cup down before he stood up.

Suffield said, "I'll go down and get it." His voice was taut with anxiety and he walked toward the door with very quick strides.

Forrester was closer to the door; he got there first and said mildly, "Then let's both go," and went past into the foyer.

Suffield's voice, behind him, gripped him as if by the elbow and swung him around. "Hold it a minute, then."

When Forrester turned he saw the revolver in Suffield's fist.

"We'll all go," Suffield said.

Ronnie sat bolt upright. "No, Les."

"Shut up."

Forrester snapped, "What the devil is this?" And Spode's

voice overlapped his: "For Christ's sake, Les, what's the flap?"

"Everybody outside to the car. You drive, Jaime, and Alan sits in the front seat with you. Now move, everybody."

"Will you all please just shut up. Jaime, pull over by the mailbox and don't move a God damned muscle. Ronnie, you collect the mail, that's a good girl."

Spode eased the car in by the side of the road and they waited for Ronnie; but after she had opened the door and swung her legs out she stopped and said, "Les, for heaven's sake—"

"Move. Eyes front, you two."

A few raindrops spattered the hood of the car and Forrester felt sweat in his armpits, along his chest, in his palms.

"I told you to sit still. I mean it, I'll kill both of you if you push me."

Spode said in exasperated bewilderment, "Jesus H. Christ."

The car swayed with Ronnie's weight and the back door chunked shut. Suffield said, "Never mind the rest of the junk. Is it in there?"

"This must be it," she said.

"Give it to me. Jaime, drive us back up to the house."

The gun was steady in the fist and Suffield leaned his back against the big door to close it. "Everybody sit down. Ronnie, you'd better open this and read it; I don't want to take my eyes off these two."

Forrester said, "This has gone far enough. Put that gun—"

"Will you all just quit yapping for a minute? I need to think."

"You don't need to think with that gun in your hand. What's come over you?"

Suffield's thumb curled over the hammer of the revolver. "I told you to sit down."

Filled with disbelief Forrester backed up till his knees struck the chair. He settled onto its edge. "All right, Les, I'm sitting down. Just take it easy now. What do you want of us?"

"Don't humor me, I'm not sick in the head."

"Just take it easy then—there's no need to fill the air with bullets. Just tell us what it is you want."

Spode folded his arms and squinted; he was by the front window. "And make it good, Les, because I can spot you the gun and thirty pounds and still take you apart—make it real good, hear?"

Suffield's red-brick lips peeled back from his teeth. "Don't you think I can handle a gun? Don't get notions, Jaime, just sit down on that windowsill and keep quiet."

Forrester's head was lifted; he was listening to the run of Suffield's voice, trying to detect the note of madness that surely had to be there; but Suffield was not out of control and there was nothing in his attitude to confirm what had to be the case: that something in him had snapped.

Suffield said, "What about it, Ronnie?"

It was so heavy it had taken four first-class stamps on the envelope. "The handwriting's like a child's."

"He was overwrought. What's in it?"

"Everything," she said. "Everything he knew. Dangerfield, Craig, the whole thing."

"I suspected as much. He must have been planning it for years. Planning to blow it all sky high if and when the man ever showed up from over there."

"It's strange," Ronnie said. "He didn't even know what it was for. He had no idea. He had to be in Phoenix with Alan and Senator Guest that morning."

"I know about that. He sent Craig to tape the meeting but Craig fell through and Trumble was right back at square one. He never did find out."

Forrester said, "Will you please—"

"Shut up." Suffield's florid face was clamped up tight; a vein showed at his forehead. "Does he name names?"

"Half a dozen," Ronnie said. "All he knew."

"Burn it," Suffield said. "In the fireplace over there. Do it one sheet at a time."

Forrester gathered his legs. "Wait just a minute."

Suffield cocked the revolver. "Sit still. Go ahead, Ronnie. Burn it."

She burned the letter sheet by sheet and stirred the ashes with a poker. Suffield stood by, vigilant over the gun. Consumed with rage Forrester cleared his throat and spoke; his voice trembled: "I think you'd better explain this. Whatever it is—"

"It isn't," Suffield barked. "It's nothing for you to know anything about." He backed up toward the fireplace so as to keep both Forrester and Spode conveniently in his view. Ronnie circled behind him and reached the couch and Suffield spoke to her as if they were alone together in the room: "We'll have to make it look like an accident."

"No!"

"Stop it. Don't get hysterical. We've got to think, you know that."

"We're not going to kill anyone, Les."

"Then tell me how else to do it. Just tell me that."

"I don't know. But there must be something."

"We haven't got time."

Ronnie said with rueful despondency, "You fool, Les. We should have destroyed the letter without anyone knowing."

"How? He wasn't about to let me go get it. Anyway they've got to be silenced now—they know too much, they can identify us, our cover's blown and the only way we can get it back is to kill them."

"But it's not Alan's fault! You're the one who gave it away!"

"You're being irrational, Ronnie. It makes no difference whose fault it is, it's done. We've got to undo it. There's too much at stake."

"I forget what they say," she said. " . . . You can't make scrambled eggs without murdering people, isn't that it? I won't go through with it, Les. I won't be a part of murder— not again. You can keep on forever explaining to me why it's necessary but I'm all through listening to arguments that prove lies are true and murder is respectable and people are nothing."

Suffield murmured, "You'd like to find a way out of it where nobody gets hurt. That's the same thing as trying to stick a pin in a balloon gradually. It can't be done, Ronnie."

Forrester understood that as senseless as it all seemed, Suffield was going to kill him. Forrester's eyes swiveled quickly toward Top Spode, and Top nodded almost imperceptibly. Forrester turned toward Suffield and started talking, to draw Suffield's attention. "I don't know what this is all about but if you're going to kill us I think we deserve to know why. If you—"

"What comfort will it be when you're dead? It won't make the slightest difference," Suffield said, but his florid frown had come around squarely to face Forrester. "Jesus, do you think I *like* this? But you and this God damned sleuth have stumbled into something and there are too many lives at stake; we just can't afford the slightest whisper of suspicion."

Ronnie's mouth was curled. "You've always had that genius, Les, for doing something inexcusable and then dreaming up high-sounding justifications to fit it. Listen to me —all we need to do is lock them up and gag them, make sure they can't get loose before tomorrow night; we'll all be out of reach in a little over thirty hours—we only need to make sure Alan and Jaime don't raise the alarm before the thing is done. After that the whole world will know what happened and it won't matter what Alan knows about us. We'll be gone, disappeared."

"No good," Suffield said. "The world will know *what* happened but it can't be allowed to find out *how* it happened. If the truth came out you could have total global war on your hands."

"My God, aren't we going to have that anyway?"

"You're talking too much, Ronnie. You're only nailing the lids on their coffins."

There was rain. It struck the flagstones outside and began to steam. Ronnie said, "If we're going to be stranded here until the flash floods subside then we've got time to think of another way."

"There is no other way."

"There has to be. Do that much for me, Les—let me have the time."

In the corner of his vision Forrester saw Top Spode close his fist around the heavy glass ashtray on the table beside the window but in that instant the storm burst like a bomb. The thunderclap drew Suffield's attention involuntarily toward the window. Suffield whipped around and spoke from a semi-crouch, pistol leveled:

"Get away from it, Jaime."

Fragmented lightning licked across the sky and metal in the hill rocks brought it down, fizzling and streaking, reflected in the windows. Thunder shattered the quiet with ear-splitting explosions; rain battered the shingles as if someone had dumped it out of airplanes in tank loads. The sky was dark and wild; Suffield spoke crisply and Ronnie went around turning on lights. "Go behind him," Suffield adjured. "Don't get between him and my gun."

Spode was by the window and when Ronnie reached up under the shade of the lamp Suffield said, "Step back away from her, Jaime," and wiggled the gun; and Spode, stepping aside, hooked his foot through the lamp's trailing electric cord and stamped down. The lamp tumbled forward and when Ronnie dodged out of its way she came within reach: Spode grabbed her wrist, yanked her around into a hard embrace. He had her arm twisted behind her back; Forrester heard her tiny outcry.

Spode talked very fast. "Now drop that damned thing before I break her arm."

In his anxiety Suffield had stepped forward; he shook his head, stubborn, weighing it, and finally he said, "I guess not, Jaime."

Ronnie cried, "Les!" Her face was taut with pain. Suffield began to walk toward them. Spode reached around with his free hand, slid his grip down to Ronnie's left hand, grabbed the middle finger and bent it back hard. "This goes first, Les." Ronnie gave a broken sound of agony.

Suffield had crossed half the length of the room, bringing

up the revolver and sighting carefully past Ronnie's shoulder at Spode's face, but Spode kept turning Ronnie in front of him. Forrester waited his chance and jumped Suffield, snapped both hands around the outstretched wrist and twisted in opposite directions with all the strength in his big fists.

The gun wobbled out of Suffield's fingers and Suffield sucked wind through his teeth.

Suffield cracked the leather rim of his shoe against Forrester's shin. Pain shot up Forrester's leg. Suffield twisted out of Forrester's grip and dived for the gun but Spode had thrown Ronnie aside and leaped forward: he butted Suffield in the kidney and the blow knocked Suffield against the brass-cornered coffee table. The table caught him behind the knees and he went over bringing the table down with a clatter of ashtrays and snapping wood.

Suffield's fist closed around the broken table leg, its brass corner still attached. He turned on one knee wielding the massive leg like a club, swinging it in a wicked circle while Spode scooped up the revolver.

Forrester, swaying to get balance, saw it from the corner of his vision in the broken instant. The jagged club whistled toward Spode and because Spode's weight was on one arm and one knee, Spode couldn't parry, and there was only one thing left: Spode shot to kill because he didn't have time not to.

The walls threw back stunning echoes of the explosion. The point-blank charge splintered bone fragments from Suffield's forehead; Suffield's mouth sagged with stupefaction and he toppled, grazing Spode's shoulder with the club. The room was instantly filled with a cordite stink.

The fierce lightning of the thunderstorm crackled around the house. Forrester's face was hot and prickly: his eyes felt sticky. Uselessly he kicked the bunched-up throw rug out of his path and knelt by Les Suffield, laying his finger along the man's wrist to feel for a pulse. It stopped beating under his hand. He reached for the rug to pull it up over Suffield's face.

Spode had turned to train the pistol on Ronnie. "I'd stand still." Spode was sweating.

Ronnie stood quivering in every rigid limb. Her face seemed all bones and eyes—huge eyes. Her hair was lank with sweat and her voice was a hollow monotone from which everything alive had been sucked. "Go ahead. You may as well."

"Nuts."

Forrester got to his feet. He could see the anger rising in Spode, the coming explosion, but Spode snugged the stubby .38 into his hip pocket.

Ronnie slid down against the wall until she was sitting on the floor. She sat hunched over, like a sick aged wreck. "Oh, Les."

Spode said, "He was your brother, right?"

She nodded. Her face dipping, the long hair swayed forward to mask it; her fingers reached the edge of the carpet and began to pick fluff.

Spode said, "Had to be."

Forrester walked across the room and crouched on his haunches beside Ronnie. "You've got to tell us everything—right now."

She pressed her hands to her temples. "They'll kill me if I talk."

Spode said harshly, "They'll have to wait in line."

"Who," Forrester said very quietly, "is they?"

Her voice was thin, far away. "I knew I was going to hurt you. I tried not to. It was the first time in years anyone ever mattered to me—I wanted to be everything you wanted me to be. . . . If you knew how I despise myself . . ."

Spode moved forward. "Snap out of it. Both of you."

Forrester put out a detaining hand. Spode stopped where he was, and Forrester stood up, gripping Ronnie's hand and pulling her gently to her feet. She smiled, childlike, but her eyes had lost focus. Spode said, "We've seen that before. Battle shock."

"Ronnie."

She did not reply and when her eyes began to roll up Forrester lifted her off her feet and carried her to the couch. Her eyelids slid shut like those of a plastic doll.

Spode said, "Let's wake her up."

"Not yet, Top."

Spode gave him a curious look. "What's that supposed to mean?"

He dragged fingers across his eyes as if to scrape away a film. "She blacked out before—when her husband was killed. She had to be institutionalized and it took a long time to bring her out of it. I'm afraid to rush her now."

Spode stared at Ronnie. "Hell, she's just fainted."

"Maybe. We'll see." Her breathing was shallow and even; her face had gone white. Forrester straightened and turned. "We can't just leave Les like that."

"We're not supposed to touch the body."

"I don't know if we want the police, do we Top?"

Their eyes locked and Spode said slowly, "I don't know what in the hell we do want."

"They said something about its being all over in thirty hours from now. Whoever they are and whatever they're doing, they've put it into high gear."

Top was down on one knee, as if by physical proximity he could vitalize the secrets that had died in Suffield's brain. "How long did we know him, anyway? Ten years? Fifteen? He used to teach math at the university, remember? There was some kid worked on your last campaign said he was the best teacher she ever had because he had the best sense of humor. I don't know what he was but I liked the son of a bitch."

Forrester said slowly, "I have a feeling if we had time to dig back we'd find Les's history stops cold eighteen or twenty years back. When he came to Tucson from wherever it was— Des Moines, I think he said. It wouldn't surprise me if there wasn't a shred of evidence in Des Moines to prove he ever lived there."

"Like Trumble, you mean." Spode scrutinized him over his shoulder. "I see what you're getting at."

Forrester was watching Ronnie and he felt as if a plug had

been pulled and everything drained out of him. She looked heartbreakingly beautiful. Spode's voice rode across the room: "Her too."

"Yes, her too." There had been no visible flaw, no slightest hint that she was a forgery. The contradiction between reason and fact was staggering. He sat down by her; her perfume was in his nostrils, and he gripped her hand although she was still unconscious. When he looked into her immobile face it was hard to regard her as the same woman she had been forty-eight hours ago, to recall her smile, her body's intricate capacity for abandon, the words that went with the expressions that chased one another across her animated face.

Everything he remembered about her had been wiped away as if by death and what was happening inside him was like an assassin's knife between the ribs. His mind observed, cataloged events, drew conclusions without believing; his scalp shrank and the delayed shock thudded into him in waves: his heart chattered with a fast violent thumping. He shot to his feet and tramped back and forth slamming his feet down hard.

"Belsky, Trumble, Craig, Les, Ronnie. God knows how many more of them. She said the letter mentioned half a dozen names."

"That might not be all of them. That's one of the rules when you're working under cover—you don't know anybody so you can't fink on anybody. For all we know there's a hundred of them."

"A hundred of what?"

Spode replied, "We have to assume they're KGB, don't we."

"You mean because of Belsky."

"Sure. Has to be."

The roots of Forrester's hair began to prickle, an outbreak of needles. "How could they possibly have operated in this country for twenty years or more without being caught?"

"That seems to be the whole point—they didn't operate. They just melted in and waited. That's the KGB hallmark—infinite patience."

The adrenalin pumping through Forrester's body made his

hands shake. He was staring down at Ronnie and the design was taking shape in his mind but the tendency to discredit the whole thing was still strong: the enormity of it was beyond acceptability, there must be some mistake.

"Got to be," Spode muttered. "Can you doubt it?"

"I can. I want to. But I don't."

"Listen, they're plants—Belsky came here to turn on the switches and get them all moving like wind-up toys. Thirty hours, she said."

"We've got to crack them, haven't we, Top?"

"How? The only name we've got is Belsky's and there's already an army of people looking for him. They don't know his contacts so they're not going to find him. And look, even if we did find one of them he'd have nothing to gain by confessing. Whatever we could do to him if he refused to talk would be nothing compared to what the KGB's people could do to him if he did talk. They're glued together and the cement's had twenty or thirty years to dry."

It was a feeling like ice across the back of Forrester's neck. "Tomorrow night. And we don't even know what to look for."

Spode picked up the phone, listening, put it back. "The line's still dead and we can't get a car out until the rain quits and the gullies flush out. Look at that stuff come down, we won't get out of here before midnight." He came away from the window, still pacing the room as if it were a zoo cage. "Listen, you got a raincoat or a poncho or something?"

"Coat closet in the hall," Forrester said absently, and then snapped his head around. "No, I'll go. You stay here with Ronnie. I'll walk out of here and try hitching a ride on the highway and get to the nearest phone that's working."

"Nuts. You ain't thinking. It's got to be me. I'm the one who knows the people in the Agency—I know who to call and what to say. You don't."

"Then give me the names and phone numbers. We're in a time trap and I've got more clout than you've got—it boils down to that, Top, I can get them moving faster."

While he talked Forrester was striding across to the foyer closet. But Spode followed him and planted his feet, obstructing the way. "Listen, Senator or no Senator, what the hell is it, your personal crusade? No infidels allowed? You know damn well where the Agency's concerned I carry more weight than you do because they know me and they don't know you. They've seen nut cases in Congress before."

"We're wasting time, Top."

"And wasting wind, but let's spell it out—you just want to be a fucking hero, don't you?"

It staggered him. "Is that what you really believe?"

"What other excuse have you got? You've got to be the one stays with her because she's the only one who can lead us to them and you're probably the only man in the world she'll spill to. That makes me the one that goes to the phone." He plucked the oilskin slicker out of Forrester's hand. "I'm sorry about what I just said. I didn't mean that. I know better."

Forrester was looking at Ronnie. "You're right—I had my mind on something else."

Spode shrugged into the slicker and Forrester turned to him. "Pay attention before you go—there was a reason I felt I ought to be the one to talk to the Agency people. If we call in the Agency we've got to do it discreetly and make sure the Agency keeps the lid on it."

"I'm not sure I get that. We don't know what Belsky's orders are but I'd say the odds against tomorrow were damned high. We may need to call out the troops before this is over—what do you mean keep a lid on it?"

"I mean our primary objective is to get to Belsky and neutralize him and get these undercover people of his out of this country."

"Go on."

"If we put everything we know in the lap of the authorities they'll put out a net—and you can only use a net when you can afford to have a lot of innocent fish swim into it. But if that happens the word will get out. You see?"

"You'd better go a little slower for us country boys."

"If the public finds out the Soviets are intriguing in our own back yard the result could be catastrophic. We've got to keep the Cold War cold, but it won't stay cold if we start a full-scale witch hunt. Another round of McCarthyist paranoia. If we can avoid that we must."

"But maybe we can't. They're planning something big for tomorrow night and it's all bound to come out."

"Not from what Les said. Remember? 'The world will know *what* happened but it can't be allowed to find out *how* it happened. If the truth came out you'd have a global war.' All right—first implication, if the truth doesn't come out we won't have a global war."

"Are you saying it's better to let them go ahead with what they're doing than to stop them?"

"Not at all, Top. I'm saying we want to stop them without anyone knowing we've stopped them—without anyone knowing there was anything that had to be stopped. We don't want to crowd Belsky into a corner where he's got no choice. If this news gets out it'll wreck whatever slim chance we may have to negotiate a withdrawal of these people in secret. If we can reach Belsky before tomorrow night we need a bargaining position and we won't have one if the public is onto it. We've got to leave Belsky an exit—convince him we won't expose this thing if he'll back away and get his people out of the country without attracting attention. When he sees the alternative—a likely war between our countries—he'll have to abort his program and pull his people out. And the public never needs to know a thing about it."

"It's a contradiction," Spode said. "It won't work unless we can reach Belsky, and we can't reach Belsky unless we get the whole world out there hunting for him."

"We've got to try it, Top. That's why I wanted to be the one to talk to your people at the Agency. They've got to realize the urgent need to keep this under wraps."

"They'll be hard to convince. I mean, what the KGB wants is to keep it covered up and if we played along with that we'd be accused of talking treason. In this game the first rule is never do what the other guy wants you to do."

"Once Belsky knows we're onto him it's no longer a question of what he wants us to do." Forrester shook his head. "I could get the President's ear, Top, but if there's any chance at all of our neutralizing Belsky it's better if the President doesn't know a thing about it until after it's done."

"It's a hell of a long shot you want to try."

"It's the only shot I've got, isn't it?"

Spode's eyes widened slowly. "Now I see what you're doing. You don't want me to make any phone calls at all, do you? Because right now the Agency only knows Belsky's here, they don't know anything else about it, and you'd just as soon it stayed right inside this room because if you can reach Belsky and get him to call if off then nobody at all has to know about it. Nobody. You'd rather never have the President find out at all. The President or anybody else outside of you and me."

Forrester nodded. In the hall mirror he glimpsed his own face and saw the hard glitter of the yellow-flecked eyes. "You had to see that for yourself, Top. The Agency is already looking for Belsky and maybe they'll find him and maybe they won't. I don't think we'd improve the chances of finding him by telling the Agency what we know. It would increase the risk of exposure without increasing the chance of success."

"But you're ready to let me walk out the door anyhow and call them if I want to, if I think it has to be done. Why? Because I've got Les's gun in my pocket?"

"No. Because it has to be your decision, not mine."

"I don't see that," Spode said.

"If you thought you could head off a world war by walking out that door, and if I told you not to walk out that door, and if I told you I was right and you were wrong and by walking out that door you would be starting a world war, not stopping one, and if after all that you were still dead certain you could prevent war by walking out that door, what would you do?"

"Hell, I'd walk out the door."

"Then if I meant to keep you here against your own judgment I'd have to kill you, wouldn't I. Because if you thought the fate of the world was at stake you'd take every chance to get away and spread the alarm. The only way I could insure your silence permanently would be to kill you."

Spode was watching him with fascinated alarm. Forrester said, "It simply isn't in me to kill you, Top, and that's why it has to be your own decision."

There was a long interval with the rain clattering on the porch steps and thunder crashing around the house and finally Top said, "Christ people are always after me to make the stinking decisions."

"It's up to you. I can't decide for you." Forrester walked away from him, toward Ronnie.

Spode said, "There's the alternative. Bring Ronnie around. She's the only thing we have to get close to the rest of them. Try ammonia. Slap her if you have to."

Forrester looked up and saw Spode belting the slicker on.

Forrester's head dipped. "You're going, then."

"Not to blow the whistle."

"Then where?"

"Outside. On the hill. I'll dig a hole for Les. If I bury him before it quits raining the storm should wash away the signs of digging. All right?"

Forrester inhaled deeply and slowly, let it out tightly and said, "All right."

☆☆☆☆☆☆☆☆☆☆☆☆☆☆☆☆☆☆☆☆☆☆☆☆☆☆☆☆☆☆☆☆☆☆☆☆☆☆☆

Chapter Nineteen

Lieutenant Colonel Fred Winslow left his underground headquarters at four o'clock Saturday afternoon and said to the
First Lieutenant in the outer office, "Just going to have a look
around. Page me on the PA system if I'm needed."

"Yes, sir. You're not going off the base."

"That's right," Winslow replied dismally and went out into
the corridor. To his left it sloped upward toward the above-
ground entrance a hundred yards and two forty-five-degree
bends away. He turned to the right, into the long ringing
concrete tunnel that went nearly three hundred yards to the
hub from which a spider of side tunnels gave access to the
several ROG commands and beyond them the silos. Enlisted
men in hard hats saluted him as they went by, holding their
ID badges ready for the checkpoints. It was hermetically cool

and dry but sweat rolled freely along his flushed face and dark circles stained the armpits of his shirt. Fatigue was gritty in his eyes; he walked flatfooted, his physical exhaustion compounded by the strain. Twenty-six and a half hours yet to go; he popped a go-pill into his mouth, knowing it would make his tongue dry and screw his nerves to a jittery tautness, knowing he would need more pills before it was done, knowing he would survive them (if he survived nothing else) because gradually he was learning that he was capable of doing and suffering things he could barely imagine.

At the door to the Communications Center he plucked his shirt away from his chest and plugged his ID card into the KMS machine and when the door clicked he went inside and nodded to the sentry.

Eight enlisted men manned the phones and radios and although only one of them had had significance for him before today, he now knew that all eight of them were Amergrad alumni. At the end of the narrow chamber the small steel door stood open so that he saw the tangle of cables and wires in the service tunnel beyond. Ludlum had his head in the doorway but the sentry spoke and Ludlum's back registered Winslow's presence; Ludlum straightened up, turned and grinned at him with the satisfaction of a workman whose hands were turning out a good job. He had been given an order and he was doing a superb job of carrying it out and that was all that ever mattered.

Ludlum hitched at his trousers with the flats of his wrists and beckoned. "Come have a look."

Winslow made his way between the radiomen's stools and when Ludlum climbed into the service tunnel Winslow followed him, folding his body over to fit through the small doorway.

Six men were at work with oxyacetylene torches, cutters, pliers, screwdrivers, soldering guns, wires and cables insulated in plastic of various hues. The smell of the sweat of the men's tension reeked in the air. One man was canted vertiginously over a bracing strut, reaching and pulling at a cable; Winslow heard gristle snap in the man's shoulder and saw a drop of sweat drip from the man's nose onto the knotted wiring below. The men were amorphous shapes in the strange light: the tunnel had ceiling fixtures but the workmen had augmented them with battery floods to get cross-lighting that would mat out the confusion of sharp wire shadows.

"We're fat on it," Ludlum said. "Christ it pays to be prepared. Like Boy Scouts, hey Fred? See, the hot-line phones come in right through here along with all the rest of the communications. Those co-ax cables there. We're taking our time, splicing and tapping into all the phone lines. We've got room enough to post our own dummy NORAD and hot-line operators in here when the time comes—they'll sound exactly as if they're in Colorado Springs and Washington. We've got plenty of time and I don't figure to cut the real lines until the very last minute. *Der Tag.* Nobody's going to have a clue beforehand and nobody's going to have time to get suspicious once the party starts."

"What about incoming calls?"

"We'll be plugged into those too. Our operators will answer as if everything was normal down here. It's no sweat, Nick got us the codes and signals right on schedule this morning."

"Isn't it a bigger headache cutting off the radio net?"

"Not as bad as it looks. It all goes out on underground antenna wire to aerials above ground. Christ some of those outside aerials are forty miles from here so communications won't get cut off if there's a direct hit topside. But nobody ever thought about cutting off communications *this* side of the aerials. Why should they? So we can cut into all the antenna wires right in this tunnel; that's the beauty of it. We hook into the relay-signal boosters and use the boosters as if they were primary sending and receiving stations. The operators won't be picking up or sending a single legitimate message on those radios, but they'll never know it because they'll be receiving from us and sending to us. When we're ready to go tomorrow night we just throw a switch and it disconnects everything and the whole wing's isolated totally from the outside world— without knowing it."

"How about contact with Dangerfield?"

"I've already tested it and it works fine. He'll be close enough to use a walkie-talkie and at this end we'll be receiving through one of the aerials we've cut off from the rest of the base."

"In other words the line of contact goes from Dangerfield to you, and then there's a break, and then it goes from you to me. So you'll have to relay orders to me?"

"No. I'm hooking a direct line from that red scrambler phone of yours into our receiver. It'll be voice amplification through a speaker and mike so Dangerfield's voice will sound metallic to you but you'll have direct voice contact. It was a little tougher to work it out that way, but Dangerfield said if there's a last-minute countermand he doesn't want delays."

Winslow's toes curled inside his shoes. "All right," he said. *Doesn't he ever sweat?*

When Winslow returned to his office he found Ramsey Douglass waiting in his chair.

"Shut the door, Fred." There was something wicked in Douglass' eyes. "Come on in, sit down. There's a chair."

Winslow wanted to seize the offensive but with Douglass he never had learned how. To sit down would be to acknowledge his servility but to remain standing would be even more awkward: it would imply he intended to walk out soon and that was ridiculous since it was his own office.

He sat.

Douglass' face was venomous but from the way his restless eyes kept combing the walls Winslow began to get the idea Douglass' venom was not directed at him. Douglass said with a sarcasm that barely masked his utter lack of interest in the question, "I've got to check you out on procedure—you want to run through it for me? A nice quick recitation for teacher, that's a good boy."

Winslow slid down in the armchair until he was almost sitting on the back of his neck. His tired eyes came to rest on the Matthewson-Ward badge pinned to Douglass' lapel and he said in a monotone, "We get a yellow alert maybe twenty minutes before ignition. Then the red alert. Then orders from the President. It all comes from Ludlum but our operators don't know that. I have various people make various calls and the computers start sending out requests for verification by land line and microwave. At the same time I hook the six ROG launch commanders into the central system and order them to unlock their master consoles by key. When we get confirmation in the proper code from Ludlum's phony NORAD people I instruct the LCs to order their operators to activate their silo consoles. The operators turn their keys in unison and that starts the countdown. After that we've got about three minutes to ignition and the only thing that can stop the countdown is a Presidential order—in this case from Dangerfield on my red phone. Assuming we don't get a countermand the missiles go off and I have something like eight minutes for Hathaway to get all our people rounded up and get them outside. Then Hathaway sets off canisters of gas in the ventilator ducts to render everybody unconscious who's still inside. We pile into the buses and get over to the airport. Does that cover it?"

"Fine," Douglass said. "That's fine, Fred." It was hard to tell if he'd been listening at all.

"What's the matter with you?"

Douglass made an abrupt and violent gesture of negation —a semaphore flash, crossing his hands over each other and whipping them apart. "Christ what a trap."

"I know what you mean. The whole thing is sick."

"It's not that. The whole world's sick; this is only a symptom of the disease. Who gives a damn anyway, Fred? In the long run it won't matter. The universe will abide with us or without us."

Winslow couldn't follow the convolutions of Douglass' wild swings of thought. Momentarily he shut his eyes and a pulse drummed blood-red behind his lids. "But what's going to happen, then?"

"I'm not clairvoyant, Fred. All I can tell you is none of it matters. What do you want to do, make a moral crisis out of it? Find some pious rationalizations to justify it so you can score a few debating points with the Almighty? Hell, I'll give you that for nothing—in war anything's permissible, most of all murder, and we're going to war. How's that grab you? Make everything hunky-dory? Do you want a pep talk to prop up your sagging resolve, some more of the repetitious rhetoric of the party line?"

"That's Nicole's department, not yours."

"Nicole is dead," Douglass breathed, and closed his eyes and wrapped his two hands together and kneaded them violently.

"Dead?"

Douglass straightened his jacket with methodical care, cleared his throat, and answered: "She got a pistol from somebody. She stuck it in her mouth and blew the back of her head off. Yes, dead is the right word. She looked as if she'd never been alive."

Winslow watched Douglass' face twist up.

"God knows why I should care. She had lousy posture and she was always complaining of headaches and cracking fingernails and backaches and corns and the state of the world. She had a face like a rhesus monkey and for Christ's sake I've kicked better ass than her out of bed. She never gave me the time of day. She used to look at me as if she was measuring me for a box."

Winslow still didn't say anything but it was becoming clear that Douglass was asking for something—beseeching. And finally Douglass stretched both arms forward along the top of the desk and looked him in the eye. "You know I'm lying, of course. The truth is when I took my clothes off and got in bed with her I had my climax before I touched her. She laughed every time."

Winslow squirmed and tried to look away but the bleak desperate eyes pinned him. "Oh, hell, Fred." And it came to Winslow quite suddenly that Douglass had come here to unburden himself because there was no one else to whom he could turn. Winslow, who had always hated him and feared him, was the closest thing to a friend Douglass had.

He said clumsily, "I'm sorry, Ramsey, I wish there was something I could do."

"Maybe there is."

Winslow immediately regretted having said it.

"Dangerfield's on my ass," Douglass said. "I've got to take over Nicole's job—rounding up all our people in the area and getting them out to the airport. I won't be able to be here tomorrow so you're going to have to take over for me. You'll have to double-check Hathaway to make sure absolutely everybody gets on those buses. Nobody gets left behind, Fred. Nobody. That was supposed to be my job. Shoot anybody who balks."

Winslow blinked.

Douglass said, "They've got dossiers on every one of us. Anybody who doesn't get on that plane can figure on being dead in twelve hours."

"I see. Yes." His mind whirled.

Douglass got to his feet. "Tell the bus drivers not to run any traffic lights but if a cop stops them, shoot him. You understand, Fred?"

"I understand that. I'm not sure I understand why you care any more whether I do it or not."

"Because it comes down to survival, doesn't it. All I want to do is keep them convinced that I'm beneath consideration. As long as they don't notice me I'll survive. If you trip up, it'll be my fault and they'll nail me for it. I need your help, Fred." He looked hard at Winslow. "Nobody cares what we intended, Fred—nobody cares what our motives are. We're judged by the consequences of our acts, not by our intent."

"Yes," Winslow said, and nodded, and Douglass strutted out.

Alone in the office he picked up the phone. "Get my wife for me, will you Lieutenant?"

He sat absolutely motionless, hardly breathing until the telephone buzzed.

"Celia?"

"Hello, darling."

"About tomorrow night. We were thinking about not going to that damned party but I guess we ought to go."

The silence was long and ragged but in the end she said, "All right, Fred," and all the life had drained out of her voice.

"I probably won't be home tonight."

"I know. I'll see you tomorrow evening then. At the party."

"At the party." He closed his eyes and his grip tightened on the receiver until the knuckles ached.

"Take care, darling."

"Yes. You too."

He depressed the cradle with his finger and released it again. "Lieutenant? Anything happening?"

"No, sir. Nice and quiet."

"I'm going topside for a breath of air. I'll be in hailing distance of the gate guard if you need me."

Along the ramp the tunnel resonated with disembodied announcements on the PA loudspeakers. When he emerged through the great steel doors the dazzling brilliance made his eyes swim. The rain had passed on toward the east and a thin steamy mist hovered along the ground, burning off; his grainy eyes squinted out across the implacable indifferent desert. He began cursing in a lackluster monotone.

☆☆☆☆☆☆☆☆☆☆☆☆☆☆☆☆☆☆☆☆☆☆☆☆☆☆☆☆☆☆☆☆☆☆☆☆

Chapter Twenty

Lamplight reflected from the night-black windows. A hard spiral of heat twisted Forrester's abdominal muscles. He glanced up and Spode stared back wordlessly, his face a studied mask. Forrester took Ronnie's hand.

She sat placid and wooden; her voice was flat. "I guess I went away for a little while."

"It's all right," he said in a low voice from which he withheld feeling by an effort of will that made him break out in a fine perspiration.

He had sat with her for hours, speaking softly and trying to reassure her.

When she had first spoken, it had been erratically. She had mumbled about the storm's end, talked childishly about her paintings.

But now she was coming back. She clung to Forrester fearfully. "Forgive me, Alan."

"Forgive you?"

"For loving you. For bringing you such unhappiness."

Her voice was stronger and he sat up. "Ronnie—"

"Les was my brother, you know."

"Yes. Top guessed that." Still he didn't prompt her with questions because he had no way of being sure what might send her off. He touched his lips gently to her forehead. She said, "You have such huge hands."

He managed to smile but her face did not change. "I have nothing more to lose, except you," she said, "and I've lost you already."

"Nonsense, Ronnie. I'm right here."

"You're here because you want to know what I know."

"That doesn't change the way I feel."

Her eyes filled with tears. "I wish it had. It would be easier if I knew I'd already hurt you as much as I was going to."

He attempted a smile. What was the answer to that?

"I'm sorry I went to pieces. We didn't have time for me to do that."

"Are you all right now?"

She had the strength to make a wry face. "As much as I'm going to be."

"Just take it easy for a while." Meaningless homilies. He had never been good at comforting.

She said, "In a way it has to be a relief, doesn't it—knowing it's out in the open. It doesn't matter what they do to me anyway, it can't be worse than what I've lived through. I suppose you must have guessed: they made me watch them beat my husband to death."

Spode's "Jesus" exploded across the room and Forrester tried not to show his shock.

Ronnie said, "I guess I'll handle it now. It was seeing Les . . ."

Spode said, "God knows I didn't want it that way, Ronnie. But Les didn't give me a choice."

She took several deep breaths. Finally she lifted her head.

"I'll tell you everything I can. I've got nothing left to lose—
I already said that, didn't I?"

"You're alive, Ronnie."

Spode said, "Help us get to this man Belsky in time to stop
them from whatever they're doing."

She was puzzled. "Belsky? You mean the man from Russia
who came to activate us? He's calling himself Dangerfield.
How much do you already know?"

"Mostly guesswork," Forrester said. "You'd better tell us,
if you feel up to it."

"I wouldn't blame you for not believing a word of it, Alan. It's
too fantastic for belief, isn't it?" Her face was wholly without
expression. She had talked for half an hour and she lay back,
drained.

"I believe it all. I have no reason not to."

"I used to think sometimes that if I just went into a police
station or an FBI office and told them the whole story they'd
laugh me right into the nearest insane asylum."

"Did you often think of doing that?"

"Betraying them? Every day. From the first day I arrived
here I wanted to explode the whole thing."

"Because you didn't believe in it?"

"I don't know what I believed in. I'd been conditioned as
if I were a laboratory animal—but I didn't recognize that at
first. I'd grown up believing in Communism. Born and raised
in the Soviet Union. I thought of myself as a loyal citizen—
why shouldn't I? I let Les talk me into joining them and
he convinced me that what we were setting out to do was
right and necessary and just. He really believed that—and so
did I."

"But you said you wanted to get out of it from the first day
you came here."

"That wasn't political conviction, Alan. It was realizing all
at once that I just couldn't live my whole life under that stress,
every moment waiting for somebody to discover the truth
about me. Afterward I began to open my eyes and see how
insane the whole thing was."

"But you still didn't try to get out."

"I asked them to send me back to Russia. They refused, of course—they said they had an investment in me."

"They?"

"Ramsey Douglass and my brother Les." Her face was masked by the weight of her hair; her voice was a monotone. "The more Les saw of American politics the more he was convinced it was an evil regime of rich men and thugs exploiting the people. He had a curious way of rationalizing the way he went on practising the kind of chicanery he claimed to loathe so much—his reasons never made sense to me but he said I just didn't have the right kind of mind to follow it."

"He was part of it, and Ramsey Douglass, and Ross Trumble, is that right? Why did they all behave like dedicated right-wing reactionaries? Was it intended as camouflage, to throw off suspicion?"

"Partly. We came here with instructions to act ultra-American. But it was more than that. We had to infiltrate the defense establishment and the political power structure, and down here they're both pretty much in the hands of the conservatives. You're not a conservative, of course, but the Republican Party has pretty firm control over Arizona's politics, and you were a Republican, so Les and I attached ourselves to you." In a lower voice she added, "Like leeches."

He clasped his hands together and scowled at his knuckles. "They refused to let you go back to Russia but you still didn't try to break loose from them. Why? Because you were afraid they'd kill you?"

"I think I could have accepted that. No, they never make do with so simple a threat as that. You see, as long as Les was loyal to them I couldn't do a thing. If I'd stepped out of line they would have killed him the way they killed my husband. They kept reminding me of that—Nicole did. They had Les and they had my family back in Russia. That's the kind of weapon they've used against all of us."

"What vicious bastards they are."

"They're frightened, Alan. Frightened people do desperate things."

Spode, at the front window, turned his head. "That's no excuse."

"I don't suppose anything excuses us," she replied. Her eyes were fixed sightlessly on Forrester's hands. Spode put his back to the window and stared at Ronnie. Clearly Top could not understand why she had gone along all these years without totting up the odds and deciding, quickly and without regrets, either to remain loyal to the Russians or to betray her comrades and take her chances: one way or the other, it would have been done, over with, a clean decision. To Spode loyalty was not divisible by two; there was no room in his mind for the idea that anyone could love two people on opposite sides of an unbridgeable gap.

Forrester knew that much about Spode; he wished he knew as much about himself. The silence was beginning to stretch, and he knew it was time to move, to act, but his attention was imprisoned by the look on Ronnie's face when she turned toward him. Her eyes had receded into dark tunnels. He felt a great rushing-out, a desire to embrace her tightly and protect her against them all: he had lost one woman he had loved deeply and now he had lost Ronnie too and it was too much to bear, too much to think about, and yet it was of no importance by comparison with the crisis Ronnie faced. The lie she had lived for twenty years had been terrible enough but at least it had cloaked her in a kind of safety; now even that had been stripped from her and there was no place left for her to turn. How could he protect her? What would happen when she began to think about the future—when the panic set in? What would she do? There was nothing.

Spode's voice clacked abruptly, directed at Ronnie: "You still don't know exactly what they're planning?"

She twisted away from Forrester. "My mind's full of gaps, Jaime—I don't remember everything. Something to do with the base—something to do with the missiles. And we're all supposed to gather at the airport to get away on a plane. To Cuba, I think."

Spode had opened the door; he pushed it shut and came back. "We can get through the arroyos, I think. There's no time at all, you know that—we ought to call the President. Put it in his lap. He can get on the hot line with Moscow and tell them to pull their people out of here or else."

"Or else what, Top? That's the point, isn't it?"

"We can't just sit on it."

"We've been over that. It wouldn't be kept secret. Once it got out there would be public hysteria. Even assuming war could be avoided the yahoos would demand war and when they didn't get it there'd be riots, armed troops, panics, shooting."

Spode said, "It doesn't have to get out. There's machinery. We had to keep it oiled when I was in the Agency. The Office of Emergency Preparedness has a chief censor with powers to clamp the lid on everything in a national emergency. We were ready to use it in the Dominican crisis in sixty-five. Once the President invokes those powers nobody can tell the American public it's under nuclear attack unless the White House clears it."

"Top, the minute I'm convinced we've got no alternative I'll call the President. But if I called him now he'd have only one thing to do—he wouldn't have time to uncover their whole net down here and so all he could do would be to slap Moscow with a war ultimatim. As you yourself put it—get them out of here, or else. But if we can pull this off without the use of the hot line we avoid that risk."

"Pull it off how?"

"Find this man Belsky. We've got an opening now: Ramsey Douglass can lead us to him. That may be enough."

"Jesus God."

Spode drove at high speed along the freeway. The whine of the tires echoed off the concrete bridge abutments and the car snickered on the bends. Ronnie sat tight against Forrester at hip and knee, her shoulder in the hollow of his armpit. Her face was drawn; she looked old. She had already withstood too much and there was no hope of release. His fingernails dug into his palms and he was filled with a wild rage—and the fearful sense of loss.

He felt the touch of her hand. When he turned, her glance locked his with tremendous impact. Her mouth trembled; she shuddered clear through to her fingertips.

Forrester stirred in the chair, groggy; something was cold against the side of his forehead. When he sat up he realized he had been slumping with his head against the window. When he looked out into the dawn it took him a moment to orient himself. They were back in his motel. Outside, the scene had a squinty-eyed hung-over aspect. Travelers were heaving suitcases into jammed trunk compartments, wiping morning dew off their windshields, slamming doors; faintly he could hear them yapping at their children. The aftermath of yesterday's flooding had left flotsam blocking the corner drains and puddles in the pavement. He saw deep tire tracks in the motel lawn where someone had sought a route to the parking lot when the water had been flowing eight inches deep.

Spode sat with his hand on the telephone. He was shaking a Coke bottle in his fist and spouting foam into his mouth from three inches away. Ronnie sat curled up in a chair beside the bed, feet drawn up under her, small fists propped under her chin.

"Nothing yet," Spode said. "The sun's up. We haven't even got twelve hours left."

"Nothing at all?"

"Orozco's got all his people out looking for Douglass. They tried to find him through Nicole Lawrence but she's dead." His teeth were showing. "Killed herself."

Ronnie closed her eyes. "Then it's got to be Ramsey, doesn't it? I don't know any other members of his cell. My brother was my own cell leader and there were only the four of us—Les and Ross Trumble and Gus Craig and me. Ramsey and Nicole had a larger group—after the first few years there was a reorganization and we were assigned to them for orientation but we never met their people."

Spode said, "Orozco's posted a few men at the airport. They'll start showing up out there but it won't be until late in the afternoon. We've got to get to Belsky sooner than that. Maybe we'll find Douglass. Maybe not. You'd better set a time limit—when you're going to call the President."

Forrester dug at his eyes, yawned wide and stood up tottering. "Just find Ramsey Douglass."

Ronnie had not opened her eyes. When Forrester had washed his face in the bathroom he returned and she still hadn't stirred. He knew what it meant: the panic had begun to hit her, she had started to think beyond the now. Her former comrades were about to get on an airplane and go back—home, Russia. But Ronnie had betrayed them and now she had no choices left. She could not go on board the plane with them because once it was discovered that Forrester was on their track they would know they had been betrayed; and Ronnie would be the logical, if not the only, suspect. They would torture her until she confessed, and then they would have their final revenge. No, she could not go with them. Yet she couldn't remain behind, because then they would send people back to find her. The only way she could be protected from them was by turning herself in, a confessed enemy of the United States.

The phone rang and Spode jerked it to his ear, grunted, listened, grunted again and put it down. "Douglass isn't home, he isn't at Nicole's, and he's not at his office. They're looking around the Air Base for him but that's a lot of area to cover. May take all day."

"Just find him," Forrester said. "Just find him."

☆☆☆☆☆☆☆☆☆☆☆☆☆☆☆☆☆☆☆☆☆☆☆☆☆☆☆☆☆☆☆☆☆☆☆☆☆☆

Chapter Twenty-One

Rykov's face had a puffed look; his eyes were shattered by bloodshot lines. Outside it was still dark, predawn; bare branches were silhouetted against the street lamps, jagged as cracks in a porcelain surface, and patches of snow had drifted across the glossy cobblestones.

Behind him Andrei said, "You shouldn't stand like that. An assassin could shoot you easily from anywhere on the roof-tops across the street."

"It hardly matters now, does it." But Rykov unrolled the blind to cover the window and turned back to his desk. The enormous room seemed mausoleumlike; the only lamp lighted was the orange-shaded one on the desk. "In Arizona now it is past five in the afternoon."

"About eighty-five minutes to go," Andrei agreed. "You've failed, you know. You may as well signal Belsky to abort."

"A cause is not lost so long as someone is willing to go on fighting, Andrei. I have not yet failed completely." He added, "I assume Comrade Yashin has recommended as a matter of public sanitation that I be quietly executed. There can be no three-judge People's Court of course. No public airing. I am to be terminated without fuss—suicided, perhaps? It would be fitting—Grigorenko would have his opportunity to trumpet that I had displayed the sincerest form of self-criticism. Or perhaps I am to spend the rest of my days in solitary confinement?"

"I shall do everything I can to see that you are comfortably maintained and that no one harms you."

"Yashin will probably order you to kill me."

"An order I should disobey."

"Irrelevant, Andrei. He can always find someone willing to do it. I am not without enemies."

"We have eighty-two minutes."

The cabbage soup had gone cold on the desk; the piece of black bread sat on the saucer half-eaten. Rykov put a cigarette in his mouth. He had to hold the match with both hands.

"You must capitulate," Andrei said. "The Chinese have already begun to withdraw their bluff. They saw it was not working."

"They need to be taught their lesson, don't they."

"The remedy is worse than the disease."

The back of Rykov's hand struck his cigarette and showered sparks over his chest. "In any case I've been discredited, I'm officially out of office—I haven't much to lose, have I? One who is already in disgrace can easily afford to indulge his principles."

He tried to catch some hint of expression on Andrei's cheeks. Andrei only said, "If I fail to persuade you to abort, of course it means my own head."

"There are worse things than death, Andrei. As the proverb has it, it is simpler to die than to live."

"Seventy-four minutes," Andrei said. "And it will require about twenty minutes for your signal to be relayed to Belsky and for Belsky to act upon it. Say fifty minutes."

"I am a patriot, Andrei." Rykov sighed with the hopeless-
ness of a failure beyond his power to correct: it was the first
time he had ever faced anything too big for him and the
knowledge was bleak. "I am a patriot."

"One of your difficulties, Andrei, is that you are constantly
thinking about the rules of the game without ever asking
whether the game itself has meaning. You cannot merely—"
He felt the warning run of heavy saliva in his mouth; his
shoulders hunched up and his throat filled and he made a
dash for the lavatory sink, limping clumsily. He clung to the
rim of the basin, vomiting with long agony.

When he rinsed his mouth and returned to the desk he
said, "An insufficiency of fortitude. I never suspected it of
myself."

"No one envies you your dilemma," Andrei said. "My dear
Viktor, please see the truth of it. The Chinese are not ready
for war. You would kill millions—tens of millions, hundreds
of millions. You would risk destroying Mother Russia—destroying the earth."

"There will be war, Andrei—war with China is inevitable.
Best it be done now when we have the opportunity to win."

"I have no cigarettes left."

"I will get you a packet as soon as you have signaled
Belsky."

"Don't be childish, Andrei."

"I have no time left for patience. Thirty-eight minutes,
Viktor."

"Will you take my place at this desk in the morning?"

"In the morning if I am alive I shall retire to the country
to farm."

"The boredom will get on your nerves."

"If you blow up the world, Viktor, we shall all be eternally
bored."

"Twelve minutes, Viktor. If my watch is not slow."

"Why do you press me when you know I have won after
all?"

"Because I believe that in the end like me you are a human being. To destroy other human beings is human. To destroy one's entire species is not. If I have love for you it is because of your humanity, not your political strategies."

"And what is it that you think makes me such a humanitarian in the end?"

"Your love for me, Viktor."

☆☆☆☆☆☆☆☆☆☆☆☆☆☆☆☆☆☆☆☆☆☆☆☆☆☆☆☆☆☆☆☆☆☆☆

Chapter Twenty-Two

The Lincoln skittered around the bend into Park Avenue, taking the curve too fast; it weaved violently on its springs. The tug pulled Forrester hard over against the rear right-hand door and Ronnie was squashed against him.

Spode was driving. "It may be too damn late."

"You've got time," Ramsey Douglass said. "Floor it."

Forrester's watch read six-ten. It was more than a mile to the airport.

Spode slowed for a red light at Ajo Road but nothing was in sight on the crossroad and Spode gunned through the stoplight. The big car lunged along the dips, bobbing and swaying. Ramsey Douglass was slumped in the front passenger seat. "See that clump of cottonwoods? Drop me there—I'll walk the rest of the way."

343

Spode took his foot off the gas and pulled off the road in the shade. "Half-mile walk from here."

"I'll make it." Douglass opened the door but Spode pointed the pistol at him and Douglass nodded wearily. "All right. He's sitting in a parked Oldsmobile on the Nogales Highway right across the road from the Matthewson-Ward front gate. I picked the spot for him because you get a good reception there and it's only a mile from here."

Spode said, "If he ain't there we'll know where to get our hands on the rest of you."

"I'm trusting *you.*"

"Yeah," Spode said dubiously.

Douglass got out of the car and Spode hit the accelerator and left him standing flatfooted by the side of the road. They broke out past the cottonwoods with the speedometer needle quivering toward eighty. "Time's it?"

Forrester had been watching Douglass cross the road and dog-trot along the shoulder in the low lancing sunlight. He looked at his watch and said. "Fourteen after six."

"Jesus."

A little more than an hour before, Orozco's men had picked up Douglass' Volkswagen coming out of the Davis Monthan gate. They had forced him off the road and taken him at gunpoint.

They had held Douglass in the bricked-in back lot of a motorboat dealership on Twenty-second Street. Forrester and Ronnie and Spode had crashed three stoplights getting there.

Top had put his gun on Douglass and told the two operatives they could go: they weren't to know what it was about.

Forrester had started without preamble: "Tell us where Belsky is."

"Belsky?"

Spode said, "Dangerfield."

"Sure," Douglass said.

Forrester told him, "You're finished anyway. You may as well."

"Why? Because this bitch has blown my cover?" Jittery or not he had absorbed a great deal very quickly. He wasn't even asking questions about Ronnie's presence; the fact that she was with Forrester and Spode was enough. Douglass shook his head. "Forget it."

"If Belsky goes through with it now the United States will know Moscow was behind it. You see that, don't you? The United States will annihilate Russia. Do you want that? You can stop it, Douglass."

Clearly Douglass hadn't thought of that. His face changed slowly; a creeping pallor drained his cheeks. But then he scowled and stabbed a finger toward Ronnie. "Where's Les Suffield?"

She appeared almost drowsy; she only shook her head, mute, and Forrester said, "Dead."

"How?"

"Accident," Forrester answered.

"That's why she went over to you?"

Ronnie's face came up. "Nicole is dead too, isn't she? You're like me, Ramsey—you've nobody left to lose."

Douglass' head shook like a metronome. After a moment Top Spode said, "Not much time. I'll have to start prying him open."

Douglass looked up with a glance of petty irritation. "You could try." Then a crafty new thought tightened his face. "Listen—what's in this for me, then?"

They had discussed that earlier. Spode wanted to lock him up, muzzle him until it was all done, but Forrester had vetoed it: *They're expecting him to show up. If he doesn't they'll get jumpy and God knows what they might decide to do.*

Spode had objected: *Outside of Ronnie he'll be the only one who'll know you uncovered their network. If he tells the rest of them it puts you in a hell of a spot. You'll get all of them on your ass like a ton of bricks, trying to shut you up.*

But Forrester had an answer to that. Douglass could hardly finger him without raising suspicion against himself: Forrester wouldn't have turned Douglass loose unless Douglass talked—that was the way Belsky would see it. No; Douglass wasn't going to say anything about Forrester. And anyhow if Forrester did reach Belsky then Belsky would know; so Douglass offered no threat to anyone but himself.

Douglass asked again, "What's in it for me?"

"Give us Belsky," Forrester answered. "We'll turn you loose. You can escape on the plane with the rest of them."

Douglass turned a slow circle on his heels, head down, thinking. When he looked up he said, "What about her?"

"Ronnie stays behind," Forrester said. He was watching her but he saw no change in her expression.

"Oh that's ducky," Douglass said, but it was easy to see his thoughts: Ronnie would be the only Russian who knew Douglass had betrayed them; if Ronnie wasn't aboard the plane there would be no one to accuse Douglass. Nevertheless Douglass said, "If she's not on the plane they'll figure she's gone over—blown all of us. The rest of us will suffer for it when we get home."

"Home," Ronnie said under her breath.

Spode said, "You'll just have to take your chances about that. Ronnie's not the only one who won't be there. What about Nicole and Trumble and Craig?"

"Dangerfield knows about them. He saw them dead."

"What about Les Suffield, then?"

"Is he honest-to-God dead? I thought you were trying to put one over."

"He's dead. So's Ronnie. They both died in a car crash this morning. That's what you'll tell them."

"Now I don't know what to believe. Anyhow Dangerfield won't buy it."

"He'll have to."

Forrester said, "He'll have other things to think about."

"Not him. He's never missed a trick, that one." Douglass ran his tongue over his lips. "Look, you're saying you'll pretend you never heard of me—you're saying I can get on the plane and nobody will ever find out you busted me."

Spode said, "You've got one other choice. You refuse to lead us to Belsky and you'll stay right here till you rot. You know what happens to you then—from our side or from theirs."

Douglass filled his chest slowly.

"You were heading for the airport," Spode said.

"Was I? You tell me."

"We'll take you down there. You'll have to walk in—tell them you had a flat tire just outside. When we let you out of the car you'll tell us where to find Belsky."

"What if I do? You won't budge him, you know. He's got his orders and that's all he knows. He's that kind."

"Let us deal with him," Forrester said. "Where is he?"

"I'll think about that. You want to drive me to the airport? Fine. I'll let you know when we get there."

Six-seventeen. After Douglass had told them where to find Belsky they had sped down to the highway and now Spode said, "There's the Olds. Douglass was telling the truth."

"Let me have your gun, then," Forrester said.

"Nuts. We'll do this my way—both of you get down below the windows back there. Belsky knows this is Suffield's car. If he sees just me driving he'll think it's Suffield. I'll pull his teeth and then you can have him."

There was a fair flow of traffic on the highway; Spode made the left turn and rolled slowly along the shoulder to ease up behind the parked Oldsmobile. Before Forrester bent down below the level of vision he had a glimpse of a man with a walkie-talkie in the driver's seat.

Ronnie trembled violently. He held her tightly down and heard Spode open the door and get out, the crunch of Spode's shoes on the gravel. Spode's voice floated back, harsh: "Remember me? Now open up real slow and step out."

Forrester whispered, "Stay down and stay quiet." And he sat up and opened the door.

There was nothing alive in Belsky's round face except the eyes: eyes hard as glass. They came around toward Forrester like the slowly swinging gun turrets of a battle cruiser.

Forrester walked forward slowly. His breathing was tight

and shallow, his sphincter contracted, his palms damp. "My name is Alan Forrester, Belsky."

"I know who you are." The eyes did not flicker at the sound of his real name: the man had learned defense and survival in a hard school.

"Call them off," Forrester said. "You can do it—with that walkie-talkie. Call them off and get them out of this country and nothing will be said about it."

"Nothing? Surely."

Forrester could hear the beat of his own heart. The twilight seemed to grow brighter, every tiny sound louder. Cars rushed past on the highway, spewing dust. Spode's gun was concealed by the hang of his coat but it was visible enough to Belsky.

Forrester said, "Your cover is blown. We know who you are. If you fire the missiles now we'll know the Russians fired them, how it was done. We'll be forced to retaliate directly and totally."

He saw Belsky hesitate for the fraction of a moment but then Belsky said, "It's beyond my power to stop what has been set in motion by my superiors, Senator. I cannot change policy; it's not my function. You may shoot me but that will not prevent anything from happening. The missiles will be ignited within five or six minutes; there's nothing you can do to stop them now. A phone call would get no results in time."

"What are the targets?"

"I can tell you that, I suppose, since you seem to know the rest. The target is China."

The design was complete in Forrester's mind now, and as he studied Belsky's bland middle-aged face with its gemstone eyes he realized his gamble had failed. He had lost.

In Silo Six Lieutenant Smith stood up and stretched; he had been five hours in the chair. Haas spoke to him, and the voice came over the electronic box: "We're going to the post movie. Want to double tonight?"

"We were thinking about going bowling."

"Uh. Okay."

"But it's never much sweat to talk Madge into a movie."

It was 1827 hours.

The red telephone buzzed.

At its base the little light began to wink.

Smith stared. A long time seemed to go by. His face flooded; pressure almost burst his throat. His hands lifted involuntarily toward his face. He whispered, "Oh dear God. Oh sweet dear God."

He reached for the receiver.

There was a piping buzz from somewhere inside Belsky's Oldsmobile and Belsky's face hardened with sudden urgency. *"I beg of you don't shoot me now!"* And he was wheeling, diving inside the car, opening a case on the seat— not an attaché case after all, Forrester realized; a radio. Spode was staring, transfixed, and Forrester saw Belsky remove something from the case and plug jacks into sockets and push several buttons. Belsky had a notepad and when the speaker began to utter dots and dashes Belsky jotted feverishly. Forrester heard the sucked intake of Top's breath and involuntarily looked at his watch.

They were like that in frozen tableau for an indeterminate time and then Belsky wrenched up the walkie-talkie and pressed a button and yelled into it: "Winslow, can you hear me? From Father Christmas abort. Winslow! From Father Christmas abort! *Abort!*"

Belsky had the earpiece at his head and it made a brief squawking sound.

"Yes. From Father Christmas. Abort—abort—abort."

He put it down and backed out of the car. "It may have been too late," he said in a matter-of-fact voice. His eyes swept past Forrester and settled on the desert brush to the northeast, this side of the mountains, where the missiles would erupt if the countermand hadn't stilled them in time.

☆☆☆☆☆☆☆☆☆☆☆☆☆☆☆☆☆☆☆☆☆☆☆☆☆☆☆☆☆☆☆☆☆☆☆

Epilogue

Smith had inserted his key; his eyes, and those of Haas, were on the countdown clock. The code envelope lay on the floor behind him and the codes lay in the tray, a perfect match for the signal he was receiving over the red telephone against his ear. The computer's voice was metallic, without expression.

The computer said, "Execute."

The last of the word was cut off by a new connection clicking in.

"Countermand. This is Colonel Winslow. Countermand has been received and acknowledged."

Smith whipped his hand from the key as if it were white-hot. Winslow's voice was going on in his ear: "We have received a Presidential order to stand down. . . . Prepare to make secure. . . ." Smith wasn't listening. He covered his face with his hands and wept.

Ensign Sakhalov broke the lock when he heard the pistol report and wheeled into the First Secretary's office with his machine pistol off safety.

He found the Second Secretary sitting in a chair drawing a plump hand across his face. First Secretary Rykov lay by the desk with his head in a puddle of his own blood. The pistol was in the Second Secretary's hand. Ensign Sakhalov stared at the scene and then said, "Why do you pretend you shot him, Comrade Secretary? There is blood on the pistol but none on your hand. You took the pistol from him after he killed himself."

The Second Secretary said, "Tell no one."

"But you will be charged with murder."

"Yes," the Second Secretary said. "He was betrayed by his subordinate, you see. Murdered by his most trusted aide."

"You wish that?" Sakhalov's jaw dropped open.

Andrei Bizenkev's eyes were wide, white circles showing around them. "I wish that, yes. You will oblige me, Sakhalov?"

"As always, Comrade Secretary, I will oblige you."

Forrester discovered he had been holding his breath: it escaped his lungs in a gust and he looked at his watch again. His eyes burned, his knees felt rickety.

Belsky was getting out of his car and putting his hands on top of his head. No expression on his bland salesman's face. "I don't suppose you will permit me to signal an acknowledgment to my superiors."

Spode said, "Nuts. Let them sweat."

Forrester covered his eyes with his palms to shut out the light. Sobs of breath racked through him. When he dropped his hands he said to Belsky in an unsteady voice, "Get in your car. Drive to your airplane. Get your people on board and get them out of this country."

There was a momentary break in Belsky's expression. "You're releasing me?"

"I want all of you out of this country."

Spode said, "We'll be watching you board the plane. We'll be keeping count."

Forrester and Spode had no way of knowing how many of them there were; but Belsky didn't have to know that.

Belsky said, "Then you don't plan to disclose what's happened?"

"We probably can't stop it from getting out," Forrester said. "There'll be people in the missile complex who know a signal came."

"All dead," Belsky said.

Spode's teeth clicked.

Belsky spoke woodenly. "By now they're dead. My people had instructions to seal off the exits, get themselves out and gas the rest."

Spode's revolver lifted into sight. "You—"

"If it matters," Belsky said, "they didn't know the gas they were releasing was lethal. I told them it would render the Air Force people unconscious long enough for us to escape. Of course it was better to leave no one alive to reveal what happened here; you see that."

Spode parked in the long shadow of a heavy mesquite clump and they watched the Oldsmobile thread the narrow service gate in the back fence; someone had broken the padlock chain and left the gate open for Belsky and now Belsky rolled across the head of this little-used runway toward the plane. The tower and terminal were two miles away; out at this end there was nothing but sun-buckled pavement and weeds. The Starlifter squatted near the fence and Forrester saw a stream of passengers descending from two Air Force buses drawn up beside the wing. They were going up the ramp in a fast disorderly flow. A figure detached itself and walked out to meet Belsky's car—Douglass leaned on the car window to talk, then shook his head and walked back to the boarding stairs and followed the last passengers into the plane. Belsky opened the trunk lid of the Oldsmobile and lifted out two cylinders that looked like aqualung tanks. He carried them up into the plane with him.

Forrester heard the ragged intake of Ronnie's breath behind him. The Starlifter retracted its stairs and the engines wound up to a shrill whine; she made a ponderous turn and rumbled down the pavement. Forrester got out of the car and stood by the fence to watch the big jet gather speed and lift off. She banked sharply to the southeast and climbed into dusk, wingtip lights blinking with lonely distance.

Spode knew what was in the canisters Belsky had carried aboard. Belsky's orders were obvious: Moscow didn't want the Illegals alive.

Spode glanced at Forrester's wide back before he turned in the seat and spoke softly to Ronnie. "He can't help you but you can help him."

Her eyes shifted toward him. "What?"

"You can get him off the hook, Ronnie." Spode backed out of the car and left the driver's door open.

Forrester was still watching the darkening sky that had swallowed the jet. Spode opened the rear door and reached in to take Ronnie's arm. She came out of the car obediently and stood trembling, hugging herself. Spode murmured, "Go on, Ronnie."

"I don't—"

"On the run." He said it gently but his face was hard.

Forrester was beginning to turn back to the car when he heard the starter mesh. A door slammed and he wheeled and then the Lincoln was curling past with its back wheels spinning for purchase. He had a glimpse of Ronnie's face, white, wide-eyed, and then the car was out on the road gathering speed, the headlamps snapping on.

He took an involuntary step, and felt Spode's grip on his arm. The tail lights disappeared at the bend and Spode's grip locked tight, arguing with him. "You've got to let her go."

The fever hit him then: a chill and a hot flush that prickled his skin, a dizziness, bright red flickers before his eyes, a trembling weakness against which he had to lock the muscles of stomach and arms. When the spasm passed he felt faint and very cold. His head was very heavy when he turned to lay his baffled stare on Top Spode.

A jetliner was taking off from a far runway with a ripping racket of power. Spode said, "They'll find those dead men in the silos. Better get to a phone." His face was a graven mask that gave away nothing of his feelings. "You've got to call the President."

Ronnie's anguished face was burned into his conscious-ness. When Spode's hand dropped away he locked his fists together. *I could get her back.*

Back to what?

They walked toward the cars abandoned by the end of the runway. He didn't speak until they had reached the Oldsmo-bile. Belsky had left the walkie-talkie on the seat and the key in the ignition. Forrester pulled the door shut and Spode started the car and aimed it toward the lights of the terminal where the telephones were. A small plane came in low over-head, landing, sliding through the airport lights.

Finally he said in a sighing gust of breath, "All right, Top."

Washington, April 9 (UPI). Pentagon spokesmen said the Air Force still has found no explanation for the crash of the cargo plane seen to plummet into the Gulf of Mexico Sunday night. It was disclosed today that the C-141 Star-lifter jet was on a training flight from an Arizona base, but the Air Force has declined to make public a list of crew or passengers, pending notification of next-of-kin.

The crash was witnessed by the crew of U.S. Coast Guard cutter *Perseus* about 2 A.M. Monday in waters 100 miles west of Key West. Crewmen reported that the plane appeared to be in a spin for no clear reason; there were no flames evident before it crashed into the sea.

The plane had taken off on a flight from Davis Mon-than Air Force Base near Tucson, Ariz. Personnel of the base were not available for comment, since the base has been closed and temporarily sealed for a routine Operational Readiness Inspection.

Washington, April 10 (AP). The President announced today that the Defense Department has ordered a sweeping reappraisal of the proposed Phaeton Three multiple-warhead ICBM system.

The President declined to comment on whether agitation by Sen. Alan Forrester (R.-Ariz.) was a deciding factor in his decision. But a high White House source conceded the step is a solid victory for Forrester.

Senator Forrester, in seclusion in Washington because of a minor virus, was unavailable for comment. But a press release from his office said he was very pleased with the President's decision.

"But we're going to keep fighting until we've brought all our intercontinental defense systems under control," Senator Forrester's statement added. "None of them is immune to the dangers of accidental discharge or organized sabotage. Under existing controls, a small group of dedicated fanatics could easily set the world on fire."